Anyone who knows Chris would agree that ne is a great storyteller. He writes as he speaks! "A spring awakening" is a good read full of perceptive observations about what makes us human. The characters are developed in such a way that we see ourselves, our struggles and our hopes in them.
Mike Pilavachi, Author and Senior Pastor, Soul Survivor Watford

'A powerful, compelling tale of one man's painful journey towards true faith portrayed with realism and insight wrapped in evocative and elegant prose. Eminently readable.'
Baroness Dorothy Thornhill MBE, Elected Mayor of Watford

To Margaret + Roy

Chris Cottee

6.5.18

A SPRING AWAKENING

Sometimes,
When things seem to be better
They really aren't.
They really, really, aren't.

Chris Cottee

instant
apostle

First published in Great Britain in 2018

Instant Apostle

The Barn
1 Watford House Lane
Watford
Herts
WD17 1BJ

British Library Cataloguing-in-Publication Data

A catalogue record for this book is available from the British Library

This book and all other Instant Apostle books are available from Instant Apostle:

Website: www.instantapostle.com
E-mail: info@instantapostle.com

ISBN 978-1-909728-79-0

Printed in Great Britain

PROLOGUE

How did we get here?
To this dark place?

David Sourbook hoped he was a nice man. He certainly hadn't been. Before.

Last Christmas he thought he was saved. Not so much in a religious sense, as in a personal one.

It was a revelation. It changed him, profoundly and wonderfully. He was approaching Christmas with his usual lonely desperation to find the festive fizz. That wonderful, soul-filling lift, when all is merry greetings and lights and magical delight. The look on children's faces, the well-wishings from complete strangers, the shared bonhomie that is itself a most special, seasonal thing. Nothing else compares to it or captures it. It is a shared wonder, designed by none but shared by all. Or those, at least, who can somehow capture it. Because it is a fleeting thing, come and gone. But if you can harbour it, even for a while, it does you such good. A soul-drenching satisfaction.

In loneliness he sought it. Mercurial it peeped, and fled from him, day after day. Like that book Song of Songs in the Bible, the lover played this game with him. Drawing, teasing, disappearing.

But then she appeared, as if from nowhere, by the pond in the lower town, a week before the big day. Like some angelic creature, Angela her name, she flitted round him and got caught up in his hair. She dragged him only half-willingly into helping her with various good works, and into her circle of friends at St Mark's Church.

From the beginning, their friendship was somewhat ambivalent.

They met a bunch of aggressive yobs, whose leader, Ruf, they ended up saving from being drowned trying to rescue his dog from a frozen pond. They arranged for him to stay with friends of hers rather than go to prison over Christmas, his dog having, that very morning, taken a sizeable chunk out of the leg of a postwoman.

Then Angela died. Of a heart condition she'd omitted to mention to David. On Christmas Eve, of all times. Three times her poorly rhythmed heart stopped, and had to be restarted. He thought she was really gone.

In the midst of all that he discovered that his dear, sweet sister, Micky, whom he'd believed to have died before he ever knew her, actually had been lost to him when he was eight and she was three, and he'd been so devastated by the loss that he'd been half-alive with the effect of it all his days. An isolated loner, resentful and lacking any strand of true kindness.

And when you lack any true kindness, you can't see what a soulless state that is.

Like Humpty Dumpty, the shell, once cracked, could not be repaired to hold the egg again, and necessary though the revelation was, at the time it was the hardest, saddest, most disembowelling thing he'd ever experienced. Yet there was Angela, and her lovely nephew Andrew, who took to him like a real uncle from the outset of their meeting, both of them pulling him in to a hope and a future and a festive reality that was nothing less than magical. Only it wasn't magical, because God was in it and behind it. The God who had called to him through The Yearning at dusk, sitting outside his little cottage, nursing his mug, time upon time.

It felt like he'd been lost and found. Split open and re-stuffed. Dead and alive again. It was the Christmas he'd never had. It promised so much.

Yet the human soul is like a large building, with many storeys above ground, and many subterranean floors below. The levels above are role-personalities for the different relationships the person inhabits – parent, child, sibling, partner, work colleague, neighbour... The floors below are uncharted regions of depth and history. Many doors are locked. Many rooms seem empty but are not. A whole past of irreconcilables is here. Memories are stored, with or without the keys that unlock them. With or without the emotions that accompanied them. With or without the present significance that loads them with power, for good or ill. Soon he would find himself asking how many levels of hell did he have to encounter down there, and how would he know when he'd reached the last?

Was there a last?

After meeting Angela at Christmas, and the changes she'd already brought, David had imagined his life would become like a chortling stream, bubbling along through open countryside to fascinating destinations unknown. Instead it began to feel like he was constantly circling the plug hole.

Still, a journey that begins so well, how badly can it end?

PART ONE

PART ONE

CHAPTER ONE

It was a week to Good Friday. Friday, 18th March.

Sometimes, the ghosts you think you've settled, overcome, and laid to rest, come back even worse than you ever imagined they could be. The cruellest of fates is when your sigh of relief that things have, at last, broken out of dark, cold winter into hopeful, bright spring, is followed by the blowing of a sour wind which sweeps away your footing and dumps you back into a more bitter and trapped place than if you'd never felt your release. Cruel is the word, and how it feels. It makes you question even the goodness of simple destiny, or God Himself.

David Sourbook, a retired schoolteacher of sixty-one with silver-grey hair and a pleasant face, leaned lightly against the railings that separated the path from the road, and felt slightly mugged. His face ached like he'd been hit and his wallet ached like he'd been robbed. £320 to remove the very tooth they'd fought together to save for three years. It added financial insult to dental injury. He looked longingly across the road at the café, but he'd been told he mustn't drink anything hot for at least an hour. And a choc-crunch-caramel shake wasn't quite the same on such a dreary day. He surveyed the sky. Grey and lifeless. Like himself. So much for spring.

'Lord, help me,' he said half-heartedly as he crossed the road to sit in the café until as near to an hour as he could get. He could order a large latte quite soon, he reckoned, and let it cool. In fact, pour some out onto a saucer like the old tramp, 'Smoky Joe', he remembered from his now-opened childhood, and blow on it till it was cool.

Memory was a wonderful thing. Wonderful and terrible.

He was pressing his tongue against his front teeth to stop himself from excavating the yawning chasm at the back of his lower jaw. He took one last blow at the coffee and sipped it. No wince of pain or sudden geyser of blood. All well. Except it wasn't. Far from it.

He took out the poem he'd written just a week ago on his phone. He read it to himself.

> You have to smile at daffodils,
> And hear their nodding trumpet peals.
> Be lifted by the breath of spring,
> And join the fresh new song, and sing!
>
> Yes, with the birds' uplifted voice,
> And with their lilting song so choice,
> With light made high and skies blue-clean,
> The whole world in a praising paean!
>
> Around my feet the crocus spreads,
> While tulips bend their glory-heads.
> A fat bee buzzes lazily,
> And all the Earth is new to me.
>
> So breathe it in, let hearts be filled,
> And all our hopes of joy, new-willed,
> And lightened be our very lives,
> Reminded, all, the world yet thrives.
>
> O buds! Burst forth! In green and blossomed praise.
> I watch you sway, in joyful, swelling days.
> O grass, release! Your newly cutted scent.
> And grow all endless summer's months, and not
> relent.

So, where did all that go? Well, with depression, it came and went, that he knew. Perhaps he should be glad for those

14

moments when the grey clouds of the mind did part and let a little spring sunshine in. He was pleased at the words, at the way it had worked out. But he remembered actually feeling it a week ago. Today was bleak, like winter yet ruled his heart. Still, he was seeing his counsellor before going to help at the old peoples' lunch. In three-quarters of an hour, in fact. The lovely Myfanwy. He had been driven to her by a deepening depression.

She sat and waited. David looked around at the usual décor. The cream carpet, the stylishly minimal shelves, the simple lamp, the bare walls with her certificates and a couple of calming scenes in huge photographs. The low, glass table between them held nothing but a box of tissues and a glass of water. You could see through it, like she through him.

He sat in his chair and she sat in hers, on the other side of a table that was transparent. What an image.

She waited. She was a picture of stillness. He reckoned she'd wait the whole fifty minutes if he said nothing. She looked at him, then at the window, then at the shelves, then back to him, and so on. Waiting. Trained to wait. To truly listen. To recede that you might break out. At last, he thought, she might say, 'So, is there anything you're trying to tell me?'

That would be clever. 'Trying to tell me' *by* your silence, or working against your silence? Silenced by your silence. He tried not to look at her nice knees and sweet, pretty face. She looked fresh as a daffodil in a light skirt and no tights. Don't stare. Always the knees, his worst temptation. Lust not!

His mind began to wander. 'She waits like very silence caught, until I can arrange a thought, and lay it out there in the space, lay bare the hurt behind my face, and let her hold it in the air, for her to see and me to bear.' Good. Not helpful. Good use of 'bear' and 'bare'.

On her lap lay her paper pad and in her hand was her ever-trusty pencil. No pen that might run out mid-revelation.

Focus, he told himself. You're paying for this. He felt his still slightly throbbing face, and a sigh escaped unbidden from somewhere.

'I'm feeling a little lost,' he said. Opening gambit. Livingstone defence.

'Lost?' she asked, predictably.

'Hmm. Lost. Deflated and defeated, perhaps.'

'You use poetry as a defence,' she observed, eyeing him.

'Do I?'

'Don't you? What do you think?'

'You mean I use the right words but arrange them in a way that robs them of real revelation about myself.'

'Do you think that might be true?'

'The dreams have come back.' There. Said it.

'Which dreams?'

'The same ones.'

'No, David, tell me which ones.'

He sighed. Both inwardly and outwardly. 'The ones with me and Michaela in the tunnel. The one where she dies. The one where I see her lying dead on the rails.' Tears welled and trickled. He sniffed. 'And the real memories of her holding my hand and looking up at me. The ones that destroy me.'

He resisted the tissues. He always resisted the tissues. Within reach but out of reach. Taking one was like admitting to – submitting to – his need of her. His need of her kindness.

She waited. She would wait now, again. Watching him and letting him lead. It irritated him. It always irritated him.

'And I miss The Yearning. I sit there, and I watch, and I look, but beyond the dusk and the trees and the sky there's nothing, now. Like discovering what it was in myself and in Micky and in God has stripped it of its power. But it's like I needed it. And now I don't have it.'

'How is your faith?'

'I'm struggling. I sit there with the Bible open on my lap and just nothing happens. I try to talk but it's like inside there's nothing going on. I don't know.'

'What don't you know?'

He thought. Let her wait some more.

'Are you sleeping?' she interjected.

'No, I'm awake.'

'We've talked about that. What did we say about it?'

'Yes. So we have. Sorry. That it isn't just deflection; I use it to make myself sound happy when in fact I'm far from happy.'

'OK, because I want to know how you really feel, because I want *you* to know how you really feel. So. At night, to be clear, are you sleeping well?'

'No. Most nights I'm woken by the dreams around two or three and then I can't get back to sleep. I get up eventually and go downstairs and make myself some tea.'

'That sounds very lonely. *Very* lonely. Is it?'

'Yes.' He sniffed and took a tissue.

'So, how's things with Angela?'

That brought the big sigh. 'Hmm.'

David was on the other side of the table from Mr Anders, serving mashed potato with a big spoon from a saucepan, when he saw it begin. Mr Anders was watching him serving, when his face sort of collapsed on the right and his whole body seemed to slump down on that side. Focus disappeared from his eyes and he slid sideways, so slowly, then fell off his chair onto the floor. Shock erupted around him. His wife, Doreen, looked down in disbelief.

But David was on it. Round the table in three strides, demanding that someone call 999 as he went. This was what they'd just sent him on the first aid course for. That was a classic stroke. Speed was the key. He turned Mr Anders onto his back and pressed his thumb against the carotid point for a pulse. Already his lips were blue. No pulse. He waited a few more seconds, feeling very carefully. No pulse.

He measured down the chest, placed his palms there, took in a calming breath and started compressions. He counted as he went. Every eye was on him. Once he'd got a good rhythm going he opened Mr Anders' mouth and saw that his airway seemed clear. He heard Mrs Anders say, 'Is he going to be all right?' and someone was comforting her.

Tilted head, sealed mouth, big breaths, five of them. The chest rose nicely. Back to the heart. Jonk jonk jonk, firm but not hard enough to break an old sternum. Hopefully.

He was aware of someone making everyone get back, giving them room and air. Mrs Stevens came over and whispered, 'Do you want me to take over?' but he didn't know if she was trained, and anyway he was in a good rhythm, so he said, 'I'm fine. Thanks.' His arms did ache, but he was confident he'd got it under control and didn't want to back off like he was incapable or didn't know what he was doing.

No response from Mr Anders. No carotid pulse. No point checking breathing if there was no pulse.

Movement by the door made him wonder if the ambulance had arrived. But then it stopped. Muttered comments around. 'He's dead.' 'Look at the colour of him.' 'Oh dear, he's gone.'

Mrs Anders' face, ashen, shocked, staring, fixed. A bit like her husband's, though less cyan in colour. Someone's arm round her shoulders.

Pump, pump, pump, check, breathe, pump some more. Arms aching now. Centred on the task, everything else sounding off, peripheral. Until a hand landed on his shoulder and a man's voice said, 'We've got this now.'

David looked up into the face of a young paramedic. He took a second to register, then moved away and sat on the floor, looking back at the obviously deceased Mr Anders.

The two paramedics surrounded Mr Anders and effectively screened off most of the fixated stares. They muttered to each other. They huddled over. A torchlight flashed. Then the second stood and said, 'I'm sorry, he's gone. He was dead when we arrived.'

Eyes turned to David. He got up and slumped into a chair like he was following old Anders.

'I doubt he survived the stroke,' the second added. 'Did you give first aid?' he said to David.

'Yes. Since less than a minute after he fell. Mostly cardiac compressions. There was no pulse at any time.'

'Well done, then. I could see you were still going when we arrived. There was nothing more you could have done.'

Still the eyes on him. Why were they looking at him? He hadn't done anything. Oh. He hadn't done anything. That was why.

Mrs Anders in particular seemed to be unable to take her eyes off him. He stood and walked over to her. She looked down at the floor as he approached.

'I'm so sorry, Mrs Anders,' he said, wondering whether to add some disclaimer or leave it at that. She didn't look up, or answer. 'If there's anything I can do...'

'You've done enough,' she mumbled.

'I tried my very best... I did everything they taught us on the first aid course, but it must have been a very bad stroke.'

She made no reply. She was just waiting for him to go away.

He retreated, unsure where to go. Everyone was standing around, staring at the paramedics working on Mr Anders' dead body. David felt really uncomfortable.

Anna Lovren at last came over to him and laid a sensitive hand on his arm as she said, 'David. Thank you so much for trying so hard to help Mr Anders. Please don't feel at all bad that he couldn't be revived. I spoke to the medics and it must have been a massive stroke. Really, he was gone before he hit the floor. Don't feel bad. I'm very glad you were here.'

'Then why is everyone staring at me?'

'They're in shock. You were at the centre of the action. They're trying to get a handle on what they've just experienced. And they don't want to stare at Mrs Anders or Mr Anders' body. So it's you. Don't take it the wrong way. You're the hero, really.'

'I don't feel like a hero.'

'People who step up and act often don't. Believe me, you are.'

'Thanks.'

The paramedics had Mr Anders covered up on their stretcher and carried him out of the door. All eyes now followed them, then went to poor Mrs Anders, still being comforted by three of her friends. He had the distinct feeling they were talking about him.

Suddenly he couldn't breathe and had to get out. He stood and his chest was on fire. He dashed for the exit and stopped outside, trying not to hyperventilate, because he knew that would just make it worse. He started to count, Fibonacci numbers, adding the last two to make the next one. He was also counting down from sixty as he reckoned it always passed in less than a minute. That double demand on his processing power robbed the panic of focus. As usual, at about forty seconds he was nearly overcome with fear that it wasn't going to go away, but he pressed on, and by fifteen seconds he could feel the pressure lessening and the sense of hope returning. Before zero he was drawing a welcome sigh of relief. It had passed. But it always felt like it would never end and he'd be stuck in it for ever. Horrible. Both depression and anxiety had that awful feature – the sense that this would never come to an end.

He rested his hands on his knees and felt a hand on his back. Anna again.

'Anxiety episode?'

'Yah. Gone now.'

'Good, well done.' She took his hand. 'Come on, you need a nice cup of tea.'

'OK.'

She let go.

He followed her, meek as a lamb, feeling fairly washed out by the whole experience. When he got back in, everyone except Mrs Anders and her two friends, Doris and Aggie, were back in their seats trying to eat their pudding. The mood was solemn.

Anna led him into the kitchen and he leaned against the worktop as she poured him a tea from the huge pot, and handed it to him.

'You're a bona fide hero,' she said. 'Angela will be so proud. How's things with you two?'

'Hmm.'

Angela was coming to dinner and he had to buy stuff and prepare a meal. That used to be a real joy. At the moment it was – something else. Worrying? Stressful? Disappointing? Something that it didn't used to be.

Anyway, shopping. He drove from the lunch to the supermarket with a vague idea of what he needed. Pasta, cheese sauce, broccoli, carrots, cheddar, French stick, butter and garlic. Not so vague, in fact. Then cream, sugar, wine, lemon and split almonds for the syllabub. And red wine to drink. And some ground coffee. And maybe a few chocolate mints.

The store was bright and clean like always, and he pushed his trolley around in a bit of a fug, with images of Mr Anders' dead stare and Mrs Anders' living one coming unbidden into his mind. He had to go back a couple of times for items he'd walked right by, but ended up at the checkout soon after 4pm.

In the car park he froze in horrified fear. Surrounding his i10 was the group of Ruf's friends, who had somehow come to the mistaken conviction that he and Angela had actually handed Ruf over to the police and got him convicted and sent away for the dog attack on the postwoman, last Christmas. So – they knew his car. One of them was just finishing off a huge 'F' on his door with the tip of a ferocious-looking knife. David decided to try to retreat backwards into the store, but they spotted him. Like a pack of wolves, they ran and pounced, surrounding him. Two of them wrestled the trolley from his grip and tipped it over so that everything rolled out. They stamped on a packet of pasta and the tub of cream, sending tagliatelle and white foam over the floor, laughing as they did so. Then others began to jostle him backwards and forwards between them, shouting filthy abuse in his face. He saw the knife.

Behind him, the automatic doors opened and two male voices yelled at them to stop. They didn't just stop but scattered, as if driven by the wind, ducking and weaving between cars.

Two security guards came up to David and one said, 'Are you all right, sir? Would you like us to call the police?'

David looked down at the ruined pasta and cream. He sighed, and felt the fear recede. 'No. They know who I am. That would only aggravate things.'

'Let us help you anyway. You'll need to come back into the store because we need to make a report, and we'll replace those two broken items for you.'

'That's very kind. OK. Thank you.'

In a moment they had the trolley back on its wheels and refilled and one of them was radioing for clean-up. They helped David back into the store, more, he reckoned, because they were concerned for his shock than that he'd try to scarper. They took him to the customer service desk and then to the café where they got him a pot of tea.

Surely this was kindness beyond necessity? And then he came over all pale and faint. He knew they could see it on his face, and he felt like he was going to throw up. He doubled over on his chair.

'Are you all right? Are you feeling like being sick?' one of them said.

'I think I'm going to be OK. Just give me a minute.'

'Try a sip of tea. Do you take sugar?' the other one said.

'Does he take sugar?' David mumbled. 'No, no sugar, thank you.'

He sat up and everything swam in front of him. He groaned. And was sick on the floor. Of the café.

One of them spoke into his radio and a moment later the tannoy announced, 'Cleaner to the café, right away. Cleaner to the café.'

Another man appeared, with a mobile mop bucket, and set to cleaning up.

'Let's move you away,' one of the security guys said, and then a woman with a clipboard appeared. She followed them and his tea to the new table, and sat down with him.

'Hello,' she said, 'I'm the deputy manager, Margaret Allen. I'm so sorry this has happened to you today. Please be assured we'll do everything we can to help you. Firstly, can I take some basic details from you, please?'

Now he looked like a shoplifter, as well as a person who throws up in a café. His dishonouring was, surely, complete.

He'd need to file a police report anyway, for his car insurance for the repair to the paintwork. Great. Another thing to do.

He sat in his seat in the front room at half past six. He was late, now, for starting the cooking. Outside, dusk beckoned. He could make a cup of tea in his WOL mug, the one with a picture of the owl from Winnie the Pooh, and go and sit outside and watch it, but what was the point? He hadn't the energy. And it no longer carried the wonder, the tear-straining beauty it used to. It no longer pulled at his very deepest being with a voice from the other side of the darkening skies, from the endless and mysterious distance of the universe. Dusk, his most extraordinary and wonderful encounter, had been bled of meaning and emptied of its call. Together, he and it were silent. Wordless, no longer in wonder but now in unshared, hollow silence. The stillness that had been awe was now just fruitless waiting. Any tears it pulled from him were of a very different sort.

The doorbell shook him. Darn. What was going on? He was confused. He'd fallen asleep and now Angela was at the door. It rang again. He stood and tottered out of the front room and to the front of the hallway. The sight of her brown coat through the frosted glass didn't lift him like it should. He half-feared the jocular jibes she'd throw at him.

He opened it and there she stood, her almost-blonde hair up in some kind of ponytail. He wasn't at all sure he liked her like that. But there was her sweet, round face, blue eyes, freckles, lovely nose. The same, yet these days it didn't seem quite the same to him. Still, she advanced for a hug and he returned it.

He clung to her. Fell into her. She said, 'I'm so sorry about George Anders. Anna told me. You did everything anyone could. You must feel horrible.'

He said nothing, but sniffed. She held him. Warm and strong. 'I guess you've got an aching jaw and you saw Myfanwy as well.'

'And ran into Ruf's old mates in the car park of the supermarket and got pushed about by them and my car door engraved with a big "F".'

She pushed him back so as to engage him with those lovely eyes, full of concern. 'Oh, David! I'm so sorry. What a horrible day!'

'It truly was. And now I haven't even prepared what I bought for our meal.'

She pulled him close again. 'Then we'll thoroughly enjoy cooking it up and eating it together, all the more.'

She was a wonderful friend. No doubt of it. He hugged her tight.

'I love you,' she said.

'Thank you.'

24

CHAPTER TWO

As they cooked together, the kitchen became a warm haven of tasty smells and secure comfort. It began to rain outside and the droplets tippety-tapped against the windows. She let him listen to Radio 4 as they worked, as long as it was fairly quiet and didn't prevent conversation. But there wasn't much of that. She seemed content to just be with him and working side by side. She even commented on the programme's ideas of 'A Theory of Everything' in physics (the subject he had taught all his working life) quite intelligently, he thought, for a non-physicist.

It was rather like winter had returned and here they huddled in the warmth of hearth and home. The truth of it wasn't lost on David.

They sat at the table, a large plate of cheesy tagliatelle with vegetables and garlic bread in front of each of them. She held his hands and said a simple grace, then they forked in. But it didn't taste right. It tasted of cheese-less cheese and garlic-less garlic. He knew the symptom. Anhedonia. A loss of the ability to experience pleasure. There was absolutely nothing wrong with the food. It tasted as it should, in fact. But pleasure had been leached out of it. A familiar symptom of depression. He said nothing.

'Is yours all right?' she said, seeing his lack of enthusiasm.

'Yes, fine. Yours?'

'Lovely. You cook up a mean dinner in your lovely cottage kitchen.'

He ploughed on, determined to eat it regardless. It was his tea. But she knew he was lacking something.

She reached out and took his hand again. 'Are you all right? I detect a certain saggedness.'

He put his fork down and looked her in the eye. Those perceptive eyes. 'I'm not doing well. Myfanwy offered me an increase in the "sten" antidepressants, but I said no. For now, at least. And I'm worried about the effect I'm having on you.' There, said it. That was twice today he'd got something out. Just blurt it. 'The way to say, is simply blurt. Don't be held back by fears of hurt. 'Tis true the words can't be recalled, but power becomes their good, un-walled.' Nice.

She looked troubled, and laid her fork to rest as well. 'What effect on me? Is this something you've been trying to say to me? Tell me, dear David, you know I only want the best for you. I love you.'

'Your life is less happy because of me. You were this bird, free and swooping, but now you're trapped in a relationship cage with me. And it isn't good for you. This is not where you should be.'

A tear welled at the corner of her eye. She studied him deeply. 'I can't believe you think that. You're the best thing that's happened to me since… since I didn't die last Christmas. I'd be lost without you. You complete me. Already, I feel that. You are my angel. You know that. Please don't back away from me for my sake, somehow thinking that will be good for me. *You* are good for me. And I will do everything in my power and God's to help you get well again.'

The tears flowed unchecked now, and she held her napkin to her face. It was a Christmas one, because he didn't get through them very quickly. Far too festive for the moment. She looked so sad. It bit into him. He grabbed her free hand.

He tried to speak but emotion choked him and his own tears released down his face, hot and tickly against his nose. What a pair, they sat there in quiet desolation, both the cause and the solution to each other's lostness.

A shadow came over her face. 'There's more to it that you're not telling me. Isn't there? You think our relationship is the cause of your depression and confusion, don't you?'

His face must have betrayed him.

'Oh, David!' There was accusation and disappointment in that.

Now he felt condemned as well as lost. He descended into a place of even darker misery. Guilty misery. Disembowelled and empty loss.

He wasn't looking at her but down at his plate, like some child caught in disgrace and unable to face the adult who stood over them. But he heard her complete distress in the small noises she was making. Small, like a dog beaten into a corner and whimpering.

They remained in this mutual prison until he said, 'Time for dessert,' and began to clear the plates. She didn't look up at him. She had her face in the hanky from her sleeve.

'I'm far too upset for syllabub,' she said as he stood with a bowl in each hand. 'David, what do you want to do? End it now or just take a break for a while?'

He said nothing. She stood and made her way into the hall, put on her coat and opened the door. He watched her, bowls in hands.

She looked at him for a few seconds, querying, then said, 'Goodbye, David.' And walked out.

The tunnel. Dark, cold, long, hopeless, lightless, going nowhere, isolated and hidden. Him, and, looking down, the upturned face of his dear little sister Micky, like a light for the whole tunnel and his whole world.

What were they doing in an underground railway tunnel?

She held his hand. It felt so comfortable and so familiar. Somehow her little face shone even in the darkness. Her eyes a beam of happy, loving brightness.

Oh! No! There she lay, against the live rail! Still, unmoving. So small. So dead. A great cry burst from him and echoed down the tunnel to the very ends, the ends of the world, the ends of his life. No, no, no!

Bitter regret and darkest sorrow came over him and covered him like a shroud. It cut him like a sweet knife, bleeding him of all but woe. The little, dead body. The stupefying sense of her loss, so complete, so unmerited, so utterly wrong. Gone without remedy, without means of recovery, without a word to be said or a kind, remorseful action to be offered. Gone, gone, gone.

It drained him then snapped him like a dry twig. Tears forced themselves from his eyes, and stung and stained his face with rivers of self-reproach. Why that? It felt like he'd never loved her properly, and now could never tell her that he did, or change it. Like those trusting eyes had found in him no strength of affection or place of comfort. He didn't understand it, but he felt it. So powerful. So emptying. So full of grievous regret. Unnamed. Unspoken. Unknown.

Now he was kneeling, stroking the blonde hair, touching the little brown coat. Yearning, yearning, yearning for her to be alive again. To move, to wake. But no. Never. Never again. 'Micky.'

Still the middle of the bleak, dead night. He went to the loo. The bathroom lights were bright enough, so if that hooded, shading effect over him in the mirror wasn't something physical, was it psychological? Or something even more menacing? It hung there like a dark presence, waiting, shadowing him. He shook as if he were cold, and looked away.

His course of action seemed somehow irresistible. Like it always had to be, and even now was simply coming to be. Drained, lifeless, this merely followed on. He was vaguely aware of being in some kind of fug, some focusless miasma.

He took the glass off the shelf that contained his toothpaste and brush, and tipped them into the sink (a thing he never did). Then he pushed out a whole strip of stenalazine antidepressants into the glass, and dropped the empty strip onto the floor (another thing he never did). He looked at them, and at the glass of water still on the shelf. He started on another strip, to be sure.

28

Then he stared at the nice little pile he'd created in the bottom of the glass. He threw the whole lot back into his mouth and followed them with a good swig of the water, then another. They slid down easily. As would he.

He looked at himself again in the mirror. Goodbye, you old misery.

He went back to bed and determined to be asleep before he began to feel woozy, confused or sick.

It was Saturday, 19th March.

David was aware of the passing of images. Rather, that images had passed. Vague sights of light and forms. People, he thought. Always, he was horizontal. And often, feeling dizzy, even sick, and very woozy. Wooozy. The word faded in and out in his mind. What was left of his mind.

Now he was propped up, and someone was holding his left hand. A blue curtain was before him, past the end of the bed. Bed. Water was being given to him through a straw. Something was sticking to him, around his chest.

Someone not quite in the picture said, 'Yes, that's nice and stable. We'll keep it on for another hour. He should be fine.'

Fortunate for someone. They should be fine.

The hand squeezed him. 'Did you hear that, David, my love? Should be fine.'

The voice was familiar. Female. Angela. Now she was patting and stroking his hand. He opened it, and held hers properly. It was comforting.

He heard a male voice ask about seizures, and when the nurse said no he replied they'd leave off the relaxant drugs.

'What was that?' he asked Angela.

'You had a seizure, a fit, brought on by the stenalazine, so they gave you a tranquiliser to relax your muscles. That's all. You're very fortunate that a stenalazine overdose doesn't tend to do any real damage. Your heart is being monitored just in case of cardiac arrhythmia. It's a possibility is all. But you heard that sounds fine.'

'Oh. I took an overdose.'

'Yes, dear David, you did.' She bent her head down onto his hand, pressing her forehead against it, and said, 'I'm so sorry. I really am.' She was crying.

'You found me?'

'I called in early before college because I was so unhappy how we left it last night, and had to use my key to get in, and there were you on your bedroom carpet and there was the evidence on the bathroom floor. And you'd thrown up in your bed, so be glad you didn't choke as well.'

He sighed. It turned into a great, deep, bemused sigh. 'Oh. I'm sorry.'

She looked up at him. Such tenderness in those eyes. 'If I'd known you were struggling so much I never would have left like that. I am so sorry, Little Noddy. Please forgive me.'

'There's nothing to forgive. You were right. In part I was blaming you.'

'I may be in part to blame. Still riding you. Pressuring you. I don't know.'

His mind shifted tack. 'There was something dark. Before I took the tablets. As I stood in the bathroom, in the mirror. It was like a dark aura.'

'Don't be dramatic. You were depressed enough to be about to try to end your life. Of course it felt sombre. Goodness! I'd be surprised if it didn't.'

'Hmm. OK.'

A tall, female doctor came into the curtained bed-space. She had long, brown hair tied severely back and was carrying a tablet before her like a clipboard, and serving the same purpose – defensive knowledge.

'Hello, Mr Sourbook. I'm Dr Levin. I'm just here to tell you that someone from the psychiatric team will need to interview you before you leave.'

'Oh. Why?'

'To assess your state of mind. We have to be sure it's safe to send you home. For your own security. They'll be along

30

sometime in the next hour or so. Maybe sooner. Thank you. I hope you'll be feeling better.'

'Right. Yes. Thank you,' he said, as she swept away past the blue curtains.

He looked at Angela as she looked at him. He said, 'Will they section me? I don't want to end up on the psych ward. Can you imagine anything worse?'

'Yes, you killing yourself all on your own in your nice little house and me at your funeral. That's infinitely worse. For both of us and lots of others, too.'

'Don't be dramatic.'

'Really?' she reposted.

It was half an hour later that Dr Saratnam materialised through the blue curtains like an apparition, all swirly sari in the most fabulous greens and lilacs. She sat on the chair at his other side from Angela and began. She asked questions and expressed concerns and ended up agreeing with Angela that he could go and stay with the Grangers for a few days as she wasn't happy for him to be allowed home on his own.

CHAPTER THREE

He looked out of the car window as she drove and it brought back so much. But this time he felt ashamed. He saw the parallel between himself and Ruf, who'd stayed with the Grangers last Christmas because he'd been thrown out of his house by his mum. Now he was in prison, serving an eight-month sentence for allowing his dog to bite a postwoman, causing some real damage. The Ruf whose friends had attacked his car.

But now it was him being taken to be supervised by them. Not to be left alone. Would they watch him surreptitiously and talk about how he was doing when out of earshot? Probably.

Would they report to Angela? Of course they would. Would he feel like a complete waste of space? Definitely. Would he try to take his life again? He wasn't sure.

Maybe he'd lose the visits to Andrew now, Angela's nephew. That would be really sad. But maybe a suicide risk shouldn't be allowed near a lad with Autism Spectrum Disorder (ASD).

That just made him feel the more ashamed. Ashamed, named, blamed. There was a poem in there somewhere. Not that he felt much like poetry. He saw a flash of himself being told by a stern-faced Mary Granger to take his feet off the furniture, like poor Ruf last Christmas. And of himself muttering under his breath, 'Feet, David.'

'Are you OK?' she said, concerned for him with that irritating, protective tone.

'Are you going to keep asking me that?'

She looked across momentarily. 'Am I asking it too much?'

'You're not my mother.'

32

'I should hope not! The feelings I have for you are certainly not appropriate for a mother.'

Silence followed. He could see she was... upset? Annoyed? Concerned?

He watched more trees in bud and blossom as they passed. His prison grew ever closer.

'Do you know any physics jokes?' she asked, out of the blue. 'Tell me one.'

'Higgs Boson became a Christian. Actually, he became a Catholic priest. He felt it was his destiny to give mass.'

She laughed.

'Another one!' she said.

'Two atoms were walking down the road. One suddenly stopped and said, "Oh! I've lost an electron. Never mind, let's carry on." The other said, "Are you sure?" and the first replied, "Yes, I'm positive."'

She giggled again.

'I know what you're doing. Lightening the mood,' he said, 'dispelling the tension.'

'Good,' she answered.

'David! Consider this your private hotel.'

It was a beaming Bill Granger, tall, thin and dressed in tweedy trousers and a bright red jumper, who descended the steps with a hand held out to shake and the other arm ready to give him a welcoming hug. Dear Bill. They met in the middle and embraced.

Mary was close behind him. She was also tall and skinny, with her hair swept back into a bun, wearing a pair of similar tweedy trousers and a dark red jumper. She hugged David and kissed him lightly on the cheek. 'It's so lovely to see you again, and that you'll be staying a few days.'

The house looked as imposing as ever, with its light browny-yellow bricks, white window frames and some wall-climbing roses already starting to bloom. Mary's pride and joy.

'Come in, come in and we'll get you billeted,' Bill said, taking David's travel bag and leading the way. Angela fell in alongside

Mary and they went into the kitchen while Bill and David climbed the stairs.

'You'll like this room,' he said. 'It's all en suite, and you've even got a TV and a tea- and coffee-making set. It also has a lovely view over the back garden to the trees, where you and I will be taking a walk later. Sound good?'

'Very much so,' David replied, summoning what sounded like enthusiasm.

They entered the room, and it was indeed lovely. It was spacious and airy, with large windows, and the ceiling in one corner angled down under the eaves. The bed was a double and made up with a large, pale blue duvet cover and two pillows each side. There were paintings on the walls of country scenes, and on a small table near the enormous TV was the tea-making stuff, with kettle.

'Now,' Bill said, laying the case on the bed, turning and smiling. 'Breakfast is at 7.30am, lunch at 12.30pm and evening meal at 7.30pm. A light supper will be available at 10.30pm if wanted. That one will be in the lounge. The others are in the dining room. We like to eat on the half-hour: it's good for the digestion. And listen, old chap, we do expect you to eat with us. That's important. I'm also hoping you're going to feel up to helping me with a small job I'm about to undertake – redecorating the small bedroom. Your help would be a real lift. I'm starting that on Monday. Tomorrow is church, of course. We'll take you. Anyway, here's your room. Unpack, then come down for a coffee in the kitchen. Any questions?'

'Can I make some contribution for this hospitality?'

'Of course you can!' he said, beaming. 'But not money. And only flowers and a bottle of red wine when you leave. No, the real contribution you can make is to be part of the family and enjoy being with us. There. See you in ten minutes.'

'Thank you. So much. I shall look forward to that walk.'

'Weather's going to lift this afternoon, I do believe. And the woods are full of bluebells and daffs.'

He left, closing the door carefully behind him.

'Bluebells and daffs,' David muttered to himself, dismissively. 'Trumpets and bells for the heralding of spring. Actually, that's not bad. Yellow trumpets and blue bells herald the glory of the approaching spring. Buds burst like cannons and birds in a choir take up an anthem of praise. Crocuses in holy crowds are the priests for the breeze-borne liturgy of life. How is it I can describe it but not feel it?'

He continued putting shirts in a drawer, then said, 'Maybe I should give up poetry and become a blues singer. Or a blues poet! "I woke up this morning. Not again, not again!"'

He gave a little laugh, and lifted himself.

He continued to chunter. 'The other day I was walking past an opticians and a girl outside said, "Come in for a free eye test." I said, "I don't see why I should need one." But I went in anyway, and they also offered me a free hearing test. Afterwards, the guy said, "You've got perfect hearing," and I said, "What?!" As I left I bought some glasses' cleaning wipes. They were really good. Spectacular. You're a funny man, David Sourbook. When I told people I wanted to be a comedian, they laughed at me. Well, they're not laughing now. That's an old one. Bob Monkhouse, I think.'

Unpacking finished, he went downstairs and met the others in the kitchen where they already had coffees at the breakfast bar in the centre. He sat on a tall stool opposite Angela. She smiled at him, a lovely smile, and it reminded him how good that smile was. How much good it had done him, in fact.

Bill and Mary made a great effort to keep the conversation jolly, and then made excuses to go elsewhere so Angela and David could say goodbye.

'They're unsure about whether to invite me for food tonight,' she said, looking just a touch sad, holding his hand.

'Ah. Up to me, I suppose. I think I'd rather it was just me and them, to get to know them a bit better, help me settle in and feel at home.' She just watched him as he spoke. 'Maybe talk about you,' he added, to try to lighten the moment.

'No, that's fine,' she said. 'I'll miss you, but I want you to feel settled here. Happy. Maybe tomorrow night. Or whenever you're ready. And listen,' now her face went really serious. 'What I said about going our separate ways, I'm really sorry. I didn't really mean that and I certainly don't want that. I want us to get through this and be together. I don't know what's exactly wrong, I will confess. But I want us to sort it out, when we're ready.'

She was trying not to stare at him for a response, but it was difficult as she was already looking hard into him. She seemed like she might crumple into tears at any second. Oh, what the hell, he didn't need to upset her. 'OK. Yes, that sounds good to me. I'm sorry too. Give me a kiss.'

They kissed, briefly but warmly, as part of a full hug, and she took hold of his hand for him to walk her out to her car.

'You know I'm worried about you,' she said, looking up at him as she got into her seat.

He said nothing.

'Are you worried about yourself?' she pressed.

He just shrugged. 'Sometimes it feels like I've just given up.'

She jumped up out of the seat and hugged him all round. 'No, no!' she said. 'Don't give up, Little Noddy. I love you and I *need* you.'

'Well, good. Thank you.'

'And I'm going to be praying super-hard for you as well.'

'Thank you.'

'And I'll see you in church in the morning. It's Palm Sunday. We get our palm crosses.'

'OK.'

She got back into the car and drove away.

He felt very, very empty. Maybe slightly guilty as well. Certainly lost. And limp. Listless and lifeless.

David and Bill both wore jackets because it might be cold in the shadier areas, and Bill also carried a small rucksack. No doubt it contained a Bible so he could show David that suicide is a sin and he needed to repent of such God-dishonouring ways.

They went through the little wrought-iron gate and were immediately in quite thick woods. The sun played a game of stripes and patterns with the trees, casting bright camouflage over bushes and pathways. A high breeze frolicked with the leaves, and the leaves played too, with their lively friend, the air. The lush carpet of bluebells around their feet seemed alive, as if attending their every step. And all above them the calls of birds sang back and forth as the occasional rustle in the undergrowth betrayed a squirrel, or maybe a fox. It was a dance of new life, a celebration of freedom from the hard, cold hold of winter. It seemed to defy you to not be lifted.

Bill said, 'Is it not beautiful – this living wood, bursting with all the joys of spring?'

'Yes, it is. I do feel it,' David admitted.

'Good for you. Let's just walk and enjoy it. We can talk when we take a sit-down for a little rest. OK with you?'

'Fine,' David agreed, relieved in fact to be able to just move at this gentle pace and take it all in. It was rather as if the wood was another place, a different world, and his sorrows had no reality here.

At length, they emerged into the light of a clearing, some forty metres or so around. David saw daffodils in a group like an old-time band, bobbing and waving as they played. Bill led him to a huge section of a fallen tree trunk and they sat down. The light was glorious as the sun hung high enough to give unfettered brilliance where they sat, and to limelight the playing daffodils. The grass was green and already verdant; indeed, it had lifted their feet as they'd walked across it. Clusters of buttercups were in cheeky attendance here and there. David swept his gaze around it all, and felt held and lifted. The very air carried that indefinable scent of spring, and filled his lungs and his whole body like it was actually alive.

Out of his backpack Bill produced a vacuum flask of tea and a packet of chocolate digestives. He began to pour tea into two plastic cups.

Bill looked around, smiling a broad and wise old smile. 'Angela is a lovely, wise, caring person. You're very fortunate how she loves you.'

'Are you suggesting I've somehow done her wrong?'

'Not at all, dear chap, merely that you are a very fortunate fellow.'

'Oh. All right, then. Bill, can I ask you something?'

'Ask away.'

'Do you know any psychiatry, and counselling?'

'Yes. A GP has to have some idea of those things, at least to be able to refer appropriately.'

'If I started to tell you about the sessions I have with my counsellor, would you feel bound to keep that absolutely confidential?'

'Yes. Not as doctor–patient confidentiality, because I'm not your doctor. But as your friend and confidant, absolutely and totally.'

David supped some tea and finished his first biscuit, took another and said, 'Can we start now?'

'No better time, dear chap. Go ahead.'

A great relief came over David. He began, 'Well, to begin with, she asked me when I started to see my childhood in more than just vague generalities – as clear and specific memories. I said that was when I saw Micky, and the loss of her. She asked why that might be, and I said because my subconscious was always desperate to prevent me from seeing that loss, and detailed memories were therefore a danger. I might stumble across a memory of her as my precious little sister, and then I'd realise that I'd known her and lost her. She seemed quite pleased with that.'

'Good for you,' Bill said, encouragingly, over half a biscuit in his mouth.

'Then she asked why my parents kept the loss of her from me. I said I supposed because at the time it had such a devastating impact on me as an eight-year-old that that was the only way they could see of dealing with it. For my own good.

She asked me why I felt the need to defend them. I said I didn't and she let that slide. So the next session she asked me all about my mum. I thought that was a bit predictable, but hey, she's supposed to be the expert, not me. I told her how I resented my mum and she probed into why that was. She centred on how I saw my mum. It turned out I saw her as controlling and maybe a bit smothering, even though there wasn't much real physical affection. No memories of actual cuddles, or kisses, or sitting on her lap or her holding my hand, that kind of thing. I would have said that was the root of the resentment, but she, Myfanwy, was trying to draw out that the real root of the resentment was how I felt dominated by her. Like she was always right and always in charge of everything, even of my dad, who I think feared her.'

David paused to drink some tea and chew on his biscuit. He looked up at the smiling blue sky and the cheery sun, and birds entertaining them with swoops and hanging glides in perfect harmony. This was a magical spot. Trees waved at him, and even the green grass blessed his feet. Was there something in the tea? He shifted his bottom on the hard wood and held his cup out for a refill, which Bill gave with another happy smile. The biscuits were offered, too. David was impressed that he didn't say, 'Carry on.' He just waited, and looked at the same idyllic spring scene.

David swallowed. 'So the next week she wanted to know all about my relationship with Angela. As I answered her questions it became clear that she was looking for me to make a connection. She was particularly interested in how Angela dominates me and makes me feel like she's controlling everything. She, Angela, calls it, "jockey syndrome" – she rides people, over-engages. Myfanwy wanted to know all about how that felt to me. And eventually the penny dropped. I see Angela through the lens of my mother. I feel a certain resentment towards her. I bridle at the way she "rides" me. Sorry, that's not a joke. But it's like it limits my feelings for her. It makes me ambivalent towards her.'

Bill said, 'Carry on, but let's get walking again. I want to show you the stream.'

Bill got all his bits back together, heaved on his rucksack, small though it was, and led the way towards the trees.

David carried on with what he was saying before. More came out as they walked, along paths between bushes and trunks under the light-splattering canopy. Until, still under the trees, they reached the stream.

Small, it was, just trickling along down its stony and brown channel, round occasional larger rocks. It was a couple of feet wide and maybe six inches deep in the centre. And it entranced David like they'd entered into a fairy vale. He stopped and stared, and Bill stood silent beside him.

'Goodness!' David said after a while.

'I know. Beautiful, isn't it?'

'Do fairies live here?'

A tiny puff of something floaty and white drifted by, and they both broke into laughter. Bill said, 'If they lived anywhere, I guess this might be the place.'

'Can we stop here for a while?'

'Of course we can,' Bill answered, taking off his rucksack. 'There's a tree over there with some useful lifted roots, just right for planting yourself on for a while. More tea?'

'Vicar? Yes, please.'

They drank tea with more biscuits and David listened to birds singing aloft. Bill said, 'How's your faith?'

'Myfanwy asked me that. I don't know. I might almost say, "What faith?" I'm not sure I'm really there yet. Despite "responding" at the course last month, at church.'

'Well, OK, that's understandable. Though on the other hand depression does have the effect of making your faith go completely flat and making God seem utterly absent. So don't be too quick to judge yourself. Sometimes you need that trust in God's robust and determined holding of you more than you need anything else.'

'Hmm.'

40

'You know when a toddler holds Daddy's hand as they walk along, and the boy slips, and the held hand holds him up from falling. They're both holding hands, but it's the strength of Daddy's grip that saves the little chap from falling, not the strength of his own tiny hand. The toddler just needs to keep holding hands. No one's asking him to be strong enough to save himself.'

'Yes, I see that,' David said.

They drank and chewed in silence and David listened to how the birds sang in discrete chirrups, waiting for an answering call. He whistled back a few times, and it was like they answered him with their next burst of uplifting song. He felt part of it, the whole idyllic setting, and it felt good. Like it was restoring him. Spring is certainly the most hopeful and hope-filled of seasons. Like as it was recreated so he, too, along with it and as part of it, was recreated. Very poetic. There was a poem in there. But, more importantly, he felt, it was very true.

David said, 'It does feel good that I've renamed the house "Dusken Views" and that I have lunch with Mrs James fortnightly, though I think she's taken a bit too much of a shine to me. And I meet up with Frank Edmonds for a drink on a Tuesday lunchtime. All that is certainly good. And the lunch club was good until I failed to revive Mr Anders. You should've seen the way they stared at me.'

'Listen, dear chap,' Bill put a hand gently on his shoulder, 'take it from a man who knows – a GP of many years' experience. Mr Anders was dead before he hit the floor. That was a massive stroke and probably a heart attack as well, and the postmortem will show as much. There was nothing I could have done, nor a full medical team had he been in the ICU. People die. Everyone dies. And no one will hold it against you. You were a hero to respond so quickly and, from what I hear, so correctly. Don't beat yourself up over it. That's the cost of being willing to step in and take action. Take responsibility. Which you did, magnificently, so well done, say I. Raising the dead is quite another ministry!'

'Thanks. That means a lot,' David said, feeling the reassurance.

Soon they set off again, and circled round to end up heading back to the house. As he saw it approaching, a darkness came over David and he said, 'I'm done in. I think I need to go and lie down.'

'Oh. OK,' Bill said, sounding a little disappointed. 'Good plan. See you at dinner, at 7.30, if not before. Anything you need, just ask me or Mary. Are you just needing a rest? Not feeling ill or anything?'

'Just the rest,' David lied.

CHAPTER FOUR

David woke from his nap feeling disorientated and depressed. He wasn't sure where he was or what time of day it might be. He closed his eyes again and hugged the pillow. Where was Bart when you needed him? Well, the big cuddly bear was at home, of course, in the small bedroom. David could hardly bring him here.

Darkness. In physics, merely the absence of light. Psychologically, an actual force. Spiritually, maybe even a presence. This, this was darkness. And he hated it.

The thoughts went around in his head. An absence of light. An emotional force. A lurking presence.

He needed a cup of tea. Alone, here in his room? Or down in the kitchen, where he might meet Mary Granger and be forced back into some sort of normality? Downstairs, before this mire of melancholy got any worse.

He shifted himself, straightened the bed, splashed some water on his face and dried it, and ventured out of his room, wondering what she would make of his assumption that the person he'd find in the kitchen would be her, not Bill. He wasn't sure what he made of it himself, though the only reasonable conjecture was that it wasn't good.

'David!' she said. 'You look terrible! You need a nice cup of tea.' She continued the preparations she was already making and carried on speaking as she did so. 'Bill has had to go out, but you can join me on the little terrace for tea and biscuits. It has a lovely view of the garden and the clematis is coming into flower. This evening we'll sit out on the patio with the heater on, under the cherry tree, which is in full blossom.'

They sat outside on the little terrace, which was some paving slabs with a few tubs under a large umbrella. The clematis was indeed just bursting its buds into pinky-red flowers. It was more promise than fulfilment but did look very pretty. In a factual sort of sense. It gave him no pleasure. He recognised that he felt better than when he'd woken up, but still very flat and dissatisfied. Mary set the tray she'd prepared down on the wrought-iron table and they sat in two of the matching chairs. She poured his tea and gave it to him.

He blew on it and took a hot sip. 'Do you believe in spiritual darkness?'

'My, what a question! Yes, David, I do, but I also know that depression often feels like spiritual darkness, for Christians, and I also know that depression is a lot more common than you might think. I speak from sad and long experience.' She leaned forward slightly and engaged him with an intense stare. 'David, look, you've been ripped open. That revelation last Christmas that you had actually lost your dear little sister who was the most precious thing in the world to you, and that the loss of her had been so traumatic it's remained buried and hidden in your inner mind for fifty years, well, that kind of trauma is bound to strip you out emotionally and leave you emptied, which I'm sure is very much part of what depression is. And the healing of it will take time. In the meantime you must be patient and hold on to the comfort that you will find a better place. Angela is there for you. God is there for you. We are there for you. You've been released from that which held you captive. The future is better, not worse.'

'Then why doesn't it feel that way?'

'Surgery cuts, but it heals. Do you see? Have you heard of a book called *The Making of a Man of God*? It's about your namesake, the Old Testament David. It shows how being honed by God into the wonderful thing He is making of you always

44

costs, and requires times of darkness and uncertainty. But He is making of you something amazing. Don't lose hope.'

'Yes, OK, I see that. But then, there's this darkness.'

She put her half-empty cup on the table, but David cradled his.

'Well, hmm, Bill would say that the mind and the brain and the spirit are so overlapping in us that it's impossible to really separate the causes of our mental and emotional problems from our experience of them. What you feel as spiritual darkness is just the emotional mess inside you. Part of depression is feeling guilty. Why guilty? No reason other than you feel, altogether and in every way, bad. Sad. Low. And the usual advice would be not to judge yourself and not to search for causes in every dark corner. That just makes things worse.'

She looked at him silently now, waiting, he imagined, but not demanding any response. Just letting him be. Letting him suppurate in his darkness.

'Would you be willing to help me prepare our dinner?' she suddenly added.

David was taken aback. 'Yes, of course, I'm handy enough in the kitchen.'

'Good. It'll taste better. For you.'

'I'm sorry?'

'Anhedonia. You know what that is. The symptom of depression where you can't enjoy anything. Well, one way to overcome it with food is to be involved in the preparation of it. I don't say it'll solve the problem entirely, but it will help. Thank you, also, for helping out.'

'That's OK. And thank you for caring that I enjoy my dinner.'

'Oh, of that you may be sure. We do a lot of catering for this group and that, and their enjoyment is of great importance to me.'

As they cooked together they settled to talking about his working life, and her experiences as a local magistrate (JP). They mentioned Ruf, but she had no particular knowledge of how he was doing in the Young Offenders Unit. She commiserated with him on the completely mistaken blame his mates had fixed upon him and Angela. But, she reckoned, they weren't the brightest pennies in the pile.

As soon as the smell hit him he registered the distant hum. Freshly mown grass. He stopped separating cauliflower and breathed it in. It lifted him like nothing had in the last hour. It was full of spring freshness and that unnameable scent of very life. 'Is Bill mowing the grass?'

'No, dear, that'll be Manuel or Rosita. Didn't you meet them? They live in the little wooden hut at the bottom of the grounds.'

He frowned. 'You're kidding me, right?'

'Yes, dear. You do like a dig in the ribs, and a dig in your assumptions about we rich and colonial religious types.'

'Ha. Well, that smell is fabulous, isn't it?' He looked across at the open back door where it was coming in. 'I suppose Bill came back, then.'

'I suppose he did. He was buying oil for the mower. He regards that sort of errand as a seasonal delight.'

'Good for him.'

'Anyway, bring back the Raj, I say!' she added.

He'd never seen her this playful. Ah, this was for his sake! Since his first question about darkness. Keep him light and away from the dark thoughts and intentions. He likes to play, so play with him. Clever. And kind.

'I know what you're doing,' he said.

'You do?'

'Yes, you're playing with me to keep me happy.'

'Trying to,' she admitted, with her usual minimum of fuss.

He decided he liked her. Just a bit. After all.

They ate in the dining room at the end of the long table where they'd had the magnificent Christmas dinner and Ruf had disgraced himself by vomiting down Mary's dress and on the carpet. David was glad there was no sign or smell of that embarrassing night.

The meal looked nice and it tasted good.

Coffees were taken down to the larger, crazy-paving patio, where the heater was on as the evening was cooling. It was underneath the great white cherry tree, with ten feet of headroom under the canopy that spread up another twenty feet and was thirty feet across at the base. Blossom in white puffs surrounded the branches, brown wood making the odd appearance along the way, and sproutings of green leaves especially at the ends of the branches. But what caught the eye was the white of the uncountable blossom flowers, as if the whole tree was a collection of poodle tails, as the blossom kept to the multiple, white puffballs, slightly oval in shape.

They sat in padded chairs a bit like deckchairs and sipped very nice filter coffee. David looked up at the branches bobbing and swaying above him. Blossom petals fell in dozens at a time, fluttering down and making the beginnings of a white carpet on the floor. Birds hidden in the foliage sang to each other songs of exquisite sadness, telling of long-lost places they once knew and held close to their little hearts, desperate to fly over again one day. Hopeful, indeed, now that spring was here.

The chorus played strings inside David and he wanted to cry, but decided to do that later, in his room, on his own.

In respectful silence they sat, and David was impressed how they could do that, and glad of not being talked at. Suddenly, such a gust of evening breeze shook the tree that a million petals left their moorings and fell, like snowflakes, on and around them. They covered the table and the floor and fell into his coffee. The air went white with them, and still they came.

It took him back to that Sunday before Christmas, at the rectory, when he had first met Bill and Mary, and snow had fallen in festive flurries such as he had seldom seen. He was there with Angela. They'd only met two days before. It was a most magical night. This was less cold, and not the season to be festive, but it held a springtime beauty and wonder all of its own. The chirping chappies seemed to up their songs in appreciation, and a chorus of cheery cheeps filled the garden, and his ears, and his heart. Hopeful spring. He must retain hope.

They chatted of normal things, and dusk soon settled upon them. David watched as the world darkened, and set the sky free by contrast to be its dusken self. A vivid crimson through the branches lit peach streaks above it. They melted into the light silver-blue, which then headed up to a darker blue peeking through the upper, half-stripped canopy of the cherry tree. The tree that had snowed all over them like it was Christmas again.

David watched in silence, deaf to their attempts to engage him. They got the message after the first couple. He watched and waited. It was empty. The Yearning that had accompanied him for so many years was absent. Discovered, it had fled from its place of calling and entreating. Even the birds at bedtime sang out for it to come back, but it was gone. Whatever and whoever its calling was, it was a deep and mysterious thing, and he missed it. He longed for its comforting passion. Its dusk phone call. Without it, the waning of the day was robbed, hollow, shallow. A displeasing thing.

'Um, David,' Mary said. 'I told Angela it was probably better to leave you in peace this evening – she wanted to phone you. I said she should just see you in the morning. I hope I did the right thing.'

'Typically high-handed and interfering,' David thought. But he said, 'That's OK.'

He turned in at ten, saying he didn't want any of the offered supper half an hour later, but agreeing to take a hot chocolate and three digestives up with him.

In the bedroom he got ready for bed, took his tablets and sat in the bed with the drink and biscuits. Then he cried. Tears of emptiness and hopelessness and dismay at the place his life had come to. The tears he'd decided not to cry earlier.

He slept, and was not aware of any dream in the night.

It was Sunday, 20th March.

David sat beside Angela in what had become their usual seats, halfway up the church on the left with him by the aisle and her next to him.

Nobody knew what had happened to him, of course, but still he felt awkward and ashamed.

Palm Sunday hymns were sung, and prayers said.

The rector ascended the pulpit steps and held up a palm cross – a strip of palm bent into a cross shape – focused intently on it, and began, 'It's wrong to blame people for things they didn't do.'

He stopped and let it sink in. 'You've probably heard sermons on Palm Sunday that have said you can take your palm cross as a reminder how fickle the crowds were in Jerusalem back in AD33. How they praised Jesus on the Sunday, then bayed for His blood on the Friday. A challenge to us not to praise Him one minute and walk away from Him the next. But that really isn't fair. Because it wasn't the same crowds. The crowds who praised Him on the Sunday, when He entered Jerusalem on the ridiculous, wobbly donkey, were not the same ones as outside Pilate's palace on the Friday.

'On the Sunday, it was a massive, self-selecting group of the people of the city, celebrating the fulfilment of a prophecy of the coming of the Messiah, caught up in holy joy, full of expectation and praise. On the Friday, it was a selected group, friends and those under the thumb of the high priest and chief priests, gathered with the specific purpose of getting Jesus done away with. Not the same at all. So don't blame the fickleness of the crowds as if they were.

'Then again, if you want to use your cross, stuck up somewhere visible in your house as it will be, as a reminder of how praise turned to punishment and worship to the whip, then do. Because it is a palm and it is a cross.'

He laid it down carefully on the top of the pulpit.

'So, I say, you shouldn't blame someone for what they didn't do. Are you awake? Doesn't that immediately make you want to say, "Hang on, vicar! Wasn't that the whole plan, the whole reason, the wonder and great gladness of the whole shebang? That there was One who would willingly be judged for what He didn't do, and suffer the consequences of what He had no part in – Jesus, on the cross?"

'"Of course!" you say, waking from your sermon slumber. Your listeners' limbo. That state in which you are merely set to allow my words to wash over you in merry trust that we're a "sound" church so it's all good. It tempts me to say something outrageous, like…'

He let it hang for a moment. 'Like the bishop who was due to preach at a Mothers' Union Lady Day service the following week and hadn't a clue what to say, imagining all those fur hats succumbing to gravity, which is a pretty terrible thing to say to start with. But at the church he was visiting on the Sunday before Lady Day, the curate stood up to preach and began with, "I spent the happiest years of my life in the arms of another man's wife!" Shock trembled through the congregation at the thought of some terrible confession. Then he said, "My mother!" "Great," the bishop thought, "I'll use that." But it was five days before the Lady Day service and his memory wasn't all that it had been, so on the great day he climbed up into the pulpit, surveyed exactly the scene he'd feared, and launched in. "I spent the happiest years of my life in the arms of another man's wife!" Shuffling ensued. Gravity lost its hold. He left it a minute, frowned, and said, "And I can't for the life of me remember who she was!"

'All right, then. You get the picture. You should be saying to yourself, "What about Jesus? Didn't He do exactly that? Suffer for the wrongs of others. Mind you, He did that because He chose to, not because it was just visited upon Him." And then I'd say, "Yes, well done. Good thinking. Take five Brownie points. Submit them at the kitchen to have with your coffee." Chocolate brownies, you understand.

'Yes, you shouldn't blame people for something they didn't do. But God blamed Jesus for everything He didn't do. Everything we all did. In one horrible, awful, stinking, desperate, painful package. On the cross on Good Friday.

'And if they had but known it, and had read the Zechariah passage more closely, they would have realised that the *reason for* the palm-waving was the sacrifice it turned into. Wasn't it? The

King who is both righteous and victorious. Humble, riding an untamed beast, an unbroken foal. He will bring universal peace, under His own rule, by the blood of the covenant.

'Yes, yes, yes! The reason for the waving of palms is that He comes to die. To shed the blood of the covenant which He spoke about in the Last Supper.

'But wait a minute! Wasn't it exactly *because* they waved the palms that He was dragged to the cross by those Jewish leaders? Wasn't it exactly that enthusiasm for Him, that welcoming of Him, that worship of Him, that so infuriated the Sanhedrin and the chief priests, that so frightened them? Wasn't it? It was all part of the plan of God. It all had to be! It all had to be!'

He picked up the palm cross again, and this time held it high. 'So there *is* a connection between the palm and the cross. Oh, such connections, indeed! But it isn't about judging other people. It's about Him who will forever be showered with palms of praises, who knew exactly what He was doing even as He set up that magnificent entry into the City of Destiny. Because He rode in to foment the very worship that would damn Him! He rode in to give up, to accept the cross, to be a King such as they had never seen, victorious in a covenant sealed by His own blood, making everlasting celebration for His people.'

He looked at it, held high, and said, 'Honour it. Rejoice at the sight of it. Wonder in deepest awe at the God who came for this. For you.

'In the Name of the Father, and of the Son, and of the Holy Spirit, Amen.'

David's astonished 'Amen' was lost in the tremble of them that rolled around the ancient building. 'Goodness!' he said to Angela.

'I know!' she replied.

The service continued with Holy Communion and the giving out and blessing of the palm crosses, but in some deep and quiet place David became troubled. 'You shouldn't blame people for what they didn't do,' he mulled. 'Well, it wasn't me that took all those tablets. I never made that decision. Sure, I'm depressed, and it had been a particularly dire day. A double dead-dog day. But it was that darkness I saw in the mirror. That's what prompted me and moved me. So what was that? They're telling me spiritual darkness is just a symptom of my depression. I can see that a feeling of spiritual darkness would be. Is. But that was something different. Something other. Something with a different, dark nature all its own. Something I really don't want inside me. Or even hovering over me.

'Yet they won't believe me.'

CHAPTER FIVE

Angela was invited to Sunday lunch. David hadn't actually been consulted on that decision, which irked him a bit, but then again it was their house and their lunch. Usually they'd have someone to lunch anyway, but today they hadn't invited anyone else because, he knew, of the difficulty it might cause for him and Angela.

After lunch they'd go for a walk. Down through the trees and the bluebells. It was cloudier but warmer than yesterday. It would still be lovely. But he was nervous.

For lunch, he and Mary had pulled out all the stops. Roast lamb, roast potatoes, three vegetables, mint gravy and mint sauce. To follow, Eton mess. Before lunch, Bill and Angela had had a nice chat, he assumed, on the patio with coffee.

David and Angela sat one side, Bill and Mary opposite them, at the great table in the dining room. David had laid a cloth for them to dine on, and set the table with the best cutlery and glasses.

'Well done, you two,' Bill said after he'd finished leading them in giving thanks. 'This is a real treat.'

'David's very handy around a kitchen,' Mary added, deflecting the glory on to him.

'I'm impressed!' Angela chimed in, smiling into his eyes.

'It was nothing really,' he replied. 'Hardest thing was catching the lamb.'

They laughed politely.

For David, it was all too trite and light. He knew it was for him, but he didn't appreciate it.

Nobody asked him how he was feeling. Was that wise, or insensitive? He didn't want people constantly asking him. But he did sort of want it to be acknowledged that he'd had a very rough time. Then again, he didn't want to be blamed for what he didn't do. He felt... ambivalent? Resentful? Flat, certainly, and lifeless.

Still, the lunch was nice, and tasted like it should, so that was good. And the conversation was light. Church and the rector's sermon started it all off, and then the plan that Bill and Mary had to deliver the church's Easter newsletters to the infamous Royal Estate that very afternoon – the same estate where David and Angela, delivering the newsletters as the very first thing they did together, had come across Ruf and his band of thugs last Christmas. That led on to the work Bill was planning on the bedroom, and what plans Angela had now her Easter break had begun. She hoped for some days out with David, including to see Thelia, Andrew and Martin. That heartened David. Also maybe a bike ride. And she wanted him to take her to visit his Aunt Mary in Cheltenham. He asked why, and she said that she was, according to him, his only living relative.

They walked hand in hand, but it meant nothing special to him. It was just a hand. She swung it slightly like a little girl, as she trod beside him with a joyful fairy-lightness under the gently swaying canopy.

When they got into the bluebell dell, Angela turned him towards her and put both her arms over his shoulders, not so as to press against him but to engage him closely and fully. By the look on her face he knew this had been planned and designed, so he listened carefully as he wrapped his arms round her waist. Straggly strands of blonde-ish hair hung down beside her round face with its deep eyes, sweet nose and the light band of freckles she said came into their own in the summer.

'David, I want to kiss you. But I don't want to upset you.'

'What do you mean?'

'Well, look, you're not just "depressed". You're suffering from clinical depression. And that makes a lot of things very difficult, not least close, personal relationships. Intimacy. It can become a minefield.'

'A mind-field,' he added.

'Just so, my dear man. So, I really want to kiss you, but I don't want to make you feel trapped or uncomfortable. I'm going to give you just a little kiss now because I really have to.'

She pressed herself fully against him and brushed his lips with hers, staying for a second, and then backed off. 'Was that all right?'

'Yes.'

'OK, but if I went for the full entanglement, you might not be so happy. Like when I say, "I love you," and you don't feel able at the moment to say it back to me. I don't want you to feel bad about that or that you've hurt me.'

'OK.'

'You're not making this easy, David. Do you understand what I'm getting at?'

'I think so. You recognise that my feelings are like balloons that have lost all their air, all limp and flaccid. And you want to know how best to negotiate that, given that we're in an intimate relationship. Fair enough. How about I report back afterwards?'

She shoved him in the shoulder and gave a snort of a laugh. 'That just leaves me quaking at the thought you're going to come back with, "Eww! That was horrible. Let's not do that again!" and all the undermining, guilty, ashamed and violated feelings I'll then have. But the very fact we've got so far with the conversation confirms my suspicion that you're not comfortable with a lot of physical intimacy at the moment.'

'Can we walk?' he suggested.

So they walked, and he thought, and she waited, and held his hand again, and swung it a little bit, which he did like.

'OK,' he said, after fifty yards in the overcast woods. 'I need your hugs. I want to hold your hand. I want little kisses. Sometimes I'm up for big ones as well. Trouble is, I'm not sure myself when that is.'

'Then I will give you massive hugs, freely available hand-holding, and occasional small kisses. Anything more will have to be up to you. How's that?'

He laughed. 'You're an amazing woman. I'm a fortunate man to have you love me. I'm really sorry I'm being so distant sometimes. I do love you.'

'Thank you,' she said, a look of breathless gratitude and relief on her face. 'You don't know how much that means to me at the moment.'

They reached the clearing and he took her to sit on the tree trunk. Despite the greyer sky, the daffodils still looked bright and happy, waving their heavy heads in the light breeze. Angela leaned against him and he put his arm around her. It was comforting.

'Do you want Bart?' she suddenly said.

'Yes, that would be nice. I might even take him to bed with me, for extra comfort. I don't like sleeping away from home.'

'I'm sure he misses you, too. I could bring him to church this evening.'

'He isn't a believer. Very sceptical, actually. I doubt he'd sit still for much of it.'

'I think he'd sit very still,' she joked. 'Anyway, I could leave him in the car.'

'I'm not planning to go this evening.'

'Oh. OK. I'll bring him over afterwards.'

'Good. Thanks. We could watch a film together or something.'

'Bart could watch with us,' she added, cheekily, he thought.

'OK. As long as he doesn't have to sit between us.'

'He's your bear!' she said. 'You'll have to speak to him.'

'Will do.'

They set off again.

'Why do you want to see my aunt?'

'Like I said, you say she's your only living relative. She could be a source of useful information about you and your family. Fill in some gaps. Connect the dots.'

'I'm not madly keen.'

'Oh, come on. It'll be fun. Cheltenham is a nice place. We'll make a day of it. Might please her to see you. When did she last see you?'

Now they were heading for the stream. 'You'll love this bit up here, back in the trees. It's a fabulous little stream. Well, I saw her maybe something like ten years ago. In that region.'

'That's about when your mum died.'

'Yup.'

She stopped when she saw the dell. 'Oh! My goodness! Oh! What a place!'

He was pleased that she was so pleased. He felt their connection doing him good. It felt good to make her feel so happy. He'd delivered her more than enough sadness, with this depression. And the uncertainty it caused, about her. About them. Which he'd tried to keep from her, but failed miserably. Miserably, for both of them. So this felt good.

'There's some raised roots over there we can sit on,' he said, and they sauntered over and sat down. 'So, I don't think we can go for a bike ride, see Thelia and go to Cheltenham all this week. Bill's expecting my help with the bedroom.'

'Yes, well, you're not his prisoner. Or slave. You could do Monday and Tuesday with him, come for a bike ride on Wednesday and we could go to Thelia's on Thursday. Then Cheltenham next week. I'm off for two whole weeks. How about that?'

'Why do you want to go for a bike ride?' he asked.

'Because it'll be a lovely day out. We could head for Sauston and have lunch at The Merry Traveller, then come home via Shadford, maybe even have a little cream tea at Poppy's Kitchen. It'll do you good. The exercise. The fresh air. Being with me.'

She did indeed bring Bart, the four-foot tall, fat, brown bear with one-foot long arms and legs and sweet little feet. Bill and Mary left them to it in the lounge, so they made up for the wine-restraint of lunch with a nice Merlot, and watched *The Peacemaker* together, with Bart pressed up one side of him and Angela the other. David felt held and actually, moderately, happy. Angela stayed right up to the supper at 10.30pm, which was toast with spreads and tea.

They stood outside in some very wan moonlight, its presence announced only by a patch of lesser dimness in the clouds. They hugged and held.

'I want you to take seriously that I *need* you,' she said into his shoulder. 'Some would call that applying unfair pressure, and I am trying to be fair, you know I am. But you got inside me, voluntarily, and there's a big hole in my heart if you're not there. "Feel wanted", at least, I suppose I'm saying. Sort of. Is all.'

He pulled her in tighter, and felt the side of her lovely face, soft and warm. 'I told you that I need your hugs. And I do. This evening was lovely. Actually, all day, with you. Wednesday, we'll go off to get fit on our bikes. Like the Famous Five. The Terrible Two. Are you coming to eat tomorrow?'

'Can do. Or I could take you out somewhere. We can decide tomorrow in the day, if you like. See how you feel.'

He hugged her even tighter.

'Careful!' she squeaked.

'Sorry. Goodnight. You've done me good.'

She pulled away a little and studied his face to discern what exactly he meant by that. 'Good,' she said, and kissed him lightly on the lips. Then she was in the car and gone.

He took Bart to bed with him. It being a generous double bed there was no problem getting the old friend right inside with him, and cuddling him did help David to feel held and to get off to sleep.

After two days of David helping Bill with the bedroom, the bike ride was OK, and David and Angela got on really well. Though he found himself a few times asking, 'Am I enjoying this?' which he'd discovered long ago was a sure sign of feeling depressed. The trip to Thelia's on the Thursday was a success, and Andrew's bone-cracking hugs had been as strengthening for David as ever. He always felt really appreciated whenever they went there. Andrew never made any secret of how much the relationship he'd developed with David, limited though it still was, meant to him. The numbers games in particular fed David in a most remarkable way. And the ferocious hugs.

Which led to that evening. The evening of Maundy Thursday. And the service of Holy Communion at church. David went more because Angela really wanted him to than because he did.

The church was dark and quiet, despite fifty or so people in there. The organ played quietly. The wood of the pews smelled of the usual spiced agefulness, as David thought of it. Spiced with so many prayers, silences, mournings and celebrations. The stained-glass windows were dark, the stones of the walls shadowed. No choir. Just the rector in cassock, surplice and red stole.

At the beginning of the service the rector produced a small dish of very dark powder, and said, 'Liturgically, this is no doubt the very darkest of heresy. But then, God is never going to ask me about my liturgical faithfulness. This,' he held up the dish, 'is the kind of ash normally used for Ash Wednesday. In case you're interested, I cut up some of last year's palm crosses into tiny, thin strips, then put them in an old pan on our camping cooker in the garden, and cooked them until totally burned. I usually only do that to sausages, on the barbecue. Then I tipped them into a mortar, pestled them into a fine powder, added a little olive oil, and put them in this holy dish. Actually, no thing is really holy, and it's an old make-up pot of Ruby's. It's ash for anointing, exactly as would normally be used on Ash Wednesday. But I've got it here because I reckon this is the day for it, not six weeks ago at the start of Lent. And all who are willing will get a smear of it on their forehead in the shape of a cross tonight.

'This is the night to be marked with the darkness of the cross. This night of darkness, and of standing with Jesus in that darkness as His disciples failed to do, 2,000 years ago.'

David's ears pricked up at the mention of what was, clearly, a kind of spiritual darkness.

'Was this not a night of darkness?' the rector continued, his tone heavy, his figure divided by shadows. 'Three times darkness enters the story, in the most sombre guises. First, when Judas left the dim and flickering light of the Last Supper to betray Jesus as he'd already decided to do, John says he went out, "and it was night". And it was night. Not just after the sun had set. Oh, no. He had walked out of the only light that really matters. He had walked out into true, lonely and eternal darkness.

'Then, when Jesus was picked out by Judas in the garden with a kiss, and the soldiers arrested him with swords and clubs, Jesus said to them, as we heard in the Gospel reading, that He'd always spoken openly, in public. But they were arresting Him in secret, because "this is your hour – when darkness reigns". Darkness was now reigning. A terrible thought. Darkness reigning on the earth.

'And thirdly, when Jesus, a bit before this, fell on to His face in the mud, in that garden, and was reduced to tears and asking to be delivered, what was it He saw? The darkness of the cross, I am sure. The three hours of darkness that came over the land the next day, under which He suffered the awful wrath of God at all the sin of humankind, and cried out, "My God, my God, why have you forsaken me?"

'Darkness upon darkness upon darkness. Do I seem a little sombre tonight? No jokes from the pulpit. This is why. Darkness reigns.

'They fled and left Him. He was betrayed. He was denied. He was abandoned. Darkness upon darkness upon darkness. But you're going to get the chance to stand with Him in that darkness. Get marked with it. Wear it home. Wear it to church tomorrow. Wear it for three days. Darkness upon darkness upon darkness.

'Will you stand with Him? Show Him you love Him? Do this little thing? This small act of loyalty and witness? When you come forward for Communion, if you remain at the rail after you've had the bread and the wine, I will mark you with the darkness of the cross. Join me. Stand with Him and for Him. Not as some ancient ritual – that's ash on Ash Wednesday. As a new sign. The ashes of darkness with my Saviour. Amen.'

David was disappointed. That was a powerful point, no doubt. And he could sense the electricity among the congregation, thoroughly grabbed by a whole new appreciation of the depths of darkness in the story and the challenge to stand with Jesus in that shadowy place. But it wasn't what he was experiencing. His spiritual darkness was something else. Different in nature from this.

When the time came, he went forward for his customary blessing, not having been confirmed yet and so unable to take the bread and wine, and he had the smudge because everyone was having it. The mark of death, so it seemed to him. A shudder went through him as he knelt at the rail. Of fear? Was that supposed to happen? But no. Not fear. Excitement? Anticipation? Actually, he was glad he had it. Marked for death. But as he lay in bed that night, comforting Bart, he'd washed it off already so as not to dirty the faithful bear.

Yet, invisibly, it remained.

He stood outside that awful door he'd seen in a dream before. Darkness surrounded and pervaded the porch of the old, isolated house. Ancient, crusty bricks had tendrils of the creepers invading their surface with a thousand unwanted, uninvited fingers. The door was ribbed and wrinkled by the decay of its wood, its natural grain now weathered and greyed by the passage of time and wind, frost and scorching sun.

Rooted, David stood. Unable to stir or hardly even breathe with stark, naked, trembling terror. His heart faltered and pressed in his straining chest. The door would begin to heave and bang and bulge any second. That thing which lay beyond it would press and burst and have him. Lick him up like vomit.

He waited, pinned, anaesthetised of all but fear. Even his widened eyes would barely move, focused as they unwillingly were on the brittle wood of the dreadful door.

There. A swelling between the ancient planks. A split of unfriendly parting. And a dark finger emerged, liquid and seeking. Like a shiny black glove, other fingers accompanied it. It pushed a widened hole in the solid door, as if creating a way from a place not of this poor substance. He watched, transfixed, feeling that what he was observing was not for mortal eyes, and would sully him forever. It swelled and grew like a fetid boil, shining curving panels of light from its bulbous surface, gentle ripples lining its face. And then the black balloon began to peel, opening to reveal an empty hollow in its true and essential being. David's horror escalated as it began to curl around his head, wrapping and enveloping him with violating intent. Darkness enclosed him until it met at the rear and sealed itself with his whole head inside. It unrolled itself down and around his entire body.

And then the stillness. Fear drained away with a feeling not unlike when they sedated him for injections in his spine. A warm, calming comfort filled him. In here, he sensed, he 'was not'. All terror, all concern, all sadness and all inadequacy were not. Instead was an intelligence, a peace, a rightness, a great calm.

It struck him as if from a wise counsel that in dreams you could feel terror, but never depression. And a voiceless, ancient thoughtfulness said, 'The only being for whom existence is natural is God. For you, existence is not natural. It is not a natural and essential thing that you "be" as He is. Existence, for created beings, is a thing of worry, of fear, of failure, of guilt and endless frustration. The injustice of being, in a world of random accidents. When God made people, He didn't consider that, to Him, "being" is unthinkingly obvious, like water round a fish. And that to you, that water would be a terrible thing. Filled with trouble. For you, nonexistence is the natural state. Here, it is calm. Here, it is quiet. Here, it is right.

'Non-being is your natural place. Come back to it.'

David woke, slowly, peacefully, warmly, and seemed to see from the corner of his eye one of those dainty, breeze-borne fairies floating from him in the semi-darkness. He was looking into the friendly, furry face of Bart, the faithful bear.

'I want to be as you are,' he said, quietly. 'I want to be no more. I want to not be.'

He rolled on to his back, searching for the floating, white fluff. 'Take me with you, Fairy Nothing,' he said, as he drifted off again, hardly aware of anything that had been.

PART TWO

PART TWO

CHAPTER SIX

It was Easter Monday, 28th March.

Easter had passed him by as if in a dream. He'd declined to go to the special 'At the Cross' Good Friday service, much to the dismay of all, and had found the celebrations of the Easter Sunday itself forced and hollow.

Yet, the rector had put a piece of prose on the service sheet for the day which took his eye and he'd found he kept looking at it. It said:

> ### The darkness of the cross of Christ.
> It's as if… It's as if… The long bright day of God's eternity is brought to an end by a terrible night. Darkness crowds the very halls of heaven. God Himself sits bent in gloom, speechless in sorrow for His Son.
>
> Dim, dingy, doom-laden, dark. No light, yet shadows everywhere.
>
> But then a dawn breaks, a new eternal day glows on the horizon, and Jesus stands at its rising, Lord of it all. He stands with His redeemed, their every hope and joy, their very life and glory.
>
> A smile beautifies His countenance, and even the Father laughs out loud. The corridors of eternity echo His happy sound. Eternity split in two? Yes, and the Day of Man with his Lord, begun.
> *Revd Canon Professor Mark Lucius*
> *'The Fires of Heaven'*

David had intended to keep it, but then it had been sat on and scrunched up and he'd thrown it away.

'Mary Stratton. Hello?'

'Aunt Mary. It's David.'

'David!'

'Sourbook.'

'Yes, I know which David.' There was an expectant pause. 'Well, I suppose I should ask what's happened.'

'Happened?'

'Yes. Have you got married? Are you phoning from jail?'

'Oh, yes. No, nothing.'

'Then I am confused. If you wanted to thank me for the Christmas card you should have done that in January.'

'Ha ha. Yes. Sorry. Only, the thing is, I want to come and see you. Or, really, my lady friend wants us to come and see you.'

'Ah! The lady friend. So something *has* happened, then.'

'Ah. Yes. I have a lady friend.'

'What's her name and what does she do and how old is she?'

'Er, OK, she's called Angela, she teaches at a local college and she's fifty-three.'

'Another teacher. Very good. What does she teach?'

'Comparative Religion and Ethics.'

'Oh. Is she a churchgoer?'

'Yes. I've started going with her.'

'Good for you. So, she's twigged, has she?'

'Twigged?'

'That there's something not right with your family.'

'Er, not more than I've told her myself, I don't think. About Micky, I know I knew her and I was eight when she died, at three. I've remembered that,' David said, puzzled.

'But she wants to meet me to find out more.'

'Yes.'

'Then she's twigged. I knew this day would come. It's just taken a lot longer than I imagined.'

'Oh.' David felt very uneasy at the way this was turning out.

'When do you want to come?'

'We thought Wednesday. This week.'

'Hold on.' There was a sound of rustling and returning. 'That's OK. Get here coffee time, stay for lunch, which I'll cook for you, take me out for a spot of tea, and be on your way to avoid the traffic. How's that?'

'Amazingly organised. Thank you, Mary. Though I have to admit I'm a bit nervous now about what I'm going to find out.'

'I'd be lying if I said you had no reason to be. Anyway, it'll be nice to meet Angela. Tell her no need to bring flowers or chocs or wine. Bye, David, thanks for phoning. See you on Wednesday. Coffee time. That's around eleven in these parts.'

'Bye,' he said, rocked back on his heels by the abruptness of it. He stared at the phone – the Grangers' landline handset. Then he put it down, very carefully, and tried not to worry. Good grief.

It was Wednesday, 30th March.

He drove and she looked out of the window at the ever-new glories of spring as the many miles sped past. She wouldn't let him have the window open on the M4 and the M5 as it was too cold and buffeting. But on the A roads it was all right, and he always enjoyed the fresh air on his face, and put on the car's heater if the temperature looked like dropping too far.

Eventually, the conversation got to what Mary had said on the phone.

'What do you mean, "twigged"?' Angela asked him.

'Realised. Fell in. Grasped.'

'No, you nit! What did she think I'd twigged?'

'That there's something wrong in my family. Some dark secret.'

'Micky?'

'I don't think so. I mentioned Micky. Something more.'

'Intriguing!' Angela said.

'That's all very well for you to think it's intriguing. To me it's terrifying.'

'Why?'

'I said she'd worried me, and she said that if she told me I didn't need to be worried, then she'd be lying.'

'Oh. What might it be, then?'

'It must be something about my parents.'

'She's your mum's sister, right?'

'Yes. There were three of them – an older brother as well, but he died first, then my mum. Now there's just her. Her husband is still alive, I think, but he has Alzheimer's, and he's in a home. My dad also had a sister, Maudy, but I'm pretty sure she's gone now.'

'What's she like? Your Aunt Mary?'

'She must be in her eighties. She was always a bit feisty. Steely-eyed. Tied-back brown hair. A little bit hunched.'

'You make her sound monstrous! I bet she's really lovely.'

'Well, you can judge for yourself in less than half an hour. This is where we turn off into Cheltenham.'

The house was a bungalow in a row of them in Sanders Avenue. There was a low front wall with a white, iron-railing fence on top of it. The house was pebble-dashed with new-looking anodised aluminium-framed windows. A driveway led to a garage on the right, and the front gate led to a small crazy-paving path between a neat lawn and flower beds. A small porch sheltered them from light drizzle.

The white door had a diamond-shaped leaded light stained with daffodils and tulips. It opened, and there stood David's Aunt Mary. She was only just over five feet tall, slightly hunched as he had said, with hair a very grey brown, loosely tied back. Yet her eyes darted like a bird in search of worms.

'David!' she said, embracing him. Then, 'And you must be Angela,' with a double-handed handshake. 'Come in, dears, come in.'

David actually trembled slightly as he passed over the threshold as if she were some kind of witch, inviting them into her lair and her cauldron.

But the inside was as neat as the outside, as she led them past the open door of a front room to a large kitchen-diner at the back. It was a bit like Thelia's house, only the front room was on the right.

In the back was a table and chairs with a central cloth of mostly white, bearing a vase of daffodils and tulips.

'You like daffodils and tulips,' Angela observed.

'I love everything about spring,' Mary said, indicating they should sit at the table. 'Coffee? White? Sugar?'

'Both white, no sugar please, Aunt Mary,' David said, and she went to the right-hand side where the kitchen section was and set about making a cafetière.

'Good trip down?' she asked.

'It was lovely, until about ten minutes before we arrived,' Angela answered, 'when it started to drizzle. Maybe it'll clear.'

'Maybe it will. So, Angela, how did you meet our David?'

Angela began to explain about the chance encounter last Christmas by the pond, and the various adventures she'd led David into, all told without any sort of diminishing of him, which he thought was nice.

'So he's started to come to church with you.'

'Yes, and he did the Reduced Alpha course. And he helps to run the lunch for the over-seventies every Friday. And he's got to know all my lovely friends there. Young and old.'

'It's made a new man of me,' he added.

'How new?' Mary asked.

That threw him. What sort of question was that? He looked at Angela, who just shrugged.

'Well, I guess we'll find out,' Mary said.

She brought the cafetière, smelling rich and fabulous, along with small mugs, milk and a plate of digestives – both chocolate and not – on a pretty tray which she put down on the table between them, then took her seat.

Angela looked at David, gave a slight frown, and said, 'So, Mary, please tell us, what is it you think I've twigged?'

Trouble shadowed Mary's face. 'Straight in, then. It's only fair, I suppose, after what I said on the phone. Well. I'm going to have to speak ill of my own sister and brother-in-law. So have some patience with me,' she answered.

'All right,' David allowed her.

Mary picked up a teaspoon and studied it in her fingers. 'I gather you've found out about Micky. Michaela. They said they did it for the right reasons. I warned them, though. You can't let a child believe they never knew their sister just because that's how that child has started to cope with the loss. You withdrew completely at first. You wouldn't speak, or respond, or hardly eat or even drink. You became almost catatonic, just staring. And when they managed to tease you out of that, you'd blanked out Micky completely. Not just her death, but her as a person. So they let it be that way – permanently. But I warned them. Oh, yes, I did, repeatedly. It's just storing up endless trouble. A person, even a child of eight, has to deal with it, not bury it. So you grew up insular, suspicious, isolated, without fellow-feeling for other people, destined to be lonely.' She looked up from the teaspoon. 'How did you discover the truth?'

'Hmm,' David said, unsure exactly how to explain it. 'There had been a pressure, like something calling to me, and something trying to get out of me, more and more for years. I think a combination of opening up to God, knowing Angela, and the incredibly insightful words of a friend of hers at church, cracked the box open that it was hidden in, in my mind. Out it all came, in a flood of memory and desperate regret and sadness. Look, OK, I didn't intend to tell you this, but here we are, so – it's also made me profoundly depressed. I'm under the doctor. I see a counsellor. I'm struggling to cope with it even though I'm really glad it's out in the open at last. I know I knew Micky and how incredibly dear she was to me.'

He stopped for a moment, then asked, 'What was she like?'

Mary's face brightened. 'She was the sweetest little thing you ever saw. Blonde hair, blue eyes, freckles, such a smile, which she kept mostly for you. My picture of her would be holding your hand, looking up into your face, smiling, you two heading off somewhere together – only round the garden, mind. She sat with you and on you much more than them, and it was hard to tell if they resented that and so were cold to her, or if they were just cold towards her so she took to you. A bit of both, I suppose. But you and Micky were so happy together. It was like neither of you needed them, your mum and dad. The lonely boy found a family. They were at fault, whichever way you cut it.'

David started to melt, inside, and the image was just too much. The pressure of the tears was huge, and they fell, burning his cheeks, tickling his nose. There was no way he could restrain them or hide them.

Mary reached over and put a hand on his arm. 'I'm really sorry,' she said. 'Maybe I should have done more to help you, but it was hard. They weren't particularly open to me, either.'

Angela sniffed and pressed a paper hanky into his hand. He bowed his head and let it flow. There was no way he could retain his dignity. His forehead rested on his fists on the table.

'I really loved her,' he sobbed. 'So much. I can see her sweet face again. Almost feel her hand in mine. Ah, Micky! Dear, dear Micky.'

'I should leave you two for a while,' he heard Mary say, and she took herself off somewhere. He was beyond caring. The sense of loss flooded him like it was new all over again. Such regret. Like having your soul stripped out of you. And her loss, so complete. So totally unrecoverable. He couldn't bear it. It was grief and loss and pain and emptiness beyond hope or redemption. She lost everything and he lost her, which felt like nearly as much.

So the tears flowed, and Angela's arms were over him and around him, his head still resting on the table. She plied him with paper hankies, and then something bigger and rougher, which turned out to be sheets of kitchen towel.

He had no idea how much time had passed when Mary returned, but she started getting lunch ready, and sharing the odd comment with Angela. Then Angela took him into the garden, and they sat on an old wooden bench which was damp, but she didn't seem to care any more than he did.

Gradually, like the weather, he dried up. Still grey and overcast, but dry. He went inside and took a trip upstairs to the loo, where the sight of his red eyes and blotchy skin shocked him. He splashed water on his face and dried it carefully. He looked OK. Hardly a living wreck of a man at all.

Downstairs, lunch was on the table. It was chicken pie, boiled potatoes, green beans and gravy. He was glad to not be over faced. To follow, there was a slice of lemon meringue pie and a cup of tea.

Conversation over lunch was about Easter and springtime and the weather and the shocking news that day of some murders in Birmingham.

'How are you fixed for a walk?' Mary asked, brightly, as they finished the washing- and drying-up.

'Good plan,' David was glad to say with enthusiasm, and Angela agreed.

They set off ten minutes later down Mary's road, made up of bungalows then full-size houses, and turned left into a small street that led to a huge open area of grass and trees, like heathland. Quite a few people were walking dogs, and families were playing frisbee or just chasing about. The sky was still grey, but not leaden.

They walked three abreast along a path not too deep in mud, and David said, 'So Aunt Mary, what you thought Angela had twigged, and you thought I had good reason to be worried by, wasn't Micky. So, having got that out of the way, for now, and only having you for today, I need to find out what else was wrong.'

'I'd spare you if I could,' she answered.

Angela squeezed his hand. Was that a warning? An encouragement?

'I need to know,' he said. 'For my sanity's sake, in all sorts of ways.'

'Yes, and I'll tell you. Only, I'm uncomfortable saying bad things about my sister and my brother-in-law, you'll understand.'

'I do. I acknowledge your loyalty to them. And I'm grateful you're willing to help me. I'm relieved you're still alive.'

'So am I!' she said, and it was unclear whether or not that was a joke.

She sighed. 'OK. Your dad did have cancer, and it was terminal. But it wasn't what killed him, and Sally, your mum, shouldn't have told you it was the cancer. At least, she shouldn't have kept it from you all those years. The truth was that he committed suicide.'

David's stomach descended into his belly like it was going to carry on all the way. A blanching dread came over him, and it felt like somehow he'd been discovered – 'outed' in some terrible thing. He imagined he went white, so he kept his head down a bit.

'Oh,' he said, after a pause, raising his head again. 'How?'

Mary looked up and across at him, and stopped. 'Why do you want to know how he did it? Isn't that hardly the point?'

'Well,' David began, playing for time, desperately trying to bluster his way out, 'if cancer wasn't his real cause of death, then how he killed himself was. So I need to know that to replace what I thought I knew.'

He saw her flash a glance at Angela, but Angela was on the other side of him and he was looking at Mary. He assumed Angela remained noncommittal.

'He took tablets. A lot of tablets.'

David's insides fell again.

She continued. 'Antidepressants. Two whole packets. There, is that enough information?'

He could almost feel Angela's eyes on the back of him. Were his legs going to give way? A hot clamminess spread over his forehead and down his neck.

'You need to sit down,' Mary said, taking hold of his arm. He did feel sick and wobbly. They guided him, one on each arm like some decrepit old fool, to a bench not far away, and lowered him smoothly onto it. He leaned forward and put his head into his hands because he felt like he just might throw up.

At least Mary didn't know anything more than that this was shock at her news.

Angela sat beside him and poured water from a bottle she was carrying onto a proper cloth hanky from up her sleeve and held it against his forehead.

'Ah, that's nice. Thank you.' He didn't feel like throwing up now.

'Why is that such a devastating revelation to you?' Mary asked.

Not the most tactful of people, he decided.

And darn it all, she'd 'twigged' this was more than just hearing about his dad.

'I think I'd better leave it there,' Mary said.

'I don't think so,' Angela answered, a little more firmly than he might have expected. 'I think David needs to hear it all. Don't you, my love?'

'Yes,' he mumbled. 'Leave nothing out. Tell me.'

Mary squeezed herself onto the bench the other side of him, putting David in a sandwich between the two women. She wriggled a bit till she was comfortable, then said, 'All right, then. You asked for this. That wasn't the first time he tried to end his life. He seemed to have an obsession with it. It wasn't just depression. Oh, don't get me wrong, he did suffer from depression sometimes. But he had good times as well as bad times. And in the good times – a whole year or two it might be when he was perfectly happy – he still wanted to end his life. It was like a compulsion. It drew him like an addiction. He never told your mum about it. But he told me, perhaps because he knew I had a faith, I don't know. But he told me.'

David had to know. 'What did he tell you, exactly?'

'It didn't necessarily have anything to do with sadness or the inability to cope or any sort of feeling that he just couldn't go on. It was an attraction to non-being. Like some state of "nothingness" had his number, and called to him from

76

somewhere inside him. He once told me that for created beings, existence was a mistake. Our natural condition is not to "be", so that's what we should choose. Therein lies not just peace, but completeness. Fulfilment. The natural order. He once said it's only God who exists always and of necessity. Only *He* naturally exists. When He created us, He made a mistake. For us, "being" is an unnatural thing, and bound to cause us trouble. I once asked him where he got this from, and he became agitated and refused to say any more. There, that's it.'

In some vague and deep place, all of that seemed to be relevant, but David didn't know where or why, so he shelved it. 'How did he try to commit suicide?'

'Various ways, the usual things. He never tried to throw himself off a building. He was afraid of heights.'

David heard Angela trying to suffocate a guffaw of laughter.

'Excuse me! He wasn't your relative!' Mary said.

'I'm sorry. I'm sorry. But the thought that he didn't try to jump off a building to kill himself because he feared heights, I mean, isn't that the height of... no I mean, isn't that just ironic to the point of being ridiculous? "I'm not going up there. I'm afraid I might... fall off!" Sorry.'

David started to laugh as well, and then Mary, to his great relief. Oh dear, this was all so bizarre.

When he'd recovered his composure, he said, 'Why didn't he succeed?'

'He did.'

'No, I mean all those times over – how many years was he like this?'

'Fifteen. Twenty. He didn't succeed because it isn't easy to kill yourself, I'd say. Could you do it?'

That was a low blow. 'Probably not,' seemed a diplomatic answer. He could hear Angela's mind whirring beside him. 'And he never said where he got those ideas about non-being from?'

Mary turned and eyed him suspiciously. 'What if I said you don't want to know?'

Was that a test? Probing to see if he knew something already? Clever, if it was. OK, then. 'I just feel I need to know. It's a strange idea. I thought suicide was normally the result of feeling depressed and not able to go on. Everything black and bleak. No future. No hope. Unending misery. That sort of thing.' '

'Well, maybe it is. But that wasn't your dad. And no, he never said where he got it from. Sorry.'

She looked across the expanse of uneven grass again, then said, 'Oh, there was one thing. He said that, sometimes, it came over him like a darkness, like a shadow over his face that he could see in a mirror. He said that once. He never explained it.'

CHAPTER SEVEN

Angela held his hand tightly around the rest of the walk. He knew she was worried about him. So was he. A breathless fear lurked around the edges of the day. The sudden loss of air and need to run and run. He recognised it. Panic wanted him. Something in his brain or mind wanted to set it off. And once it was set off, it couldn't be stopped until it stopped.

That darkness. He'd certainly mentioned it, asked people about spiritual darkness. But how much had he said? Owned up to? He wasn't sure. Now it felt like some guilty thing to be ashamed of. He'd mentioned it in the hospital with Angela there. So she knew. Probably that was a good thing. But now it suddenly felt like a dark secret.

Nothing pleased him as they went round. Not the breeze, not the sky, not dogs playing or children chasing or Angela's soft hand. All was empty of meaning or pleasure. Anxiety teased at him. Darkness wanted him. Greyness surrounded him.

They spoke of ordinary things. Oh, the dullness of ordinary things! But Angela was thrilled that Mary had taught philosophy at a local sixth-form college. They shared insights about education and the current state of legislation and recruitment. Form-filling and box-ticking. He just half-listened and wished it was all over. There was tea yet to negotiate.

The tea Mary had arranged was in a small tea shop in a nearby village, and she drove them there in her car. They sat at a round table with a frilly cloth and shared a pot for three with scones, jam and cream. When conversation between Angela and Mary slowed, David said, 'What else can you tell me about my dad?'

Mary looked at him for a moment then said, 'Well, OK, he had that dark side, but he was basically a good guy. He and Sally were happy until you came along.'

'Oh!' Angela said. 'Just what every son wants to hear!'

'Sorry. No, that's not what I meant. Let me rephrase that. In the early days, despite him having troubling episodes of depression that worried Sally because she'd never encountered it before, they were basically happy. A while after they married there was a short period when he refused to get out of bed. For two or maybe three days. Wouldn't eat, wouldn't say much, wouldn't get up. For a young married woman – she was only twenty – that was hard to understand. She was on the phone to me sometimes with this stuff. But, that aside, basically, they had some happy times. They were both working, they made friends, they saw some of his old friends, they had days out, they took simple holidays to the coast in Kent, they drank wine and went cycling and were quite romantic.

'But when she knew she was pregnant with you, something changed. I think – do you really want to hear this?' She took a bite of scone and looked out of the front window of the tea shop.

That startled David. Did he? 'Yes.'

'OK, then, I think you were a mistake, and I got the impression he didn't want a child. And Sally did want one, until she realised how set he was against it. It was like they'd never discussed it. And in those days a termination was out of the question, so you were born resented and unwanted. There. Said it. But then the strangest thing happened. Having practically split them apart, once you got to about one, your dad, Derek, changed completely and thought you were really sweet and great fun. He started to take more interest in you than in her. So she resented you, even though at first she'd quite liked the idea of having a child.

'So, basically, you and your mum never got on. She pushed you away and then resented you for inclining more to your dad. She'd go off in the evenings to her groups and classes, and you

80

and your dad would go down into the basement and play stupid games. Pub skittles, toy soldiers, cards, darts – which sent Sally ballistic because she said it was far too dangerous, but really she was only trying to get at the two of you. Jigsaws. Board games. Some of that stuff got packed up in a box when your dad died and your mum didn't so much keep it as refuse to touch it, like she was afraid of it almost, and it's in my loft somewhere, I think. It was. It said, "Derek's basement stuff" on the box. I expect it's still there.

'Anyway, then Michaela came along. I didn't think they'd have any more, after what happened with you. She was another mistake. Sorry, "unexpected blessing". But a mistake as far as they were concerned. So neither of them wanted her. From day one you took to her. You'd be the one cuddling her, feeding her from a bottle, even changing her nappy. You took her out in her pushchair. You saved up and spent your pocket money on a little teddy for her. They refused to let her have it as it wasn't really child-safe.

'But the games continued with your dad. So you and he retained some level of friendliness. I guess there just wasn't much else to do of an evening back then. You had no telly. You had no friends. Not any that I knew of, anyway. They kept you very much at home even before Michaela died.'

'Oh!' David said. 'I thought that was just as a result of losing her.'

'It got worse then, and you became very isolated, like I told you, but it started before then. For some reason, they didn't like you to be out of their sight. I reckon they feared you telling people how they treated you. It was abuse, really. Negligence. You see, you asked what your dad was like. Well, he played with you. Almost like you were his little playmate, but he never cuddled you or sat you on his shoulders or kissed you. Never once, as far as I could see. He was totally non-demonstrative. You *were* emotionally neglected.'

'Goodness!' Angela said. She stroked his arm. 'Poor little fellow! Such a lonely little chap.'

'Except there was Michaela,' Mary continued, 'which meant when she got meningitis and they wouldn't let him even see her, and she got whisked away into hospital and he literally never saw her again, it wasn't like she died, I suppose. It was like she had never existed, or something, in the mind of an eight-year-old. I don't know exactly what they told you, David, but I'll bet it was something unhelpful to "protect" you, and you ended up like I told you before. Like reality as a whole had been stripped from you. Like the world you'd known didn't really exist. And you had to form a new one, based on what you could see. And that didn't include Michaela. So they concocted the story, in case you came across evidence of her, that she'd died before you were born. I warned them. But they were set on it. I even said it would come back to haunt you. But no. They were resolute. And there you are. No photos, no talk of her, nothing that might connect you to her.'

David was stunned. Angela just looked at him with a sympathetic expression on her face, and kept her hand on his arm on the table. Then she paid, and they were heading back to Mary's car.

Drizzle surrounded them all the way back to Mary's house. David felt it described him perfectly: wet, grey, uninspiring. Dull.

Mary spoke. 'I know you didn't really like your mum much – my sister. But you haven't really asked me about her. Don't you want to know about her as well as your dad?'

'Go on, then,' he said, resigned to it.

'Don't sound so enthusiastic. All right. Before she married she worked as a secretary in a large tea firm. She had few if any real friends and tended to stay mostly with our parents. She lived at home till she married Derek. They met on a train when he fainted and she helped him. I'd say she tended to be rather selfish. Maybe self-obsessed would be nearer to the truth. We never really got on while she was at home. She was the bossy big sister. When they married and she moved out we had a more mature relationship of mutual something. Respect? Shallow

82

affection? Something like that. I think she needed someone to talk to so we used to talk on the phone, right from after the honeymoon in the Isle of Wight. When you arrived I wanted to be the nice aunty, but they weren't really up for that, even though we lived less than an hour away. My husband, Alan, never really liked her much, or your dad, and resented the way they treated me, as he saw it. He wanted to punch your dad once. Or twice. So we didn't see them much. Family parties, mostly.'

'I wasn't christened, was I?' David suddenly interjected.

'Yes. Your dad was dead against it, but Sally thought it was a sort of insurance policy, just in case. But he hated anything to do with religion. When Sally tried going to church with a friend he made it so uncomfortable for her she soon stopped. He regarded it as worse than bunkum.'

'How did he make it uncomfortable?'

'Comments. Criticisms. He belittled it and belittled her for going there. It just ended up as one more resentment between them. One of so many.'

'Resentment seems to be the thing,' Angela put in. 'Listening today, it's a word that comes quite a lot. They resented each other, they resented David, he resented them, they resented Micky, Alan resented Derek. I may be overstating it. But it's the pattern I see.'

'Not sure if it's a pattern,' Mary answered.

David was waiting for her to qualify the comment, but it was just left hanging.

'Well, goodbye, then. It was nice to meet you, Angela.'

They were standing by David's car, on the footpath. They didn't even go back into the house. She'd told them they should get going to beat the traffic. Now it felt more like telling them to get lost. Like she'd had enough of this whole meeting of them. David wondered if the hug on greeting was to be repeated. Then Mary gave Angela a polite one, so he gave her the same. Then, what? 'See you again'? 'You must come to see us'? 'Come down again in the summer'? He felt awkward.

Angela spoke up. 'I hope David and I can come down again to see you.'

'Any time you like. David can just call me again. I'm here, mostly. I might look out that box of Derek's bits and see what's in there.'

'OK,' he said. 'And if you think of anything else that might help me... And thanks for lunch.'

'Goodbye. Drive safely now,' she finished, and headed for the house. David watched her as they got into the car and he started it up. No turn. No wave. Strange woman.

'How are you?' Angela asked as soon as they got going.

'Ragged. Battered. Abused. Negated.'

'Change the first two round and you have the acrostic "bran" – something indigestible you eat because it does you good. Clears you out. Maybe that's what that was. An unpleasant brown flaky powder that'll clean out your insides. What do you think?'

'Possible. You remember I said to you once, long ago, it was like The Yearning had my number – it connected to my internal receiver frequency. Well, now it feels to me like something bad and dark has my number. And I don't like it.' He looked across at her as they came to an intersection and he stopped the car. He didn't want to sound too negative with her. 'Anyway, it's stuff I needed to know. What did you make of it?'

'Bizarre. Deeply, troublingly bizarre. And she thinks she's normal.'

'Huh. I know. Imagine trying to live with someone like that. No wonder he's in a home.'

'That's maybe a little harsh. But yes, she's quirky and not in a good way. Definitely on the Wobbly Way.'

He just drove. After a few minutes she said, 'Are you going to be OK or shall we stop?'

'Maybe stop for a coffee halfway. I'll be OK till then. Thanks so much for coming and for being there for me. You were in my corner.'

She stroked his neck. 'That's not hard. I love you. I'm here for you.'

'Don't pity me, though.'

'No. I know. I don't. I won't. I'm sympathetic, is all. Same as I'd expect from you.'

She put her hand on his knee and left it there. It was nice.

It was like he could feel the pressure building. Somehow, he knew what she wanted to ask him. For some minutes. Longer. Was it something about the agitated way she was looking around her and at him? Then it came out.

'She mentioned the darkness. Your dad's attempts at suicide had that darkness you mentioned.'

'Ah, you remembered.'

'Must have hit you like a brick.'

'Yah. Frightening. Makes me wonder what it is.'

'I think it's still depression, even though she said it came when he wasn't depressed. Depression has many symptoms, as well as feeling depressed in mood. It's a complex illness that doesn't all just flow from feeling down. That's true, isn't it? I reckon it was still depression that caused the feeling of darkness.'

'It wasn't a feeling. She said it came over him and he could see it in a mirror. That's exactly what I experienced. I saw it, over my head and face, like an invisible cloth descending over me. And did you hear his rationale for suicide? The call to non-being. That sounds familiar to me, like I've heard it somewhere. But I have no idea where. Maybe a seminar or a discussion or something. But that's intellectual, not emotional. That's not depression.'

'Can't depression affect you intellectually?' Angela asked.

'I'd say not. It's a neurosis not a psychosis.'

'I know that, but the distinction is between rational thought and non-rational thought. That sounded perfectly rational to me; I just wouldn't agree with it as a position.'

'There's nothing in depression that would lead you to that philosophy. Such a way of thinking isn't naturally part of depression. That's a philosophical position, not a depressive frame of mind.'

'So where *did* it come from, then?' she said.

'Exactly! Where did it come from? That and the darkness. They aren't characteristics of depression. They're something else. Something frightening.'

'I think maybe you need to get a grip,' she said.

'Maybe,' he said, but inside that hurt.

From then on she chatted away happily but he said little.

When they arrived back at the Grangers', he told Angela he was tired and she should just go on home. She looked at him with concern and puzzled sadness, but didn't complain. He offered her neither kiss nor hug, and his demeanour told her he didn't want that sort of farewell, he supposed.

He used his key and went in, and walked into the lounge where they were reading newspapers.

'Ah, hello, dear chap,' Bill said, looking up. 'No Angela?'

'No. She had to go.' It was the first time he'd told them an outright lie, but he felt justified by the way she'd treated him. Telling him to get a grip had really stunned him.

'Oh,' said Mary, clearly disappointed. 'We'd hoped you might both be here for some supper.'

'No,' David repeated. 'I'm going upstairs for a lie down.'

'Oh. OK,' Mary said.

He left them and climbed the stairs. He listened for their comments but he knew they'd keep them until he was well out of earshot. Heavily and slowly his legs pushed him upwards. He fell onto his bed and enfolded the lovely and faithful Bart in a huge hug.

'You don't think I need to pull myself together, do you?' he said. 'No. Clearly you would never say such a thing. "Get a grip." What a terrible thing to say to someone when they're being open and honest about their troubles. Their fears. Who needs friends like that? Not me and not you.'

For an age he lay there. Not sleeping. Hardly moving. Warm against Bart-the-faithful. Comforted against them all.

At 10.25 David went downstairs for some supper. He resented the fact that he couldn't just go down when he liked and raid the fridge. But Bill and Mary were resilient over the mealtimes thing. So he joined them in the lounge.

It felt as if they would have liked to greet him with more enthusiasm, but all Bill managed was, 'David! You feeling any better?'

'I'm fine,' he said.

'You didn't look fine when you came in,' Mary insisted.

'Well, then, I hope I look better now.'

'Anyway,' she said, 'the hospital want to see you tomorrow morning at eleven for an assessment so they can release you into your own custody. Psychiatric department, a Dr Sweeting.'

'Oh,' David said, taken aback.

'Looks like your sentence is over, dear boy,' Bill added, clapping him soundly on the shoulder.

'Oh,' he said again.

'Cheese and crackers? Tea? A French Fancy?' Mary asked, indicating the tray on the coffee table.

'Thanks, yes,' he said, and knelt on the floor to load up a small plate.

'How was the visit to your aunt?' Mary asked.

'Interesting. She's a funny old thing, even more so than I remembered. Quite feisty. I discovered stuff about my dad, some of which I might wish I hadn't.'

It was Mary's turn to say, 'Oh.'

He continued to relay the basic story of the day and the revelations. Should he tell them about the darkness?

No.

CHAPTER EIGHT

David retired to bed at about half past eleven. He did all his usual tooth-brushing and tablet-taking, then slid into the large bed alongside Bart. Bart-the-faithful. Bart the cuddlesome bear. He put his arms around the great, warm middle and felt Bart's soft snout on his cheek and his comforting arms on his sides. Bart was not one of those floppy bears that had heads and appendages that fell this way and that at every whim of gravity. Oh no. Bart's soft, furry arms, legs and head stayed firm, so you could cuddle him properly and be cuddled back. This was the secret of a truly fine bed-bear.

David felt held and comforted. Maybe a good bear was all that a man truly needed in his life and in his bed. Perhaps a cat as well. To sit on his lap and be another faithful, furry friend.

He settled quickly. Depression was always at its worst in the mornings. Now, with the addition of some red wine to the tea of supper, he felt drowsy and even vaguely happy. He eased into sleep.

As David stood, serving pan in hand, looking across the old people's lunch table, he was staring straight into the face of Mr Anders. Like a flash of X-ray, he saw the blood vessel burst in Mr Anders' brain. He almost felt the heart stop as the rush of blood flooded the synapses and clogged the system. He saw with his own eyes the sudden look of surprise, replaced in half a second by the defocused eyes and slack expression. As Mr Anders began to tilt sideways in slow motion, his lips turned blue and his skin went grey.

Move! David put the pan down on the table and was already heading to his left to go round the end of the table, past all the horrified stares. But he wasn't moving. Caught in mid-stride, he was unable to go any faster. He saw the seconds ticking past as he urged his body on, but time held him. Mr Anders continued on downwards in the slide of death, but David was moving at a centimetre in ten seconds. Impossibly slow. He hurried, he rushed, he pushed himself to speed up, all to no avail. It was going to take him for ever to get round that table to Mr Anders, now nearly horizontal as his chair scudded away from under him.

What was that? On his forehead? A smudge. Two dark smudges, in the shape of a cross. And a voice without words said, 'Marked for death. Dead already. Marked for death. Dead already.'

His body hit the floor with a terrible plop, like something made of jelly held in shape only by his clothes.

And then the press of a finger on his own forehead. A cold finger. Smudge, smudge. David was falling. He put his hand to his forehead and brought down a black smear on his fingers. Still falling, only not onto the floor, into a dark, deep, rectangular pit cut into the floor. A grave. Falling, falling. 'Marked for death. Dead already. Marked for death. Dead already.'

He was nearly in, and noticed that the grave wasn't empty. It was full of a shiny black substance, a gloopy liquid, with swirls and lines on its surface. It split and opened, welcoming him, and he slipped inside. The cavern was full of quietness, and peace, and rightness. The fulfilment of all his deepest dreams. The answer to all his hardest questions. To not be.

It closed over him, and he rested, in peace. In not being.

He woke, and was amazingly and warmly calm. He was still cuddling Bart. No sweaty limbs, no shaking terrors, no tangling in the straining sheets.

'You are my comforter,' he said to Bart.

And a voice from nowhere said, 'The Lord is your comforter.'

David replied, 'I need my comforter to be here. To be real, warm, soft and cuddling me.'

He stood before the mirror in his en suite bathroom and stared into that familiar, and yet somehow so unfamiliar, face. Bedraggled, of course. Bed-raggled. Grey hair hanging sideways in flying tufts. Eyes bleary. He hadn't intended to be here. Except that he'd relieved himself and was splashing his fingers under the cold tap, and the mirror was right there behind the sink. But he didn't need to be standing here, staring.

'Who are you?' he mumbled.

The dark shadow caught his eye. Just descending over his forehead, to the right of centre, like a shadow from another place. It flowed down over him until he was covered by it, and the invitation was clear. Be not.

He stood there, running his mind over the practical options for ending his life. He was mesmerised by the visions of them, playing out in front of him, so it seemed.

'Come back.' It was Bart, calling to him from far away

'Come back here.'

He woke with his nose pressed against Bart's fluffy snout, his arm over Bart's body.

'Faithful bear,' he said. 'Bearer of faithfulness.'

This time he remembered everything.

It was Thursday, 31st March.

David met with Dr Sweeting to see if he was safe to send back to his own home. He 'fenced' with her and covered up whatever he thought might lead to him having to go to the psychiatric unit. It seemed as if she couldn't really be bothered to fence back, and she discharged him.

He sat in the coffee shop with a large latte. And a large, half-chocolate-covered Viennese biscuit. And he began to laugh. He was recalling how he'd been waiting in a queue in the bakery one time and had been eyeing up the Viennese biscuits, but got distracted, and when the girl serving suddenly asked him for his order he'd said, 'A large latte and a Vietnamese biscuit.' Much hilarity.

It was good that he could still laugh. Then again, it didn't mean much. You can feel like death and still go round whistling. That was the true 'whistling in the dark'.

And he'd deceived Dr Sweeting about the darkness. Well, there was no point telling her. She'd hardly understand. He remembered the dream last night. And the mirror. That was a spiritual thing. It was the same inviting void his dad had discovered. The naturalness of non-being. Nobody understood that. Nor were they likely to. So, yes, he'd lied to her face about being in danger of trying it again. This thing had his number. What to do?

Would they stand around his grave, sobbing? Really? Would they say it was a desperate shame, what a fine fellow he was, sadly missed, you broke our hearts, the like will never pass this way again? No, they'd blame him for upsetting Angela and say he was a rum sort from the beginning. That he never really became a Christian and had dark spiritual forces at work in him. Good riddance. Let us not be taken in by the likes of him again. That sad fellow.

He supped his frothy coffee and bit his crumbly biscuit. Next, to face the Grangers. And Angela. Good grief, what was he going to say to her?

On the way back to the Grangers' he picked up a nice bunch of flowers and a bottle of a decent red wine from the supermarket.

When he walked in holding one in each hand, they knew immediately what the news was without him having to say.

'We'll miss you,' Bill said.

'It's been a joy having you here,' Mary added.

'And if you decided to stay a little longer…' Bill continued.

'No, no,' David replied. 'You've been too kind already. I told the psychiatrist woman. You've kept me busy but also given me my freedom. I'm more than grateful. I'd like to take you both out for a meal one evening, at The Old Rabbit's Warren in Tilsby.'

'That would be lovely!' they both chorused, and then laughed.

'Are you upping stumps immediately?' Bill asked.

'Yes, strike while the iron's hot, I need to get home and sort myself out.'

'No lunch, even?' Mary enquired.

'Thank you, no. I'll do some shopping and get some lunch in the café there. Thank you.'

He headed up the stairs. So far so good.

His invitation to a meal out was genuine, even though he doubted he'd be around long enough.

Bill appeared while he was packing up.

'You'll want a lift,' he said.

'Oh. Yes. I hadn't thought.'

'No problem.' He sat on the bed. 'Perhaps I could share a thought or two with you?'

'I've got five minutes. Share them all.'

Bill gave a gentle laugh. 'OK, yes, why should I think I have any right to impose my supposed wisdom on you? Anyway… there's a couple of things I believe need to be said. So… look, if you and Angela have problems in your relationship, we won't ever just take sides with her. You are our friend now, as well. But that said, you do need to know that she's really cut up about whatever it is that's happened, which she hasn't exactly said, and she's not sure what to do to make it right, and she's very vulnerable at the moment so if you could just try to be careful and kind with her. I'm not saying you have to keep it going if it's really over between you, just that she needs you to be gentle, you understand?'

So she'd picked up fully the intent of his moody silence when they drove back. 'OK. I hear you.'

'I suppose I'd hoped for something a bit more affirmatory than that.'

'I suppose you did.' David zipped up the small bag. 'I'm ready; let's go.'

'Can I take one of those?'

David handed him the small cabin luggage bag and Bill set off. David gave the room a final look around and followed with Bart under one arm and pulling the suitcase on its wheels with the other hand.

Mary was waiting downstairs in the hall and gave him a hug and a kiss on the cheek. Then Bill and he proceeded to the car. David put Bart on the back seat, sitting up, with a seatbelt round him. It seemed appropriate.

On the way in the car, Bill said, 'There's something else I need to tell you. If you'll bear with me.'

'I have a bear with me,' David joked. 'OK, go ahead.' He made it sound less weary than it felt.

'This morning, while I was praying, I had an image of you. You were alone in the middle of the night, staring into a bathroom mirror, and some shadowy thing started to descend over your head. It told you that you want to be dead. But it was deceiving you. *It* wants you dead. That's its nature. It tells you that you want to be dead. Because it likes suicide. It wants you to die ahead of your natural time, and by your own hand.'

'Creepy,' David said.

'But David, if there's any reality to that, you need to know there is a solution. Nothing like that can stand against the power of the Name of Jesus. It can be defeated. Don't despair.'

'I won't, then.'

'You asked Mary, my Mary, if she believed in spiritual darkness.'

'Yes.'

'Are you encountering something dark like I've just described to you?'

'No.'

'Because depression has its own kind of darkness, but that would be something quite different.'

'I thought you had a thing about how complex we are inside – how much the different elements of us mix up together.'

'I do hold to that view, but something like I just described to you isn't part of you. It's something else. Something from outside of you. A dark, nasty, invasive and evil thing.'

'Hmm.' David looked out of the window at the passing trees. He reflected that before, he hadn't wanted to mention the darkness because they wouldn't understand. Now, it was because they might understand. What a complex fellow he was sometimes.

Bill shut up.

They got to David's house without a further word being spoken. It was an uncomfortable silence. David knew that he and Bill were far from seeing eye to eye. But Bill was a big enough man to let that go. Bill helped him to the front door with his stuff, gave him a manly hug, and offered the wish that he'd see him in church on Sunday.

He wouldn't.

David let himself in and breathed a great sigh of relief. Home. Alone. It didn't bother him in the slightest that this was where he'd tried to end his life.

He unpacked, made tea, and read the pile of mail that Angela had put on the little sideboard in the hall. That was kind of her. She was kind. But she'd overstepped the mark, and all Bill's fine hopes couldn't change that.

CHAPTER NINE

David was having tea on his lap tray with the news on the television when the phone rang. The landline. He was inclined to leave it but decided to put his tray down and answer it.

'David. It's Aunt Mary.'

'Hello, Aunt Mary.'

'David, I found the box of stuff that you and your dad used to play with. It was mostly bits of pub games and jigsaws and toy soldiers, but there's one item that did concern me.'

She waited but he said nothing. Surely his 'Oh, what was that?' could be inferred.

'It was an Ouija board. Do you know what that is?'

'Of course I know what it is. It's a piece of occult equipment for speaking to spirits.'

'I've burned it. It was a very dangerous thing.'

'Mark gave it to him.'

He heard her breath catch. 'Mark? You met Mark?'

'Yes, he was dad's friend. He gave him the board and they played it sometimes.'

'David, Mark was a spiritualist. Of the most dangerous sort. He believed in contacting the dead and conjuring up spirits. Did you ever play the game with them?'

'No.'

'Because if you did, that would be a very – unhelpful thing for you.'

'Why?'

'Because evil spirits, unhelpful spirits, are real. They only wait for an invitation to latch on to you. Even infest you like rats in a house. You didn't play with it with them even once, did you?'

He wasn't going to be interrogated like a naughty child. 'I said no.'

'It might have been the source of your dad's obsession with suicide.'

'Why?'

'Because that's the kind of thing unhelpful spirits do.'

'Ha. OK. Anyway, it's gone,' David said casually.

'Yes and so is he. Mark. He came to a sticky end. A very sticky end. He threw himself off a high section of Tower Bridge onto a passing pleasure tour boat. He crashed right through the plastic canopy and decapitated himself on the back of a seat. It got a lot of media coverage at the time. Do you remember?'

'No, why would I?'

'You didn't stay in touch with him after your dad died?'

'No. Listen, Aunt Mary, this is all very fascinating but I don't see what it has to do with me.'

'I just thought you should know.'

'OK, well, thanks for phoning. Bye now.'

'Bye, David.'

Most of that was true, at least.

He had a clear image of himself, sat with the two men, in the basement underneath the single, hanging bulb, with the Ouija board on a small table between them. Each of them had a finger on the heart-shaped, wooden planchette. His dad had said, 'What shall we ask it?'

Mark had replied, 'Nah, that's for sissies. If you want to really use this thing, you need to call up a spirit.'

'What kind of spirit?' David had asked.

Mark had turned his sneering, facetious face towards him and said, 'Any kind. Whatever comes.'

Angela rang his mobile. She sounded nervous and upset. She had reason to be.

'Hello, David. Can we speak?'

'OK.'

'How are you? I gather you're back home.'

'Grangers told you, did they?'

'Yes, of course. It's not a secret.'

'No, it's not.'

'Are you happy to be home? Can I come round?'

'I'm just settling back in, and I'm a bit tired. I'd rather not.'

'Oh, David, we've met up when we've been tired before. Let me come round. Don't push me away.'

'I rather think you did that yourself.'

There was a deathly silence.

'Look, dear David, I've been so upset and I really need to see you. Please don't do this.'

'I'm really sorry but you've hurt me, really hurt me. I still can't believe what you said to me. That I should pull myself together, basically. What a thing to say. It cuts deep, that does.'

Again, a hanging silence.

'You know I didn't mean that.' He said nothing. She continued, 'David, are we...' there was a terrible pause, 'are we over? Please just tell me if we are.'

'No. I'm not saying that.'

'Oh, thank you.'

'But then again, I'm not sure I'm going to be around long enough for that to mean much.' Where had that come from? He hadn't intended to reveal that.

'Oh, David. I'm going to get everyone praying for you. Right now. I'm so worried about you. I'm going to get everyone praying.'

'You do that if you think you need to. Goodbye, Angela,' he said, and pressed 'end'.

It was Friday, 1st April.

David awoke with bright sunshine making a white screen of his bedroom windows. It forced its way even though his curtains, causing them to almost throb with vital colour. The yellow and white shone with a false hopefulness.

He looked at his alarm clock. It was just before eight.

Bart was on the floor, looking up at him. 'Morning, faithful bear,' he said, and reached out to stroke his friendly and furry cheek.

He reviewed the night. Nothing. He'd slept soundly, could recall no dreams, and no trips to the loo. Doubtless he'd made one or two, but they'd been so unremarkable as to not have been recorded in memory.

OK. Good enough. He got out of bed, threw on his dressing gown and slippers and made his morning call to the bathroom. No darkness lingered there, no suicidal shroud, even though he now knew where this thing had come from, and why it clung to him.

He descended the stairs, aware of the dull hopelessness of morning depression. It mattered little. He knew the solution now to life's frustrating aggravations. And soon it would be over. Fear lay in being alive, not in the fulfilment of being no more.

Being. No. More.

As he passed the front room he looked in as he always did to check he hadn't left the telly on or the fire the previous night in a half-asleep state as he'd headed for bed. And there on the little table was his poem pad. The big one. The one for completed and written-out-neatly-and-in-full poems. With a poem covering the whole front page. A pen lay beside it.

That wasn't right.

He went in and picked it up. In large capital letters it was titled, 'DEATH WAITS FOR ME'.

Without reading any more, he held the pad down and looked for the notes that always accompanied any completed piece. The pages from the smaller notebooks. The rejected scribblings. The first attempts. The screwed-up pages of half-formed ideas and verses. But there were none. He searched the bin, and then carried the pad with him into the kitchen and checked that bin. He took it outside, fearful that if he put it down it would disappear, and looked in the big bin. No discarded notebook-size pages. Or any size. There was the writing. But there wasn't the writhing.

Mystified, he carried it inside and made a pot of tea. Why wasn't he reading it? Because it was in his handwriting and yet he had no knowledge of having written it. And that, frankly, frightened him. So he took the tea with him and it, into the front room, and sat in his chair, and even put on the TV news. He blew on the tea in the WOL mug with the large owl relief that Angela had bought him, and took a sip. And another. He looked at the pad in his hand without focusing on the words. Only the title was clear. Yes, death waits for me. I know death waits for me. I thought I knew what it was. So what is this?

Steeling himself to be proved wrong, and for revelations from, or at least about, his own soul, he held it up at a comfortable distance and started to read. It certainly read like one of his, quite apart from the distinctive hand.

It was framed as the voice of death, calling to him. But this was death uncovered, laid bare of its pretences. Death as pain, as decay, as defeat, as hopeless loss. As darkness in a most overwhelming and troubling defeat. Judgement, in fact.

It was the best, most compelling, most darkly real piece he'd never written.

He shuddered. That kind of darkness wasn't what he'd been shown. That was a terrifying, lurking, painful, danger. A death-darkness to be wary of. The darkness of being wrapped by a spider in its silky cocoon, waiting for it to inject you with its disgusting digestive juices.

Unsettled, he put it down. He'd written this, last night. He had come downstairs, all unknowing, and poured out this warning. This grim gushing.

He gave a small snort of derisory laughter. So much for Angela getting them all to pray.

Dressed and breakfasted, he reviewed it again. A fine piece, no doubt, by his meagre standards. Written by him, last night, also no doubt, from both its handwriting and its form. Yet written as a whole, delivered pre-formed, as if not from him but from some deeper source. And it chilled him. This was a different style of darkness from the one that had called so comfortingly to him. This was an unnatural darkness, a dark enemy that wanted to destroy him with poison and suck him dry.

Shaken, he decided to go out and find something to do. The early depression had lifted, and he was able to face the day with some sort of equanimity. Some modicum of hopefulness. He would walk into town and wander about, taking a coffee at the bakery and seeing what he could see. It was clearly a lovely spring day, bright and warm, and the birds might even lighten his mood, who knew?

He put on a light jacket and his brown shoes and set off up the lane. Mrs James was holding Sparks, the new Boston terrier, in her front garden. 'Hello, David,' she said brightly as he passed.

'Hello Mrs J. How's Sparks today?'

'How are you today, you silly old thing?' she asked it, tugging at the scruff of its neck. It barked in reply. Or annoyance.

'And how are you?' she asked. 'You've been away.'

'Yes, but I'm back now, and I'll no doubt see you soon.'

He'd managed the whole exchange without actually stopping, and he sped up again up the lane.

'Byeee!' he heard her cooing after him.

He started with a coffee and a croissant at the bakery, and then wandered round the shops, counting how many sold ibuprofen and codeine tablets. Enough, he reckoned.

His appointment with the lovely Myfanwy was at eleven, but he wasn't even sure he'd go. Still, it got to half past ten and he couldn't think of anything better to do, so he walked up to her offices. Throughout their encounter he was resistive to the point of being rude, and scoffed at her suggestion that they should start meeting three times a week. He eventually left with the session not even finished.

He took lunch at his favourite bakery – an egg sandwich and a large coffee – looking out of the front windows at the town and the people.

Then he set off to the largest chemist on the High Street. He went up to the pharmacy counter and said to the woman serving, 'I've been taking paracetamol and codeine for lower back pain, but I wonder if ibuprofen and codeine would be better.'

She was in her thirties, darkly pretty with black-brown hair tied back away from her face, and she looked very professional in her white lab coat. 'Yes, probably, because of the muscle-relaxant effect of the ibuprofen. Is it muscular pain?'

'I think so. What's the biggest size of ibuprofen and codeine you sell over the counter?'

She turned and picked up a box from the shelves behind her to show him. 'This has 200mg of ibuprofen and 12.8mg of codeine in each tablet.'

'The dose is two?'

'Yes and not more than six in twenty-four hours. And you shouldn't take them for longer than three days because they can be addictive and the codeine can cause gut problems. In fact, if you've been taking paracetamol and codeine you've already been taking codeine so probably you should see your doctor before changing tablets.'

'How many in a box?'

'Sixteen or thirty-two, but I can only sell you one box of thirty-two or two boxes of sixteen.'

'OK, I'll take the large box, please.'

She charged him, he paid cash, and she said, 'Do see your doctor before starting on those.'

'Thank you,' David said, walking away. No chance of that.

He went on to all the other places he could buy them – chemists, department stores – and headed home at about 4pm with five boxes of thirty-two and four boxes of sixteen. He was calculating as he walked home. That's 224 tablets. That's forty-five grams of ibuprofen and nearly three grams of codeine. That must be enough. He'd sink into a lovely snoozy state with the codeine and the ibuprofen would see him off.

Once home, he took all the plastic and aluminium film strips out of the boxes and dropped the boxes in the bin in the front room under the small table. Should he press them all out now? Probably not. Their gel outers might attract moisture from the atmosphere and spoil them. So he left the strips on the table on top of the poem and went into the kitchen to make tea.

He ate his pasta and cheese sauce with green beans in front of the TV news, then washed up and made sure everything was tidy. He grabbed Angela's house key from the hook by the front door as he left, and got the car out of the garage. He arrived at Angela's house at six as intended.

Standing at her door, he pressed the bell. She opened it and surprise turned instantly to happiness. She didn't look very well. Dark rings under her eyes. Red eyes. Puffy cheeks. She looked generally puffy.

'David…'

He held out his hand. There was her key. 'I'd like my key back, please.'

Her whole body seemed to deflate. 'Can't you come in? Can't we talk?'

'I need my key back, please,' he repeated, indicating for her to take the one in the palm of his hand.

'I don't want my key back,' she said, trying to be brave with him.

'I need my key back. Now.'

She turned and picked it up from her little hall table. She put it in his hand, but didn't take hers. So he dropped it onto her welcome mat and walked away.

'Why are you so angry with me?' she called.

'I'm not angry. But I am very hurt.'

Now she couldn't come snooping around in the middle of the night.

Merlot in good measure made the TV seem quite jolly as he sat at home, relaxed and surprisingly happy. The house phone rang a couple of times but he left it. Also his mobile. He didn't care who it might be.

But then at 8pm his front doorbell rang. Darn it. At least they'd used the bell, which always put people slightly more in his favour. He was mightily inclined to just ignore it. It might even be some of Angela's church friends come to save him from himself. Especially as she'd had them all praying for him.

Blast, it went again. So he got up and walked into the hall. A brown-coated figure stood the other side of the frosted glass. It didn't look like a salesman.

He inched the door open. There stood the rector, collar and all.

'Hello, David. Can I come in?'

'Colin. Hello. Er, I'm just having a quiet evening on my own really, so…'

'Perfect. I won't keep you long.'

He almost barged past David. Were clergy supposed to do that? Did they have some sort of ancient right of entry to homes on their patch? Their parish patch?

David followed him saying, 'It's not really…'

'David!'

He'd seen the evidence.

'Oh, David! Look at this!'

He was standing beside the table and scooping a box out of the bin. 'There's enough here to kill ten people. Oh dear, what *are* we going to do?'

His face was full of sadness rather than judgement.

David just stood there, hands at his sides, discovered.

'We prayed for you last night.'

'A lot of good it did,' David said.

'We prayed for this thing to reveal itself. What's this?' He pushed strips of pills off the poem. He picked it up and read it. David watched his lips moving as he read. Horror spread over his face. 'Oh my goodness, did you write this?'

103

'Last night. But I don't remember doing it.'

'This is the spirit revealing itself – its true nature of destruction and fear.'

'Did Angela send you?'

'Not at all. I believe God did. The God who loves you and wants to spare you all this.'

'And how would He manage that?'

'Sit down, David.'

David stayed standing, rather taken aback.

'You're not possessed, but you are being oppressed, by a dark spirit that wants you to commit suicide. I don't know how it got its claws into you. Have you ever tried to contact spirits?'

'No.'

The rector just stared at him.

'OK, yes. As a child a friend gave my dad an Ouija board and we played with it and both my dad and that guy committed suicide later. There. Is that what you want?'

'It's what I need. Not at all what I want. Nor do you want it. What I want is to pray over you right here this evening and set you free from this thing, in the mighty Name of Jesus. Will you let me? I consider myself your friend, David, and I only want to help you, if you'll let me.'

A huge urge to swear the most awful blasphemies rose in David like sick rising up from his guts. A hot and acid gorge felt like it might expel itself from his mouth any second. He shook and went very cold. Sweat broke out on his palms and his forehead. He started to mumble and mutter, such was the fight inside him over the horrible words.

'You need my help. You've just gone as white as a sheet and broken out in a sweat. And you don't dare speak, do you? Spirit of suicide, I command you in the Name of Jesus to be silent and I do not allow you to speak at all.'

The folding, roiling words of abuse to God fell flat, like broken letters, silent in his head. He slumped into a chair.

The rector continued. 'I mustn't do this alone. I have two friends in the car outside waiting for me to call them in. Bill and Mary Granger. You know they love you. Can I call them in?'

David nodded.

In less than a minute the rector was back. Bill said, 'Hello, dear chap,' but looked grave, and Mary had her most serious expression on her face. She tried to smile at him but it hardly dented the steely mask.

Bill and Mary sat next to David on the settee, while the rector stayed standing.

'David,' he said, 'we love you as a fellow follower of Jesus Christ, and all we want to do is prise open the grip of this unhelpful spiritual presence you've picked up. There will be the minimum of mumbo jumbo. I have no bell, book or candle, apart from the Bible in my pocket. I carry no stole, cross, crucifix or salt. No anointing oil or holy water. I come armed only with the Name and the word of Jesus, and that is more than enough. But David, I do need you to completely renounce the playing with the Ouija board, the intention to commit suicide, any blasphemous thoughts and any kind of spiritual darkness that you know of. You need to hand them all over to Jesus to take away and destroy. Will you do that? Only say yes if you're sure.'

Now he was terrified. The whole room seemed to be full of a thick atmosphere of dread. The darkness of death was no longer a thing of peace and refuge, fulfilment and solution, but rather a gaping horror of flesh-flaying evil. His thoughts went back to the sermon of Maundy Thursday, and the pit. This felt like a mini version of the pit. That darkness, which he hadn't recognised then, but did now.

He cleared his throat of the stinging and stinking gorge, and said, 'Yes,' firmly for them all to hear.

'Now we will pray for you. We will all stand over and around you – don't worry, that's a surrounding of protection and care – and we will lay a hand on you and tell this wickedness and darkness to let go of you and leave. You might feel something; you might not. If anything frightening or uncomfortable happens – it doesn't usually – you can ask us to pause. But once we start, we're not going to stop. Is that OK?'

'Go ahead,' he said.

They gathered round him as Colin had said. David bowed his head and shut his eyes and said in his heart, 'Dear God. I didn't ask for this thing, but I realise I've maybe not discouraged it as I should have. I've been bad these last few days. Disrespectful and unkind. I've upset people and challenged people that I shouldn't have and I'm sorry. Please forgive me and help me to make it right. Take this deceitful thing away from me.'

He realised they were muttering in the 'other languages' he'd heard spoken of once or twice. Prayer languages that weren't human. The tongues of angels. Angela spoke them. Though he imagined that angels actually knew what they meant. It wasn't frightening. A warmth seemed to spread out from their hands and began to fill him up like the feeling of codeine or red wine. He felt amazingly relaxed and comfortable, like he might easily sleep. It was a filling, strong, healing and holding peace.

Suddenly the rector spoke, not loudly, but firmly and confidently. 'Foul spirit from darkness, I name you – you are a deceiving spirit of death. In the Name of Jesus Christ of Nazareth, God's Son and the Living Lord of all, defeater of all evil, reigning on the eternal throne of heaven, you will not speak. Release your grip now and leave this home and never return.'

Silence. The quiet prayers stopped. What were they waiting for?

Then he felt Colin's hands on his head. 'Lord, thank You for setting your servant free. David, the Lord bless you, the Lord shine His face of peace and love over you, the Lord drench you in His unfailing love and unimaginable peace, in the Name of the Father, and of the Son, and of the Holy Spirit,' and all three of them said, 'Amen.'

Liquid love did indeed drench him, in outpourings from heaven itself. Love bathed him and held him. He knew then that he was smiling like some vacant fool, but that kind of foolishness he didn't mind.

Mary said, 'I see the love is flowing. Thank You, Lord.'

They took their hands away and the rector said, 'How do you feel?'

'Utterly different,' David said. 'So relaxed. So ashamed, though, of what I was planning to do. I'm so sorry as well for how I've been these last few days.'

'That's all right,' Bill said. 'We've all been in dark places. Perhaps not quite as dark as that one.'

'I'm going to ask you a question and I want you to answer it without thinking,' Colin said. 'Who is your Lord and Master?'

'Jesus,' David answered, without hesitation.

'Good. Indeed He is. That's all good news. Now the bad news. I'm afraid I'm going to ask you to go and stay with the Grangers again for a few more days.'

They both laughed. 'Sorry,' Mary added.

'This will have taken it out of you – I mean not just the unhelpful spiritual presence, but left you drained, and maybe a bit vulnerable, so you should have some real support for a few days.'

'Is everyone at church going to know about this?' David asked.

'Good grief, no!' Colin said. 'Not at all. This is nobody's business but ours. And Angela's, I suspect.'

'That was surprisingly easy,' David said.

'The Name of Jesus is amazingly powerful. It shouldn't really take more than a firm application of it to such a spirit, usually, in my experience,' the rector answered.

'You're an extraordinary minister,' David said.

'Actually, no, I'm really not, nor would I ever wish to be. I want to stand back, not to stand out. The power isn't mine, so neither must the glory be. It's all His.'

'OK,' David said.

CHAPTER TEN

David packed a bag, picked up Bart and followed Bill and Mary down in his own car this time.

At the front door they greeted him with warm hugs and ushered him in. They took him into the kitchen and gave him a coffee. He sat up at the breakfast bar on a stool with them. He felt a little odd.

'David, you may still feel depressed,' Mary said to him. 'What we just did won't necessarily affect that. Though it might. Anyway, how do you feel?'

He looked at his coffee mug while he tried to get his feelings in order. 'Well, this is kind of new territory, so, let's see. I feel blessed. By which I mean I actually feel like something good has been done to me. But also, embarrassed. And relieved. And, er, set free. Hopeful. Ashamed. Guilty. But not at all anxious or, at this moment, noticeably depressed. Or suicidal. Oh, and thankful to have such good friends. I think I'm going to have some apologising to do in the next day or so,' David said.

'Well, we'll take ours as read perhaps, old chap,' Bill said.

'No, no! I was rude and dismissive and even dishonest. I treated with disdain your enormous hospitality by being that way over the last day or so and I'm very, very sorry because I am enormously grateful for everything you've so kindly and graciously done for me. You've been wonderful.'

'Yes, well, unlike the rector we *are* wonderful!' Mary said, and they all laughed together again. It was a delightfully warm moment, and made David realise how safe he felt. Safe from darkness, safe with friends, safe with God and Jesus. Safe with

Angela? It was more of a question of whether she was safe with him. He suddenly felt so sorry for her, and the way he'd treated her. He looked at his watch. It was not yet 9pm.

'I must ring Angela,' he said.

'You might do better to go round,' Mary offered.

'Yes. I will. Thank you. I'll go now. I'll just throw my bag and bear in the bedroom and go straight away.'

'Good man,' Bill said.

Bill followed him up for a word.

'Now, David, mealtimes are as before. But also, we'd very much like you to join us, Mary and myself, at our morning prayers and Bible study at 7am in the kitchen where we just were. We just take half an hour before breakfast. Also, Rector Colin left us some intentions for you. He'd like you to be at morning and evening services on a Sunday, and to come to the Wednesday morning Communion even though you can't take Communion yet, and with that in mind to do the full Alpha course in the autumn so you can be confirmed at the service in January. He knows you did the mini Alpha but he thinks doing the full thing will help you.'

'That all sounds fine to me,' David answered, happily.

'Good. And whatever you have to say to Angela, do it with love, eh?'

'I hereby affirm and undertake that I will do so, with all kindness and affection.'

'Good man!'

This time she dwindled as soon as she saw him.

'I am so sorry,' he said straight away, and handed her his key.

'Oh!' she said, staring at it, then back at him.

'Can I please come in?'

'Yes. Of course. Do you want mine back?'

'I certainly do. Have you heard?'

'No. What?'

'They came and prayed for me this evening and it's gone.'

'Oh. Goodness. Really?'

She'd been in her front room with the telly on. She turned it off and said, 'Glass of Merlot? Oh, no, you're driving, I guess.'

'A coffee would be good. We can Merlot together another night.'

She threw her arms around him in such a hug he thought he might not be able to breathe. 'Oh, David, I've missed you *so much!*'

'I've hurt you and been so cold and mean. I cannot believe I treated you that way. Nor can I begin to describe the state of mind I was in. It was like I'd just let everything go and nothing meant anything or mattered any more. It was like I was addicted, like an alcoholic on a bender, and it was all I could see or think about. I was driven by it. I was even rude to Bill and Mary. And Myfanwy. And Aunt Mary. It was like I'd set myself on being dead and that was all I could see. All that mattered. It was awful, but when I was in it I couldn't see it. I am *so sorry!*'

His arms were right round her, holding on to her. She was warm and soft and comforting and smelt of Angela. They stood like that for happy moments.

'This is dangerous,' she said. 'All I want is to take you upstairs and lie down with you. Which isn't going to happen. So we'd better decide what is going to happen.'

'Pub,' he said. 'Normality. Cheerful atmosphere. Moderate imbibition of alcoholic refreshment. Walk to The Lion. Maybe even have a plate of fries between us. What do you say?'

'I say to hear you say, "imbibition" is a heartening sign and we should leave for the normal world immediately. Let's go!'

She pulled herself away, threw on her light coat and boots and they were out of the door in two minutes. They held hands as they walked up the road and she swung them like a little girl.

'I'm sorry, David, but… I love you,' she said.

'Then I'm even more sorry, Angela, but…' he let it hang. 'I love you.'

She stopped him and kissed him, full on the lips, careless of their previous agreement. He was happy to respond. He really wanted her to feel cheerful again.

'Mary said I might still feel depressed,' he said. 'What they did isn't a cure for depression, necessarily.'

'Fair enough. If you feel you must,' she said. 'But I'd *so* rather you didn't.'

'Ha. Me too.'

It was Saturday, 2nd April.

David didn't like to be up before 7am, but he was determined to make a good start with Bill and Mary on the morning prayers before breakfast.

Greyness leaded the curtains, but at least it was light. How did he feel? He turned on to his side and looked at Bart.

'Morning, bear,' he said. Would he keep Bart in his bed at home, instead of in the spare room?

So, how did he feel? Not sure. He'd slept well. He didn't feel particularly depressed, which he often did first thing in the morning. Whatever they'd done to him last evening had maybe lifted that, at least for a while.

He felt hopeful. He'd had a really good time with Angela last night. Better than for a while. Was it just the depression making their relationship so dead recently? Probably. But that was exactly the problem with depression. You just couldn't tell. Anyway, it definitely pleased him enormously to make her so happy.

Oh dear! He'd made her so sad these last days. He'd been so horrible to her. And she was so faithful, trying so hard to help him and be patient with him. He felt she'd never let him down, never give up on loving him. 'Faithful, like you,' he said to Bart, who just looked at him.

Anyway, up, get up.

At the table, Bill and Mary sat with a couple of Bibles and small booklets.

'Good morning, David,' they both said.

'Good morning, both,' he replied, and sat.

He looked at the booklets. They were titled *Daily New Life Bible Notes*.

'You use daily Bible notes?' he said. 'I though those were for beginners.'

'No, dear chap, they're for everybody, and they're very good,' said Bill.

'And,' Mary chimed in, 'if you don't use them yourself how can you recommend them to others?'

Mary opened up a page to the day's date. It had a theme for the day, a suggested Bible passage and a thought on it, and a prayer.

Bill began with a short prayer. They read the Bible passage carefully, dwelt on the thought and discussed it, and said the prayer from the book together.

'Breakfast time!' Bill announced.

'That's not our main time of prayer in the day, I should say,' Mary said, getting up, 'it's just a good start to the day. I commend both to you.'

'Thank you,' David said, feeling slightly chastened.

'How did it go with Angela last night?' Bill asked as they headed into the cooking area. David had slunk in after midnight, and not seen them.

'Absolutely wonderful. I made her happy, you'll be glad to know.'

'That is good news. Long may it continue. And did she make you happy?'

'Very.'

'And I can assume you're still chaste, despite the hour you rolled in?' Bill asked.

'Very chaste, sir,' David replied.

'How did you sleep?' Mary asked over toast, marmalade and coffee.

'Very well. Like the proverbial log.'

'No bad dreams? No dark shades bidding you to do things you don't really want to? No terrors of the night?' she continued.

'No, but you see, that was the problem. They weren't really terrors. They were a warm, comforting invitation – "End this suffering. Be fulfilled in not *being* any more." It was the poem I'd written that really shook me.'

'Ah,' said Bill. 'That was because we prayed for this thing to reveal itself. Reveal its true nature. It was deceiving you into thinking it was somehow benign, a blessing. In the poem it revealed itself. How do you feel?'

'Hard to say. A little shaken. A bit frail, I suppose. Like, I'm not sure exactly what's happened to me.'

Mary took it up. 'Do you know the passage in the Gospels where Jesus talks about a man who has an evil spirit cast out of him, but then it comes back and finds the house all neat and tidy, so it goes and gets a bunch of its worst mates and they all move in?'

'Vaguely. Like *The Young Ones*.'

They laughed. Had they actually watched *The Young Ones*, that riotous comedy of revolting students?

'Yes, well, firstly, don't worry about it because that spirit was clinging onto you, on the outside, not infesting you on the inside. But secondly, take the encouragement that it won't come back if you fill up the space with something else. Maybe in your case there isn't really such a space, but the principle still applies, I think. What do you think, sweetie?' she asked Bill.

'Definitely the principle applies. That's why Colin has all those requests of you. Make sure you fill up the space with relationship with Jesus.'

'I do feel a bit vulnerable,' David admitted. 'I'm not sure if that's a feeling of emptiness or just that something unprecedented has happened to me. Like finding myself in zero gravity. Or doing a space-walk. Or like I'm in new territory without a map. I'm not expressing myself well, but something feels a little odd.'

'Well, good, you've recognised it, then,' Mary said. 'So just be sure to keep your thoughts on the Lord and take every opportunity to feed on Him.'

'Wise words, my dear,' Bill said, and David watched as he took his wife's hand on the table and gave it a warm squeeze. Their eyes met with a look of great closeness and love.

'So, it's Saturday,' Bill said. 'Any plans?'

'Not really. We thought we'd contact each other once we were up. About eight or nine.'

'So she hasn't got you directing traffic or cleaning the town or ferrying elderly folks to the shops?'

'Not that I know of. But then that's the delight of Angela, isn't it? You just never quite know.'

They met in the bakery in town for a coffee at eleven. They shared a croissant, both having breakfasted already. He looked at her as they ate – not too obviously as she didn't really like him staring at her. It made her feel uncomfortable, she said. She looked lovely in a just-above-knee-length brown skirt, tan boots, a green jumper and her brown spring coat. A straggle or two of her light-brown-almost-blonde hair hung down carelessly at the sides of her round face with the lovely deep-set blue eyes. The freckles were still waiting for a bit more sunshine before they came out of hibernation.

'You're looking at me,' she said.

'Sorry. You should be glad, after the way I've been.'

'Hmm. Maybe. Even so, you know how I feel about being stared at.'

'What shall we do today?'

'We have this morning. This afternoon I'm bringing Mrs Stead and Miss Latham up to the shops.'

He laughed.

'What?'

114

'That's exactly what the Grangers thought you might get me doing.'

'Well, they were wrong, I'm not expecting any help.'

'I'll help. Gladly.'

'Oh. OK. They'll like that. Handsome young feller that they think you are.'

'Know me to be.'

She smiled. She touched his cheek. 'Know you to be.' She leaned across and kissed him. Croissant flakes exchanged in the moment but neither of them minded.

'And tomorrow, after church, we're going to see Andrew,' she added.

'Oh. Are we?'

'Yes. Thelia rang and invited us to lunch.'

'Very good. That's definitely something to look forward to,' David said, pleased. They seemed to fit together, and David sometimes reflected that in both the fascination with maths and the need to be thoroughly hugged, there was something very good. For both of them. Andrew met another need in him, which was a surprising thing to discover.

'There's that little smile,' Angela said.

'I'm not a child,' he replied.

'I know, sorry. I don't like to be stared at and you don't like to be spoken to like a child. Little Noddy.'

She nudged him and he nudged her back and they both nearly fell off their tall stools and started laughing, leaning in a heap on the counter.

It was Saturday evening.

'Hello, Aunt Mary.'

'Hello, David.'

'How are you?'

'I'm fine, thank you. Why have you rung?'

'I'm ringing to apologise. You were right about the Ouija board and I lied and I was rude to you and I'm very sorry.'

'Well, all right, then. It was me tipped off your Rector Colin, I was so concerned. I had to ring a few churches in the town before I found one which recognised your name, and that was him.'

'That was "he",' David muttered under his breath.

'Oh, *David!* I heard that. Don't be such a grammatical Nazi! You didn't even teach English; it was physics and maths.'

'Sorry, Aunt Mary, I don't know why I said that. You're quite right.'

'I'm not your mother, you know. You don't have to carry your resentment at her over to me.'

'Sorry. Anyway, I'm feeling much better. I don't know what came over me before.'

'I know. Your rector was good enough to ring back this morning and say you were going to be much better even though he couldn't give any details. He's a nice chap.'

'Yes, he is. And thank you for being concerned for me, Aunt Mary.'

'That's OK. You look after that nice Angela.'

It was Sunday, 3rd April.

Church had felt good to David. Better than for a long time. They were still celebrating the resurrection and David had encountered a real sense of it this morning. Lifted, he was, especially when the rector played the Lighthouse Family song, 'Lifted', and he'd realised how appropriate the words could be.

People had greeted him just like normal. No sense of secrets spread. And then he and Angela, after coffee, of course, had got into her car, and even now were heading towards Lifford. It was a bright spring day with high, streaky clouds and vibrant greens bursting out about them. She was singing with her sweet, high voice to a CD of classic rock tracks, because she knew he liked them, and she'd found out she did as well.

She was wearing her nice white jeans. They'd had an argument once about her wearing clothes that were too young for her and he would never have it again. What an idiot he could be. Best forgotten. Or remembered. Whichever.

Without staring, he reflected what a fortunate fellow he was to have a lady friend of her age who was, in his eyes, such a lovely shape. That was far from the most important thing about her, or their relationship, and he adored her for their meeting of minds and souls, but this mattered to him as well. Or was it just part of the way he saw he as a whole? No matter, really, she was just lovely.

'What?' she said. She had a radar about him looking at her.

He decided it was best not to deny it. 'I was just thinking how lovely you look.'

'Aww,' she said, cocking her head slightly towards him. 'And you look very handsome in your Sunday shirt and tie. Though that collar is beginning to fray a little. We should get you a couple more good ones. Maybe a couple more ties, as well.'

'Huh! I see. I look smart but shabby and outdated. Seven out of ten for trying.'

She sighed a great, dramatic sigh. 'OK, I'm sorry. Just don't resent me for it.' She paused. 'Do you remember how that word came out so much with your Aunt Mary? I've been thinking over that. So, think about this. Is resentment more like hatred or like anger?'

'I suppose hatred. But not a lot.'

'No. Resentment doesn't even really have the energy to be hatred. And nothing like anger. That takes real energy. Passion. Resentment is a pale thing. Did you ever hate your mum as a teenager?'

'No, I don't think so.'

'Did you ever tell her you hated her in a moment of sheer frustration?'

'No. Did you ever say that to your mum?'

'Yes, a few times. And I didn't always apologise. Not straight away, anyway.'

'Why is this interesting?' he wanted to know.

'I think it's significant. How you handle, or rather how you don't handle, frustration. Your mum was a continual pain in the butt to both you and your dad, and you couldn't even work up any good, honest anger.'

'Isn't that a good thing? That I kept it to resentment?'

'No, actually, I don't think it is.'

'Yes, well, you're not my counsellor.'

CHAPTER ELEVEN

Thelia met them at the door of the pebble-dashed house as she always did. She was a little shorter than Angela, with fashionable glasses, and her hair hung down at the sides of her face in straggles not unlike Angela's.

Martin came up behind her. He was tall, well-built because he worked out, and always smiling a great, gracious smile. His face was clean-shaven and already tanned from time abroad sorting out his company's computer issues.

Thelia ushered them in, hugging Angela then David, and Martin administered his usual hug to Angela and warm handshake to David.

'Andrew!' they both called, but there was no response.

'He's in the front room having some Lego time,' Thelia said. They walked in there and he was sitting cross-legged, with pieces of Lego strewn about which he was arranging into small piles. But he didn't even look up. He was wearing a candy red shirt and pale brown shorts. The pleasant features under the mop of red hair were drawn into something like concentration. Angela seemed quite cool about that but David was disappointed, even though he knew it didn't really mean anything.

He went over to Andrew, knelt on the bright red and cream carpet, and touched him lightly on the arm. 'Hello, Andrew, my good friend,' he said.

Nothing. In fact, Andrew stopped playing with the pieces and let his hands flop into his lap. He looked down at the carpet.

Thelia spoke up. 'Andrew. How about saying hello to Aunt Angela and David? They've come to see you.'

Nothing.

David lowered himself further and leaned on his elbow, trying to get a look into Andrew's face.

'Do you remember last time we came and we built that tower?' he asked.

Nothing.

David looked up at Thelia but she just shrugged. This was Andrew. They lived with it all the time. But she gave a little nod towards him as a way of encouraging David to keep trying.

'Can I use some pieces from the box?' David asked.

Nothing.

Thelia spoke. 'Andrew. Give David a nice big hug, you know you both want one.'

Nothing.

'Maybe you should give him one anyway,' Angela offered.

David was uncomfortable with that. 'No, I shouldn't. That's forcing myself on him, regardless of his feelings, isn't it, old friend? If you want a hug, you'll soon enough let me know.'

Nothing.

This was exactly what David had feared. He really didn't want to force himself on Andrew and make him feel uncomfortable, but he really did want Andrew to know he was glad to see him and up for a hug. Difficult.

'Come and have a coffee in the kitchen,' Martin said.

Hmm. To stay and play or go for coffee and chat. He looked at Andrew, and suddenly he seemed forlorn, all alone on the floor, just sitting there.

'Oh, just give him a hug,' Angela said.

'No, I'll stay here and play with Lego with my friend Andrew, and see what happens,' David replied.

'Fine. Andrew, be nice,' Thelia said, and they trooped off out of the door. David kept his distance from Andrew, a couple of feet, and started to build a bridge out of the Lego, using Fibonacci numbers for the sizes of the columns – rising then reversing the numbers so that the bridge came down again.

Andrew was pretending not to watch, but he had his eyes at a level where he could see.

Minutes passed. 'How are you, Andrew, my good friend?'

'Mmm.'

'That good? OK!'

'Mmm.'

Andrew started to build again, and David tried to see a pattern but couldn't. 'Have you got a number progression going there, old buddy?'

'Mmm.'

'I can't see it. Help me out. You're the clever one. You can see what I'm doing.'

'Fibonacci. Again.'

Suddenly Andrew launched himself right at David and flattened him against the carpet with his slight but full weight. The hug that ensued from Andrew was enormous and tight, and David had difficulty breathing. It always amazed him how such a light frame exerted so strong a grip.

He hugged back, firmly and warmly.

'Uncle David,' Andrew said.

'My dear little Andrew,' he replied, and felt the warmth of the hug in its ferocity.

'Sweets time,' Andrew added, and loosened his grip.

'Ah well, that's not up to me, is it? Let's go see.'

They disentangled themselves and Andrew took David's hand as they went into the kitchen. Everyone looked up and Thelia said, 'Persistence paid off, then.'

'Could say,' David replied. 'This young fellow thinks it's sweets time.'

Thelia looked at the big clock and the list on the wall beside it of events and timings for the day. 'Hmm,' she said. 'Andrew, that would be fifteen minutes early, so not on schedule. What do you want to do?'

Andrew squeezed David's hand tight and looked up at him. Such a picture of the young Micky, it almost made David want to cry. Then David realised – Andrew was looking him right in

121

the eyes. David felt a broad smile spread across his face from somewhere deep inside his head. He squeezed the little hand back carefully and said, 'So, maths genius, have them now but off schedule, or wait and have them on schedule. Which is more important to you? The having them now, or the schedule?'

'Now. Now. Now.'

'I think that's your best choice, matey, but I'm waiting to hear it in a sentence.'

'I'd like to have them now, please,' he said, but he was no longer looking David in the eye. Too much to expect. The sentence was great.

'Good sentence!' David said, with a shake of the little hand.

Andrew smiled and shook the hand as well.

Thelia took the bag of sweets from the fridge and let Andrew take three out. They were ball-shaped boiled sweets. He put all three in his mouth and crunched them with an enormous chomp.

'It's a wonder his teeth survive!' Martin observed.

'Kill or cure. I think it makes them stronger, if they don't crack and splinter, which they haven't. He could probably eat wood!' Thelia said.

'Which is good enough reason not to get your fingers in there,' Angela said, indicating the scar on her ring finger. 'And that was when he was little. I think he could probably chew right through the bone now.'

'Don't give him ideas,' Martin warned.

'Well, lunch will be at two, so you've got half an hour to play, you boys,' Thelia suggested.

'What shall we do, champ?' David asked him.

Andrew shrugged. Then he said, 'Garden,' looking out of the French windows at the sunny day.

'Well, you are privileged,' Thelia exclaimed. 'It's not often he'll opt for the garden. Just don't let him spend all the time counting things and don't let him get filthy dirty. Or climb. That tree looks potentially rotten to me.'

'OK,' David agreed, and led the boy by the hand out through the French windows, which were already open. Then he stood looking at Andrew and waiting for some indication of what he wanted to do.

'Piggyback. Fast,' he said.

'Piggyback OK. Fast not so OK. Let's see how we go.'

Andrew stood on one of the wrought-iron chairs by the table and David backed up so he could climb on his back. The arms round his throat nearly choked him, so he tugged on them and said, 'Loosen up there, rider! I can't breathe. OK. Here we go.'

He set off at a brisk walk. Andrew started to choke him again, so he stopped, tugged at the little hands and said, 'Andrew, not so tight. I have to be able to breathe, matey!'

Off they went again, but half a minute later the problem returned.

'Andrew. I'm going to set you down, and put you on my shoulders instead.'

He started to lower himself but Andrew squeezed harder and said, 'Piggyback!'

He used the calm but firm voice he'd learned from Thelia and Angela. 'Andrew, no. Shoulders or nothing.'

He prised the hands apart with difficulty and set Andrew on the ground. He turned to look at him. 'When you squeeze that hard I really can't breathe, mate. I'm not blaming you. But I can't do it that way. So, shoulders?'

Andrew walked back to the chairs, and stood on one with his back to David and his legs slightly apart. David lifted him on and off they went again.

'Fast!' Andrew said.

'Not gonna happen, dude!'

He managed a bit of a trot, but was very careful, being aware that if he were to stumble it would be his passenger who would bear the brunt of the fall. Andrew started playing with his hair, as he'd done in the past, but not grabbing handfuls, thankfully.

'Wash up for dinner!' came Thelia's voice from the house. David was relieved.

'Hear that buddy? Wash time!'

He set the boy down on a chair and Andrew grabbed his hand as they walked back through the French windows and into the house. They both took off their shoes and went upstairs to wash, where David helped Andrew in just the way he remembered his dad's big hands helping his small hands as a child.

The Sunday dinner was roast chicken with all the trimmings, followed by apple pie and custard.

'Oh, yes!' Angela suddenly said at one point. 'Ruf is getting out.'

'Already?' David said.

'Next month. Good behaviour, I guess. His sentence was eight months given that it was a first serious offence and he went to the police with us, and pleaded guilty, and the dog was dead. So he'll have served just under half.'

'I wonder if we'll see him,' David replied.

'Well, now, I've been thinking about that. You know what he and his mates need? Some sort of youth club. And you know who's in a position to run one for kids like them? We are, at St Mark's. We've got the hall, we've got the helpers, we've got the equipment the younger kids use, like the footie table and table tennis and balls and bats and Wi-Fi, and video games, and you and I could do it. You've got experience with kids, a lot more than I have.'

David was taken aback. 'Clearly, you've been thinking about this. You haven't said anything.'

'No, well, I was letting it go round in my head for a while, and I've been praying about it even before I knew he was coming out soon. Since you were attacked by them, actually. His mates.'

'So that's how we react to me being attacked? Look after the people who did it?'

She let the question hang in the air, and he heard himself, and added, 'OK, yes, I know.'

She smiled, that lovely smile, and said, 'I knew you would.'

'Hmm.'

'It's no good just wishing they wouldn't roam the streets looking for trouble; you have to give them an alternative.'

'Are there no workhouses? No prisons?' he asked.

She picked up a chicken leg from her plate. 'If the next words out of your mouth are, "I just don't see why it has to be me", I'll hit you round the head with this chicken leg.'

David looked at the threatening piece of meat and said, '"Reports are coming in that violence has erupted at a suburban Sunday lunch. We go over now to our reporter on the scene. Hannah, what's happening there in leafy Lifford?" "Well, Dale, details are still coming in but apparently there's been an incident involving a chicken leg. A rather poultry excuse for violence, if you ask me."'

'Oh dear!' Martin said.

'Angela, I think you've left yourself without a leg to stand on,' Thelia added.

'Stumpy the chicken will have her revenge,' she insisted.

'Stumpy!' Andrew said, and chuckled in his private way, prodding a piece of chicken with his finger.

'When were you planning to tell me about this venture?' David asked.

'Soon. Now. You know.'

'I see. I'd need to get a new DBS clearance, I guess.'

'With Charles Sears at church, yes. He's the Safeguarding Officer now. And you'd need to do the deanery training morning, to bring you fully up to speed on current practice and policies and such. And I reckon if we got a shift on we could start next month. Roo and Alan Trench would help us. And Miss Spencer. She'd love it. And she's really good with bolshie youngsters.'

'Don't tell me you've been having conversations with these people already.'

'OK, I won't. Only in passing. You know. Casually.'

David huffed. 'I see. Is this casual and in passing as well?'

'No! I'm *asking* you.'

'Should I feel privileged?'

'Always!' she said, and reached over and squeezed his hand. He sighed. He made it sound weary and resigned.

'So, will you?' Angela asked him.

'You know I will.'

'Pushover,' Thelia said, with a wink at Angela.

'Hoi!' he said. 'That I am not. You don't know the trouble she used to have with me.'

'OK, don't get your feathers in a flurry!' she replied, leaning over and prodding him in the arm.

'Chicken's feathers!' Andrew added with his lovely bright little chuckle.

The walk was very pleasant after lunch. Andrew immediately asked to go on his dad's shoulders and there he rode happily most of the way. David noticed that occasionally he grabbed a handful of hair and had to be dissuaded. David was glad Andrew hadn't done that to him. His might have come out in clumps.

About twenty minutes from home he got down, and five minutes later he asked to go on David's shoulders, which pleased David. He carried him happily the rest of the way, holding on to his knees to keep him safe.

Back at the house it was time for a cup of tea, which the adults had outside while Andrew played with his Lego in the front room. When Angela said they'd be heading off soon after the tea, Martin announced he'd like them all to pray together for a few minutes beforehand. Then he added that they should do that in the front room as they liked Andrew to be included in times of prayer as much as possible. So, fifteen minutes later, they sat around, and Andrew jumped up onto David and held on to him like he was about to disappear – which, David supposed, from Andrew's perspective, perhaps he was.

Martin began with a short prayer thanking God for Angela and David and praying for safe travelling for them. David was moved by this, and prayed next. 'Dear Lord, thank You so much for Andrew. He's such a special little chap, and such a joy to spend time with. Please bless him in all the ways that will be best for him, and make him the best that he can be. And for me and Angela, Lord, strengthen us together as a couple, whatever that takes.'

Angela kicked him softly on the shin. Unaware of what he'd done, he just continued. 'Lord, strengthen us and show us what You want for us. Guide us, we pray. In Jesus' Name. Amen.'

Soon the prayers were over, and the goodbyes, for which Andrew didn't come out of the front room. And David was being driven homewards.

'Why did you kick me?' he asked.

'Don't you know some prayers are very dangerous? Like, if you pray, "Lord, humble me," then He may answer you by doing something, or allowing something, that humiliates you. So if you pray "strengthen us – *whatever it takes*!" that could be pretty dangerous too. You have to think seriously about what you ask God. Because He does. Who knows what might result from that prayer.'

'Oh,' he said, somewhat diminished. 'Sorry.'

'Well, all right, but some prayers are dangerous. Not because God is bad in some way but because He takes seriously what we say to Him. So we need to as well. Anyway, why wouldn't you hug Andrew when we arrived?'

'I told you. I don't want to put him in a difficult position. I mean, you're related to him. I'm not. And I'm also aware that a hug from him does me good. So I need to be careful I'm not just taking advantage of him. After all, I'm the adult. I've got all the power. At least, that's how he would see it. Any kid would.'

'But you know he wants a hug from you and it does him good.'

'No, I don't know he wants a hug from me. Kids are notoriously changeable in what they want and need. Parents sometimes say they don't know which version of their son or daughter they're expecting to come down the stairs in the morning.'

'That's teens, surely,' Angela objected.

'Oh no, younger than that, too. Look, there was no meanness in my reluctance. I love Andrew and always will want to give him a good hug. But I need to be sensitive to the fact that his wants and needs can't just be assumed by me.'

'You've given this some thought.'

'Not a lot. It's worried me once or twice. But I haven't spent ages mulling over it. I'm just trying to be careful and sensitive towards him.'

'Well, then, I must commend you for that,' she said, and turned towards him with that smile that was just for him.

'He's a lovely lad, and very special,' David added. 'He deserves the best treatment.'

There was a period of silence while she drove when they both just enjoyed the late spring afternoon. The sun was starting to turn golden and clumps of remaining daffodils and yellow crocuses seemed particularly encouraged by that hue, and danced with sheer pleasure in their bright glory. Small birds swooped and swept, and a light blue sky began to take on shades of silver.

'So, David, a youth group for some proper misfits. Are you up for it?'

'Where will Ruf be staying?'

'I've heard with one of his mates.'

'We need him to convince them we were helping him, not handing him in.'

'True. He'll do that, I'm confident. So, are you up for it?'

'With you and some other good leaders, yes.'

'I think we should meet up with Ruf and his mates when he comes out and straighten everything out and invite them to the new group.'

'I agree,' David said. 'Good plan. He never answered your letter, did he?'

'No. I might have got the wrong detention centre, or he might just not have wanted to be in touch. Or maybe he just doesn't write letters.'

'So who do you get your information from?'

'Lucy Wright at church. She's a police liaison officer, or something.'

They were back in time for the 6.30pm service and afterwards they approached Rector Colin over coffee in the small hall. He sat on the edge of the old stage and they stood in front of him, all with mugs of church coffee in hand.

'OK, what's this great new idea?' he asked.

'Well,' Angela began, 'you remember the young lad whose dog got drowned – Ruf – and the Grangers put him up for a while? Well, he's coming out of detention soon and he and his mates will be as bored and up for trouble as ever. And I was thinking, seeing as we've got to know him a bit, we could start up a youth group for them and kids like them – admittedly, some fairly rough sorts – and try to give them something more constructive to do.'

'Never anything obvious or easy!' the rector said. 'That's part of what makes you such a treasure. Sure, why not. Who've you got as leaders?'

'Me, David, and I was thinking of asking Roo and Alan Trench and Miss Spencer.'

'Five isn't enough,' Colin said. 'Ask Philip and Rachel Hughes as well. And Den Kirkham. He runs the tuck for the younger group, and they'd probably be happy to share it with you. Go for it. Get everyone OK'd with Charles Sears, of course, and we'll run it by the PCC at some point. There's a meeting in three weeks. Have something concrete for them to look at then. Good. It might affect our insurance. I'll speak to the wardens. What day are you thinking?'

'Friday nights, 8pm to 10 or 10.30.'

'Good. That fits. Alpha's on Thursdays now. The younger group finishes at 7.30. Whatever equipment you're going to share can just be left out. Also, if you get a sudden emergency of not enough leaders, a couple of them might stay on to help. You know them, Angela. OK. Good. Keep me informed.'

He slipped himself off the stage and, as he walked away, David said just loud enough for him to hear, 'What a nice man!'

He turned and replied, 'You two deserve each other.'

David replied, with a cheeky grin, 'Does that mean you'll take the wedding?'

Colin didn't turn again but said, 'Next year, maybe.'

It was Friday, 22nd April.

The meeting was held at Angela's house, all squeezed into her front room. Present with Angela and David were Philip and Rachel Hughes, a couple in their mid-thirties; Miss Spencer, a devout and very sprightly 78-year-old; Roo and Alan Trench, late twenties; and Den Kirkham, who was in a very smart suit as he'd come straight from work. He was forty-something. Miss Spencer was scribbling notes on a pad on her lap.

'What shall we call it?' Roo Trench asked, from the long curtain of black hair she allowed to fall freely around her head.

'Any ideas?' Angela asked.

'What does it matter what we call it?' Rachel said.

'Oh, it does, dear,' Miss Spencer said, having been watching the conversation closely. 'It can attract, a good name. Or repel. It can inform expectations. A good name for a group is like a good name for a person.'

'All right, have *you* got any good suggestions?' Rachel asked her.

'Well, let's see. Then again, no, not really!'

'How about, "Later"?' Roo suggested. 'They say, "Later" meaning "see you later", so it refers to meeting, and to being later than the younger kids.'

'And it sounds kind of cool. Slightly disrespectful and casual. Like "whatever",' Angela put in.

'Yes,' David agreed, 'I could go with that.'

'Well, you're bound to agree with Angela,' Rachel said with a bit of a wink and a cheeky grin.

'Later,' Miss Spencer said, weighing it up. 'They'd like that. Not religious, casual, it says they're older, and not to be constrained. Like they can stay out as late as they like. Which most of them probably can. Slightly rebellious. Slightly "in your face". Imaginative. Not staid or churchy. It's good. I say go with it.'

Angela took it up. '"Later" it is. OK, let's start on a rota. By the way, are we all DBS checked?'

They all were.

'And have we all done the deanery training morning?'

They all had. David had done it at St Luke's the previous Saturday.

'Is anybody currently first aid certified?'

Den was. As well as David, of course.

Angela spoke seriously. 'We want to communicate Jesus to them informally in conversation and action, not by sitting them down and telling them, like at school. It's important that this isn't school, isn't it, because we are seeking to introduce them to a relationship, not just impart information, and that requires relationship with them, above all else, doesn't it?'

A murmur of agreement followed.

'So then,' she continued, 'we won't need a programme as such. Apart from which equipment to put out on any week, which can be *ad hoc*. There's no need for a term's programme; in fact, we won't even keep to terms because they're not going to. Even those who are still at school.'

'Yes, good point,' Rachel agreed. 'Just turn up and do what needs doing. Play with them, get to know them, don't be in a leaders' huddle, ever. Be with them. Love them. That's the crucial thing.'

'Good, yes,' Alan Trench said.

'And to safeguarding matters,' Angela announced. 'Apart from the little kitchen to be used for tuck, which only Den will go into, or someone to help him from among us if needed, there are no separate rooms for us to remember not to be in alone with one of the members, so that's easy.'

'Apart from the toilets,' David pointed out, 'which are single occupancy, so if you're in there with a member you're out of your mind.'

'OK, accidents,' Angela continued, with half a glance in his direction, and no smile. 'We have an accident book, which is in the kitchen with Den, and we'll follow usual procedures.'

All agreed.

'And we've all signed up for the parish's safeguarding policy, so there we are.'

'Are we charging them to come in?' Den asked. 'And are we selling tuck at cost?'

'I think both,' David said. 'They don't value something they pay nothing for, but they'll know and like that the tuck is at a lower price than in the shops. We'll give them tea and coffee for nothing at some point in the evening though, right?'

'Yes,' Angela agreed. 'Maybe free biscuits, too.'

'But only two each,' Miss Spencer advised.

'Why?' Roo asked.

'Because, believe me, otherwise they'll eat through five packets and still be looking for more.'

A laugh erupted. 'Probably right,' Alan said.

'What about sanctions?' Miss Spencer asked.

'Exclusion. That's all. And definitely no shouting at them or belittling them or physical attention unless it's to restrain them, and then only *in extremis*. Like, real danger.'

'When do we start?' Rachel asked.

'As soon as Ruf is out and we've been able to meet up with him and his guys and invite them along,' Angela said. 'And he's out in the middle of May. Start by the end of the month, I'd hope.'

Things were so much better. So sorted out. Like a lost future had become his again.

CHAPTER TWELVE

It was Monday, 16th May.

Ruf had been out since Friday.

'We just need to trawl the streets till we find them,' Angela said, swinging her legs from the high stool at the bakery like a little girl. 'They'll be hanging around somewhere, sooner or later. Might take a bit of walking, is all.'

She brushed a piece of croissant from David's chin. 'Messy chap,' she said.

'Explosive confections,' he replied.

'I reckon we should start with the High Street, just because that'll be a safer place to encounter them than some quiet alley. We don't know for sure he'll stop them from attacking us for handing him in. That's just a reasonable assumption. Reasonable from our point of view, I hasten to add.'

'Hmm,' David said. 'They were pretty angry when they saw me that day.'

'Yup. So we need to get him to acknowledge us as quickly as possible. I think he will.'

'Let's live in hope.'

A few minutes later they were finished with breakfast and they set off up the High Street. They had no luck there so they headed towards the Royal Estate on the biggest road, Greenleigh Drive. It had some fairly large shops and a good few people walking about. But they weren't there either. So next they went on to Selhurst Place, a square of shops and offices round a central fountain and war memorial. And there they were, lounging about the fountain. Eight of them, including two girls. Ruf was holding the lead of a large, black dog.

On the sight of them, four of the boys immediately shouted angry abuse and ran towards them. David's heart sank as his guts did the nasty descend into his bowels and a hot swirl began in his head.

He was pushed to the ground and Angela was pinned against a wall by a hand on her throat. David was then punched straight in the mouth and tasted blood. He heard Angela squealing in pain. Then he was grabbed by the shoulders of his coat and sat upright. Ruf was sauntering over to them. He stopped some yards away.

'I think you misunderstand our relationship,' he said. 'I'm not your friend.'

David was punched in the back, which knocked the breath out of him. Angela spoke. 'We hoped you might hear us out. Your friends hate us because they think we handed you in to the police. You know we didn't. We hoped you might tell them that.'

'Bring them here,' he said.

'We don't follow your orders!' one of the girls said, and slapped Angela hard around the face, causing her to yelp again.

'Bring them here!' Ruf shouted, his voice powerful and angry.

They were dragged to their feet and hauled over to the edge of the fountain. There they were sat side by side on the low wall, with Ruf in front of them and the rest making a circle around, some standing right by them.

He spoke. 'They attacked you before anything to do with the cops, last Christmas. So don't blame me for them just not liking you.'

'But we–' David got out before another punch in his back took his breath away again.

Angela tried again. 'Tell them the truth about us.'

'All right,' Ruf said. 'These two didn't hand me over to the filth. They did take me to them; in fact, they made me go or they wouldn't help me with somewhere to stay. And friends of theirs put me up until I went to the Youth Unit. But they didn't report me and they did help me. But they're not my friends and I'm not about to defend them.'

'We've come with an invitation,' Angela managed to get out before the other girl got hold of her hair and yanked it. Angela caught hold of the girl's hand and pushed it away, causing the girl to spit on her head.

Ruf said, 'What invitation? Another dinner party with your fatuous friends?'

The whole group went, 'Woo!' and a couple said, 'Fatuous,' and one voice said, 'Fat you is!'

'We know they make you sick,' David sent back.

'Funny man. What invitation?'

'We want to start a new youth group,' David continued, 'for you lot, at the church, just to come and hang out and play games on a Friday night. Give you something more fun to do than hanging around doing nothing.'

'We like hanging around doing nothing,' a boy said.

'So, is this some police thing to keep us off the streets?' the girl beside Angela said.

Angela answered, 'No, it's a police thing to get you all in one place so they can arrest you.'

The girl began a torrent of foul abuse but Ruf cut her off with, 'No, fair comment, that was a stupid question.'

'Oi!' she turned her anger at Ruf. 'You can't speak to me like that, you...'

'Shut up, Kerry, and go home. It's past your bedtime.'

'Oi!' she said again. 'Don't use my name, you...'

'Shut up and go home!' he shouted. She slunk away, mumbling.

'Who's it for, then, this Friday night thing?' another boy asked.

'You. We waited for Ruf to be out before starting it. This Friday, eight o'clock. You and anyone you like and want to invite along. And it's a pound each to come in,' David answered.

'I see,' Ruf said. 'What if it's twenty of us?'

'Fine!' Angela said.

Ruf tugged on the dog's lead. 'You might be lucky. If we're not busy rolling old ladies for their pensions.' Then, 'What's the temperature of that water?'

'Quite mild,' a boy said.

'Pity!'

David was pushed sharply backwards so that he fell off the low wall right into the water. He didn't panic as it was only a foot deep, and when he stood up, there was Angela, equally wet, beside him, and the gang heading off down the road, laughing and jumping about.

She looked at him. They started to laugh and embraced each other in the water.

'You're going to have a fat lip in the morning,' she said, 'but this might just have reduced it a bit!'

They set off at a slightly breathless jog and by the time they got to Angela's house, which was nearer than his, they were beginning to shiver a bit. They held each other in the kitchen and let the warmth of their bodies ease the chill.

'Are you OK?' he asked.

'They pulled my hair twice but it hasn't come out – it's just made my head ache a bit. I'm all right. How about you?'

'No teeth loose. Fat lip, I guess. But a success, I'd say! I reckon they'll come.'

'We're like the apostles in Acts 4,' she said, 'rejoicing to have been found worthy to suffer for the Name. Or was it chapter 5? Anyway, it's all good!'

'Maybe that's God's answer to my dangerous prayer,' David said.

'I'll be glad if this is the whole answer.'

'I thought you were the reckless one.'

'I like to be reckless *for* God, not *with* God. Let me look at that lip. Ooh, it is beginning to swell a bit. Tell you what, you put some ice on it and make some coffee while I take the fastest shower in history and get changed, then you can shower and I'll put your clothes on a fast cycle.'

'OK,' he agreed.

She kissed him on the cheek, and fled up the stairs. In five minutes she was back, to see two nice coffees and him with ice in his handkerchief pressed against his lower lip.

The heat of the coffee made him wince, but he drank it thankfully and was warmed.

'There are towels up there – throw your clothes down the stairs once they're off and come down in my spare dressing gown which is hanging over the landing bannister when you've showered.'

'OK,' he said, and headed off. The warmth of the shower was lovely, but his back began to ache where he'd been punched. When he got downstairs in the yellow dressing gown, which fell to just on his knees, feeling ridiculous, she was in the front room with the fire on low. She didn't laugh. Or even comment.

'I was surprised at Ruf,' she said. 'I thought he'd be more grateful and friendly than that.'

'We're just not his people. We're their natural enemy. Posh sorts. People who look down on them. Friends of the cops. Snitches and accusers. Teachers and judges.'

'Yah, I guess. I hope they come. We should pray they do, now we've seen them.'

David agreed, and they settled down for a few minutes to say a couple of prayers each for them and for the new group.

It was Friday, 20th May, 7.30pm.

The younger kids were being urged out smartly today as David and Angela stood outside with Philip, Rachel, Roo, Alan and Miss Spencer. Den was already inside doing the tuck for the younger lot.

Dean Wright, who ran the younger group, leaned out of the door and said, 'All good! Come on in.'

This, the larger of the two halls, had a vinyl-type floor in a light brown colour, and high, double-glazed, modern windows all along one long wall. There were some store cupboards and the kitchen on the opposite long wall, and all the brickwork was painted a very pale yellow. It was well maintained and clean, with rubbish bins at both ends. The toilets were off the end wall at the opposite end to the kitchen.

David and the leaders walked in the main doors, in the centre of a long wall with the kitchen on their right, the window wall opposite, and the toilets down to their left past the cupboards. The floor area had a table-tennis table near the short wall on the left, a football table and a mid-sized pool table. A table in the far corner next to them held a screen and some games. The opposite corner had a small chill-out zone with some beanbags and a CD player. The main area was clear for football, and a small goal was positioned at each end of it. Some moveable screens right along the bottom end of the hall gave that zone and the computer games some element of protection from the football.

Along the far wall were three gas heaters, not currently on, and around the walls were dotted blue noticeboards for the various organisations that used the hall.

'This is great,' David said to Dean. 'You had a good evening?'

'Twenty-five kids, no trouble, some nice conversations, lots of tuck sold!'

'Great!' David agreed.

'I really hope this goes well. Stick at it if it doesn't take off at first.'

They drank coffees and agreed the roles. Angela and David would operate the welcome desk by the entrance doors. Miss Spencer would somehow lower herself onto a beanbag and wait for kids to come over to her. She smiled as she asked for help later to get up again. Philip and Rachel would hover near the computer games, and Roo and Alan by the bigger games.

Angela and David started to set up the registration desk. She would sit behind it and write names in a register book, while he would get them to fill out a card with name, date of birth, address and phone number, and any allergies. He would help them with that if necessary.

David kept looking at his watch. As 8pm approached he got more and more nervous. Would anyone come? Would there be trouble? Would Ruf come? Would they wreck the place and leave, pockets stuffed with stolen tuck?

Ah well, it was all a matter of faith. Let the Lord do what He will do, he told himself.

At five to the hour three boys came in through the door. Ruf and two boys David didn't recognise from the gang. Signing them in, Angela discovered their names were Stewart Digby and Andy Norton. Stewart was short and overweight, Andy was tall, thin and troubled with zits. Neither looked particularly happy to be there. They went straight to the computer games table, while Ruf hung by the door, waiting, apparently.

A few minutes later, three boys trouped in that David did remember. McConley, Davis and Law. They signed in as Alex McConley, Mike Davis and Scott Law. They went with Ruf to the football table.

Girls followed, in a giggling gaggle of four. One was strikingly good-looking with carefully applied make-up, flowing light-blonde hair and a perfect complexion – her name was Sandy Elman. Her friends, sheltering in her shadow somewhat, were the very dark, short and pretty Elena Rost, the smiling but cautious-looking and chubby-faced Zee Tarrant and the bespectacled, tall and slightly stooping Abbie Coltrane. They paid no attention at all to Angela and David other than to answer questions. They focused entirely on each other and then went to the tuck shop and bought some sweets which they took to the chill-out zone. Ruf, Alex, Mike and Scott were giving the football table a fairly rough workout. A 'Ruf' workout, David decided.

All these were aged from fifteen to eighteen. Ten minutes after them, two younger boys came in; they were fourteen, both quite friendly and easy-going, called Chris Stott and Ben Garry.

David realised that the girl who'd got a bit of abuse when they'd met them, Kerry, wasn't there.

When all were in, David sauntered over to the football table and said, 'Hi, Ruf. No Kerry?'

'Out with her boyfriend. What's it to you? Liked her, did you?'

The other three gave a little jeer.

'I felt a bit sorry for her, that's all.'

'Well, she's thirteen and he's sixteen and yes, they do have sex, if you're wondering.'

'Right,' David said, and thought, 'So this is how it's going to be.' He felt that Scott Law, in particular, looked at him with singular dislike in his eyes.

'Right,' they all repeated, tittering like idiots.

'Hi, guys, you good?' David said to the other three.

They all gave a little laugh like he was some kind of fool, and he decided to leave them to it for now. 'OK, see you later,' he said, and headed for the two younger boys who were talking to Alan Trench by the tuck. He noticed that Angela had joined Miss Spencer with the girls in the chill-out zone, and they all seemed to be in good conversation already. So much easier with girls, he thought.

'Hi, Chris and Ben. Have I got that the right way round?'

'Yes,' they both said. 'Are you the vicar?'

'No!' he and Alan both laughed. 'I'm just one of the people who started this group. Do you live nearby?'

They did, and the conversation progressed about school and friends, and then he and Alan challenged them to a game of table tennis, which was fun, though slightly chaotic as the two boys weren't very good. David and Alan tried not to beat them too soundly, but still did.

After that, David tipped off Den to prepare for the 'coffee break', and ten minutes later he called everyone together to some chairs to get their drink and biscuits and sit around with it.

Getting them to quiet down enough to speak to them was a trial: as soon as he had them quiet, one person would laugh or comment and that would set them all off again. Finally, without losing his cool, or reverting to 'teacher mode', he got a reasonable level of listening.

'OK, hi. I'm David, and this is Angela, and we lead this club; in fact, we started it. It's called "Later" because there's a younger club that meets before this one.'

'Is that called "Earlier"?' Andy Norton said, and everyone laughed. David saw in him the joker of the group.

'No. Thank you, Andy. And this is called "Later" because it sounds kinda like you're the older group who can stay out and chill out and be a bit more grown-up. Working with us in the tuck is Den – thank you, Den – he made these drinks as well. Then there's Roo and Alan, Philip and Rachel, and Miss Spencer. We plan to be open every Friday, at least in term-time, from eight to 10.30. It's a pound to get in, as you discovered, but all the tuck is cheap so buy plenty. Each week we'll have this little get-together and sit-down time for a chat, with our drinks and biscuits. So, anybody got any questions?'

'Do you get chocolate Hobnobs?' Andy Norton asked.

Everyone laughed. 'Well, we just might, seeing as you've asked,' David answered. 'Any more serious questions?'

'Is she your girlfriend?' Ruf asked, and they all bellowed with laughter.

When it died down, David said, 'Ruf, my old friend, you know she is.'

'Ooh!' they all went. 'Old friends!'

Ruf coloured up and said, 'Shut up.'

Scott Law was still eyeing David with malicious intent. Nobody else seemed to notice. He tried to ignore it. It was 'veiled' but definitely there. It worried David because it didn't seem to be a passing annoyance, but, rather, something fixed and deliberate. Perhaps he was just imagining that. Or perhaps not.

'Can we bring friends?' Elena asked from under her dark mop.

'Yes. Anyone in Year 7 and above. As many as you like.'

'Do we have to come every week?' Sandy followed up.

Angela fielded that. 'No. But we would like you to come as often as possible just to give a sense of being a group, belonging together. It may be we'll do extra things as well like go on a walk, go bowling, have a Christmas party, you know the sort of thing.'

'Cool!' the two younger boys said.

'What time does it finish?' Elena asked.

'I just said – 10.30. Or is that too late?'

'We told our dads 10pm. They're going to pick us up, like, one each week,' said the young Ben Garry.

'No, that's fine,' David answered. 'Basically, you can leave if you need to.'

'Like, now?' Andy said, and once again tittering followed.

'We'd miss your sparkling wit,' David reposted.

That seemed to be the end of the discussion time. Mugs were returned, and everyone went off to some sort of activity. The younger boys started kicking a football in the main area and after a while the girls joined them. Then all the boys joined in and it became a bit of a free-for-all, so David organised two actual teams and refereed it, and it continued for a good while, until it was time to go home.

The leaders said as many goodbyes to the kids individually as they could, and then sat down with another coffee to talk. They were happy with the evening, but David commented, 'Did anyone notice how Scott Law was giving me the evil eye?'

Nobody had.

'Are you sure?' Rachel Hughes asked him. 'I would have thought I'd have noticed.'

'Definitely. A sort of veiled hatred. Slightly unsettling, actually.'

'We'll keep an eye on it. On him,' Den said, and they all agreed.

After some clearing up, they went home.

CHAPTER THIRTEEN

It was Friday, 17th June.

Over four weeks the club had grown, and on this evening twenty-six young people turned up.

David got into a game of table tennis with Alex, Mike and Scott, Ruf's three friends. David had played on previous weeks as well and the kids were generally impressed with his level of skill; they normally expected anyone over forty to be useless at anything sporty.

Everything was fine until a new girl, Sam Lazenby, walked past the table and Scott called her an 'Effing slut'.

David was shocked at the abusiveness of it, especially as she was at least a year or two younger than him, and said, 'Scott! You can't speak to her like that. Control your language.'

He swore and said, 'You're always picking at me.'

'I've never heard anyone speak in such an abusive way in this club before. I don't pick at you. But I'm shocked at what you just said to Sam.'

Scott repeated what he had said to Sam. David was speechless for a moment and then said, 'Scott. That just isn't acceptable. You're going to have to stop it.'

Scott threw his table tennis bat on the table, swore again and stalked off. As they were playing doubles, that was the end of the game, and anyway the other two boys went off after him.

David was exhausted and slightly sweaty. He went and sat on a chair which was against the wall by the tuck shop hatch, and the next minute there was a queue of kids wanting tuck. The queue was quite close to him so he was about to get up and move when Scott said, 'Hey! You just grabbed my bum!'

David thought it was a sick joke and said, 'You shouldn't say that. It's not funny.'

But Scott was looking right at him and said even louder, 'You just grabbed my bum, you paedo perve!'

Now the whole queue was staring at him as he stood and said, 'I didn't touch you.' He looked at Mike, right behind Scott and said, 'Did you touch him?'

'I didn't do anything!' he protested.

'What's this?' Angela said, approaching.

'He grabbed my bum, just now,' Scott repeated.

Angela just looked at David.

'I saw him. He did it,' Alex threw in from immediately behind Mike. 'He grabbed his bum with his left hand.'

'Why are you saying this?' David asked, a sudden turmoil gripping his guts. This was serious.

Angela said, 'Look, Scott and Alex, if you insist on this then there's going to be a lot of really serious trouble. This isn't some silly joke. Are you sure that's what you want to do? Scott? Alex?'

'Yes,' they both said, and Scott added, 'I want the police called.'

'Did you see this?' she asked Mike.

'No, I was looking over there.' He indicated the main part of the hall. 'I don't know anything.'

'I want to complain to the police,' Scott insisted.

Angela looked at David with real sadness in her eyes. He hoped that wasn't some sort of disappointment.

'Ok, Scott, you need to come with me and Alex you need to go with Philip so we can make a note of what you're saying. Philip, you need paper and pen. You know the drill.'

David watched as Angela took Scott off to the computer games table and Philip took Alex into the tuck. Den came out to give them space. There was a horrible hush around the hall, and a lot of eyes were on him. A lot of whispering was going on as well. He felt like it said 'Abuser' across his forehead. A muted semi-hush seemed to focus everything on him. He saw Angela asking brief questions and simply writing down the answers, without investigating, just recording, exactly as the procedure required. After five minutes she came over to him and said, 'I'm really sorry. I'm going to have to call Charles Sears and the police.'

'I know,' he said. 'I didn't even touch him.'

'I know you didn't,' she said. 'But we have no choice, do we?'

'No.' He felt sick.

'Where do you think you should be?'

'I think I should go home.' He recognised the kindness in her asking him rather than sending him home.

'I agree. I'll see you there later.' She took his nearer hand and squeezed it. 'Try not to worry,' she said quietly. 'I love you.'

The drive home was torture, and the trying to sit down and not worry at home was purgatory. David felt awful. He felt accused, sullied, guilty, shamed, and that his work with young people might come to a sudden and inglorious end. Indeed, the club might fold. It might get into the papers. These days, he might be found guilty and sentenced. All because of the way an allegation was weighted now, in these days of safeguarding to the extreme. Nowadays, various bodies felt the need to prove that their past mishandling of abuse was over. Including the Church of England.

He had the news on but he wasn't watching it. He took a WOL mug of tea outside and watched the dusk descending, but its beauty had fled. He stood and walked over the road to the fence, and looked across the fields there, but felt no better and came back and sat down again on his little bench.

'Oh, God, why is this happening?' he asked.

Depression hit him like a brick in the guts from the hand of God. All joy and hope drained like he was bleeding out. He felt like he hadn't the energy for this. To fight it. It was all too much. He should just let it overwhelm him and carry him away. He got up and went inside, hoping to feel better in the safety of his little house, but it made no difference, and he thought of going back outside. Then he recognised that old enemy of depression, the thought that you'll feel better if you go out, and when you go out you feel worse and think you'll feel better back at home.

Without really intending to, he started to rehearse in his mind, and then out loud, what he would say. 'I'd just finished playing table tennis with some of them. I needed a sit down for a breather, and there was a chair by the tuck shop. There was nobody queuing there at that time. Then suddenly there was quite a queue, standing quite close to me, so I was about to get up and leave when one of the boys, Scott Law, accused me of grabbing his behind. I didn't touch him at all, not even accidentally. There was no contact between me and him. At first I thought he was making a nasty joke, but he persisted with it.'

That seemed satisfactory. He went over it a few more times, just to see how it sounded, very aware that he was going to be repeating it in all sorts of unpleasant situations.

The doorbell rang. He opened the door and there was Angela, smiling at him but clearly upset. She hugged him hard and said, 'I'm so sorry about this, David. This is horrible. Charles Sears is on his way.'

They went into the front room and sat together on the settee. She took his hands in hers and said, 'We should pray and ask for God's protection.'

'OK,' he answered.

They bowed their heads and she prayed. In the silence that followed, he didn't manage to find the energy to say anything. After a while she said, 'How do you feel?'

'Terrible. Like a ton of depression just landed on my head. Why would they do that to me?'

'Maybe because you told him off about the appalling way he spoke to Sam Lazenby. I heard about it. That was awful. And you said he's had it in for you for a while.'

'Yes, but this. And Alex saying he saw it.'

'I know. David, try to be strong, OK? Don't just crumple under this. It'll get sorted out.'

'These days? I doubt it.'

She leaned over and kissed him, full and warm on the lips. He breathed her in. Constant, faithful, always there for him. 'David, there are going to be so many people on your side in this. So many.'

'Maybe, but that doesn't count, does it? The system swings into action. What must be done must be done, with the weight automatically behind the accuser. The "alleger". The "alligator". He who bites. Who rolls you up and drags you under, to drown in suspicion and unprovable smears. Who tarnishes you with suspicion whatever the outcome, and mires you in incapacity whatever your innocence. Tell me it isn't true.'

'You know I can't,' she said, sadly, squeezing his hand, her head against his shoulder. 'Anyway, I need a coffee.'

'We might need more than that.'

'We might, but let's be sober for when Charles arrives.'

They went into the kitchen and made her a coffee. Then they sat at the kitchen table and talked. But not a lot was said.

The doorbell rang. David got up and answered it, closely followed by Angela. There stood Charles Sears in his work suit and tie, looking very smart and smiling. He offered David his hand, and they shook, and he said, 'Hello, David.'

David said, 'Hello, Charles. Come in,' which he did. They led him into the front room and all sat down, David and Angela on the settee and Charles in the armchair.

'Can I get you anything?' David asked.

'No, thanks, let's get straight down to it, if you don't mind. David, I'm very sorry about this but, as you know, once an allegation has been made a certain necessary and legal procedure begins, regardless of the rights and wrongs of the matter. A boy called Scott Law has complained that you grabbed him in a sexual and inappropriate manner at the youth club this evening and another boy, Alex McConley has supported that allegation. Angela and Philip Hughes then took statements from them both, and Angela did as she is supposed to do and rang me. I in turn rang the diocesan Safeguarding Officer, Alistair Bream, and also the local police, where I was able to speak to Detective Chief Inspector Steve Drane who heads up the SGU – the Safeguarding Unit – to make an initial report. He says he will be in touch with you. They will also contact the social services department. Do you understand all of that?'

'Yes.'

'Just to fill you in, the police unit will investigate the claim under the 1997 Sex Offenders Act and will decide whether a prosecution is necessary according to three factors: whether or not a criminal prosecution is in the best interests of the child. Whether it is in the public interest that proceedings should be instigated against a particular offender. Whether or not there is sufficient evidence to prosecute. On the basis of their findings the church will act accordingly. Is all that clear to you?

'OK. Now, in terms of St Mark's, we have our own policy, of which you are aware, based on the diocesan guidelines, and that says that until such an allegation has been cleared, you cannot continue to work with children or young people, and that you have to try to avoid contact with the church's children and young people in the meantime. That means you shouldn't come to the morning service, and at the evening service you should sit away from the young people at the back and not engage with them after the service. Do you understand that?'

'Yes.'

'But the church's policy goes further. Even if you are cleared by the police, the church may still decide to remove your permission to work with children and young people if it feels that you may be a danger to them, and put in place an agreement with you about maintaining your membership of St Mark's while separating you from the church's children and young people. Is that clear?'

'Guilty despite being found innocent.'

'Not really. In many cases the criminal proceedings are inconclusive or fail to get off the ground owing to lack of evidence, but the church still has the right to make a decision about who will and will not have access to its children. If a

148

person is convincingly cleared of any wrongdoing or bad practice then the church would fully reinstate them, but in any other case the church is left with its responsibility for its vulnerable members. You know that.'

'Yes, I do, but can you imagine how it feels right now being told it?'

'Very hard, I imagine, and I'm truly sorry for that, but this is the way it is in safeguarding these days, like it or not.'

'Hmm.'

'So, David, please tell me in your own words what happened this evening.' He took out a pad from his side suit pocket and a pen from an inner pocket.

David related the story, brief as it was. His mobile rang before he could quite finish.

'Hello?'

'Mr David Sourbook?'

'Yes.'

'Sir, this is Detective Chief Inspector Drane from Veery Lane Police Station. I have a report of an allegation brought before me this evening that a child of fifteen at the youth group at St Mark's Church says that you touched him in a sexual and inappropriate manner this evening. You are aware of this?'

'Yes. I did no such thing.'

'OK. Thank you. I am going to need to have a formal interview with you, on Monday at 10am at the Veery Lane Police Station. You can bring someone with you who at this time doesn't need to be a lawyer if you'd prefer to bring someone else. Ask for me, DCI Drane. I assume you're not due to travel anywhere distant in the next few days?'

'No. I'll be at home.'

'Good. Then I'll see you on Monday at 10am. Goodbye for now, sir.'

He relayed the information to Angela and Charles, and Charles said, 'Would you like Daniel Ilonuba to come with you? He's a lawyer and he's offered to help anyone at church with this kind of thing.'

'No, I'd rather Angela came with me.'

'Oh!' she said. 'What use would I be?'

'Well, first I don't want to get "lawyered up" sooner than I need to – maybe gives a bad impression. And secondly, I want you with me. I trust you. You know me. And you know the situation.'

'I'll have to take the morning off from college.'

'Well, if that's a problem…'

'No, no,' she said quickly. 'If you want me there, I'm there.'

She put her hand on his and stroked it with her thumb. 'Once again, if you hadn't met me you wouldn't be in trouble with the police.'

'A bit more serious this time, but a lot less your fault,' he replied.

'David,' Charles spoke up again. 'That's the duty of my office discharged, for now, but I am also concerned for you. This could be a very trying and difficult time. You know we have supportive counsellors at church who can be there for you, and I just want you to know this will be kept on a need-to-know basis, and those who do know will be praying for you and looking for you to be completely exonerated. You are among friends, despite this horrible business.'

'Thank you,' he managed.

'How are you doing so far?'

'Not good. Rather depressed, actually.'

'I'm sure that's understandable. I should go. Do use the help that's there if you need to.'

He bade them both goodnight on his way to the front door, and left.

They stood in the hall and looked at each other. She said, 'I'm so sorry, David,' and with those words something inside him slumped again and the awful weight of it fell upon him as from a bruised sky. A tear appeared in his eye and she scooped him into a great hug and held him.

'This is so… words fail me. I feel like some pariah. Just when everything seemed so much better. I feel like everything is collapsing and nothing will be left. Nothing. And like it's really all my fault, somehow. I did something. I deserve this.'

'You don't, you don't!' she said, pulling his wet face into her neck.

'Well, that's how it feels. And everybody will hate me. And the kids will already be telling everyone about what I've done and the club will close and the church will be damaged and people will look at me with thinly veiled suspicion. You could tell Charles doesn't think I'm innocent.'

'No!' she insisted. 'He was just doing his job. Doing his best. He's not judging you.'

He pushed her away a little and looked into her face. 'There's a big difference between not judging and believing you're innocent.'

'Well, *I* know you're innocent and I'll stand by you through thick and thin. Whatever.'

'Whatever it takes,' he said.

'Whatever it takes.'

They sat outside and watched the dusking skies, but they were grey and patternless. They went back in and she stayed till nearly eleven, watching television and trying to talk normally. He felt anything but normal. He felt dreadful. This great machine had started up against him, and all the weight and power lay on its side, not his. He was disgraced before anything more could be done. His name was sullied. There would always be suspicion now, whatever the outcome. And that assumed the highly unlikely possibility of a good outcome. A clear vindication. But how would that be? Scott and Alex would hardly be able to back down now, and they had no reason to. They must be laughing their heads off. And the chances that someone was watching him just at that moment when the alleged groping took place were minimal. No, it was stacked in their favour, and he would be the loser.

He took himself to bed, despite lacking the energy even to do that. He stared at himself in the bathroom mirror and waited for

151

that dark shadow to descend, but it didn't. He watched for his face to transform into some hideous half-fleshed skull, but it didn't.

In bed, he picked up Bart and hugged him ferociously. But he found no words for the faithful bear. And Bart retained his silent wisdom.

He dared not turn out his bedside light. Its steady glow somehow gave him a little comfort. So did the furry embrace of Bart. A little. But not enough to enable him to fall into the friendly arms of slumber. He tried to content himself with the fact that he'd have to wait. But as the first hour crawled by he became more and more afraid that he wouldn't be able to sleep at all. He would be in such a state in the morning that it would be the beginning of losing his mind. Rationality would flee in a fretful fug. Anxiety would overwhelm him in that breathless desperation to bolt. He would find himself standing against the fence over the road feeling like he would never be able to breathe again. Trying desperately to calm himself down. That awful feeling like this would never pass. It had hold of him and he was stuck in gasping panic, like a fool to the eyes of all who stared in pitying amazement.

He got up as an airless heat hit his chest. It was starting. Oh God, let it stop. Don't let it rise right up to full, chest-thumping, winded horror. Stop panting. Calm it down. Don't overbreathe. Oh God, let it slow down, please!

He started to calm, and decided to go downstairs and get a glass of Merlot and self-medicate. A glimmer of hope returned. It was fading. He would be OK. He would go down, put on the TV and drink some wine. He would still get some sleep tonight.

Let it be. Oh, Lord, let it be.

CHAPTER FOURTEEN

It was Saturday, 18th June. Not that he cared.

In the dull light of a leaded dawn it all hit him afresh with a renewed vigour. And horror. It was true, not a dream. He'd been accused of molesting a young boy. A young boy! Of all things!

How he would be hated. How they would laugh at him. Would it get in the papers? Would his neighbours shun him? Would the church throw him out? Would Angela lose faith in him? Would he never see Andrew again?

Would even Bart pack a bag and leave? He reached down and picked up the great bear, who had fallen out of bed as he sometimes did, and looked into his friendly face. 'I'll always have you,' he said, and it was like a voiceless word came to him from heaven. 'You'll always have Me.'

That stopped him. He stared at Bart but listened to God. Nothing more. What more was needed? 'Thank You, Lord. Father. Thank You. I need that right now.'

Still, he really didn't want to get up. He really didn't want to face the day. Was that depression, or the situation, or both? Both.

Anyway, what was the point of getting up? There was nothing to be done. No remedy to be found. How he hated this life. Anyway, what time was it? He groaned. It was half past five.

He hugged Bart and turned over, trying to get comfortable enough to sleep. But the reality and awfulness of it all played in front of him like a drama. And he began to rehearse again what he would say in his defence. So he decided to focus on something else. He recalled their last visit to Thelia and Andrew, and the fine time they'd had that Sunday afternoon. But before he knew it he was revisiting the events of last night, the images of police and social services, the dire outcomes, and he was running through his defence again.

It was no good. He might as well get up. He levered and dragged himself out of bed and groaned his way into the bathroom. A haggard and weary face stared blankly back at him in the familiar mirror. 'Hopeless,' he said. 'Hapless and helpless and… and… happyless. Happyless. "Oh, I know who you are! You're that paedophile. You're that pervert that touched up the young lad in the church youth group. Disgusting. Disgraceful. We'll put your windows in. We'll paint 'abuser' on your garage door. We'll abuse you on Twitter and Facebook. There's no end of ways we can get at you. You're going to wish you'd never been born."'

He had a shower and shaved, and brushed his teeth. But he felt no better. He went downstairs and made a pot of tea and took his WOL mug outside to his bench and looked at the grey sky. So grey. Unrelenting in its leaden misery. The whole world was held in its grip of gloom.

The whole world was against him.

'Oh, God,' he said into the uncaring heavens. 'Will You be on my side? Will You be with me today? I think You spoke to me and said so. You said I'll always have You. I have to hold on to that. Please be faithful to me. God, I need You.'

He looked at the empty WOL mug in his hands and decided he'd feel better if he went for a walk across the fields. He went in and got his wellies on, but no coat as it was mild. Then he set off across the road and onto the slightly squishy footpath alongside the field. He got maybe 200 yards when he realised this was no good and he'd feel better back at home, so he turned back.

As he returned he tried to remind himself that this sort of depression was always at its worst in the morning, and he'd feel better as the day got properly under way. Then he reminded himself that that would make absolutely no difference to the

154

reality of what had befallen him. Blackness descended like a hammer. The bruised sky scowled at him.

He went in and decided to go and lie on his bed to see if he could get some more sleep. He lay there, cuddling Bart, and drifted in and out of some sort of dreamy state, afflicted by images of himself being jeered at and locked up.

He woke to his mobile phone ringing. He picked it up and saw it was Angela calling.

'Hello, Little Noddy,' she said, a smile in her voice. 'Wakey wakey. I shall be there in ten minutes with four fresh croissants from our favourite bakery, so get dressed and get the tea on. OK?'

'Actually I've been dressed since before six. OK, see you soon.'

He laid Bart comfortably in the middle of the bed, checked his image in the bathroom mirror and went downstairs. Kettle on and plates out, he fetched butter and marmalade, knives and mugs, and set up the table in the kitchen. He opened the front door so she could walk straight in.

The kettle had boiled so he made a big pot of tea and put it on the table. She grabbed him from behind with a warm hug and a kiss on the back of his neck.

'Hello, my love,' she said. 'Have you had a rough night?'

'Very rough.'

She held on to him, nuzzling the back of his neck, and wouldn't let him move. 'I'm sorry. Tell me about it.'

'OK. Let's sit down.'

They sat. He poured tea while she put the croissants on a plate.

'Well, I didn't have any dark shadows in the mirror, so that's all right. The worst of it was waking at half-five and being unable to get back to sleep with the whole horror of it playing in my mind. So I got up and sat outside with a WOL mug of tea. That was just grey and dreary. So I went for a walk. But I felt I'd be better if I came back. So I came back. And tried to sleep some more. But it was fitful at best.'

'You recognise that pattern?'

'Yes, worse in the morning, and that thing of "I'll feel better if I go out," then after ten minutes out, "I'll feel better if I go back." And now, added to that, I can't clear my head of the accusation. It goes round and round and I can't focus on anything else.'

'Perhaps that'll improve.'

'Perhaps it'll get worse.'

They ate and she looked at him with sympathy and smiled. 'Well,' she said, wiping marmalade from her chin in that childlike way he usually so loved, 'I'm planning to take you for a walk today. Along that lovely path we found after Easter. Forget the grey skies. It'll do us both good. We can have lunch at The Old Fox and ramble back though those two villages… Hadford and the other one… along by the little river, and we can stand on the bridge again and even play Poohsticks. And it'll take us out of ourselves.'

'You mean it'll take me out of my pit of despair and hopeless injustice.'

'And me out of my pit of concern and painful love for you. Not the love. The pain and pit. I need it, too.'

He felt resigned to her mercies. Much like he had at first, before Christmas, when they'd met and she'd ridden him round town in her 'jockey syndrome'. 'All right,' he said, with some resignation.

'Good, thank you,' she said, rather than, 'Don't sound so enthusiastic!'

They finished, washed up the dishes, tidied the kitchen and he decided on wellies again, plus a peaked cap and a light jacket. They got into her car and she set off.

'Can you imagine how much I hate this?' he said, looking out of the side window as the grey world sped by.

'I can imagine, yes. I was accused once of becoming too fond of one of the female students who'd taken rather a liking to me as her tutor. I had allowed her to spend some time with me, only at college, mind, before I realised what was going on. One of the other staff complained about me to the safeguarding guy. I had to defend myself. Fortunately there were other staff who stood by me, and the girl herself never made any complaint – it was just Barry Yates, the miserable old so-and-so, who eventually had to back down and shut up. But it ruined that year for me at college. It was miserable. I feared for my job and my reputation. All sorts of horrible outcomes assaulted my nights and my dreams. At one stage it seemed like I might be suspended. So, yes, I do have some insight, my love.'

'Great,' he said, and went quiet. He didn't know why he made no response to her revelation.

The miles sped by.

They walked through countryside, from which all the colour had been sucked as if by some lingering death. She tried to make conversation, but he wasn't interested.

From time to time a brightening came over him and for a few minutes he felt hopeful and at peace, but then it relentlessly closed again and left him in gloom. He knew that symptom, too.

At length he stopped and said, 'I feel so tired. That heavy tiredness. And it aches right across my shoulders.'

'That'll be tension,' she said. 'Here, sit on that bench and I'll massage your shoulders.'

He sat, she pressed her thumbs and fingers into his shoulder muscles, with both firmness and gentleness, and he could feel the pain starting to leave and the knots easing.

'Thank you, that's a lot better,' he said.

They set off again.

Sun started to lighten a patch of the clouds, and as they walked the grey thinned like an old man's hair and the bright dome shone like it should. Shadows leapt into being as brightness coloured the trees and grass, and even the birds began to sing.

By their lunchtime stop it was getting hot, and the only cloud was a few wispy strings unreachably high in the heavens. They were both thirsty and began with a flavoured cider each, then their lunch of wraps with salad in a shady garden.

After lunch they went across the road to an open grassy area and lay down. They slept. He woke first and looked at the straggles of her near-blonde hair, unruly as ever round her pretty face. It had been said that in the first half of your life you wore the face nature gave you, but in the second half you wore the one you had fashioned yourself. Angela's face showed laugh lines at the sides of her eyes rather than frown lines in the middle of her forehead, and an upturned mouth at rest rather than a downturned one. She had fashioned a happy face.

She woke and saw him looking at her. She gave a little frown.

He said, 'At least I've got to sleep with you now.'

'Hmm. You know what you're going to have to do to really sleep with me.'

'Yes. Arrange for conjugal visits.'

She laughed, and nudged him in the ribs with her elbow. 'Don't be such a pessimist.'

'Well, if the glass *is* half-empty…'

'Even pessimists have good things happen to them sometimes,' she countered.

'Just because I have a persecution complex doesn't mean they *aren't* after me,' he said.

They both lay back again on the soft grass and stared at the awesome sky, so bright in its blueness, its open grandeur. Children could be heard laughing somewhere, and a dog's bark was carried to them on the bending air. It was like the world had stopped, just for them. And beautified itself in its best and brightest clothes. 'That's You, Father,' he said, under his breath. And he loved Him then, in that moment.

A fat bee buzzed lazily by. He loved the way its bulky body somehow bobbed along on the still air. A cabbage white butterfly flapped past on its ridiculous, papery wings, searching for someone's prized brassicas. Somewhere a lawnmower gave an impossibly calming and tuneful hum as a backdrop to the dreamily buzzing, songfully chirping day.

She was looking at him. She'd turned stealthily on to her side and was smiling broadly at his peaceful frame. She gave a little laugh.

'Right now, you feel a whole lot better,' she said.

'Right now I do. Have you ever thought about us getting married?'

'Oh!' she said. 'What a question out of an admittedly blue sky. OK. I'm aware of it as a future possibility, and I like it as a future possibility, but I haven't given it a great deal of deliberate consideration.'

'Why not?'

'Because such a thing should not be forced, but left to take its natural course.'

'And what do you think?'

'Well, that raises a bigger question, doesn't it? Are we the sort of a couple where a proposal is made in a unilateral fashion, or the sort of couple where we discuss it together?'

'I tend to see myself as a traditional fellow.'

'Hmm. I tend to see myself as a woman who considers and discusses major decisions with her partner before action is taken.'

'OK, I see that,' he said, and continued to be happy for the moment.

At length they got up and carried on, stopping for tea at the quaint tea shop in the middle of the tiny high street of Upleigh. It was between there and getting back to the car that he started to ask himself, 'Am I enjoying this?' which he knew was a bad sign.

They'd agreed to have dinner at his house, but as soon as he walked in he knew he didn't really want to. But he didn't want to start upsetting her again so he was going to make all pretence at being happy and chatty.

They prepared the meal of lasagne, garlic bread and a light salad together, commenting about the day and avoiding the subject of marriage. They ate it in the front room on their laps, side by side on the settee, watching the news on the TV. After mugs of tea and chocolate biscuits she surprised him with, 'Can we sit outside and you can tell me about The Yearning?'

'Oh. OK,' he said, unsure about that. By now he was definitely feeling the downward drag of depression and didn't want to do much, but he was very wary of starting to retreat from her as he'd done before.

So they sat there. It was a warm evening and the sun had become an enormous, fiery ball of orange gold. Not unlike what it looked like in space pictures, he reflected. It hung just above the horizon and behind the trees, breaking through their leaves and branches in precious shards. The sky was turning yellow around it and high clouds had turned peach. He knew it should have moved him, as it clearly did her, but it failed.

'Well, you know I don't seem to get it any more?'

'Yes, you told me that. A few times. I'm so sorry about that because it sounds like the most beautiful thing. But maybe it was like the ringtone and now you've lifted the receiver.'

'Good analogy. Yes, maybe. Though I can't but long for it. I would sit here and just look out across those fields, and past the trees, and sometimes the sheer beauty of it, especially in winter, would nearly drive me mad. I would burst into tears of sheer joy. Yet a yearning joy, like it offered more, called me to something it only hinted at. It met something inside me with a sense of belonging, like the inside and the outside were part of the same thing despite being separated by trillions of miles. Sometimes it seemed like I was seeing right across the universe – past the trees and the world and the sun and out, out, out, across seas and oceans of space to somewhere I belonged, somewhere I should be, some awesomely and unspeakably fabulous place that was my true home. Transcendent. Numinous. Stirring in some impossible place and reaching out to me as its call made me reach out to it. It was both deeply unsettling and deeply fulfilling.'

As she listened she just stared, across the fields, trying to see what he was describing.

'And it's gone,' he added.

It was Sunday, 19th June.

They couldn't go to St Mark's in the morning because of all the children. He felt ashamed and embarrassed. She saw that, clearly. They would go in the evening and avoid the young people.

For lunch he drove them out to the carvery restaurant near Meoping and they ate a hearty meal, even though his didn't really taste of much. There was nothing at all wrong with it. And he couldn't have wine as he was driving.

The weather dulled as forecasted after lunch and they went back to Angela's house and started on a large jigsaw – a 1,000-piece picture of St Peter's in Rome, which seemed a bit of a betrayal, but he liked to think he was open-minded.

Tea was just a pot of tea and some cake Angela had made. Then, off to church, which he'd been dreading all day. He couldn't help wondering who knew and what the reception would be like. He'd suffered images of being stared at and whispered behind. Angela had robustly dismissed such images and even prayed for him to be free of them.

They arrived as the service was just about to begin and sat on the right because the young people always sat on the left. There were about thirty people in. When the rector entered he gave David a very deliberate smile, which was heartening.

The service had some familiar hymns, which was strangely comforting, and the reader gave an adequate sermon. The real encouragement was at the door as they left without going through for coffee. Rector Colin grabbed David's arm and took him aside.

He said, 'David, I want you to know you have my complete support. I, personally, don't believe at all this ridiculous allegation, and I pray for you to be completely exonerated as soon as possible. But, you know, the process has to go forward. That's just the way it is these days. Don't blame Angela, or Charles Sears, they're just doing what's required. But if there's any help I can offer, please just get in touch with me.'

'Thank you, Colin,' David said. 'That's helpful.'

CHAPTER FIFTEEN

It was Monday, 20th June.

He'd slept only fitfully, with a repeated and horrible dream of standing in court being accused on all sides of horrible things. He eventually got up just before 5am and sat outside with a WOL mug of tea. He looked at the image of Owl from Winnie the Pooh, standing out with his big, wise face, just as Eeyore had done on the previous mug that he'd broken in desperate sadness last Christmas. Had wisdom replaced sadness? Certainly not. But Angela had been very kind to get it for him. She was very kind. Kindness ran through her like letters through a stick of Blackpool rock. And he was learning. He needed her for that among so many things. But one-sided needing wasn't a good basis for any lasting relationship. Except parent and child, which this sometimes seemed a bit like, and that was no good. She seemed to encourage that sometimes, with her 'Little Noddy' and ruffling his hair as she occasionally did. All very affectionate, but it left him feeling like a child, and he hated that. Then again, he was the needy one. Well, no, she said she needed him just as much as he needed her. That her deep love for him made him pretty much essential to her happiness of life. Was that true? Well, why else say it?

He was drained with heavy sadness and unable to lift his anticipations of the day. Should he go back to bed? Angela would call at eight with croissants, which he wouldn't want but would eat rather than argue. He looked at the sky. He supposed it was rather lovely. The sky beyond the trees was silver, streaked with thin, grey clouds in horizontal wisps. A lonely crow, sitting in the top branches of one of the trees, called its 'Caw caw' as if from far, far away. But it left him unmoved. He went inside, put his mug in the sink (a thing he never did) and climbed the stairs with heavy steps. He lifted Bart into his arms and fell with him onto the unmade bed. He closed his eyes and tried to not be. Just absent himself. Leave a man-shaped ripple in space-time for a second and be gone.

The sound of a text arriving on his phone woke him from a heavy doze. Where was he? What had just happened?

Fortunately his mind had been trained by now to reach for his phone in any circumstance and he saw the text from Angela. The usual thing – arriving in ten minutes, get decent and get the kettle on.

When she arrived, carrying a brown leather briefcase, she took one look at his haggard appearance and they fell into each other. Kissing followed and they went and sat on the settee and kissed and cuddled and generally comforted each other. He realised he wanted her. Fully wanted her, right now, in his bed. He had no idea where that came from except as another distraction from the reality of the day. And, as she liked to say, 'That's not gonna happen.' Better not to mention it.

It didn't help that she was wearing a light summer dress, pulled in at her waist with a belt of the same light yellow colour, and it fell to a good two inches above her knees, so sitting as she was she was showing a good five inches of lovely thighs. But if he put a hand on there she'd be suspicious. And rightly so.

'Bad night?'

'Terrible,' he admitted.

'Croissants!' she said, picking up the bag and holding them beside her head with that cheeky grin that made it look like she'd stolen them. Then *she* looked like the child. Maybe that was a subtle part of the reason he loved her round face so much in that pose.

'Come on,' she added, and led him by the hand into the kitchen.

Sitting at the table as usual, she said, 'How bad? Your night?'

'Probably the worst since the dark shadow nights. Horrible. Nasty dreams. Kept waking. Sweating and sticking to my sheet. Up at five. Back to try to drift off. Heavy dozing. Woken by some idiot texting me.'

'Hoi!' she said, and nudged his arm like she did. 'Woken for a nice breakfast and to break the dark hold of the night for the bright hope of the day.'

'Bright hope!' he said. 'Some hope. That's a nice line, though. Dark hold, bright hope.'

'Thank you. I'm going to be with you throughout. No matter what. And maybe this is what God has allowed to strengthen us in answer to your prayer. But because it's from Him, it's for good, for our future, together.'

'Hmm.'

'You know Paul says in Romans that God works everything for our good. For those who love Him and are called for His purpose. Well, that means through tough times. And don't forget Isaiah 43: He goes with us through the rivers and in the fire so we aren't either overwhelmed or burned. He doesn't prevent us going through floods and flames. He goes with us and protects us in them. So I'm a bit like a picture of God for you today. Going with you into the waters and the fire. In me is a picture of Him. Try to be encouraged and brave.'

'Brave?' he said. 'Am I not brave?'

'I think you are. You just need to summon it today.'

'Have you been reading up on motivational speaking?' he asked her.

'No. I spent half the night praying for you.'

That silenced him. Now he felt a bit ashamed. 'And I never asked you how your night was.'

'That's OK. I am truly invested in this and deeply sad for you, but I know it's you who's in the firing line. Summon your faith and your courage and be ever so brave.'

'Ever so brave!' he repeated.

She smiled. It was that winning smile that she never gave to anyone but him. Eyes engaged, face alight, hair in throw-away twirls, inviting him in. She took his hand on the table as well, and held it as she continued to eat.

'How is it that I have someone as lovely as you?' he asked, partly because he knew it was the best thing to do, partly because he felt it, a little.

'I do not know. To be sure 'tis a great mystery,' she said.

He still felt basically awful. But the food was sensible, the tea refreshing, her presence and her words comforting. A little. Better than facing it alone.

They sat in the waiting area, which was painted a boring pale blue, with a chequer-patterned vinyl flooring, looking at the advisory posters, having told the young woman behind the glass that they had arrived for their interview.

Police and Legislation Monthly incorporating 'Crime Statistics Review' didn't attract him particularly. He remembered how he'd seen a magazine in the doctor's waiting room once called *Gas and Pipeline Monthly* and been so amused simply by the title that he didn't need to actually pick it up for its riveting content.

10.05 arrived and passed. 10.08. Every minute was an agony. At just after 10.09 the door beside the reception windows opened and a female officer appeared. His heart leapt, but she called for the boy in school uniform with his mother sitting on the other side of the room. He definitely looked guilty.

10.10 came and went. An eternity of anxiety. At 10.12 precisely the door opened again and a short man in a smart suit said, 'Mr Sourbook, would you follow me, please?'

They stood and followed as he led them into a small room with no natural light, just a strip light in the ceiling. This must be the room for the worst sorts, David thought. It was painted that grey they used for battleships, with a floor of mid-blue, vinyl tiles. At one end was a metal table, pressed against the wall, around which stood four wooden chairs and on the far end of which, against the wall, was a taping machine. It looked to be digital.

Already sitting at the table was a female officer also not in uniform. They both had cards round their necks on cords. David and Angela were made to sit on the opposite side of the table from them.

The male policeman in the suit pressed a button on the recording device and began. 'This is a record of a formal interview at Veery Lane Police Station on Monday, 20th June with Mr David Sourbook. Present are myself, DCI Steve Drane, head of the Safeguarding Unit, also Detective Sergeant Alissa Myers, Mr David Sourbook, and you are?'

'Miss Angela Adams.'

'Who is accompanying Mr Sourbook. The time is 10.15am.'

DCI Drane was about forty, clean-shaven and had intense eyes of a dark brown in a square face. Sgt Myers was younger – maybe thirty, and blonde with a pale skin and a thin face.

In front of DCI Drane on the table was a brown cardboard-covered file which he now flipped open and looked at. 'Mr Sourbook. Last Friday, 17th June, you were accused by Scott Law of touching him on the buttocks at the youth club run by you and Miss Adams. Another member of the club, Alex McConley, said he witnessed the assault. Would you like to tell us your version of what happened?'

David sighed inwardly and began his so-often rehearsed telling of it. 'I had been playing table tennis for half an hour with Alex McConley, Mike Davis and Scott Law. Table tennis, played properly, is not "ping-pong". It's exhausting. I was tired and sweaty. I went to the chair that sometimes sits by the tuck servery and sat down for a breather. In minutes there was a queue there for tuck. I was about to get up and move, when Scott looked back at me and said, "You just grabbed my bum!" I thought it was some kind of sick joke and I said, "That's not funny. You shouldn't say that." But Scott wasn't joking and said even louder, "You grabbed my bum, you paedo perve." I said, "I didn't touch you." And I asked Mike who was right behind Scott, "Did you touch him?" thinking it was he who was having a laugh. He said he didn't. Then Miss Adams came over and asked what was

166

going on. Scott repeated that I'd grabbed his behind. Then Alex, who was behind Mike, said, "I saw him do it. He grabbed his bum with his left hand." I asked them why they were saying this. Then Miss Adams warned them. She said, "Scott and Alex, if you insist on this there's likely to be a lot of serious trouble. This isn't some joke. Are you sure that's really what you want to do?" and they both said yes and Scott said, "I want you to call the police." Scott said again, "I want to complain to the police." So Miss Adams took Scott, and another member of the youth group team, Philip, took Alex so they could listen to them separately and take notes.'

'Here are the notes,' Angela said, taking the notebooks out of the briefcase she was carrying. She laid them on the table and DCI Drane took them up and placed them squarely and precisely beside his folder. David wondered why the woman, Alissa, was so passive. Was it a form of 'good cop, bad cop'?

'So, Miss Adams,' Drane said, 'thank you for these. Could you tell us your recollection of these events?'

'I was with two of the other boys. The first I knew of it was raised voices at the tuck shop. I went over and asked what was going on. Scott Law was accusing David of touching him, and David was replying that he hadn't. Alex joined in saying he'd seen it happen, and I asked them if they wanted to take this seriously. They said they did and I took notes from Scott while Philip Hughes took notes from Alex. Those are the notes, and they confirm exactly what David has told you.'

'Which is that Scott Law claimed you grabbed his behind and Alex McConley said you did it because he saw you.'

'But I didn't touch him,' David insisted.

'Then why would he say you did?'

'Because he is one of a group of lads who have attacked us in the past, and on that very evening, while we were playing table tennis, a younger girl walked past and Law called her an "effing slut". I was shocked and I told him he couldn't speak to her like that and he should control his language. He swore again and said I was always picking at him, which isn't true. I told him I was shocked at such abusive language, so he repeated that she was an effing slut. I told him that wasn't acceptable and he must stop it. He swore at me, threw his bat on the table and stormed off. The other two boys we were playing with went off after him, and that's when I went and sat down.'

'I see,' Drane said, and looked across at Myers, who looked back and gave him a tiny nod. 'I expect you think that somehow explains his action in accusing you. But it's really not that simple, is it? Paedophiles are notoriously subtle and calculating. A paedophile would see that bust-up as a perfect cover for an abusive action. Almost an invitation. "It explains why he accused me, so it gives me the ideal opportunity to touch him." Not only so, but there's the chair. Conveniently situated by the tuck. It's a reasonable assumption, I would think, that after a hot and sweaty game of table tennis, they might like a cool can of cola. You say there was no queue when you went and sat on it, but you might have guessed they'd be there in a few moments. Isn't that so?'

'No. Not necessarily. They play games all evening, and they don't go to the tuck after every one.'

'But after such a strenuous half-hour, surely it's a reasonable guess?'

'I'm sixty-one. They're in their teens. I get sweaty and puffed a lot quicker than they do.'

'I see. We will of course be interviewing them all, with their parents, in detail.' He slid the folder across to Myers, who suddenly came to life. He started reading the notes Angela had brought in.

Myers said, 'Mr Sourbook. We've taken a look into your school teaching records.' She pulled out a photograph and showed it to him. 'Do you recall this young lad?'

His heart sank. 'Yes, that's Paul Fox. I taught him about twenty years ago.'

'Just so. He's a good-looking lad. Blond hair, pleasant features, freckles there across his nose. That's quite an attractive smile he has. Tell us what happened with him.'

He deflated inside. So this was how it was going to be. 'I taught Fox physics when he was in Year 10, so he was rising fifteen. He was a very friendly and well-behaved lad, and I began to notice that everywhere I went in the school, there he was. He only ever wanted to ask about physics, but it gradually occurred to me that it was too often. So I reported it to the head and started to find ways of avoiding him. But another teacher had already noticed it and reported it.'

She laid the picture down on the desk. 'And unfortunately there's no way of us knowing if somehow you'd found out about the other teacher and only reported it yourself to cover your back. And you want us to believe that this lovely-looking young lad was taking an unhealthy interest in a middle-aged teacher and not the other way round.'

'I never said he took an unhealthy interest in me.'

'What was it, then?' Now she was getting quite attacking.

'He obviously took some sort of liking to me, but I'm not about to put a label on it. Kids do that sometimes. For a short while. It passes.'

'Sounds like you think it's a crush. Maybe that's what you fantasised about him.'

'Oh, for goodness' sake! That's just insulting and ridiculous!'

'There's no need to get abusive and angry, Mr Sourbook,' she said. 'That won't help your case at all.'

He could feel Angela beside him bridling at the fact that he hadn't said anything to her in the car when she'd told him such a similar tale about a student of hers. He'd wondered then why he hadn't mentioned this. Now he really wished he had.

He was sweating. He was sure Myers could see it. And Angela, out of the corner of her eye. Now he felt guilty.

'All right, then,' Myers said. 'Moving on. More recently, there was an incident with this student, do you remember his name?'

She held up another picture. It was Stephen Birks, looking greasy and spotty under that unruly mop of dark hair. He slumped inwardly again. They'd been doing their homework already.

'What's the story with this one?' she said. 'Story' was made to sound like 'fabrication'.

David sighed again. More obviously this time. 'He was a Year 11. I was on lunch hall staff duty. I was sitting on a chair at the end of a table. Some messing broke out and suddenly he was sitting on my lap. My hands were resting in my lap. I pulled them out, and pushed against his back to get him off me. But he said I'd fondled his buttocks. I hadn't – I'd just removed my hands from under him. Then he changed his story and said I pushed him off with a great shove. I didn't. I just gave him enough of a push to get him upright. That's it.'

'Once again, an allegation, but you're totally innocent. Once again, a teenage boy,' Myers said. 'Seems like a pattern to me.' She looked at Drane, who nodded in response.

Drane spoke again. 'These notes seem perfectly consistent. Why would McConley say he saw something when he didn't?'

'Beats me,' David replied. 'You'd need to ask him that. I'd say it's because they're friends, and both part of the group that attacked us last Christmas, and more recently when they attacked me outside a supermarket, so they were allies in attacking me again. Simple as that.'

'I see,' he said. 'Simple as that. Let me ask you, Mr Sourbook, do you have any other young lads you're close to?'

He was trying to think what to say when Angela answered. 'My nephew, Andrew. David is brilliant with him. He has ASD and David is superb at relating to him. My sister, Thelia, and I are really impressed with how he handles him.'

David couldn't understand why she'd volunteer such information to them.

'Well, letting go of your unfortunate use of words, how does he "handle him"?'

'He plays Lego with him. He uses maths questions with him. He's incredibly patient with him. Andrew took to David straight away when they first met last Christmas, but Andrew has a habit of throwing himself at people sometimes and hugging them so hard it feels like bones might break. David puts up with that and is very patient with the fact that Andrew can also be very emotionally distant and non-communicative.'

'Sounds like he's a very vulnerable child. How old is he?'

'He's eleven.'

'Sounds like a very vulnerable young man. So, he isn't related to David?'

'No, he's my nephew, my sister Thelia's child.'

'I see. And is Mr Sourbook supervised at all times when he's with Andrew, or is he allowed to be with him out of sight of yourselves?'

'He's totally allowed to be with Andrew any way that's necessary. He plays with him in one room when we're in another, he takes him up to the toilet to wash his hands, they go in the garden sometimes. And it's wonderful. Thelia and I, and her husband, Martin, are really pleased how good David is with him and for him.'

'He's a very vulnerable lad. Non-communicative. Hardly best able to report that Mr Sourbook has touched him in some inappropriate way.' Drane slid a small notebook and a pencil over to Angela. 'Write down your sister's full name and contact details, please.'

Angela did, and slid the notebook back.

Drane looked across at Myers. There was the tiniest nod, and she said, 'Is there anything else you'd like us to know at this point?'

Angela said, 'Only that David is completely innocent and these allegations were made out of spite.'

'Well, Miss Adams, Mr Sourbook, we now have to start the process of interviewing the members of the youth club, and the leaders, and anyone else we find we need to. I see that these previous concerns didn't lead to any action against you, but we will need to revisit those as well. That may take a while. I warn you, Mr Sourbook, to stay away from all children and young people you're not actually related to until this is resolved, and that includes Andrew. We will certainly be interviewing his mother and father. Did you by any chance bring the youth group's leaders' and members' details, Miss Adams?'

Angela reached into her briefcase and handed over a folded sheet of paper to her.

She opened it, scanned it, folded it again and handed it to Drane.

He spoke. 'Then for now we're done. We will be in touch, and I cannot say when that will be. But on that occasion we will let you know whether we will be charging you under the 1997 Sex Offenders Act. The interview is terminated at 10.43am.'

He switched off the recorder and they were ushered from the station.

CHAPTER SIXTEEN

The silence in the car was heavy as they sat in the station car park at the back of the building.

She stared forward, then she turned towards him and said, 'I can't believe you didn't tell me about you and that student when I told you my story. Why not? Why didn't you say a word? How can I trust you if you don't tell me things?'

That stung. 'How can I trust you?' She shouldn't need stories to trust him. He was mystified. 'Why is it a big deal? It isn't a big deal. Just because I have a story similar to yours. So what? That just means I can sympathise with your experience.'

'Then why didn't you say so? Did you not want me to discover your previous record?'

'Don't say "record". It isn't a record. Two silly misunderstandings, similar to yours. But you… Why on earth did you tell them about Andrew?'

'I had to tell them about Andrew.'

'And me taking him to the toilet, and playing with him out of sight. It sounded like you wanted them to bust me for abusing him.'

'Don't be neurotic. No it didn't. I was being open and honest. They will value truthfulness and transparency.'

'Those two! I don't think so. They were out to get me. You heard how they spoke to me.'

'They were just doing their job. In the scheme of things this isn't a serious case. Charles Sears told me that. I told you. Once they find out this isn't the tip of the iceberg they won't be interested. It isn't the tip of the iceberg, is it, David?'

He refused to answer.

'Is it, David?'

Still he said nothing, but stared forward at the car park wall of cracking and flaking bricks. She was clearly angry. He felt... what? Disappointed. Resentful. Yes, he resented this.

He said, 'Did you ever fall emotionally for one of your female students and become too close to her?'

'What's that a prelude to?'

'It isn't a prelude to anything. It's meant to show you what an insulting and ridiculously needless question it is. Yet you ask me if this is the tip of the iceberg.'

'No, I didn't. I asked you to just confirm, once, that it isn't. I don't think that's too much to ask of you.'

'Really. Really? Not too much to ask. So it's too much for me to ask of you that you just trust me.'

She was silent. He opened the car door and started to get out. 'I can't do this,' he said.

'Stop, get back in.'

'No. You know what you need to say to me. See you.'

He shut the door, firmly, not with a slam, and walked away. He didn't look back. He was too full of resentment.

The walk home was blurred by a torrent of thoughts and repetitions of actions and statements. He was on autopilot. Everything else was a foggy backdrop to the internal monologue. Depression weighed on him like a stifling cloud of noxious gas, sucking the life out of him.

He didn't even go in but sat on his bench and wondered how he'd got home. He could remember almost nothing of it.

Alone again. Sat here. Staring at... what? Nothing, really, truth be told. Nothing out there. A blank universe of multifarious irritants. Large and small.

Angela's car drew up across the road, its wheels on the grass verge. She opened the door and began to get out, looking over at him. He stood, and walked inside. He shut the front door after him. He heard her car door bang shut and he stopped and listened. Was she coming over, or driving off? The engine started, and he heard the car pull away.

So be it.

He sat in the front room with a glass in his hand containing two fingers of whisky. The TV was off. He stared at the brown liquid and swirled it around the inside of the cut-glass tumbler. He took a good sip, savouring the vanilla, toffee and wood-smoke flavours as it warmed him inside. He took another. Larger this time. He wanted it to soothe him.

So now he was being nasty to her again. Well, she started it, childish though that sounded. But she did. Accusing him of withholding information, of being untrustworthy, and her revealing all about Andrew in a way that was bound to make them suspicious. Ridiculous! What was happening in her head?

She wasn't his mother. She wasn't even his wife.

His phone alerted him to a text. It couldn't be Angela – she was driving. He opened it. The text was from her. It read, 'I'm back outside. I'm really sorry. Please let me in.'

He considered it. Didn't she realise they'd contact Thelia and he'd never be able to look her in the face again? She didn't have to say anything about Andrew. They wouldn't necessarily have found out. It stung. Badly. Anyway, he didn't have the energy to get up and answer the door.

Another text arrived. 'I'm coming to the door. Please don't leave me standing outside like an idiot.'

He texted back, 'I'm too depressed to get up. Use your key.'

A moment later she walked in. She knelt at his feet, rested her head on his legs, took his hand in hers and said nothing.

Minutes passed.

'I said I'm sorry,' she said. 'And I really am. Please forgive me. I shouldn't have said what I did about trusting you. I do trust you. You don't have to tell me anything. I trust you. And I'm very sorry.'

More minutes passed. She seemed content where she was. Demanding nothing of him. Just resting with him and on him.

'This is all I want,' she said.

She knew him so well.

He drained the whisky and waited as the warmth spread through his chest like it was going down every artery and capillary. Wood-smoked vanilla toffee floated around his throat and mouth, along with a rapidly fading burning. He put the glass down and rested his hand on the side of her face. She made a small appreciative noise and he began to feel the alcohol lifting his mood. Just a little. A dangerous thing, but right now he needed it.

She nuzzled his legs with the side of her face. But she said nothing. Like Job's comforters at their most wise, before they opened their mouths. Then in that old story, it all went downhill. The blame game came. But not Angela. She was content.

After a while, she uttered softly, 'Just to be clear, don't expect me always to be as compliant as this.'

'Don't expect me always to be as depressed as this.'

'I certainly don't. Have you got an appointment with Myfanwy coming up?'

'Tomorrow.'

'Good.'

Then she went silent again, and kissed his hand.

He woke to find her gone. He cleared his head, and called, 'Angela!'

'Coming!' she said. 'With coffees.'

She walked in with a tray holding two mugs of coffee and some of his shortbread biscuits. When she put the tray down he saw a new mug – a Piglet mug, from Winnie the Pooh, just like his broken Eeyore one and his current WOL one. It was as large as the WOL one, holding about a pint.

'Nice mug,' he said. 'Is it for me?'

'No, silly, it's for me to have here. Goes with the one I bought you. One each now.'

He took WOL and two biscuits.

'I'm sorry, too,' he said as she sat on the settee. 'I really am. I've been so depressed, but I know you're doing your best. And I felt so sad that you mentioned Andrew.'

'Don't you worry about Thelia. She'll agree with me. You're the best for Andrew and nothing will change there. She isn't stupid. She won't be swayed by some copper ringing her up with stupid allegations. She knows what's what.'

'Good. Thank you. I have really taken to Andrew and he makes me feel useful.'

'I really want to help you not be so depressed, but I don't know how,' she said.

'I know. I don't know how either. Except to be there for me. Keep being so kind to me even when I'm being bad-tempered and sulky. Full of slumpedness.'

'It was the slumpedness that first drew me to you, if you remember.'

'I do remember. By the pond, on that moonlit night a week before Christmas. Never to be forgotten.'

She smiled. 'So,' she said, 'it's good that we're not at odds, not least because Miss Roberts and Mrs Jackson both need a tour round the shops this afternoon, and you know what we say about that.'

'Helping helps,' he said. Slightly wearily.

'Helping helps. It does, though, doesn't it? Even if just a bit. It lifts you to do something constructive and particularly something kind. So, that's on the agenda for this afternoon, if you will be so kind as to help me. They do take a bit of watching, those two!'

'I know,' he said, remembering the last time when they suddenly wanted to go in opposite directions from an island in the middle of a busy road in town. One of them had been so insistent she'd stepped into the traffic while it was still moving and had to be saved by a quick reaction on his part. Like a couple of birds in a bag, they were. Or out of a bag. Or something.

On Tuesday morning, 21st June, he woke at around 5am, heavy with lack of sleep and all the worries of the coming day. Everything felt dire and without remedy or hope. He turned and screwed himself around the bed for the best part of an hour, then got up, made tea, washed and shaved, sat outside, and went back up to try to get some more sleep.

But that day he had an appointment with the lovely Myfanwy, at 11am.

She sat in her chair, knees revealed by her grey-green skirt that fell a good four inches above them. He tried not to stare. She knew nothing of the events of the past week, but saw immediately what state he was in. She waited for him to tell her.

He told her, in unspared detail, and she listened with her usual attention, and occasional questions. When he finished, she said, 'And you say this has left you very depressed. Why?'

He was puzzled. Had she not been listening? 'I just told you why.'

'No, you didn't. You told me what happened and how you reacted. But you didn't tell me why you reacted that way.'

'What happened is why I reacted that way.'

'Hmm,' she said. 'You're a physicist, so I'll ask it like this. Is it possible that in some other universe in the multiverse there is another David Sourbook who reacted differently to those events?'

'What, like, he just shrugged and said, "Whatever"?'

'Possibly. Or some other reaction.'

'Can't you give me a clue?'

'No, David, you have to get there yourself. This is significant. Something terribly unfair and unjust has been done to you. How else might you react than to slump into a depression?'

He considered. What were his options? Ignore it? Mount a massively impressive defence against them? Revenge?

Oh! Maybe many people, rather than slumping into a depression, would get very angry. Shout, gesticulate, insult and hit out.

'I suppose I could get angry,' he said.

'Aha!' she responded. 'A little half-hearted, but yes. Do you think other people might get very angry about such a thing?'

'I would say yes.'

'Is there anything inside you that might react that way to such an injustice?'

He looked inside. Had there been even one moment when that had been his uppermost thought? Not that he could recall. Or even any sense of anger at all? Not really. 'No,' he said.

She sat back on her chair, having been leaning forward in apparent enthusiasm for this new discovery. 'OK, tell me, as a teenager did you ever shout at your mum, or tell her that you hated her?'

'No. I don't think so.'

'Or your dad?'

'No, I wouldn't have dared do that to either of them.'

'Or anybody else?'

He tried to remember. 'No, I think not.'

'Can you remember any time in your youth that you became so angry with something that you smashed it?'

'Oh, once. I was about ten, and I was making a plastic model of a Spitfire with glue and the wing wouldn't stay on. I hadn't at that point discovered that the glue actually melts the plastic so adding loads more makes things worse. I tried, over two days, having built most of the rest of it, supporting the wing on knife-handles, scraping the glue off and starting again, adding on a small piece of plastic as a brace, but nothing worked. And in final fury I smashed my fist down on it on the table.'

'Good. And what happened?'

'I hurt my hand and the model hardly cracked.'

'Right,' she said, 'so the only time you can remember really letting your anger out the only effect was that you got hurt and nothing changed. Interesting. Your anger was impotent. But I also bet that somewhere inside you is a box of anger so full the lid hardly stays on. And one day it's going to fly off.'

'Really,' he said, intrigued.

'David Sourbook doesn't have to react to the events of four days ago with depression. There are other options. Maybe, from our perspective, this is an opportunity for you to get in touch with your anger.'

'I need to find my anger?'

'Don't you?'

'But anger is a bad thing,' he said, sure that that was right.

'Is it?'

'Yes, anger makes people fight and swear and destroy and treat each other badly.'

'Does anger have no positive elements? Could it be right to be angry about some things?'

David thought. 'Well, yes, I suppose if you're angry about poverty and injustice and you act to make things better.'

'Then why are you so afraid of anger?'

'Am I?'

'Aren't you?'

'I don't think so.'

'Well, I see our time is nearly up. I'd like to see you Tuesdays and Fridays for a while. Is that OK?'

'Yes, I suppose so.'

'And, David, I'd like you to do a bit of homework for me, for next time. Can you consider the question, "What are the reasons it's better to feel angry than depressed?"'

'OK.'

'Make those appointments with Sarah as you go, please. Goodbye, David, we've done good work today.'

'She wants you to get angry?' Angela asked over spaghetti bolognese at her kitchen table. It was warm and safe in her kitchen that evening and it smelled pleasantly of the cooking they'd done together. The curtains were closed. Drifts of drizzle scratched occasionally against the windows outside.

'Well, not exactly. She wants me to get in touch with my anger, which is in a box inside me with its lid about to blow off. Apparently.'

'Your anger about these allegations?'

'Again, not specifically. She takes the fact that I've responded with depression as a sign that I'm not in touch with anger and not able to feel or express it and I wouldn't feel so depressed if I was able to feel the anger.'

'And what does she expect you to do with all this anger?'

'Crack heads. Beat the living do-dos out of him until I feel better.'

'OK. What does she really expect you to do with it? Unfocused anger is surely not a good thing. Isn't getting angry just going to make things worse? I mean, with the police situation?'

'That's what I tried to tell her, that anger can be destructive. But she was insistent – I must find my anger. Oh, and she gave me some homework. It's a question: "What are the reasons it's better to feel angry than depressed?"'

She wiped bolognese sauce from her chin with her paper napkin. 'Ooh! She wants multiple reasons. Not just, "Why is it better?" but "What are the reasons it's better?" Any ideas?'

'Not yet. But I'm angry that she's set me homework.'

'Why?' she said, then, 'Oh, ha ha, very good. Am I dim or what?'

'I'll take the fifth.'

She laughed. 'It's amazing how you can be so depressed and yet still so funny.'

'Actually it's not amazing at all. It's a classic syndrome. The sad clown. It's well known. Some of the greatest comics have been depressives.'

'True. Two cannibals were eating a clown and one said, "Does this taste funny to you?"'

'Oh, that's an old one. There's also, "Why don't cannibals eat clowns? Because they taste funny."'

'Well,' she said, mopping up the last sauce with a piece of garlic bread. 'Feeling angry is better than feeling depressed because it's just less soul-destroying and painful. And less likely to make you want to kill yourself.'

'Always better to want to kill someone else,' he agreed.

'Maybe. Also, anger leaves you the energy to deal with it, whereas depression strips you of that energy. Though, again, what you then *do* could make things worse, rather than better. Like in your situation.'

'You said to me something before about anger requiring energy, and resentment not. So you're saying being angry is an energetic thing which shows you have energy. But there's a problem with anger. It commits you. Once you've shown anger about something, you can't so easily go back and say, "I was only saying," or, "Well, OK, maybe your view is right after all." Being angry commits you to the view you've taken.'

'Hmm,' she mulled. 'Whereas with depression you just slink off and lick your wounds. Maybe anger takes courage.'

He didn't like that very much. The image of the coward, the wounded animal, the keeping silent as having nothing to say.

She continued. 'And, I suppose, there's the sense of unworthiness and failure, self-loathing and guilt that that response can partly come from and partly feed into.'

'Oh, thanks!' he said.

'No!' She put her hand on his arm on the table. 'I'm not talking about you. I'm just trying to answer the question.'

'Same difference, surely.'

'No, sweetie! I'm just considering possibilities, I'm not describing you.'

He felt slightly better.

As they talked on he was warmed by some wine, and later he actually enjoyed sitting on her settee and watching some TV. She then walked him home, insisting that she wanted to and didn't at all mind having to walk back after. They sheltered together under an umbrella as the drizzle kept coming and going.

But that was followed by yet another night of squirming dislocation, and another early morning full of colours of gloom and expectations of doom. He tried reading the Bible notes the Grangers had given him but he couldn't concentrate on them. He thought of last night, but what struck him most was that he wasn't telling Angela how increasingly anxious he was becoming at hearing nothing from the police. He was desperate to get some message back, and there was nothing he could do to speed it up.

Day after long and weary day went by, and no word came.

And, like Angela said, wasn't 'finding his anger' just setting him up to make things worse?

CHAPTER SEVENTEEN

It was Friday, 24th June.

Nothing had been heard from the police.

The day had started with high white cloud, at around 5am, but it was brightening and clearing as the morning got under way. The usual routine had left David heavy, drained, lacking hope and fearing all manner of problems.

He sat looking at Myfanwy in her high boots and sensible, brown skirt right down to her knees. She waited, as was her wont.

'I think I know why to feel angry is better than to feel depressed.'

'Go on, impress me.' She smiled. She didn't smile often, but it was a bright, engaging smile when she did.

'OK. One, feeling angry is less unpleasant than feeling depressed. Two, feeling angry is generally more short-lived than feeling depressed. Three, feeling angry is empowering while feeling depressed sucks energy out of you. Four, feeling angry leaves you or gives you the energy to act, while depression takes away the energy to act. Five, feeling angry doesn't affect your ability to think and concentrate, necessarily, while feeling depressed does. Six, feeling angry comes out of a sense of self-worth and maybe feeds into that sense, while feeling depressed comes out of and feeds into a sense of unworthiness and guilt. Seven, feeling angry takes courage because it commits you to a position whereas feeling depressed is maybe even cowardly – slinking off and licking your wounds. There, seven good reasons. Oh, and eight, feeling angry makes you want to kill someone else, while depression makes you want to kill yourself. Always better to want to kill someone else. Are you impressed?'

'I am! That's very good homework. That's eight out of ten. And how much of that is about you?'

His dais as the teacher crumbled instantly into dust. 'About me?'

'Yes. OK, let's take them one at a time. One, feeling angry is less unpleasant then feeling depressed. What does anger feel like, to you, David?'

Sneaky woman! Straight in under the radar. What does anger feel like? It feels like being angry. He tried to imagine, or recall. It was hard. He couldn't just replace 'anger' with 'annoyed' or 'fury'. So he tried a practical 'actualising' of anger. That might please her. 'It feels like wanting to hit out, to hurt, because you've been injured in some way.'

She had waited for the answer and now she eyed him and said, slowly, 'Tell me what you think of that answer.'

'It's not very good. It sounds too theoretical. Not like I'm actually feeling it.'

'Good. That's a helpful answer. Let's skip to number three. Feeling angry is empowering. What does that feel like?'

'It makes you want to act. Hit out. Say something sharp, maybe hurtful.'

'When did that last happen to you?'

He thought. She waited. She said, 'Who was the last and most recent person to make you feel angry?'

He considered. He felt a heel saying it, but he said, 'Angela.'

'OK, good. Tell me about that.'

'When we went to the police station. She told them about Andrew, her nephew, and how they leave me alone with him and even let me go up with him up to the toilet to wash his hands and how huggy we are, which was bound to make them suspicious, and they've effectively banned me from seeing him. And then outside in the car afterwards she practically said she couldn't trust me because I hadn't responded when she'd told

185

me of an incident she'd had with a student and I'd had a similar one.'

'OK. Tell me exactly about your conversation when she annoyed you.'

He recalled for her in great and accurate detail the events requested, right up to their final reconciliation in his house.

Myfanwy continued to look at him with the listening regard, pencil now still against the notebook on her lap. 'When you got out of the car and later got up and went inside the house, what were you trying to do?'

'I wasn't trying to do anything. I was reacting to the loss of relationship that I felt. I couldn't be near her if she was going to be like that.'

'What were you trying to do *to Angela*?'

'Nothing, I...'

'David, I want you to accuse yourself, and accept no evasions or excuses. What did you intend for Angela to feel?'

Something inside him broke, allowing a light to penetrate. 'I wanted her to feel sad. Hurt. I wanted to hurt her. There, that must be the truth.'

'In which case what you felt towards her was what?'

'Anger. I was angry at her.' Suddenly it wasn't just a word. He felt it.

She looked pleased. So she should. That had not been easy. That had cost him, somewhere in his mental landscape.

'Was I wrong to be angry with her?' he asked.

'That doesn't help you and is irrelevant to me,' she said. 'Though it might be interesting that you ask, "Was I wrong?" rather than, "Wasn't I right?" The important thing is, you were angry with her. What did that feel like?'

'OK, I wanted to hurt her. I was looking for her to feel upset. I was punishing her, taking pleasure of some sort in her discomfort. I wanted her to feel sad and to wonder if our relationship was over. I was cruel and unkind.' Saying it felt awful.

'Try to stick with how it felt. All right. You were angry with her so you punished her. Did punishing her feel good?'

'I don't think so, no.'

'Then what did it feel like?'

'Bad. Guilty. Unkind. But justified.'

'It seems to me she caved in and said sorry very quickly. Does she tend to do that?'

That upset him. He didn't like to hear Angela spoken of negatively. 'Well, maybe she has a real humble streak and doesn't like to prolong us being against each other.'

'Maybe you need her to stand up for herself a bit more.'

'It's a good thing she's so willing to compromise and not blame.'

'Is it?' she asked, to his surprise. 'I'm not sure it's helping you very much.'

'Why not?'

'You tell me why not.'

'I don't know.'

'Well, what might happen if she didn't back down and apologise so easily?'

'We'd continue fighting. And what's the good of that?'

'What might be the good of that?' she asked, cool as usual.

'I suppose I'd get more angry and recognise my anger for what it is.'

'Well done. Maybe she's not so good for you after all.'

'What?' he said, nearly shooting out of his chair. 'You can't… you can't dictate what relationships I have.'

'Nor would I. But I might well raise a question about whether they're healthy for you.'

'That wasn't raising a question; that was a comment, a criticism.'

'Was it?' she asked, unmoved as ever. 'When she asked you to tell her that this allegation wasn't the tip of the iceberg, I imagine she asked you just to confirm to her once that that was the case. Yes?'

'Yes. So?'

'Well, why didn't you answer her?'

'Because I shouldn't have to confirm that. She should just know it.'

'How? Why? Aren't there wives out there who've known their husbands for twenty-five years and have no idea they're covert paedophiles?'

'Maybe, I suppose so.'

'Do you think I assume you're innocent of this allegation?'

'Yes.'

'But why?' she pressed.

'Because you know me.'

'Do I? I know what little I've managed to prise out of you over these months. But I don't know the things you might have kept from me. I don't know that you're innocent. Nor does Angela.'

'Well, if that's your attitude… I thought you would have my back, give me support, be there for me. I might as well just leave.'

'Now,' she said, 'that's better. You feel like stomping out of here and slamming the door. Good. What's that I've managed to stir up in you?'

He clicked, and felt a little foolish. 'Anger. You've made me angry with you.'

'Good. And what about those two young men who deliberately accused you of abusing one of them and turned your life into a living nightmare for nothing more than their own perverse amusement?'

'What they did was wrong. Very wrong.'

'Give me some more. What do they deserve for laughing with their mates about what they've done to you? Making you a laughing stock as some kind of perverted paedophile?'

'How dare they? Who do they think they are? How dare they drag my good name through the mud when all I've tried to do is help them? I wish they'd end up convicted of making false accusations.'

'Once this is over, do you think they should be able to stay members of the youth group?'

He felt he'd like to slap their stupid, laughing faces. 'No, they should be shamed and thrown out. They should be the laughing stock.'

'Do you deserve this treatment from them?'

'No.'

'And what about the church, what action have they taken?'

'I'm not allowed to be in the morning service, so I can't be near the children. That's an insult. I've never done anything to suggest I can't be trusted with them. I hate that. It's so unfair. I don't deserve that.'

'And who's to blame?'

'Scott and Alex. They're the ones who should be thrown out, not me.' He felt it now. The desire to see them get their comeuppance. The righteous indignation at the way he'd been treated.

'Were the police fair to you?'

'No! They deliberately put the worst light on everything, with nasty insinuations and veiled insults. They should get to feel it from the other side of the desk.'

'And Angela?'

That flummoxed him. 'Well, she shouldn't have demanded that I tell her it wasn't the tip of the iceberg. For that matter, neither should you. I don't have to demonstrate my innocence. I'm hiding nothing, so leave me alone.'

It felt good. Speaking with such confident judgement. Delivering his condemnations. Calling forth the downfall of his enemies.

'How does that feel?' she asked.

'A lot better than being the victim.' He swore, mildly. 'No more Mr Nice Guy.'

'That's maybe taking it a little too far,' she said.

'Sorry.'

They both laughed.

'Be careful,' she added as he got up to leave, 'how you take this back to Angela. Or even *if* you do.'

'I will.'

'Well,' David said in response to Angela's query. She was able to meet him on a Friday evening as the leaders of 'Later' had all agreed it was better for her not to be there at the moment. 'That's a little sensitive, as some of it was about you. And she told me to be careful how I relay it back to you.'

'Sounds like it might have been critical, then.'

'No, not really.'

She looked up from her plate of spaghetti bolognese in the Italian restaurant. She didn't speak straight away but took a sip of her Chianti, eyeing him, warily. 'Not *really*?'

That had been poorly handled. Now what? 'Well, no, nothing critical exactly. Nothing suggesting blame to you. No.'

'What, then? Not blame, but...?'

'Questions. Always questions, you know how they are.'

'Questioning my... intelligence? Integrity? Suitability? Compassion? What?'

'Ha. Well. No, not really.'

'Again, not *really*. Then what, David?'

Why did he do this to himself?

'Just tell me what she said, David, or I'll only imagine worse.'

That was probably true. 'All right. She said you don't stand up to me enough and that stops me feeling and expressing my anger, and maybe you're not good for me after all.'

He immediately regretted the 'after all'.

She registered instant shock. Mixed with... what? Anger? Disappointment? More shock?

'Oh,' she said, plainly unprepared for that revelation. 'I see. Do I see?'

He felt sorry for her. 'She isn't God, you know.'

'Yes. I do know. I know that. But she is an insightful and trained therapist. I can't just ignore... well,' and then she went silent. Her face was slightly red. He recognised the fledgling flutterings of her tears. At least he saw those these days.

She toyed with her spaghetti. Then she spoke, as she continued to stare idly at it. 'I suppose I've assumed that we've found each other, and we're destined to be together. I liked it when you said that about getting married. But maybe I'm assuming too much. Maybe that's a necessary wake-up call. Maybe I'm not even good for you.'

'It was only a thought. Her thought. But she also said you were quite right to insist I give you an assurance, once, that this allegation thing isn't the tip of the iceberg of a pattern of abuse. She reckoned you shouldn't give in to me and apologise so easily. So, here you are, no, this allegation isn't the tip of the iceberg either of a history of complaints or a history of abusive behaviours, at any level.'

'So I could be good for you if I was tougher with you, and you need to find and express your anger. That's going to lead to some right set-tos, isn't it?'

'Somebody said you should never marry someone until you've had at least one proper row with them.'

'Yes, well, you can forget about getting married. For now, at least.'

'Oh.'

'Yes, oh,' she said, and a tear slipped down her soft cheek.

Now he felt really sorry for her. Why was he such an idiot? 'I didn't mean…'

'You didn't mean. You didn't mean. You never mean. Maybe I should just kiss it all goodbye and go. Maybe I should just get up and leave.' She dropped her fork on the spaghetti and looked utterly miserable. Her head went down and a single tear dropped from the end of her nose onto her bolognese sauce. His heart broke for her.

Why did he do this to her? Should they really part company and stop hurting each other? He saw so graphically again the desolation and desperation he had brought into her life. It seemed to happen so easily. Now what? He really hated to hurt her, and he needed to stop doing it for both their sakes. But was the solution to end it? Or apologise? Or stand his ground? Or get angry? Or talk it through some more? That sounded right, but it was that which had led to this. He was staring at her. She didn't like that either. But he was captivated by the sheer totality of her sorrow. 'Lord, help me,' he sighed, somewhere inside.

'Look, Angela, it was Myfanwy, not me, who suggested maybe we're not good for each other. I think we are good for each other. Nothing has done me so much good as you in twenty years. Nothing matters as much to me as you. Nothing gives me as much hope as you. So it isn't just some assumption that we've found each other so we'll be together. It's so much more than that. So stop crying and pick up your fork. And wipe your face on your napkin, for goodness' sake. *You* wanted to know what *she* said, and I told you. She has many reasons for the things she says, and not always the obvious one. It's not fair that you throw your hands up in horror and burst into tears. I gave you the assurance you wanted, now you should calm down and give me a break. It's me facing allegations of child abuse, not you. So give me a bit of leeway.'

He surprised himself. That was quite firm, and clear, and even commanding. How would she react?

She was staring at him now. She wiped her face like he'd said, and picked up her fork. He waited, determined to say nothing more until she'd gathered herself and spoken. Then he changed his mind, stood up and walked round to her. Impervious to the stares of the nearby diners, he lifted her chin, bent down and kissed her full on the lips, his hand on her cheek. When, after a good, long kiss, he pulled back, he wiped the remainder of the tear smears from her cheeks with his hand, then went and sat down. She looked a little surprised.

'You eat,' he said, 'while I catch you up on the rest of the session.'

'OK,' she mumbled, smiling a weak smile now.

'She gave us eight out of ten for our homework, but I think that was just because we had eight reasons. She was impressed, mind you. Then she started asking about them one by one. Number one was that feeling angry is less unpleasant than feeling depressed, and straight away she asked me what feeling angry is like, to me. I found that hard to answer without resorting to a thesaurus. So she moved on to number three – feeling angry is empowering whereas feeling depressed takes your energy away.'

He took a bite of garlic bread and continued to talk as he chewed.

'She asked what that feels like and I said it makes you want to hit out. So she asked when that last happened and again I was flummoxed, until we hit upon the conversation you and I had outside the police station, and what happened when you came to my house, and she pinned me with, "What were you trying to do to Angela when you got out of the car to walk home and when you got up from your bench and went inside?" I said I wasn't trying to do anything; I was just feeling I needed to not be with you at that moment, but she insisted with what was I trying to do *to you*. And I realised I was trying to hurt you. I was lashing out at you. I was angry with you. After that she led me on to how angry I was with Scott and Alex, and the church, and the police, and then she deliberately made me angry with her by saying we maybe weren't really good for each other. Then it was time to go. There. In a nutshell.'

'Well, that certainly puts the "me being not good for you" in a better context. And you seem different.'

'How different?'

'More… forthright.'

'Forthright? That's a funny word.'

'Less like a victim.'

'Ah! She'd like that. Being angry is taking charge. I'll use that next time.'

'Sounds to me like you're using it already.'

'I do feel different. Not angry, actually, but energised. Things seem clearer. I'm really sorry I upset you again. But maybe you need to not get upset so easily.'

He felt forthright. Confident. Surprisingly in command of himself.

Back at her house, coffees in hand, they sat on her settee and watched some late news. Then she put her mug down and rested her head against his shoulder. She felt warm and nice. She slowly slid her hand up his chest and pulled his face round to hers, and kissed him, languidly and deeply. She sort of melted into him. Then she slid her hand down his chest and all the way to his belly. She stopped there, but it was warmly arousing. He put his nearer hand on her thigh, firm and soft though her skirt. Then she slid her hand round his waist until she found an opening and tugged his shirt till she could get her hand onto his skin underneath. He was breathless. He started to pull her skirt upwards.

Then he stopped, pulled slowly away, and said, 'You don't really want to do this.'

'Speak for yourself.'

'OK, I really *do* want to do this and I really *don't* want to do this and in the morning we would *both* really regret it. And hardly be able to look at each other. And usually it's you insisting we be more careful than this but if this is my turn, well, fair enough.'

She slid her hand out, but looked hurt.

'I'm really sorry,' he said. 'This is as hard for me as it is for you. I'll meet you for breakfast at the bakery at nine. But now I'm heading off home. And,' he kissed her again, a proper kiss, 'I love you. And thank you for being so understanding this evening.'

'Hmm,' she said. 'Can't Little Noddy stay a little while longer?'

'No, and we need to keep you off the Chianti in future.'

'Until we're married anyway.'

'Until then at least. Goodnight, my dear one. Let me go.'

She released him, reluctantly, followed him to the front door, holding his hand, and watched him into the night.

He walked home less racked with mixed regret than he expected. He'd done the right thing. Well done, mate. She would respect him for it. He respected himself for it.

Something had changed.

CHAPTER EIGHTEEN

Dreams of court scenes and being disgraced assaulted him, but he woke at seven feeling more refreshed than he had in ages.

It was Saturday, 25th June. The half-year anniversary of Christmas Day. Maybe their six-month anniversary.

He lay in bed, looking at the curtain patterns on the ceiling, and reviewed the dreams. He realised he'd felt stirred to annoyance by the accusations, not crushed. Today he would ring the station and ask if there was any progress to report. It was five days, after all. Only five days. It felt like two weeks. Waiting, waiting, waiting, for your fate to be decided by rule-bound and inconsiderate idiots. What did they know? They didn't know him and they didn't know the situation. They knew some pc rules for PCs. They'd have to muddle through them until they came to some sort of confused conclusion. And he just had to wait. And *that* wasn't fair. Maybe along with all their courses on the law and the sneaky ways of paedophiles they should be made to go on some courses about ordinary people and the experience of being accused.

He got up, showered and generally got ready for the day, then took tea outside to his bench. The day looked set fair. He went back inside after a while and read his daily Bible notes. The Bible passage for the day was from Psalm 73 about when the psalmist had been stupid and ignorant and yet God held his hand and was bringing him to glory. It calmed David from the ever-present anxiety of being caught in a Kafkaesque accusation-world. He prayed for help and for himself and Angela. He prayed for the church and the youth group. He prayed for the town and the nation. He prayed for the poor and the world.

It was time to go. He walked into town and saw that Angela wasn't either outside or inside the bakery, waiting. He hoped she'd come. He hung around outside, and soon enough she appeared. She looked rather quiet and uncertain. His heart hit his boots. Was this the break-up?

'Hi,' she said, and kissed him briefly on the lips.

'You OK?' he asked.

'Let's go in.'

Not the answer he was hoping for. They queued, bought coffees and croissants and sat on the stools in the window. He waited for her to say something.

'I think I may have got overly amorous,' she said. 'I seem to remember getting a bit fresh last night.'

So that was it. Relieved, he replied, 'I think it was the Chianti. Maybe stick to the Merlot in future.'

'I'm sorry,' she said. 'And I'm embarrassed.'

'Don't be. Just be glad I was up to the task of fighting you off and escaping with my decorum intact.'

'It wouldn't do to lose one's decorum.'

'Well, we didn't, so all's well. I slept better.'

'Oh, good! What time did you get up?'

'Not till seven. Then I felt OK as well. Anxious – that never leaves me. But not depressed. Dreams of being in court and found guilty and universally shamed, but nothing major.'

She nudged his arm. 'Good, I'm glad.'

'So, who are we taking out this afternoon?'

'Are you sure you want to?' she said.

'Yes. Who's on your list?'

'There's Mrs Timms, Mrs Lane, Mr Frack and Mrs George.'

'Oh!' he said. 'Mrs Timms and Mrs George.'

'They are entertaining, I have to admit,' she said. 'By the way, Thelia wants us for lunch tomorrow. She also has beef.'

'Are you sure?' David asked. 'Have the police spoken to her yet?'

'Yes, she'll tell you all about it. I bet they wished they hadn't bothered. She really wants you to come. She said, "I'm not letting some plopper cod stop Andrew seeing his best friend."'

'Plopper cod?'

'Copper plod.'

'Ha. Popper clod. Plopper cod.'

'What a ridiculous hat!' Mrs George said as soon as they pulled up outside the almshouse where Mrs Timms lived and she saw the very-wide brimmed, circular thing on her head.

David got out and opened the nearer door for Mrs Timms, who thanked him and got in, holding on to the hat to keep it in place.

'I was just saying, what a ridiculous hat,' Mrs George repeated.

'It keeps the sun off my neck,' Mrs Timms replied, happily.

'Looks like you're off to Wimbledon.'

Angela drove off.

'Oh, Wimbledon!' Mrs Timms responded. 'Will you be watching it? I'm so looking forward to watching that Frenchman – he's a handsome fellow, isn't he?'

'You shouldn't be noticing at your age – it's not proper,' Mrs George said, sternly.

'Noticing keeps me alive. He's a chunk.'

'I think you mean he's a hunk, dear.'

'No, I mean he's a chunk. I'd sit on his lap, given half a chance,' Mrs Timms insisted.

Mrs George tutted. 'Disgraceful,' she muttered.

'Don't you watch it, though?' Mrs Timms asked her.

'Sometimes. I like that Slovenian woman. Or Lithuanian. Or whatever it is. I want her to win.'

'Do you watch it?' Mrs Timms asked into the front of the car.

'I manage some, not much, usually' Angela said, and David added, 'I'm not really a fan.'

'I need to go to Homeson's, if that's all right,' Mrs Timms announced.

'Terrible, cheap place. I never go there,' Mrs George commented.

'That's no problem at all, Mrs Timms,' David reassured her.

'Well, I need to go to Newsome Bros,' Mrs George announced.

'That's not a problem either,' David added.

'But I certainly won't be buying a hat like that one.'

They travelled on in silence.

'I like your brooch,' Mrs Timms commented out of nowhere to Mrs George. It was gold inlaid with stones in the shape of concentric rings, and set off nicely her silky green summer frock with the plunging neckline.

'It didn't come from Homeson's. Or Woolworths,' Mrs George retorted.

'No, I should think not. It's from a proper jeweller's, I should say.'

'Yes, it is. My late husband gave it to me for our fortieth wedding anniversary.'

'My Charlie gave me a plant in a pot for our fortieth.'

'Well, there you are, then.'

'I went to Wimbledon once, many years ago.'

'Did you?' Mrs George said, unimpressed.

'Yes, Charlie and me queued for an age, then we got in and got a place to stand on the centre court right by the net and Chris Evert came on to play but after half an hour the heavens opened and there was no more play on any court that day.'

'My Teddy used to take me every year. We'd always have debenture seats and strawberries and Pimm's and go for a dinner afterwards. It was very special.'

'Ooh, sounds lovely,' Mrs Timms agreed.

'Maybe we should make up a trip next June,' Angela said.

'Oh! Wouldn't that be lovely?' Mrs Timms exclaimed.

'You sound like a show tune,' Mrs George said, sourly. 'Eliza Doolittle in *My Fair Lady*.'

'Or a show!' Mrs Timms exclaimed. She started to sing in a strained cockney accent.

'Oh, goodness! Saints preserve us,' Mrs George said, turning away to face out of the window.

Once they were parked in town, Mrs George said, 'I need to go to Newsome Bros first.'

So they went. When they got to the doors, Mrs Timms said, 'I'd better not go in. It's much too expensive for me.'

'That's probably best, dear. I'll meet you all back here in twenty minutes,' replied Mrs George, who hurried inside.

'Have you never been into Newsome Bros?' Angela asked.

'I don't think so, no. Not in a good while, anyway.'

'Well, come on,' Angela said, offering her arm. 'There's often things on offer.'

Twenty minutes later they were at a checkout when Mrs George rolled up behind them. 'What's that you've got?' she said, referring to the basket of goodies, and sounding rather like, 'What's that you've stolen?'

Mrs Timms was proud to show her. 'They had these biscuits at two for one. And these marmalades at reduced prices. And these nuts – well, I've never seen the like! I shall have to come in here again.'

Mrs George rolled her eyes. 'I may have to start going up to town, to Harrods,' she said.

'Harrods! What an adventure that would be! Oh, let's, please!'

Back in the High Street, Mrs Timms asked to be taken to Homeson's. When they got outside, Mrs George announced, 'I'm not going in there. I'll sit on this bench and wait.'

'I'll wait with you,' Angela said, so David escorted Mrs Timms inside. She took him to the plumbing section, and selected a small tap washer in a see-through bag.

'Do you know what to do with that?' he asked.

'Of course I do! I've done it before. I turn off the stopcock under the sink, then I use the spanner to unscrew the top of the tap, turning it the right way, of course, take out the old washer, put in the new one, screw the tap back on and turn on the stopcock. Done. Five minutes. That would be £10 a minute plus VAT if I got a plumber in to do it.'

'Well, I am impressed,' David said.

'Well, dear, perhaps you shouldn't be *so* impressed because you make it sound like you think someone who's eighty has no marbles left.'

They paid, less than £1, and left, him feeling justifiably admonished.

When they got back into the High Street, Mrs George announced, 'I want an ice cream.'

It wasn't a terribly warm afternoon and Mrs Timms said, 'Isn't it a touch breezy for an ice cream?'

'If I want an ice cream I'll have an ice cream and I don't need a weather report to tell me if I can!'

In the middle of the street by the war memorial was often an ice cream van. As she approached it, Mrs George opened her purse, looked in and, after a big sigh, said, 'Does *anyone else* want an ice cream?'

'No, thank you,' they all muttered, not wanting to find themselves in her debt. So she bought a large one with chocolate and strawberry sauce drizzled over the top. Satisfied, she rejoined them, and they set off towards the supermarket. A sudden gust of wind caught Mrs Timms' hat and swept it off her head straight into Mrs George who was behind her and who hadn't even taken a lick of her ice cream. The hat threw the ice cream off the cone and into the top of her silky green summer frock, which showed a large area of décolletage. It immediately began to melt and disappear down inside the frock.

'Oh! Eek!' she said, waving her arms and flapping her hands like she was beginning a dance. 'Don't just stand there, get it out!'

David looked in horror at the prospect, then sneaked a glance at Angela who shot back a look of equal disinclination. Mrs Timms said, 'I don't think any of us dare put our hands down there, dear!'

'Don't you call me "dear"! You did this deliberately! I should sue you. Oh! It's sliding down to my stom… oh!' and she started to jiggle and wiggle, making the dance take on a disco effect.

'I shall have to get this dry-cleaned,' she moaned.

'Oh, I wouldn't bother to get that old thing dry-cleaned,' Mrs Timms said, all innocence. 'I shall just sponge my hat off in the sink.'

Angela took out a tissue and held it out to Mrs George, but she spat, 'What the hell do you think is the use of *that*? I need to get to a toilet.'

'There's a customer toilet in Newsome Bros,' Angela offered.

'I can't go in *there* looking like *this*!' she said. 'There must be another one.'

'There's one in Homeson's,' Mrs Timms said, quite sweetly.

'Then my dissolution is complete,' she replied.

They never got to the supermarket. Angela drove them both home with assurances they'd take them again tomorrow, but Mrs George declined in a most firm manner.

'Take *me* home first,' she said.

'But you know you're all invited to my house for tea,' said Mrs Timms. 'I've got French Finger Fancies.'

'I'd rather eat my own fingers, one by one.'

'Oh, you have them too? I love the strawberry ones, and the lemon ones.'

Mrs George responded with a low and growling grunt. 'I don't know why I do this,' she said. 'I have plenty enough money to get a taxi. I don't have to rely on *charity*.'

They pulled up outside her gate. She opened the door before David could get out.

'But then you'd have no one to talk to,' said Mrs Timms.

'Exactly.'

She shut the door firmly and walked away.

'I do hope she won't sue me. I'd hate that,' said Mrs Timms, looking a little disconsolate.

'I think any court would find it an "Act of God",' David said.

'Definitely!' Angela agreed, and they all burst into gales of laughter.

'Drive away! Drive away! She's looking!' David said.

They went and had a very nice tea with Mrs Timms, and reassured her that it really wasn't her fault about the hat and the ice cream. Then they went to the supermarket for their own shopping and spent the evening reading together at his house. After Angela left he sat with a small whisky and reflected on the day. A remarkable day, for which he thanked God, which had put a whole new spin on his life and situation. He took himself up to bed at eleven, feeling more hopeful than he had in a while.

People were all around him, looking with accusing stares, shifting and shoving each other to attack him. Suddenly they were on him, pounding him and pouring out curses all over him. He fell from his bed onto the floor with such a grip on one of Bart's ears that he was about to rip it clean off. Sweaty sheets were around his legs as he struggled and fought to get free, and Bart looked most miserable.

'Bart!' David said. 'No, no! Here, let's check that ear.'

To his great relief, it was all right. He lay back on the carpet, his legs still in the tangled sheets on the bed, and Bart lay beside him. 'I'm so sorry, faithful bear, it was a dream, a horrible dream. Never leave me, bear of bears, bearer of faithfulness.' And it seemed like a voice without a voice said, 'I will never leave you, nor forsake you.' And he remembered when he'd had the same sense of, 'You'll always have Me.'

'Is Bart a sort of sign of You, Lord?' he asked into the bedroom ceiling, but it remained darkly silent.

He got off the floor and found his phone to check the time. 2.38am. No way he was getting up yet. He went to the bathroom, relieved himself and splashed water on his red face and rheumy-looking eyes. No dark shadow descended, at least.

Back in bed he cuddled Bart for comfort and said, 'Lord, let me sleep.'

It was Sunday, 26th June.

He woke at nearly 8am feeling really not too bad. Then he remembered the accusation and his stomach roiled and churned. Then he remembered the dream and felt physically sick with echoed stains of fear.

He showered, hoping it might somehow wash away. He looked at himself in the mirror as he shaved. Who are you? What's happening to you? You used to be this simple character, this cold-hearted poet, this isolated intellect untroubled by others and not troubling them much either. But now, since last Christmas and meeting Angela and her crew, the things that have surfaced! OK, The Yearning was already in there. But that was quite pleasant, and had no face and no name. It made him cry, but they were tears of a sweetly unidentifiable longing, a distant call, and of a beauty that was almost spiritual in character, numinous and wondrous and searching.

But now! Evil spirits from his childhood, and the police, and getting mixed up with reprobates, and the eyes of accusation at his failure to save an old dying man, and his unwanted attentions to a young boy. And depression. And anxiety. And banishment from the church, of all things.

Ah, but he had a new weapon. A new friend. Anger. Even this very morning he didn't feel so depressed. Even with the anxiety of the police investigations, he was angry about it.

Downstairs, smartly dressed with shirt and tie, and with a WOL-full of tea and two slices of seeded toast and marmalade, he phoned Angela.

'I think this morning I'd like to go to Christ Church.'

'Oh. OK. Why?'

'They have no children and young people and it'll be a nice straightforward Anglican service and then we can get off to Thelia's.'

'Fair enough. 10.30 service?'

'It is indeed. Can you pick me up at say ten past ten?'

It was indeed a straightforward Holy Communion at Christ Church, with an ageing congregation.

As she drove them south he said, 'I want to start going to Christ Church.'

'You mean instead of St Mark's?'

'Yes.'

'Oh, that's my church.'

'I know it is.'

'And they're only following the necessary protocol that's insisted on by the powers that be. They're just doing what they need to.'

'I know. But I also need to make it clear that from the point of view of someone unjustly accused that's just not acceptable. I need to make a statement as well. About being treated that way, whatever the reasons.'

'But they're only doing what they have to do.'

'And I'm only doing what I have to do in response to that. Someone has to stand up for the little man. Someone has to start the cry of "Enough!" Someone has to make them listen to the voices of the unheard and dispossessed. It's too easy to just lock into the system and shunt them off. It won't do. I'm not going back to St Mark's, lovely people though they are, until this is over and I get some apologies, and maybe not even then.'

She was quiet, brooding over the steering wheel. He watched patches of sun and cloud pass by.

'Are you starting a movement?' she said.

'Not a bad idea, if I could.' He thought. '"JUST". J-U-S-T. Justice Under the Safeguarding Trial. Why not?'

'No, I agree. Maybe it's about time. The knee-jerk madness to cover up past horrors doesn't justify the way people are being treated. Managing by regulation is being seen as a cover-all to cover one's butt. There is no understanding, no subtlety, no appreciation of how the best youth and children's workers relate to children. It is thoroughly flawed. It's a shotgun to shoot three flies and to hell with the bees and butterflies that get in the way. But St Mark's is my church.'

'Then this is a trial of your loyalties.'

'Isn't it?' she said, wisely.

Thelia flew out of the front door and hugged him with one arm while holding Andrew in the other, and he likewise squeezed David in a strong grip. Then she put him down, saying, 'Ooh, you're getting heavy, young man,' at which point Andrew put his arms up to David like a much smaller child. David very happily picked him up.

'Uncle David,' he said.

'Aww! Nephew Andrew.'

'Really?' Martin said, emerging from the dark hallway.

'What? Oh, no,' Thelia replied, seeing his assumption of what was being said about Angela and David's relationship. 'Well, not yet, anyway!'

'Thanks,' Angela said, stroking Andrew's hair as she hugged her sister.

'Coffee time!' Thelia said. 'Come in.'

CHAPTER NINETEEN

'He said he wanted to advise me – no, what was the word he used? Appraise me, appraise me of the situation. He said an accusation had been made, di-da-di-da-di-da. And he needed to make me aware that you might be a danger to Andrew, especially as he has limited ability to tell us if anything occurred. So I told him that Andrew is perfectly capable of making us aware if something upsets or disturbs him, to which officer what's-his-face said paedophiles sometimes get the young people to trust them – it's called "grooming" – like I'd never heard the word – and so Andrew wouldn't make any indication of being upset. So I told him that kids that have been groomed still register concern when something untoward happens and that you've been coming here for six months and in that time you've been enormously good for Andrew and in all that time there has been no indication, not the tiniest, slightest sign despite our proximity with you and Andrew together, of anything untoward and in fact the way you are with Andrew is an example of wise care of someone with ASD. He said, well, you should be wary because paedophiles are notoriously clever and I said so am I and it's a pity you aren't. Then I bade him goodbye and put the phone down.'

They all laughed out loud at Thelia's tale over their coffees in the back room while Andrew played with Lego on the carpet.

'What a jerk!' Martin commented. 'Every time you tell me it just makes me wonder what's going on. Is the point to protect young and vulnerable people or is the point really to protect the institutions that have been found out pandering to paedophiles in the past?'

'Pandering to Paedophiles in the Past!' Angela said, emphasising the ps. 'It's a Pity to Paint such a Picture!'

Andrew made a strange noise, looking at David, almost into his eyes, and pointed to the rows of Lego towers on the floor. It was an odd shape of towers of bricks, many just one brick, around the left-side edge, but one or two quite large ones on the right side. David frowned, slipped off the settee onto the floor and did some counting. The others fell silent and watched. David assumed they were intrigued.

'OK, genius, what have we here? We have ones all down the edge, in a straight line. Then a two in there, then a three, suggesting Fibonacci numbers, but then a four and a six side by side. Ah, it's in rows and each row as it goes down is slightly shifted to the left. So underneath that row is a five and a ten. Then a six, a fifteen and a twenty. Finally a seven, a twenty-one and a thirty-five. And the two, the three, the five and the seven are all red bricks – the primes, but the ten, twenty-one and thirty-five are all green, whereas everything else is yellow. Hmm. What am I looking at, little man?'

Andrew was impassive, waiting, staring at his creation.

'Tricky Dicky!' David said, seeing. 'That's hard to recognise because it's the left-hand side only of a Pascal's triangle. And the primes are red but also the numbers on the primes' rows that would be in between the primes and are divisible by the primes are shown in green. Sneaky beaky! I don't imagine you're going to the next row down because that means a stack of... seventy in the middle and two fifty-sixes either side, so let's fill in the right-hand side of the triangle and show off the pattern. Then you can show me all the integers and the triangle numbers.'

Andrew squealed with delight and threw his arms round David's neck, nearly strangling him.

'Andrew,' Thelia said, warning, and he slacked off a bit. David patted his back so he knew he wasn't being rejected.

The others started to chat again, and after David had finished the work with a happy Andrew, he said, 'I'm thinking of leaving St Mark's until this is all resolved. Going to Christ Church where there are no children or young people, at the moment.'

'But that's Angela's church,' Thelia said.

'She doesn't have to come with me.'

'Is it a sort of statement of discontent?' Martin asked.

'You bet it is!' David said, firmly. 'Someone has to speak up for the little guy. The person who's *actually* being abused in all this. It seems to me that whatever the agenda and the requirements of the institutions, the individual who's been accused is just thrown to the wolves. Discarded as irrelevant. Well, how can that be right?'

'I see that,' Martin said. 'I agree, absolutely. And that includes your church, even if they're very apologetic about what they've had to do.'

'Yes. It has to start somewhere. The position of the accused has to be more fairly taken into consideration.'

'This is a bit of a new you, isn't it?' Thelia said, with that considered carefulness he so admired in her. It was clearly not a throw-away comment, a joke or a criticism.

'His therapist told him to get angry,' Angela answered, unhelpfully, and not with careful consideration.

'Not quite the point,' David insisted. 'She said I need to know and acknowledge when I *am* angry and have every right to be, and express it appropriately. Which gives me a sense of control, not just collapsing into depression as a victim. I'm pushing back because I think that's right.'

'Good for you!' Martin agreed.

'But it leaves Angela with a quandary,' Thelia said, quietly. 'How do you feel about that, Angela?'

'Quandaried. Divided. I suppose I could go to St Mark's in the morning and join David at Christ Church in the evenings. But I don't much like the idea.'

'Or you could throw your weight behind David and go with him,' Martin observed.

Thelia said, 'Or David could feel this is too much to ask of Angela who's been at St Mark's for years. Ten years, isn't it, about?'

'Yes.'

Thelia continued, 'Or Angela could see that this is part of David needing to take control, to step up, to make his point, and she might feel that that is so important to him that she'll thoroughly support him even if it costs her.'

'And that's not impossible,' Angela added, helpfully.

They ventured out for their usual jaunt after lunch, and Andrew immediately wanted to sit on David's shoulders, which pleased him. But the boy had certainly put on some weight. Not a great deal, but enough that David wondered what aches and worse he might suffer later.

He was holding on to Andrew's little socks – the boy was in shorts. He sometimes held him by the knees. They were all discussing holiday plans, and whether or not Angela and David would try a holiday together. But David was very distracted just giving Andrew his ride and being careful not to trip.

'Are we boring you?' Thelia said, noticing his silence. 'Come on, you don't seem terribly keen on spending a couple of weeks in the sun with my lovely sister.'

'To be honest,' he said, feeling content, 'I've never even considered it. And with all this hanging over me at the moment, it seems a frivolous hope.'

'Aww,' she said, 'come on, David.' She put an arm right round his shoulders, underneath Andrew. 'Don't let it hang over you so heavily.'

'It's like a snake that's wound itself round your arm and won't let go, and you're just waiting for it to bite. And it's terrifying, truth be told. You try to get away from it. Have a nice walk. See a film. Have a red wine. And you imagine you've shaken it off. But as soon as you look down, there it is again, squeezing your arm with its disgusting body as it writhes and coils.'

'Well, nobody likes to talk about snakes,' she said. 'So let's talk about where you two honeymooners might take a nice holiday.'

Angela nudged her and said, 'Don't push.'

'I'm not pushing. Just speculating. It must be, what, six months now.'

'We met on the 18th of December,' David said, 'and started our relationship maybe a few days later. Maybe Christmas Eve, or even Christmas Day.'

'That's right,' Angela agreed, with a warm smile at him. 'So it was six months, oh, the day after the incident.'

That shut them all up for a while.

'You really enjoyed being with Andrew and he really enjoyed being with you,' Angela said as she sped them homewards on a bright summer's evening with a red and purple sunset over to their left. It was after 9pm. She was straining any respect for the speed limit.

'I did. And Thelia and Martin were lovely. So, thank you. That's done me good. What do you really think about a holiday together?'

'I like the idea. Majorca in August is magnificent. The beaches, the nightlife, the mountains, the blistering central plain, the little villages, the shopping in Palma. We should do it. But in separate hotels.'

'Separate hotels? That's a bit extreme, isn't it? Just separate rooms, even on separate floors, would surely be enough.'

'I knew a couple – she was my friend – they went off for two weeks, separate rooms, and she still came back with a souvenir she hadn't planned for. It's too easy. You have a nice meal, some wine, a cocktail or two, a romantic walk along the beach, back to one of the hotel rooms...'

'But we're too old to get pregnant.'

'And that's hardly the point!'

'Anyway,' he concluded, 'I'll need to get this allegation that's hanging over me cleared up before I can think about that.'

'That's a shame. Surely it would give you something to look forward to.'

'I can't.'

She stopped outside his house and they leaned in and kissed each other. It became a drawn-out kiss and he liked it. When they parted she said, 'Kissing in the car! I still can't feel right about it.'

'You could always come in for a cocktail or two.'

'Get out.'

She touched his lips with hers and he left the car, waving after her as she drove away.

He had a Merlot, watched some late news, sat outside for a while and then went to bed. He slept peacefully, but was disturbed a couple of times by noises outside. Dogs or drunks, he imagined. There was no repeat of the horrible dream.

It was Monday, 27th June.

In the morning he woke at half past seven and got up, feeling a touch depressed, but not much. As he descended the stairs he looked through the frosted glass windows in the door and it seemed like there was something across them outside. Then he heard voices. Puzzled, he opened the door and saw the paint. People who had gathered on the footpath looked at him suspiciously, muttering among themselves.

David walked the length of his path, turned and saw it all. On the garage door was spray-painted, 'PEDO PERVE ABUSER'. On his front door, 'KIDDIE FIDDLER'.

His heart sank. His neighbours were seeing this. Mrs James was standing there, holding the new dog, Sparks, and both she and it seemed to have reverted to the old, disapproving sneer of the previous dog. She spoke. 'What's all that about, David? It's hardly nice, is it, in our quiet street?'

'Some kids from the youth group at church. I annoyed them by telling them off, and this is what happens.'

'Disgusting,' she said. 'Disgraceful.' But it sounded so like it was aimed at him, not them.

Hilary Bleaks (mother of the screaming Bleaks – her many, high-volume children), was standing there, latest baby in her arms, and she said, 'People complain about my boys but they never done nothing like that. Should be strung up, little... Why they got it in for you? What you done?'

'Nothing,' he said, lamely. 'I told them off in the youth club and this is what happens.'

Then he saw a man getting out of a car with a large camera. From the *Clarion*, no doubt. That was all he needed. He was asking around, surely for the homeowner. Someone pointed in his direction. He swallowed hard.

'Mr Sourbeak, is it? I'm Dillon Dewar from the *Clarion*. Can I get a picture of you in front of the graffiti?'

'Are you kidding? No, you cannot. I'd rather you didn't take any pictures at all.'

'I'm sorry, but I will be expected to come back with photographs of the damage at least.' He let the camera hang loose on its neck-strap and took out a pad and pen. 'Can I get your name right?' he said, clearly used to getting it wrong.

David spelled it for him.

'Any idea who did this?'

'It would be wrong to speculate publicly because I might be pointing the finger at someone who's innocent.'

He scribbled furiously.

'I see. Have there been any allegations that might have led to these words?'

'Again, it would be wrong to speculate. Listen, doubtless you need a good quote, so let me say this. I am extremely angry to see this desecration of my property. It's a disgraceful thing to do to someone. I shall be calling the police immediately and I'm obviously going to have to spend a lot of time and trouble cleaning up this mess. Got that?'

'Sorry... "obviously going to"... there.'

'Do please quote me exactly. I hate it when papers put what was said in quotes and it wasn't actually what was said. It's a real failing of the local news sheet. I mean all local news sheets. Maybe you could stand out from the rest.'

'And you didn't hear or see anything in the night?'

'I may have heard noises, but thought nothing of them.'

'Thank you, Mr Sourbook. What's your first name?'

'David. Thank you.'

He went off to interview others. David looked at the writing and his heart sank. All that work. He could try to get a painter in but that could take weeks. He'd have to have a go at it himself.

'Should be shot, anyone who does that,' Mrs James said, but it still wasn't clear whether it was he or they, and what he had done or what they had done.

'I'm going in to phone the police,' David replied. The dog eyed him suspiciously.

The police-person took a note of the details and gave him a crime number for his insurers, but offered no assurance of any kind of investigation. The crime number made him realise he should contact his insurers. So he took his phone outside and photographed the two doors, then went down to his shed, threw on some overalls, grabbed a tin of white emulsion paint and a reasonable brush, and went out and painted over the words. Then he phoned the insurers, made the report and got their permission to get in a painter to make it all good. Next he went online, and by coffee time he had a man due to come in the morning.

The crowd had dispersed. No words to gawp at and shake their heads about.

Sustaining his feelings of anger about the boys who, he was sure, had done this, he decided he'd done well and should get away from it. He changed into cycling gear (no Lycra, but old trousers and shirt) and set off on his bike to head for Hadford for a coffee. It was a nice day, and a nice ride. Or it would have been if images of the local paper and the graffiti on his house and the reports of what they'd discovered didn't keep flashing in front of him.

Angela had some work event so they didn't meet that evening. He phoned her later and told her about the graffiti. She was understandably upset. But she reminded him about the need to keep trusting God through it all, because He promised to never fail or forsake us. David recognised the truth of it.

He slept badly with dreams about being publicly shamed and chasing vandals but somehow being unable to move fast enough. He woke in a tangle of sweat and disarray, both inner and outer.

It was Tuesday, 28th June. It was a Myfanwy day.

She sat in her green skirt and brown boots with a brown jacket over her light green blouse, and waited.

He started straight in. 'I've been less depressed. I feel much more in control.'

'That's good. Tell me more.'

'It happened surprisingly quickly. I discovered some anger, like you said. I felt it. I admitted it to Angela. I started to react to the situation with this allegation with proactive resistance rather than reactive withdrawal. I've even suggested to Angela that I'm not going back to St Mark's until I get an apology and someone acknowledges how appalling it is to be treated this way.'

'How did she react to that?'

'She was taken aback, and is uncertain whether to back me or persuade me to change my mind.'

'How do you know that Angela and you are right for each other?'

That blindsided him. 'Oh, the usual things, I guess. The way we talk together. Common interests. Mutual attraction. Having fun together.'

'You misunderstand my question. Which is revealing. You assume that what lies behind it is my belief that you are right for each other. I wonder if you carry around an assumption that you and Angela will be together, when maybe you're just holding on to that because of some experiences you've been through and some need of a friend. You assume that I think that your relationship is somehow bound to be. I don't. It's exactly that that I'm questioning.'

'Are you saying that just to make me angry, like last time?'

'Did I say it last time just to make you angry?'

'That's a typical therapist's response.'

'A typical therapist's response is to make you question what you've said.'

'OK, yes, last time we met you were deliberately trying to provoke some anger in me. Or get me to connect with the big, bubbling pot of anger that's in there. While, no doubt, doing other subtle therapist tricks at the same time.'

'You regard me as some kind of witch.'

'I am capable of getting angry,' he insisted.

'Yes, you are, we've seen that before. But it tends to collapse too quickly because you always see yourself as being in the wrong for being angry.'

'Now you're giving me the answers.'

'Now you're fencing with me. Why?'

'Because however well-intentioned, the way you question me can be irritating.'

'And isn't that a real part of the whole counselling process? An emotional response. Some real contention, where it's needed?'

'So you *are* trying to make me angry!'

'I'm trying to make you *real*. There's a story told about a child who's in a restaurant with his parents, and when the waitress comes over the child expects her to just talk to his parents, but instead she goes straight to him and engages him in conversation and asks him what he'd like. When she goes away, he says to his mum and dad, "That waitress! She thought I was *real!*" It's a revealing comment. Are you real, David?'

He said nothing. He was annoyed, but also confused. She waited, then she said, 'This isn't level one therapy, I'll admit, but what am I really asking you, David?'

Light shone. 'You're asking me if I think I have the right to be angry and stay angry.'

'I love it when I earn my salary!' she said, and smiled a big smile at him.

'Ha!' he said, taking it in. 'There's two kinds of anger. There's anger as an instant and passing reaction, and there's a settled anger that remains. The one I need more of is the second. But to have that, you have to know you have a right to it. That you're real, in some sense. You have the right to be angry.'

'Maybe so,' she said, still smiling.

They discussed that for a good while.

Eventually, she said, 'Not a witch after all, then.'

'And I need to be sure I'm real. Because then I'm allowed not just to *get* angry but to *be* angry.' Something suddenly occurred to him. 'It's like I'm working my way through levels of darkness inside me. Levels of hell down there. How many levels might there be? How do you know when you've finished the last of them?'

'That's entirely another question, for another time. I feel I've led you a bit more than usual today, but that's been necessary and now requires you to go away and mull it over.'

'I thought the mulling was part of what I'm paying for.'

'It's your homework.'

CHAPTER TWENTY

He was doing a bit of gardening when Angela arrived. She helped him for a little while, pulling out some weeds and dead-heading some nasturtiums and mimulus in his tubs in the front garden, then they went inside for a cup of tea.

'I see the painter didn't turn up, then.'

'No surprise there. He did ring a while ago to say he'll be here in the morning.'

'Anything from the police?'

'No.'

'You should ring them again and take the opportunity to ask about the investigation.'

He swore, mildly, and added, 'Much hope there.'

'You can only try.'

They took their teas out and sat on the bench. A swollen globe of pure sunshine lit the horizon red behind the trees and shot shafts of crimson and peach up into hanging wisps of cloud in the pale heavens. It was awe-inspiring. It stilled them for a while, and David appreciated the fact that she could just be quiet and enjoy it with him.

He decided not to tell her that Myfanwy had, again, questioned their rightness for each other.

'Veery Lane Police Station, how may I assist you?'

'Hello, this is David Sourbook. I rang yesterday about graffiti sprayed on my cottage. I was hoping someone would be in touch with me, but no one has.'

She took his details to check and said, 'Don't worry, Mr Sourbook, I'm sure someone will be in touch when they can.'

'Has my complaint been referred to a named officer?'

'Not at the moment.'

'All right. Would it be possible for me to speak to DCI Steve Drane, or Detective Sergeant Alissa Myers?'

'DS Myers should be available. Hold on, please, while I try to connect you.'

There was the usual pause. No music.

'Mr Sourbook, this is DS Myers. What can I do for you?'

'I'd like to know whether we're anywhere near a resolution to the allegations made against me.'

'These things take time, Mr Sourbook.'

'That's all very well for you to say. For me, just waiting, dangling on a thread, it's an extended torture with no end in sight. Do you understand that, Ms Myers? Every day is another anxious wait for news, and no news comes, and so the next day it starts all over again.'

'You're going to have to learn to be patient, Mr Sourbook. Such investigations take time. They have to be done properly.'

'Can you tell me how far you have investigated? Who you've spoken to? What you've discovered? How it's looking?'

'No, I'm sorry,' she said quite firmly. 'I can't reveal any of that as it is an ongoing investigation.'

'Well, Ms Myers, I suggest you have a good look in the *Clarion* this Friday. It might just help you to see what it's like to be at the mercy of your leisurely progress.'

'We will be in touch at the right time, I can assure you,' she said, and the line went dead.

It was on page 18 of the paper. It took up about 40 per cent of the bottom half. The reporter had managed to get a decent picture of him looking at the graffiti, as well as a good picture of the words. The article read:

LOCAL MAN ACCUSED OF ABUSING
TEENAGE BOY

Mr David Sourbook of 27 Lower Lane woke last Monday to find his cottage sprayed with the words, 'Pedo Perve abuser' and 'Kiddie Fiddler'. Mr Sourbook declined to comment on who might have sprayed the words, but Mrs Doreen James, who lives two doors away from him and was among the crowd of people who had gathered at the scene, told our reporter that Mr Sourbook blamed some boys from the church youth group to whom he had recently given a telling-off. Mr Sourbook is a leader at the youth group at St Mark's Church.

Further investigation revealed that a boy who cannot be named for legal reasons has accused Mr Sourbook of abusing him at the youth club on Friday 17th June and that the matter is in the hands of the police. A spokesperson at Veery Lane Police Station refused to comment, as did Rev Colin Barber, the rector of St Mark's Church.

It was Tuesday, 12th July.

The evening, though overcast, was still light at 8.30pm, which was when the rector had managed to squeeze them in. His study was lit by a single side lamp, giving a welcoming illumination to his wall of bookshelves, his great desk and filing cabinet, his desk chair and two light brown armchairs. He offered them the armchairs and went off to make coffees.

'All right, then,' he said, once all were settled. 'Fire away.'

David spoke. 'We're leaving St Mark's until this allegation is settled and will return then only if there are adequate apologies. I feel that the way I've been treated is appalling and someone has to stand up for the little man, the only person who is really being abused here.'

'Yes. I understand. As I told you, David, I am personally completely convinced of your innocence. Myself and Charles Sears are completely bound by the rules currently in force. Your situation *is* appalling. In a case like this where there's no real evidence either way, and a low-value case as far as the police are concerned, they won't find convincing evidence, and it could drag on for who knows how long. Weeks or even months. They might call you back in and try to rattle your cage. They might try to apply a bit of pressure to the two boys. At the end of the day there will be no resolution and the diocese will have to carry out a risk assessment to see if it's safe to let you back in contact with our children and young people. In fact, they'll do that even if you are totally exonerated. And my beliefs about the matter don't count for diddly squat. So if your message is for me, then I'm afraid it's wasted. If your message is for those who hold my lead, I'll happily pass on this latest development with a full explanation of why you feel this way and are taking this action. What about you, Angela?'

'I'm totally with David on this. It's appalling to be treated this way. Someone has to speak up for the person whose rights are being trampled under a stampede of political correctness. I'll go with David and I won't come back until or unless we both come back. And I'm sorry about that because I love St Mark's and owe it a huge amount. But there it is.'

The rector spent a while asking them how they were and listening carefully.

'I hope you come back. You will always be welcome. And I don't disagree in any way with the action you're taking. Something has to change. You, David, shouldn't be made to suffer, now, for the *Church's* failings in the past. Let me pray with you before you go.'

Day after weary day the same hope, the same wait, the same unease, the same disappointment, the same going to bed expecting the same tension tomorrow. An increasingly weary round that gradually wore him down and seemed to destroy all hope or optimism, colouring more and more of each day with anxiety and apprehension.

At least Angela was on holiday from the college now. He'd started to notice that people seemed to be looking at him from time to time, and that made him feel like some disgusting outcast. But he decided to keep his head up and be bold about it. He noticed that having Angela with him made him feel much more secure in those situations. But it wasn't pleasant. Occasionally people seemed to see him and turn to each other and comment, or point. 'That's the paedo guy from the paper whose house got spray-painted.'

Days went into weeks.

And then the phone rang.

'Hello, Mr Sourbook, this is DCI Drane from Veery Lane Police Station. We need to ask you to come in for a further conversation, and I'm scheduling that for this coming Friday, 29th July at 10am. Can you make that?'

'Yes. Do I need to bring anybody? A lawyer?'

'You can bring whoever you like. Friday at 10am at Veery Lane Police Station. Goodbye, Mr Sourbook.'

David's 'goodbye' was cut in half.

He and Angela sat in the little interview room again opposite DCI Drane and DS Myers. The tape machine was started. The usual preliminaries were announced.

'Mr Sourbook, and you, Miss Adams how well do you know Mr Rufus Masters?' Drane said, slightly sourly, David thought.

'Ruf!' he said. 'He was part of a gang of youths that we had the misfortune to bump into as we were delivering church newsletters on the Royal Estate last December, a week before Christmas. They roughed us up a bit and Ruf's dog, Charger, bit me, though Ruf wasn't in charge of it at the time. That was the second time we encountered them, in town. But we were saved by some police who turned up, doing their job.'

'Yes, all right, carry on,' Drane said, more sourly.

'Doing a very good job, so they were.'

'Yes, I get it.'

'Doing the job they were paid to do.'

'I'm doing the job I'm paid to do, Mr Sourbook.'

'Or are you just following orders?'

'You think I'm some kind of Nazi?'

'Yes, actually, that's exactly what I think.'

'That was the exact day we first met,' Angela piped up, pouring oil on the troubled waters.

'I see,' Drane said. 'Please continue with how you both know Rufus Masters.'

'Well,' Angela obeyed, 'a couple of days later we were having a walk on a very snowy and icy day down by the trees and the lake opposite David's house on Lower Lane, and there was Ruf, with Charger, looking very cold and dejected. So I asked him what was the matter and he said Charger had bitten a postal worker, quite badly, and the police had been called, and his mum had thrown him out of their home, and he knew Charger would be put down and he'd be in trouble. So I told him I have some friends, the Grangers, a JP and a GP, who would happily put him up for a while, but only after we'd been up here so he could give himself in. At that point he let Charger off the lead, and the hare-brained thing chased off and fell through the ice into the pond and drowned. David had to rugby-tackle Ruf to prevent him from falling in as well, and then we took him back to David's house as he was wet and cold and in shock. Then we brought him here, then to the Grangers, and after Christmas he was sentenced to a custodial sentence. We wanted to start a youth group for him and his mates, so we waited for him to come out of the Young Offenders Unit and went to find him. We thought he'd be really friendly given all the help we'd given him, but he was really bad-tempered and made it very clear we weren't his friends. But they did come to the youth group.'

'When did you last see Rufus Masters?'

'The night of the allegation.'

'And not since?' Drane pressed.

David spoke. 'No, not since. Not once. Not even a little bit.'

'But it could be alleged that you might have some sway over him.'

'If it were so alleged it would be alleged wrongly. He isn't our friend, despite our assumption that he might be. He lives in his world and has little respect for ours.'

'Even your friends the Grangers.'

Angela said, 'As far as we know he hasn't had any contact with them, either. Where is this leading, anyway?'

Drane looked across at Myers, who said, 'Rufus Masters reported to the rector of St Mark's that the two lads who made the allegation, Scott and Alex, boasted in his hearing of how they had "stitched you up" with a false accusation, and also he heard the whole group boasting of how they had damaged your car and roughed you up while he was still inside.'

'Oh,' David said, immediately heartened.

'We have interviewed Mr Masters and warned him that one of the conditions of his early release was not to be associating with known criminals, and also checked his story. As far as we can tell, it sounds firm.'

'So?' David said.

Drane spoke. 'Of course we don't know – indeed, there is a real question mark over – whether you have been in a position to influence him, but he told the story pretty much as you did and denied that there had been any collusion. We have visited the two boys and their parents or step-parents and discussed it with them, and they have withdrawn the allegation. For now, the case is closed.'

'What do you mean, "for now"?'

'It will remain on file in case of future allegations, of course.'

'Whatever happened to "innocent until proven guilty"? I thought that was the bedrock of our whole legal system.'

'Indeed it is. But safeguarding sometimes requires a more careful approach. In any case, this is the end of our investigations.'

'So I'm completely exonerated?'

'There is no case to answer.'

'So I'm not completely exonerated?'

'No. The complaint was withdrawn. You didn't go to trial. You weren't found innocent. There is no longer a case to answer. But a record of the allegation remains.'

'Did you see the local paper?' David asked. 'They aren't going to print some "no case to answer" follow-up. There's no story in that. "Local man completely exonerated" might be worth a couple of inches, but not this.'

'The local media is not our concern.'

'Nazi.'

It was Sunday, 31st July.

The rector stood at the front of the church in his robes, the choir seated behind him, and after his welcome he deviated from the normal course.

'I'd like to ask two people to come up and join me. David and Angela, please come up.'

David and Angela knew it was coming, and stood beside him on the top step of the chancel.

He explained everything that had happened, in some detail, then he asked, 'And the question is raised – who is really being protected here? The vulnerable, or the church? And when such an approach to our work with children and young people makes us stand away from them, not daring to touch them or show them affection, are *we* not guilty of spiritual neglect by denying them a true expression of the affectionate love of God for them in Jesus Christ? Churches are not schools. Our calling and mission to children and young people is to model and express the love of God, not to convey information, merely.

'David will be assisting the PCC in a thorough review of our safeguarding policy in an attempt to make it a positive rather than a negative document, enabling confidence and affection rather than fear and disengagement. I look forward to that work. I apologise to David and Angela for the way they've been treated, even though we had no freedom to act differently. I absolutely agree that the situation of the accused is wildly underrepresented, and needs to be addressed as a matter of urgency. I welcome them back into our fellowship with open arms and an open heart. As, I trust, do we all.'

As he turned to hug them both, there was a great cheer and the whole congregation stood to applaud, then started crowding forward to greet and embrace them. By the time they could get on with the service it was a quarter of an hour late.

It was Tuesday, 2nd August.

It was a Myfanwy day.

To begin, he told her all about the conversation with the police and the announcement at church. She reacted positively to all that. He told her about how being with Angela made him feel much more confident when he was out and about, when people seemed to be staring at him, or noticing him, at least.

She didn't react positively to that. She said, 'Why do you need Angela for that? Why can't you hold your head up on your own?'

'I don't think you understand how soul-destroying it is. To feel that people all around you are identifying you as some sex pervert freak. I can bear it, but it's awful, and having someone to talk to distracts me from it and enables me to ignore it or maybe just not notice it or imagine it so much.'

'David, you asked me about levels, a while ago. "How many levels of hell are there in a person?" What did you mean by that?'

'Well, it's just that, in the last seven months or so, I've had to confront so many... excavations of my soul, revealing so much depression, and guilt, and spiritual oppression, and anger (apparently), and darkness. And suicidal desires, and deception, loss, discovery (much of it unexpected and unwanted), and even my own bitterness and nastiness and soulless lack of kindness. And I'm bound to wonder – where does it end? *Does* it end? Because I'm not sure how much more I can take. Frankly.'

'It is a list and a half. Much of it revealed in your dreams, but not all. Where do you think it's leading you?'

'Leading me? Is it the gracious Hand of God leading me into revelations and strengths I hadn't imagined? It doesn't feel like it.'

'You know I don't share your faith, but I do understand it, and the role it plays. So, laying God aside for a moment, where do you think all this revelation is leading you?'

'I suppose… to being free. Free of all the things that have tied me down and limited my life.'

'Limited your life. I like that. What things have been limiting your life?'

'Depression. Depression makes you lose some of the rooms of your mind, and you can't necessarily get them back. And lack of concern for my fellow man. A basic lack of any kindness. I was a soulless and solitary grouch. I'm so much more in touch with people now. Depression had me trapped. And I was looking in all the wrong places. I was looking in outer space and listening to some nameless "yearning" so when the person I needed came along I couldn't even recognise it. I see people now. Really see them. More and more I see them – how they really are. And I've stopped being some wet wimp in my relationship with Angela and become a real partner. Firm and stable and able to stand up for myself, making it easier for her to stand up for herself. Which, you were right, she did need to.'

'But is she helping you to stand up for yourself, or making you dependent on her? Is she a comfort blanket, preventing you from really engaging with these issues you face?'

He was annoyed. Here we go again. He had expected this, and it stung. 'People need people,' he said. 'Do you want me to return to being some kind of hermit, licking his wounds in his solitary cave? Angela has opened up vistas to me, and relationships, and faith. And I'm opening up things to her.'

'Are you?' Myfanwy asked, seriously. 'I see you overcoming on level after level. I see the levels of hell falling before you. I see something special in you that will help and engage and enable other people even without you being trained. I think you have a unique gift that is being honed and shaped by these necessary pains. I see greatness in you. But Angela stops you standing on your own two feet.'

'Don't you do that? If she does, by her support, then don't you, even more?' He knew it was a slightly lame argument.

'No, I'm trying to get you to stand up for yourself.'

'You're making me dependent on you, rather than her. On Angela.'

'That isn't my intention.'

'I think I need to stop seeing you.' He had come with that in mind.

'Why?'

'Because of the way you keep challenging my relationship with Angela.'

'I believe you need me to challenge that relationship. I think she holds you back from all you could become. I believe you will end up frustrated and resentful of each other.'

David stood. 'This is our last session. I am very grateful for all the ways you've helped me. But I have made a decision.'

She stood also, and faced him, then walked over to stand right in front of him. 'I've never pushed you to choose between me and Angela.'

David saw a tremor of sadness in the shape of her mouth. Like she might cry.

'Haven't you?' he said. 'I think to be fair to her, I need to separate from you.'

'Well, I don't believe we're finished.'

David noted the ambiguity of 'we're finished'. She seemed to be wanting to hug him, but he couldn't believe she would. Then she did. She stepped forward and put her arms round him, and held on.

'You'll be back,' she said, still holding him. 'But at least I won't have you staring at my knees twice a week.'

'Trying not to stare at your knees twice a week. Isn't this highly inappropriate?' he asked.

She put her hands up to his shoulders and pushed him away but kept her hands in place. With a steady and frightening stare, she said, 'Be careful.'

'Of what?'

'Be careful of Micky.'

He was speechless with astonishment. She watched his face.

'Micky's been dead these nearly sixty years.'

'Not in you. In you she's still alive. And she's not as much your friend as you think she is.'

'Are you mad?' he said.

'Be careful.'

PART THREE

PART THREE

CHAPTER TWENTY-ONE

It was Monday, 15th August.

A hot Mediterranean sun beat down upon them even as they sat at breakfast outside a small café near her hotel in Palma Nova, Majorca.

Across the road lay the wide beach with palm trees at the road-edge, then a huge expanse of clean, golden sand, and then pure blue water bedecked with white vessels of many kinds. Sun-seekers were already batting small balls back and forth or lying half-shaded by big, straw umbrellas. Young women wearing only the skimpiest of thongs strolled back and forth or lay on the sand, and he wondered at the lack of natural shame that allowed them to do that. Maybe it was his age. He certainly wasn't looking at them – not even their knees!

The cloudless brightness of the sky was a wonder of the natural world, and the sun gave crisp shadows and blinding reflections. They were having coffees and *ensaïmadas*, a local pastry-like confection, dusted with powdered sugar. Angela was dressed in very short shorts and a T-shirt saying, 'I (heart) the sun', while he was in longer, men's shorts and a short-sleeved shirt with buttons and a top pocket, because he preferred that sort of shirt and liked pockets. His shorts had six of them as well – for wallet, money, keys, camera, his little box of pills and so on. It left him free from the encumbrance of a jacket or any sort of bag. Angela had a small over-the-shoulder bag in sand-yellow.

They'd arrived at Palma airport on the Friday three days ago and were starting to feel relaxed and settled in. She hadn't lied about the freckles – well, she didn't lie. Her honesty was one of the things he most loved and treasured about her. A couple of days in the sun and a broad streak of them went across her nose from cheek to cheek, and blonde highlights had appeared in her hair. With her brown legs and cheery face she looked a treat. He'd brought his gran's ring with him. The only question was the timing.

Today they were taking their hire car into the central plain for a visit to some of the towns, in particular Santa Margalida. Angela had told him about the great church and the paved area beside it that looked out at some height over the surrounding fields, which in this weather roasted in the sun and was absolutely breathtaking in its panoramic stillness. He could hardly wait. This was going to be the most perfect day ever. He would remember it for the rest of his life.

It was her turn to drive and he rested his hand on her thigh. It seemed appropriate in this relaxed situation and hot weather. He reflected that for a woman of her age, she still had very nice legs. Firm and smooth and soft. She was altogether a vision of loveliness, but he didn't stare. She hated that.

'I know what you're thinking,' she said.

'That's a clever trick. Prove it to me.'

'You're thinking I've got very nice legs but you mustn't stare.'

He laughed.

'So you know you've got very nice legs.'

'I like yours.'

He looked down at them. 'You can hardly see them.'

'I've seen them. Those shorts are not as demure and protective of your modesty as you think!'

'You've been staring up my shorts?'

'Constantly,' she said, smiling her cheeky smile. 'Your legs are muscly and smooth and faintly hairy. They're not old man's legs – all stick-like and bent. Well, not yet!'

The excellent motorway network quickly took them past Palma and onto the recently built east–west motorway, but as soon as possible they turned off that onto the small roads and the sparsely populated centre of the island.

What sped by were fields of gold and dried-out light-brown earth, with scrubby bushes and white farmhouses, hedges of stones and occasional gaggles of goats. Groves of olive trees stood in small gatherings, their trunks surrounded by scattered chunks of rock on the hard earth. The high sun that bathed them was at the same time threatening and glorious.

They passed through tiny villages, each with a church and a café bar and a few houses, occasionally seeing old women dressed entirely in black, and old men, unshaven, smoking, in shirts and trousers, often a bit bent, sometimes sporting a cap to spare their ageing eyesight.

David could see the imposing, tall, rectangular church building and tower in Santa Margalida over the low fields long before they began the ascent to the little town. It stood like a spiritual guardian over the plain, which, no doubt, was exactly the point. They navigated the narrow streets and parked in the large town square, finding a safe spot to leave the white hire car. A coffee in a bar in the square under the parasols refreshed them, and they stared in wonder at an ancient olive tree with many holes in its thick trunk. Then they set off on foot to the church. All the houses seemed to be a very pale pink. Many were old, some had an internal courtyard; all had shuttered windows and doors in painted wood to keep the heat out. The road had a series of small trees in a line that led up to the big open area in front of the church itself.

When they arrived at the church, they stood and wondered at such a large building for such a small town. They went inside for a few moments, awed at the detail and splendour of the many statues and paintings, altars and ancient pews, in a refreshing coolness as the heat was kept out by the thick stones of its construction.

But soon they were outside again and standing against the low wall, three to four feet high, of the paved area to its side, staring over the fields and villages of the plain. In the near-distance on the left side of the view were low hills, looking green, but more directly in front, in the far distance, were mountains in their bluish-grey haze. She had brought a wide-brimmed, floppy hat in off-white for the relentless sun. He, a straw hat with a less-wide edging.

They stood in hushed reverence at the silence of the bristling cauldron before and below them. They could see for miles around, and distant sounds were wafted to them on the air that arches sound high and far when so hot. Angela went and sat on a seat near to the church building, but David needed to stand at the wall and watch. No one else was there with them at this highest hour of the day. No locals would be so foolish. It quietened him. It pulled at him. Such emptiness. A sense of something 'out there' in that dangerous, invisible fire. A yearning. Just like the old yearning. Not so strong, but definitely there. Definitely here.

He leaned his hands on the wall as his back began to ache, and after a while Angela rejoined him there.

'You OK?' she said.

'Hmm? Oh, yes, fine. You standing up to the heat?'

'Wilting a bit. You look like you'd stand here all day. Are you OK?'

'Sure. I love that view. It's just like you said. But it is somewhat energy-sapping. Let's walk back to the square and get some lunch.'

'Good plan. You're buying.'

'Did you see the bike hire shop? As we came into the square?'

'No.'

'We must look at it.'

'Are you feeling suicidal?'

'Not especially. But what better way to get into that fabulous countryside for an hour or two?'

'OK,' she said reluctantly. 'We can look.'

The shop was just shutting for siesta but hired them two bikes, sold them two plastic water bottles for a euro each, and filled them with water for nothing. The hire included helmets. Still full from Majorcan bread with tomatoes and cheese, olives and

234

Serrano ham, they set off downwards through the little streets to the flat fields and small, dusty roads below. Angela brought the satnav from the car in the bag slung over her shoulder.

Once they were moving and the air was flowing around them, it was quite cool, as David had suspected. He led the way despite knowing nothing about the geography, and she cycled about ten yards behind him.

It was magical. They met hardly any traffic and pedalled the flat lanes easily, looking over stone walls or squeezed in by high hedges. He was so happy he began to say hello to the creatures they encountered.

'Hello, bird. Hello, bee. Hello, flies. Oh! Hello, snake!'

A medium-sized snake, about four to five feet long and a good two inches thick, was curled up on the right side of the road, and he had to swerve out into the middle to give it a wide berth. Just at that moment a car came round the bend at an unreasonable speed. Both he and the car had to adjust swiftly, and the car driver shouted something at him in Castellano as he sped past.

'Hello, car!' David heard from behind him as he cycled away from the snake. He loved the quirky sense of humour they shared.

'Have you ever seen that before?' he shouted back.

'No.'

He drove back slowly, following as much a country route as possible until they drew near to Palma and then they had to join the motorway again. After that they were back at the hotel in twenty minutes, seeing the high and magnificent Palma cathedral and the busy Bay of Palma where yachts jostled with boats as they went.

They were both tired, and after a *zumo naranja natural* from a bar (it was becoming his favourite phrase as it meant a freshly squeezed orange juice which was fragrantly fantastic), they separated for a rest in their respective hotels.

He'd found a nice restaurant in Port d'Andratx at the western tip of the island for their special meal that evening. Not that she knew yet just how special it was to be. Just that they would meet at six to drive out for a walk and a drink and then the meal. And that she should look a bit smart.

He lay on his bed in his nice, airy room, with the air conditioning on, and felt all warm and happy. It had been a fabulous morning and afternoon, a perfect holiday day, and there was the prospect of a lovely meal and a very memorable evening ahead. Now he could have a nice rest. He texted Angela. 'I love you. See you later.'

She texted back, 'I love you. Can't wait. Smart clothes out!'

This was indeed shaping up to be the best day of his whole life. A day he would forget hardly a moment of. Had he ever felt so justifiably happy?

He drove, as he reckoned he might need a snifter this evening and then she could drive back. The ring was in its box in his pocket.

As soon as he could he got onto the coast road. They both loved the views of the sea as the sun still hung fairly high and the day remained hot. Sky, sun, sea, sand, all the holiday 'Ss', and Angela beside him, beside him for ever. It was so good. She chirped away happily about this and that because they were away from it all. All the things that had hurt and frustrated them.

He checked the small box in his trouser pocket from time to time. Smart trousers. A light cream colour, and nicely tailored. He was very proud of them, and the tan-coloured, tailored jacket carefully laid out on the back seat. The car might be an economy model, but once out of it they were going to look like the visiting glitterati. She wore a knee-length and very attractive skirt of a similar colour to his trousers, and a lovely cotton blouse of a pale, sunshine yellow. Her hair fell free, as usual, straggles by her tanning and freckled cheeks, blonde streaks throughout.

She had her hand on his thigh, warm and tender.

Sunshine blessed them and Mediterranean evening views uplifted them. New experiences encouraged them, and the encountering of a snake earlier in the day excited them. A future that looked and felt like this emboldened him.

They were going to eat traditional paella and drink traditional sangria in this rather nice quayside restaurant to make it especially memorable. He'd been told it was a quality place with a wonderful sea view from the tables under the awning by the water, one of which he'd booked.

They parked up at the car park off the road and walked into the town, right by all the fishing boats moored at the high, concrete edge over the water two metres below. The quayside was strewn with nets and floats. The boats were real working ones, doubtless due to be out again in a few hours.

As they strolled, hand in hand, he continued to feel uncommonly happy, and checked again the little bulge in his trouser pocket. He was carrying the rather smart and unnecessary tan jacket over his shoulder.

As they progressed along the dockside, the boats became more pleasure boats in white, with masts and swept lines and multiple decks, though the really big ones were all further out in the bay. It looked fabulous, and the various restaurants along the quayside all seemed to have outside seating under awnings by the water. They found theirs and stood until a waiter approached them, as most of the tables were taken. He checked their booking and seated them right by the water, holding their chairs for them to sit and unfolding their linen napkins for them. He asked what they'd like to drink, and when they said, 'Sangria' his face lit up and he told them the house sangria was a real speciality. He fetched two leather-covered menus from a central station and left them with those while he went inside the restaurant, which was, as they all were, over the other side of the pathway, which also seemed to be a road that led nowhere much beyond where they were sitting. David realised it was the road for driving the catch away in the morning, the other way, towards Andratx itself.

Back came the jug of sangria. It was in a lovely, curved, fat jug and was dark red with oranges and other fruits floating in it. They ordered the traditional paella for two before the waiter could disappear again. And then they sat, looking out over the water and towards the land they could see over the other side of it. The main entrance to the harbour was to their left.

They talked of what a fabulous day it had been and what a wonderful time they were having and what a beautiful island it was, and David was just beginning to register what a large table this was for just two people when the paella arrived, and his eyes were opened. It was in an enormous, shallow, black pan, which one waiter carried as another cleared the table for it and helped him set it down. Then he put two plates down, and asked if he should serve some out, to which Angela replied in the negative. They beamed with pride, draped their white cloths over their forearms and wished them to enjoy it, before walking away.

David looked in astonishment. A sea of yellow rice was dotted with prawns, mussels, other shellfish, tentacles, peas, long green beans, smaller white beans, and lemon wedges on top. A spoon lay beside it for serving, which Angela took up and said, 'Anything you don't like?'

'Being so full I can't move! No, all looks good to me,' David replied, and she served him as much as she dared, then herself.

They lifted their tall glasses of the sangria, chinked them together and she said, 'To a wonderful holiday!'

He added, 'With you!' and they drank. It was unexpectedly powerful.

'That's got something in it!' David observed.

She laughed. 'I'd better be careful.'

The paella was hot, tasty, dangerous in parts (he found he didn't much like the tentacles) and very satisfying. As they slowed in eating-speed, he said, 'We should be thinking about the future. We're not getting any younger.'

'No one is,' Angela replied.

'No, but it happens faster as you get to our age.'

'You mean "not getting any younger" happens faster?'

'Exactly. It does.'

'Well, laying aside that that makes no actual logical sense, I suppose I'd have to say I know what you mean. And that it's... moderately true.'

He laughed out loud. 'Moderately true! That's funny. The perfect repost. I love the way our minds work together.'

'So do I.' She reached out for his hand past the huge pan, and they held them together.

'So, by the future you mean... ?'

'I mean getting married.'

'Oh! Well, surely you should consider such a serious matter when at home where it has to work, not in an "escape" reality which is hardly reality.'

He knew exactly what she was going to say, and replied, 'Some say distance gives perspective.'

'True. True. But you've rather sprung this on me.'

'No, I haven't. I've been dropping hints for weeks. And I haven't just thrown myself at your feet, ring in hand.'

'Also moderately true. At least.'

'Should I interpret this as reluctance?' His heart hammered against his sternum bone.

'No, no, not at all.' She squeezed his hand and held on tight again. 'I want to marry you. I see us as being married. I love you and I would die if I lost you.'

'OK, then.' He put his fork down. 'What was it drew you to me that night last Christmas by the pond? I've never asked you that. I hope it wasn't that I looked like some lame duck that needed saving. Especially when I think about how you tended to treat me like a child sometimes. And what were you doing out there on your own by the pond at night a week before Christmas?'

She looked a bit troubled, then put her fork down (a good sign?) and said, 'I didn't feel well and I went for a walk. I was feeling in a very fragile state that night. I'd just had a big bust-up with Thelia. You remember I told you that she set Andrew's regime and I didn't agree with some elements of it. We'd had a big argument over it. So you see, in answer to your first question, I was in need of some company. And I felt like the heart condition might be starting up. I got upset and then anxious, which can do that. Fresh air and a gentle walk can help. So that's why I was there and why I spoke to you. It wasn't an act of kindness to some poor, lost fellow so much as the need of some human company.'

A dreadful realisation hit him. 'Hang on a minute – you told me that you never mentioned the heart condition to me because you tended to forget about it. So that was a lie. You'd been very aware of it just days before you told me that, on Christmas Eve in the hospital.'

She looked him in the eye, and a tear began to form. 'I know. I'm sorry.'

Something very hot flared inside him. 'But that means you lied to me from the very start. From the beginning of our relationship you lied to me. What else have you lied to me about?'

'Nothing.' She looked miserable.

'Nothing. How can I believe that?'

'I don't know.'

He felt like he was standing in the waves of the sea and an unexpectedly big one had just broken against him and made him gasp for air. And it wasn't sea-cold, but confusion-hot. 'But I've always really respected your honesty and integrity. I've depended on it. I feel like… a big chunk of the wall of our house just fell away.'

He felt like saying 'I can't do this' and walking out. But he wasn't going to. Not now. Not now he knew he had the right to be angry and, therefore, to stay angry. He recognised that that didn't sound like it made logical sense, but somehow, somewhere, it was right.

In fact, not only was he not going to react that way; he wasn't going to react and spoil the evening at all. For her sake, at the very least.

He said, 'I'm sorry I said that about "what else?". I think I've probably been less than honest with you sometimes. And you had every right not to tell me about some condition you had, when we'd only just met.'

'Yes, but I had no right to lie about it, which I did.'

He looked at her and made himself squeeze her hand to stop her looking so sad. And he reckoned this was one of the happiest days of her life, too, and he wasn't about to spoil that for her. He smiled, and she smiled her lovely smile back.

'Don't be sad,' he said. 'Let's forget about it.'

'I love you,' she replied.

But the ring stayed in his pocket.

CHAPTER TWENTY-TWO

Walking back from her hotel and the parked car through the streets still full of light and activity, he brooded. He wanted to express the anger he felt, by some act of destruction or rebellion. But nothing that would actually be immoral or illegal or upset the Lord too much.

He passed a vape shop, then decided to go in. He bought one that tasted of vanilla. Outside, he sucked on it and released a huge cloud of white vapour into the street. A passing couple frowned at him, and commented in German.

It made his lungs feel strange, like a very slight sense of drowning. Well, so what. He took another huge draw and released another fragrant cloud. Now he felt tight in there. Like asthma. He refused to worry, and walked on towards his hotel.

He also refused to blame, curse or belittle her. Her.

Sprawling on his balcony in a white plastic chair, polluting the world with yet more vanilla vapour, he wondered at the world he was creating. Could he trust her? Should he trust her? Where was God in this? He took the box out of his pocket and flipped open the top with a careless flick of his finger. The ring fell out and began to roll on the concrete floor. The third-storey concrete floor, towards the edge. Over the edge where there were trees and bushes at the side of the small garden area, where he would never find it if it were to fall. He watched it roll.

Maybe it was a sign. Maybe Myfanwy was so totally wrong because in fact he would have to be stronger to deal with Angela, rather than finding her a comfort blanket. Surely there was truth in that. Well, no, some people did just let their partner comfort them. But that didn't seem at all like him and Angela. He and Angela. Them. Her.

'Lord, what was that tonight? I know that through the whole incident with the boys you have made us really strong together. Answered that prayer. That dangerous prayer I prayed. She stuck with me throughout and I trust her. That is, I trusted her.'

Slowly, gently, tenderly even, a voiceless voice, a wordless word spoke to him. 'It isn't Bart.'

It isn't Bart? What isn't that faithful bear? That friendly comforter to the lost and lonely. What isn't him? Isn't he?

David stared out towards the sea, too dark now to actually image, but shore lights and boat lights twinkled under a million stars. He recalled that old sense of yearning on the shimmering plain, and it was as if the scene in front of him opened up to reality. And he knew that 'it isn't Bart' was the same message as before. God telling him, 'It isn't Bart who will always be with you, by your side, watching over you; it's Me'.

He recalled the question – is Bart a sort of sign of God, a pointer to His presence? Or is Bart a threat to putting his trust in God alone? 'It isn't Bart' suggested the latter.

Yes, well, that had better not mean Bart had to go. The faithful bear. He hadn't done anything wrong. Not a thing.

So, OK, it isn't Bart, but it is You, Lord. My faithful friend and comforter. What? Does that mean to tell me I don't need Angela either?

That frightened him. He did need Angela. But not at any cost. The realisation crept upon him that because of the path he was on, he really did need God more. Jesus more. The Holy Spirit more.

But if God's purpose was for him and Angela to be together, then that was fine.

Was it God's purpose?

'Is that Your purpose, Lord God of the stars and the seas and the light and the dark and the endless universe and The Yearning? Because if it is, let it be, and if not, then not.'

A peace came over him. Almost like a dreamy sleep. He might need that tonight.

'It isn't Bart.'

'OK, Lord, I know I'm not marrying Bart, but what's the message here?'

He listened. Nothing. A gentle night breeze stirred the bushes below him. He watched into the darkness, and waited.

'OK, so, it isn't Bart; it's You, to be my faithful comforter. So maybe I need to be that to Angela. A faithful friend. And your faithful friendship means that You forgive me, constantly and totally. So I have to forgive her, constantly and totally. Aha. Every marriage needs that, surely. On and on and on, forgiveness of each other. Who doesn't become cranky, awkward, demanding, needy, opinionated, selfish, self-righteous? She's needed to forgive me when I've been hurtful – very hurtful sometimes. And I haven't been 100 per cent honest with her. There are things I've kept hidden away. So, OK, I've put great store in her honesty and integrity. Well, maybe there's times when she feels the need to cover some things over. She hadn't done any wrong. She kept to herself about the heart condition because she didn't want me to know. Yet. Well? Then I asked her, and she lied. So that challenges the picture of her I've made up. I can't easily reconcile that. But I can forgive her. Completely and totally.

'But I'm still left feeling she's not quite the person I thought she was, in a very important way. That's my problem. There's my problem.'

He brooded. He stood, walked over, picked up the ring and put it back in the box. It was unharmed. He put the box on the table and threw the vape on the floor and crushed it with his foot. Stupid thing. Stupid, childish reaction.

'I shouldn't have asked her what else she's lied to me about. Partly because that's logically pointless, but more because that's unnecessarily undermining of her. What else do I think she's lied to me about? Nothing. I think she may have not always told me everything about everything, but that's her right. And if we get married, the "no secrets" thing is silly. Of course we have secrets. She doesn't want to know all the bad and stupid things I've ever done. Nor do I want to know hers. And, come to think of it, she was lying in a hospital bed just come back from the very jaws of death when she told me that about her heart condition, in answer to a question she perhaps wasn't ready for. Has she ever deliberately and in a premeditated fashion lied to me? No. She hasn't.

'Lord,' he said, 'if I'm not to be a terrible hypocrite, I have to forgive her, Angela. Actually, maybe not even forgive her; just accept the circumstances of what she said to me and let it go. Yes, that. She did no wrong. Maybe that is a form of forgiveness, I don't know. Not usually. Anyway, she has no case to answer. No complaint to satisfy. And with Your blessing I will ask her to marry me. Not tomorrow, nor the next day. No, Thursday. Seeing as today's opportunity had been missed, Thursday must be next in line. Because it's the 18th. Eight months to the day since we first met. That fateful day. When my life got turned upside down and the ground was littered with change. Clever. Ha ha. Change fell out of my pockets as I was held upside down, change was all around, but was the change useless litter or valuable coin?

> 'You turned me upside down.
> The ground was litt'red with change.
> Even now I'm not sure,
> Which way up is less strange.

'Hmm. Has possibilities maybe.'

It was Tuesday, 16th August.

The plan was to travel across the island to Cala Ratjada and swim in the sea, then take a 'Glass Bottomed Boat' tour in the afternoon.

By 11am when they arrived at the beach, the heat of the day was well under way. They were able to park just across the road from the beach and walk past a large beach bar onto the sand. It was hot underfoot. They found a nice spot, not too crowded, over to the left, next to where the path led round to the town centre and shops. They stripped down to their swimming costumes (which they had put on under their outer clothes earlier). Angela was in a lemon-yellow one-piece with green, diagonal stripes. He was in plain blue swimming shorts. They put on their goggles and started into the water. It was cold, but not sufficient to cause any discomfort. Soon they were diving below the surface and looking at the white and grey fish all around them, many a good six inches or more long. David loved it. The fish didn't shoot off, but happily allowed him among them as long as he didn't get too close. He'd never done anything quite like it before.

After the swim, they lay down on large beach towels in the shelter of a beach parasol stuck into the sand. Still wet, they lay looking at each other, maybe a foot apart.

'You look lovely,' he said.

'A tad thick around the middle,' she replied, grabbing an inch and just about managing to make it wobble.

'No. You can't expect to have a waist like a twenty-year-old. Anyway, I've got a proper belly.'

'Of course you have. At least it's not a beer belly. It's just a natural pot.'

They laughed at the state of themselves.

'Anyway, you're a lovely shape,' he said, 'very desirable.'

'Shall I reprimand you for putting too much value on external appearance, or take the compliment?' she said, grinning. She lay back on the towel. 'I'll take the compliment. And you are a very handsome fellow, and not in bad shape at all.'

'I'll do, then.'

'You'll do.' She leaned up again.

He leaned across and kissed her, enjoying the feel of her skin. He edged over closer and pressed himself against her, all the way down, though his clinging, wet, swimming shorts came down to his knees. She didn't try to shuffle away, as he half-expected. She felt really lovely – soft and smooth and firm and enjoyably curvaceous.

When they parted, she said, 'I'm serious about you.'

'Angela, I intend to ask you to marry me. When you think we've talked about it enough.'

'I hope you're not expecting me to give the answer before you ask the question. That's the coward's way out.'

'No, but I recall our conversation about me just asking or both of us discussing it first, and you were more inclined to the latter course.'

'I was.' She looked him hard in the eye. 'When you pray about it, what leading do you get?'

'Nothing very specific. I believe that along with God's guidance there's still the responsibility to think it through and make a wise choice. I certainly get no sense of being directed away from you. I can't see a future without you. I think we're really good for each other. I know I love you. And we seem to fit together – our faith, our sense of humour, our fun with words, my relationship with Andrew – lots of things.'

She looked at him, not intensely, maybe slightly sadly, or just thinking. Hard to read, in that moment. 'I love you. I've never loved anyone like I love you and that's the truth. You complete me. I respect your intellect and I've seen you grow in kindness and come to faith and overcome some incredible obstacles. And you've been very patient with me and very courageous. And I think we're incredibly strong together. And, like you, I get no sense that the Lord is at all unhappy with any of that. I think we have His blessing.'

He leaned over and kissed her again.

'But I'm not promising what my answer would be,' she said, with her cheeky grin.

They dozed for a while and, before getting dressed and finding some lunch, asked Jesus to guide them about their future together.

The boat cruise from the town's harbour was a revelation of the shallow waters around Cala Ratjada. They drove back in the late afternoon and went for a siesta in their hotels, then ate at a lovely restaurant in the small town of Calvia. Angela was thrilled at the views back towards the coast, which gave David ideas.

On Wednesday 17th August they drove into Palma and took the scenic old railway up to Soller, high in the mountains. It was a steam engine pulling a train of rickety, wooden carriages. After a light lunch they took the tram down to Port de Soller and walked up and down the waterfront until it was time to retrace their rickety steps. Once again, she was entranced by the mountain views, which confirmed his thinking about the restaurant he'd found for Thursday night.

Thursday, 18th August. The big day. The new big day. No matter.

They'd decided to stay local that day, and strolled along the shops, then played some mini-golf at a fabulous place with three courses and waterfalls and fish, which took the rest of the morning. Mushroom omelettes with salad followed, and a lazy walk back along the beach, paddling in the sea, watching the very energetic beach volleyball, sitting under the palm trees and chatting, chatting, chatting all the way. Hand in hand they strolled, and David got more and more to feeling that this was the most natural thing in the world, and so was the next step.

After siestas, and later that evening, he drove them up into the mountains and to the restaurant he'd found that had a balcony that felt it was like the edge of the world. They got a table right against the railings and looked out in wonder at the coastline stretching to either side, the tiny boats so far below them, and the horizon that gave the sense that they could see the curvature of the earth. Because the drop beneath the balcony was so steep, they could see nothing directly below them and it seemed like some utter precipice, hanging off an unforgiving edge of mountainous rock.

The sky was blue, the sea was shades of blue and green, and the coastline to north and south was rugged brown and green. The sunset, when it came, was in the fullest and least obstructed view imaginable. Perfect.

Angela was wearing a very airy, cream-coloured dress, which let some light through when it was behind her, but he wasn't about to complain. He was in his smart jacket and trousers again, with a crisp, short-sleeved, white shirt. He felt he looked the part. When he took the jacket off and hung it on the back of the chair his arms looked really brown.

Her eyes were on him, all the time, as if she knew what was coming. Such intense affection. Such warm attention to him.

They didn't serve paella – it wasn't that sort of place.

When they were sat at their table, drinks menus in hand, she looked at the incredible view over the endless ocean and said, 'Now that is something!'

'I was just thinking, "That is something else!"'

'Well, it is,' she affirmed.

'You look lovely,' he said.

'Here we are all smart again,' she answered, like she was on to him. How transparent was he?

They ordered orange-juice-and-lemonades, and looked over the food menus. He ordered a cheese salad, feeling the need for something light, while she ordered half a roast chicken and fries, obviously not feeling any such need. How she stayed so trim when she did eat quite a lot, he reflected, and did little proper exercise, was a wonder. It must be her metabolism. Which is a bit like a doctor telling you you have a virus. Sounds good but tells you nothing.

As they ate, the sun began to set, and glowed blood red on the horizon, turning tiny, high, wispy clouds peach and apricot, and reflecting off the distant sea in orange and purple and gold. It changed as the dusk progressed, and he knew that when the dusk was fully come, that was his moment. He felt really nervous. Eating was hard.

'You all right?' she said, looking up from her carnivorous feast.

'Hmm? Yes, fine, not just very hungry.'

'Not just?'

He laughed. 'Just not.'

'Relax,' she said. 'Enjoy the view. Have a whisky. I can drive back.'

Busted, surely. She knew.

The lights along the balcony canopy glowed bright, and he knew his moment had come.

'Angela,' he began, 'I have something to ask you. Perhaps you'd like to stop devouring that poor bird and wipe your hands.'

'If it wasn't going to be eaten it never would have existed,' she defended herself for enjoying meat so much. 'There would be, like, ten chickens in the whole world happily pecking away and no breeding of them to eat. So as long as it had a happy life, we're both content.'

'OK. Point taken. I love meat too. Are you clean? All right. Here we go.'

'Here we go?'

'Don't make it harder than it is.'

'Oh, it's something hard. Are you ill? Leaving me? Have you run out of money? Is it a confession of something awful?'

'All four. Stop it. Just listen.'

He took the little box out of his pocket and put it on the table. She looked at it, then up again into his eyes.

'Angela, today is exactly eight months since we met, though it didn't take me eight months to fall in love with you and to realise how wonderful you are. Look around you. Another dusk. Look at the sky, the sea, the sunset, the colours of dusk all around us. See how high we are. You have lifted my life up, so much higher than it was or ever would have been. Angela Adams, I cannot live without you, I love you tenderly and passionately, I want to marry you. Will you marry me?'

He flipped open the ring box as he said the question. She clasped both his hands and the box on the table and her face glowed with happiness. Her eyes sparkled in some reflected light, and she said, 'David Sourbook, I was beginning to wonder if you'd ever ask. I suspected you were my angel, and you are. Sometimes it's seemed like I'm the one who's "OK" and you're the one who's "Not OK", but that simply isn't true. I am awed at your strength and courage, and your insight and wisdom. You have gifts yet hardly seen. I love you with all my heart and I respect you with all my mind, and yes, I will marry you.'

He took the ring from the box and slid it on her finger. Applause broke out from around them. Glasses were raised and 'Well done' and 'Congratulations' called out. Somebody even said, 'A lovely young couple', which was heartening.

The waiters didn't know, but quickly brought them a bottle of champagne in an ice bucket, all smiles and congratulations as well.

They toasted each other, and she looked at the ring on her finger. 'Oh, David, it's lovely,' she said.

They kissed over the table, and more applause was set off.

'Goodness! What a night!' she said.

'I wanted it to be very special,' David said.

'You managed that!'

'You knew it was coming.'

'Did I?'

'OK.'

They sipped and looked at the view. She'd lost interest in the remains of her chicken. They looked into each other's eyes like teenagers in love and David's heart swelled and throbbed at the sight of her. His fiancée.

'I have two conditions,' she said.

'Oh?'

'First. In the marriage service you must promise to obey me.'

He laughed. 'I thought that went out with the old service.'

'The "old service", as you so casually call it, the 1662 Book of Common Prayer, is licensed for use for all perpetuity. Other services may come and go, but it will always remain.'

'Sounds like we'll be using it in heaven.'

She smiled a broad smile. 'Any good Anglican will tell you we will.'

'And the second?'

'Is serious. From now on we must aim to pray together every day. Even if only briefly.'

'I agree. I have one condition,' he said.

'Oh? OK, what is that, then?'

He leaned in and whispered, 'No sex until we're actually married!'

She kissed him. 'Agreed.'

She stared at the ring and turned her hand to make the light shine off it.

'It was my grandmother's ring. You'll like this,' he said, holding her finger up for her to look at it. 'She called it the "Last Supper Ring" because the ruby in the middle is Jesus, giving them the red wine and about to shed His blood on the cross, and the twelve small diamonds are the apostles. It's worth quite a lot of money.'

'Oh, now you've got me worried. Can I take it off when it might get lost?'

'You must *never* take it off!' he said, very firmly, then he smiled. 'Of course you can.'

'I love you,' she said. 'You are such fun!'

David was quite sure nobody had ever said anything like that to him before in all his years. It felt like this was, finally, the resolution of all his troubles.

Could it really be, at last? Why not?

CHAPTER TWENTY-THREE

It was Monday, 22nd August.

He'd brought a little camping stool so he could sit right at the edge and watch, and wonder, and wait. The three holy 'Ws'.

Heat blasted down in searing waves, threatening to burn up the whole plain before he could find what he was looking for.

Angela sat behind him, in the shade of the church, but he had his hat and that would have to do for now.

A dog barked, sounding like a universe away, and its sound was carried high on the curving air and dropped onto the great balcony where he sat. Was that all it was, this yearning? Was it The Yearning, or just something like it? That's what he'd come back here to find out.

After half an hour, Angela came up to him and said, 'I'm going to walk back to the café and get a coffee. I'll see you there when you're done. Unless I start to feel I can't wait any longer – like it's getting dark, or the café is closing, then I'll come up to get you.'

She leaned down and kissed him on the cheek, very tenderly.

'OK, my love,' he responded. 'See you later.'

'Not too much later. I'd prefer "soon".'

'See you sooooon.'

She went away. He turned and watched her go. So precious. His fiancée.

Now, focus. Or un-focus. Whatever he used to do. Maybe just watch it and enjoy it and let it take him up and in. Yes, that.

He waited. He looked at the scene and was awed again at the sense of stillness, and the heat. And how it seemed to make everything seem very near, or very far away – he wasn't entirely sure which. And the stillness seemed to enter into him and touch him somewhere very deep. It lifted him. Exalted him like he could fly up and be part of it. Like the sound that curved, he knew as a physics teacher, in the heated layers of air, and came back down sounding far from its source. That gave the feeling of distance. But more than the distance involved. Great distance. And something inside him did react to it. Like he was being called. Like the old 'The Yearning' he used to feel on his bench looking at the sunset in the dusk. The Yearning that had so subsided, even disappeared, since his journeys of relationship, self-discovery and faith in these recent months. The Yearning he really missed.

Well, here was something very like it. Its younger brother. And it felt good.

He submerged himself in it, let it wash over him, closed his eyes and heard its call, and was greatly heartened by the fact that whatever it truly was, it was still there. In part, it was divine. But what else?

It was Wednesday, 24th August.

The holiday was coming towards an end, with their flight back on the coming Saturday. They agreed they'd had, and were having, the most amazing time, and the period away from all the pressures and worries had done them good. They felt increasingly comfortable together as an engaged couple. Confident, in fact. David admitted to himself, though not to Angela, that in a strange way being engaged made him feel grown up, at last.

It had done something to him. Myfanwy, though, was totally and completely wrong.

At about 5pm that day, David and Angela were having some drinks in a café bar and enjoying them, despite the noise from a toddler being fed in a high chair from a jar of mush by his mum. His dad sat slightly away from their table, watching football on the large TV screen. David had registered that football was always on the TV in Spanish café bars.

David looked across at the mother and saw in her frame the tension not just of the last half hour, but of the recent months. She really needed this holiday, but she maybe wasn't getting it.

'Come on, Jonathan, open up, it's nice,' she said.

Jonathan sometimes took a mouthful, sometimes spat it out, got it on the back of his hand, rubbed his eyes, squealed, and so on. The father paid no attention, engrossed in the football. Or, rather, David observed, he intended to seem unaware, but he wasn't at all.

David saw, with a surprising clarity, and had to act. He went over and sat at the table where the man had rested his beer glass. The man reached out to move it, but David said, 'It's OK, leave it. Hello, my name's David, I'm here on holiday, as I guess you three are.'

'Yes. So?' the man said, not turning.

'Well, excuse me for saying this, but what you need is exactly the same as what your son there needs.'

Now the man looked at him. 'What are you talking about? I'm not about to help him eat his "beef and tomatoes".'

David stifled a 'I'm surprised you even know what he's eating' and said, 'No, I'm sure you'll have something much more interesting later. No, what he needs is to sit on your lap. Which is also what you need. And you're trying to control your frustration and resentment at his relationship with his mum. And she needs a decent rest.'

The man spoke quietly. 'What the hell makes you think any of that is true?'

'I've been through a lot myself, and it's given me a sort of sensitivity to what's going on inside people. Nothing spooky. And I'm a follower of Jesus and He seems to have added to that insight by His Spirit who lives in me. That's not spooky either, it's just the original Christian Faith that's been around for 2,000 years. Forgive me for intruding, but I just wanted to help. I hope you have a lovely holiday and a real rest, which your lady there really needs, I'm thinking. I'm going back to my lady now and I'll say nothing – you can even pretend I was talking to you about the football. Who is it, by the way?'

'Athletic Bilbao.'

David got up and returned to Angela, who had been watching him. The man sat very still, apparently still fixed on the football, then he stood up, wiped something surreptitiously from beside his nose, and went over to the high chair.

'Come on, Jon boy,' he said, and lifted the squirming child up and into his arms. He quietened almost immediately.

'You need a cup of tea, Sal, and one of those buns,' he said to the woman.

She just looked at him, then said, 'Yes, thanks, Ian, I do.'

He carried the boy to the bar, ordered her a tea and a Spanish-style bun, and took the boy, nestled nicely into his shoulder, back to a seat near to her but a more comfortable style that he could recline on. Within minutes the boy was fast asleep lying on him and the woman was mopping up tears from her face as she enjoyed the tea and the bun.

'What came over you?' she asked him, quietly.

'I just realised,' he said. 'Jonathan needed his dad.'

'More than you know,' she agreed.

When she finished her tea and bun she slipped over to sit next to him and leaned against him, and she too closed her eyes.

The man looked at David, who gave a little wave and a thumbs-up as he and Angela left.

'What was that?' Angela said. 'What did you see?'

'How do you know I saw anything?'

'Well, I could see from her shoulders that that much tension wasn't just today's. But you saw more than that, tell me you didn't.'

'Yes, I did. I saw… him desperate to hold the baby, the baby desperate to be held by him, him resentful of the mother for their closeness, her resentful of him for not taking his share of caring for the baby, all in an instant like a photograph. That's the best description I can give right now. But I saw it all just like that in a flash, like when a thought comes into your mind complete in an instant even though it has various stages and parts. It was a revelation, an insight, and not just from me.'

'Ooh,' she said. 'What's happening to you?'

'I know.'

It was Saturday, 27th August.

They were sitting in the Palma airport departure lounge. David was just waiting, drinking a coffee with Angela. On a table two away from them was a couple in their mid-thirties also waiting and drinking coffee. David couldn't hear their conversation, but he was drawn to them as the woman got up and walked away while the man stayed in place.

David saw. He stood, went over, and sat down opposite the man who, he now realised, looked deeply miserable and quite angry.

'Please excuse me for saying this, but you're full of bitterness towards your wife and it leaks out far more than you realise.'

'What? Who are you?'

'I'm just a man going home from my holiday like you are. You think you've got it fully under control and that everything you say to her comes across as kind and pleasant, but from time to time – in fact, quite often – it's like a knife and sticks into her.'

The man looked amazed. He went slightly pale.

'Now, you think that whenever she speaks to *you* that way that's just because she's a bitter and horrible person, but in fact she's doing exactly the same as you are. You're both doing exactly the same to each other – leaking bitterness and using that as a reason for feeling bitter towards each other.'

'Well, what if that's even true?' the man said.

'There is a solution, but I have to tell you it's costly.'

He looked around like he might be being watched, and said, 'What is that solution?'

'The solution is that you have to both forgive each other totally and then continue to forgive each other totally.'

'How on earth is that possible?'

'It is possible if you yourself have been completely forgiven.'

'And how is *that* possible?'

'That is possible through Jesus Christ who came as the Son of God among us and died a horrible death on a Roman cross to take upon Him your sins and wrongdoings just so that you can be completely washed and forgiven. So much so that even in the sight of a pure and holy God you are totally faultless. That is what Jesus Christ offers you and that is what opens the door to complete forgiveness, and that is what holds out hope for your marriage, which you think is hopeless and have given up on.'

The man lost David's gaze, looked down at the table and began to cry.

'How do you know that?' he said.

David continued. 'Also, sometimes do you think of her but in your mind see your mother?'

'Yes!' He looked up into David's eyes.

'You need to get help to disentangle them. Your wife and your mother. A bit of counselling would help with that. Just google "counsellor" when you get home. Make sure it's a properly certified one. There is hope yet, for you and your lovely wife, but you need to act.'

The man put a hand on David's arm and said, 'We've just had the holiday from hell. Thank you.'

'You're welcome. First thing you can do is go and apologise.'

'All right, I will.'

David went back to Angela. She was watching him intently. 'What was that?' she said.

'I saw. Again.'

'Oh, my goodness!'

'I know.' Illumination hit him. He grabbed her hand. 'You know in Acts when the disciples suddenly looked hard at a person and then healed them – like Peter and John with the crippled man in chapter 3 and Paul with the lame man in – where was it – Lystra? Lystra – like they were seeing something about to happen – maybe this is like that. God's gift to me.'

'But why now?'

'Maybe because you complete me. Even just being engaged somehow gives me the right platform to exercise the gift.' Myfanwy was so wrong. He would never see her again. Surely. 'Though, to be honest, I'm not sure about doing this – going up to complete strangers and delving into their problems. I don't want to be some creepy weirdo who bothers people all the time.'

'If it's God's gift to you…'

'Well, if it's going to be happening, maybe I should get cards printed, to give to people, saying, "Please let me know how it turns out", with my contact details so they can contact me for more help as well. Or tell me I was completely wrong.'

'Then,' she said, staring at his face in wonder, 'if this is happening now already, what about after we're married?'

'I know!'

It was Sunday, 28th August.

Everyone at church wanted to gawp at the ring and say how amazing it was and congratulate them both. And say how brown they were. Rector Colin got them both up to the front of the church during the notices to congratulate them and lead a prayer for them.

'We were wondering,' Angela said to him in a quiet moment over coffee, 'if we could be married on Easter Saturday next year. Is that a possible day for a marriage?'

'Unusual, but quite possible. And I guess "unusual" suits you two down to the ground!' he said.

'Can we book it?'

'Come to the rectory tomorrow evening at six and we'll start the process then. And David, the youth team have agreed that those two lads can't come back to the club, and at the first meeting after the summer the truth about the situation will be told. Are you up for coming back to help lead that?'

He smiled. The rector had been such a backbone in all this. 'Yes, happy to.'

Now, so much to do!

It was Monday, 29th August.

Rector Colin's study was lit by the evening sun, and Ruby brought them all a coffee. He sat at his computer on his desk and called up his wedding booking file. Then he grabbed a large A4 box file from his shelf, opened it and took out a great sheaf of papers bearing the signs of having been used and then wedged together. He put them on the desk and pulled out a fresh sheet from underneath in the box. 'So much for the paperless office,' he said. 'Still, the French invented the paperless toilet centuries ago.'

He swung his swivel-chair back towards them and said, 'Ah, David, but first, share with me your thoughts about a positive safeguarding policy.'

'Oh. OK. It all starts from the position that what we are trying to communicate to our children and young people is the love of God, in Christ, through the Holy Spirit. Schools, colleges, other institutions, whatever information or training they're trying to convey, it isn't primarily love. That makes us different and it means we have to have a different approach to working with children and young people. We cannot just say, as I've heard some say, "It's the same for us as for schools." That's comfortable for those who want to keep children and young people at arm's length, but it cuts out the really good workers who want to form relationships with them and "become somebody to them". Do you know, I was even told not to talk in terms of "relationships with young people", because it sounded suspect. Workers keep them at arm's length for fear of all the policy-carried terrors of an allegation. And the ones who truly suffer are the children and young people, because they don't any more receive the kind of personal love that leads them to Christ.

'We should have policies that we give to the parents saying that we intend to love their children and young people as an expression of the great love of God, and convey that love to them in natural ways that are age-appropriate.

'And our main safeguard, apart from the things that are obviously unsafe or unwise, is that everything is done in the public arena – never hidden away – and that our teams work together and support each other very closely.

'The whole thing is love-driven, love-orientated, love-protected and love-conveying. Otherwise we've failed before we've even started because we are conveying a message of love without a context of love – that is, experienced love – and that just confirms the human suspicion that the love of God is just words. And then that's all we've taught, along with a few Bible stories.'

'Can you write that down for me so I can take it to the PCC next Tuesday?'

'OK.'

'Right. When do you plan to get married? Oh, yes, Easter Saturday, which is… April 15th next year. Why Easter Saturday?'

'Well,' Angela began, 'because it speaks of hope and victory and resurrection. And, well, I don't know if this makes sense, but we, David and I, started out at Christmas, and Christmas has to lead to Easter – Jesus' birth to His death and resurrection, and that seems like the journey we're on. Also, we intend to go wild on the flowers for the wedding, having them professionally arranged as well, and will leave them in church for the next day, so that'll be a specially huge display for the great day, and save the flower arrangers a job – if they don't mind, that is.'

Rector Colin smiled. 'I wasn't asking to be convinced. You can have the day. But your explanation is certainly a joy to hear. I'm sure the flower arrangers have more than enough other things to be setting up, like the empty tomb scene.'

'There is something else I wanted to mention to you,' David said. 'Since Angela and I got engaged, something has happened a couple of times. We've been in some ordinary place, and suddenly I've had a vision of someone's situation – some complete stranger. And when I've spoken to them about it, it's been right, and seemed to help them. Even gave me the opportunity to mention Jesus. What do you think about that?'

'Sounds like a gift from the Holy Spirit to me. Just the kind of thing we need. Speak to Louis Perrotti, he's had experience in that area. Why do you think this has started since you got engaged?'

'I'm assuming our relationship provides some sort of platform for it, psychologically maybe. Like I feel more confident.'

'I complete him,' Angela said with a smile, taking and squeezing his hand.

'Sounds good to me,' Colin concluded, with a broad smile of his own. 'So, David, you're starting the Alpha course on Thursday evenings, yes?'

'Yes.'

'Angela, are you going to accompany him? I know you've done it before.'

'No, we feel that's something that'll be good for him to do on his own. Give him a bit of space. Do his own thinking.'

'Not that he isn't capable of thinking his own thoughts!' Colin put in.

Later, at his cottage, they sat on his bench outside with mugs of tea and looked at the dawning of dusk and the brightening of the sky as the darkening earth gave it contrast and colour. A plain white sun held on to the horizon while birds over in the trees made a last dash for home, sang an evening chorus and settled in for the night. They sat in silence for a while, hand in hand.

'I do see it,' Angela said. 'The pull of that view. The sense of something beyond. And the sheer beauty of it.'

'I know.'

'So here we are, back from holiday, engaged, throwing ourselves back into the youth group…'

'Wondering if Ruf will be there.'

'Yes, and you starting Alpha, and a wedding to plan, which will be enormous, and confirmation for you in January, and this new gift you're experiencing…'

'Which I'm a bit unsure about.'

'I know, but go with it, and us praying together every day we can, and the whole allegation thing firmly behind us...'

'And my very nice repainted doors, windows and garage...'

'Yes, that too, and Andrew and Thelia and Martin to go and see, and I just have this feeling.'

'Feeling?'

'Like this is new territory,' she said, swinging her empty mug on her thumb.

'Well, it is.'

'Yes, but more than that. Like, this is a big, unknown future. You're changing. We're changing. Life is changing. And we'd be fools to think all our challenges are in the past.'

'True,' he agreed, wondering where this was heading.

'I just think these coming months, like, up to Christmas initially, will be, sort of, laying foundations for our life together.'

'I suppose they will,' he agreed, now swinging WOL, until she stopped him in case it fell and broke like Eeyore had.

'No, David, more than that. I feel we stand at the threshold of something, a dawning, a dusk, a new path, an adventure, a time to get serious. Do you feel it?'

He thought.

'No.'

'OK. But I think you will.'

He wasn't quite sure what to make of that, except that it sounded like a slight note of warning, and he'd had enough of warnings.

CHAPTER TWENTY-FOUR

It was Friday, 16th December.

Youth club was finishing for Christmas. They had a big party with thirty kids in, and all the leaders – Angela, David, Philip and Rachel Hughes, Den Kirkham (still in tuck), Roo and Alan Trench and Miss Spencer, who still wouldn't let anyone call her Olive.

They played some silly party games and were heading for the nibbles and cakes with fizzy drinks, which had been laid out on a couple of tables by Den and Miss Spencer. Ruf turned to David and said, 'Any chance of an invite to the Christmas dinner at the Grangers this year?'

David stopped, looked at him, smiled, laid a hand on his shoulder and was about to say something when Ruf said, 'Nah, I s'pose not, after last year!'

'Oh, don't put yourself down,' David answered. 'You hang with a different crowd now. Mostly. I'm thinking that's Lisa's influence.'

'Sure is.'

'But you can't get her to come here?'

'Not yet.'

'Any chance of seeing you in a service over Christmas?'

'Now you're reaching.'

'Ha. OK,' David said.

It was Monday, 19th December.

The previous evening, after church, Angela had happened to mention she had to have one of her regular ECGs in the

264

morning, and David had asked if he could come. They were both trying to be part of and see as much of each other's lives as possible.

Afterwards, they went across the road for a coffee and then set about delivering the St Mark's Christmas newsletter to Morgan Terrace and Alister Road. They delivered them side by side, doing alternate houses, so they could talk.

An old man opened his door even as David retreated up his front path. He was holding the newsletter and looking very annoyed. He was small, and dressed in a casual shirt, off-white cardigan and creased, dark trousers. 'Did you not read the notice on the door?' he said. 'It says, "No Junk Mail". So why have you given me this rubbish?'

David stopped and looked at the angry, twisted, hateful face. He wanted to say something really cynical and cutting back. But he calmed himself and said, 'It's not junk mail, sir. It's not selling anything. It's the parish church newsletter. It's got good news in it, and it's all about Christmas.'

'Well, I don't *want* it!' the man said, and threw it at David. It fluttered to the floor. David really wanted to hit him right in his miserable old face. As he stooped to pick it up, he said, 'Well, a Merry Christmas to you,' and under his breath, 'you tedious old grump.'

'Get off with you, out of my garden,' the man said. 'And don't bring any more.'

'Shall I make a note not to deliver you one again?' David asked.

'You come here again and I'll call the police.'

Angela was waiting for him at the next gate. 'I don't think you handled that very well. I think you baited him a bit.'

'Miserable old… OK, yes, I got angry with him. Sorry. He just pushed my buttons.'

They carried on. 'I don't think that's a helpful type of anger,' she said.

'I know. It was his vicious little face. I could have hit him.'

265

'David! That's not how we react to people. Especially little old people, even if they are being annoying.'

That evening they ate with the Grangers, as they wouldn't be able to go to their big Christmas dinner this year.

The dining room was decorated differently from last year. No lights and no tree, so the room lights were on. But they'd gone for paper streamers across the ceiling in every bright colour David could imagine, and small items hanging down from them – swirly items, 3D paper balls and delicate cards, all swinging merrily in any small breeze.

Around the walls they'd attached a myriad of fascinating festive icons. Pictures, cards, small Santas and angels and crib scenes, each suggesting a different cultural background. Some had gold and silver reflections, some were plain colours; some were fluffy at the edges, some straight; some were irregular in shape, some more disciplined; some had borders in many fine colours, some just ended at the painted plaster of the wall. It was like a room in a small and enthusiastic Christmas museum.

As they ate, David told them about Ruf's comment, which pleased them both, but they agreed he wouldn't be on the list even if he had improved a lot. And David found himself wondering if Bill Granger should be his best man. He said nothing, but registered him as a candidate. On a very short list.

Back at her house afterwards, quite late, David said, 'Love, are you going to have bridesmaids?'

'No. If I wanted bridesmaids that would be sorted already. Just one page boy.'

'Andrew!'

'Yes, the dear Andrew.'

'And who's going to give you away?'

'Nobody owns me.'

'Don't be awkward.'

'Thelia. Do you want Martin as a best man, complete the set?'

'I don't think I really know him well enough. He's a fine fellow for sure, but tonight at the meal I was wondering about Bill Granger.'

'Bill? Yes, I can see that. He'd do a fine job and not embarrass you too much in his speech.'

'Mind you, he's a canny old bird and could probably dig up something,' David reflected.

'Who else is on your list? You should get on and ask them. It's no good having the photographer, flowers, reception, cars, invites and service order all done if you've no best man.'

'Philip Hughes – we get on really well at "Later". Or my Aunt Mary from Cheltenham. She is my only living relative.'

'So she is. I have no comment to make on any of them. But I thought you'd sorted it out already. So get a move on.'

They were in the tunnel again. Micky beside him, picking her little feet carefully over the sleepers, avoiding the live rail. It was so dark. And dank. And dangerous. Why on earth had he brought her down here?

Some sort of half-light reflected off the shiny, apparently wet, brick walls. He stopped. Was that a train? No. Smaller, like scuttling. What if Micky saw a rat and panicked?

Why were they down here? What were they escaping? Or searching for? It made no sense.

No! As he looked, the young David slipped his hand out of Micky's trusting grip and placed his hand behind her shoulders, as if to push her. He couldn't read his intentions, but it didn't look like it was to steady her.

No, no! He shoved her forward, down, onto the live rail. A bang and a bright flash led to a shower of sparks and he was looking down at her twitching little body. She didn't even look up. She rolled onto her side off the rail and was dead.

Fury. He saw fury in his face, and then triumph. Then the earth beneath him began to open like an old mineshaft and he was sliding down, rock and rubble no help to his scrabbling fingers as the devil's very breath sucked him down to hell. He was screaming, screaming, screaming as the hole got deeper and seemed to close over him with nothing but hopeless loss beneath.

And grinding fury with desperate loss inside him.

Bang, bang, bang.

What?

Bang, bang, bang on his front door – he heard the hinges shake.

'Mr Sourbook! Mr Sourbook, it's the police, please open up.'

Police? What now? Oh, he felt awful. His belly griped and pained. What was that awful smell? Why was he on the floor?

He put his hand out and met wet slime. He lifted it before his face and saw thin, pink vomit.

'Mr Sourbook, are you in there? Please open the door, this is the police.'

Bang, bang, bang.

'OK,' he tried to say, but his throat burned and nothing beyond a hoarse, thick whisper came out.

He tried to stand and his head banged like a hangover. What did he drink last night?

All around his bedroom was vomit. Yellow, brownish, pinkish. He fought his way into his dressing gown, covering his slimy pyjamas, and started down the stairs.

At least Bart was on the other side of the bed, the clean side.

He opened the front door and bright light stung his eyes.

A male and a female police officer stood there, both in uniform.

'Are you Mr David Sourbook?' the man asked.

'Yes,' he managed.

'Sir, we're here from the local police because your neighbours heard such loud and sustained screaming that they thought someone was being attacked. Was that you making that noise?'

'Eh? I don't know.'

'Well, is there anyone else at home?'

'Here? No. I'm alone.'

'Sir, we need to come in and check and to make sure you're all right. Can we come in, please?'

'Of course. Come on in.'

They followed him into the front room. He sat on his chair and drew his dressing gown around him.

'Mr Sourbook, something has clearly happened to you. It looks like you've been ill. Is there someone we can phone for you?'

'Yes, my fiancée. Angela. Her number is 0778 – err – 078 – no.'

'Is there a mobile with her number in?'

'Upstairs, in my bedroom. It's not locked. The phone. Adams.'

'I'll put the kettle on, then go and find it,' the female officer said.

She came back down with it, to her ear. 'Here, speak to him yourself,' she said.

David took the phone.

'David, what's happened?'

'I have no idea. I woke to banging on the door and police here and I've been sick everywhere. The woman's gone.'

'What woman?'

'No woman. Just joking. Oh, I feel awful. Confused, actually. It's frightening, like my brain isn't working properly. Perhaps I've had a stroke.'

'I'll be there in ten minutes. I love you. Try to be calm.'

'She's coming,' he said, handing the phone back, he knew not why.

'Then I suggest you go upstairs and shower, get dressed, and come back down for this tea,' the woman said.

He got up without a word, and obeyed. His bedroom was a stinking disaster area. He hoped the fresh clothes in the wardrobe didn't smell.

Downstairs, he couldn't sit. For some reason he had to stay standing up. And on the move, round the front room and kitchen. His mind was vague. He started to feel breathless. Like he couldn't get enough air in his lungs. His heart began to pound in his chest. His mind raced over nothing, going nowhere. It was a panic attack brought on by his feeling that his mind had gone blank, his thinking had somehow stopped working properly, which he found a very frightening experience.

'Mr Sourbook,' the policewoman said, holding out a mug of tea. 'I advise you to sit down and try to stay calm. You've had a horrible experience. You feel shaken by it. But in half an hour you'll be fine. Just sit you down on the chair and sip your tea. Here.'

He took it and stood, sipping it. He tried to sit down but stood straight up again.

She said, 'Mr Sourbook, have you been alone all night? Is this just a dream of some kind?'

'I think so. I think it is. But I can't remember it.'

'Nothing?'

'No.'

'Did you wake up in the night in a state?'

'I don't think so. You woke me, banging on the door.'

He tried again to sit down, and managed. He tried to relax, and did, a little. He looked forward to Angela arriving, and drank more of the tea.

Angela walked in, looking very concerned. She sat next to him, took his hand, and said, 'David, sweetie, are you OK?'

'Better now. Stay with me. Something horrible happened. But I don't know what.'

'You're shaking!' she said, and put her arm right round him and held him close. 'Drink some more tea.'

'The bedroom upstairs is in a bit of a state,' the male officer said. 'He's been sick rather a lot. Like he was in some sort of dream panic – he says he can't remember it at all. It'll take a bit of cleaning up.'

'Oh, sweetie!' she said. 'That's terrible. I'll stay with you. I'll make some more tea for us both.'

'My stomach really hurts,' he said, as empty griping set in.

'I'll make us some toast.'

'We should be making a move,' the female officer said.

'OK, yes. I'll look after him now.'

'Thank you,' he managed.

They left and she said to David, 'Maybe you're actually ill. I'll take your temperature.'

She fetched his forehead thermometer from the kitchen. His temperature was normal. 'Do you feel ill?'

'No. Just very shaken and fuggy in the head.'

'Let's get some breakfast in you and see how you are then.'

They had tea and toast at the table in the kitchen and he began to feel more normal. His mind began to function better as well, which was a great relief.

'It must have been a dream,' he concluded.

'But you have no memory of it?'

'Not a glimmer.'

'Well, that's unusual. For you.'

'I know. And worrying.'

Taking out Mrs George to do some shopping, with Henry Totter, who was a much better match than Mrs Timms because he also liked Newsome Bros and avoided what he thought of as 'the cheapo stores', was a festive joy.

They wanted to go into town in the late afternoon to see all the lights aglow. That pleased David and Angela well enough, not least because by then he was feeling much better. It had taken most of the day. Underneath he was still unsettled by the mystery of what had befallen him in the night.

The centre of town was clean. The floor wasn't awash with litter. Angela's efforts were, perhaps, beginning to have an influence in the minds of the council.

The great tree in the centre of the High Street was festooned with light of many colours – not just red, green, blue and yellow, but gold, orange, lilac, a sandy brown, silver, and a very light green and blue alongside the usual green and blue. David stood and marvelled at it. There must have been 500 bulbs, he reckoned. Thin, swirling, plastic strips hung around them, reflecting the colours as they turned and flashed. The lights were sometimes still, and sometimes flowed across the tree in patterned waves.

'Come on,' Angela said, after a while.

'I can't,' he replied. 'I'm mesmerised. I'm in a festive mesmer. It's fabulous, isn't it?'

'So you've said, five times, but we're here for Mrs George and Henry, so come on.'

At that moment a band started up. It wasn't the Salvation Army band, as was often the case; it was a group with a large sign on the ground in front of them saying they were from Churches Together. David recognised one or two of them. He really should start taking that collection of churches more seriously.

A carol sprang to life with music and voices – 'O Come All Ye Faithful'. He couldn't help but join in. Then he heard Mrs George and Henry belting it out as well. So there they stayed, a good twenty minutes, singing their festive hearts out and taking in the lights on the shops as well, in streams of white and multicolours, and the council's displays that went across the street high up with scenes of snowmen, children, trees, Santas and the rest in flashing colours and descending, white snowfalls.

David and Angela linked arms, keeping an eye on the two in front of them, and just rolled around in the moment, fully festive as it was. It brought back to David last Christmas in particular, and how he'd found that magical joy for the first real time, and how much a part of that was the precious lady to his left, now his 'intended'. A sort of warmth came over him and made him tremble. 'Thank You, Jesus,' he muttered, for all sorts of reasons.

After a while that didn't seem at all long enough to David, Mrs George turned and said, 'Can we go on now?'

'Yes, I think we've stood long enough,' Angela agreed.

A shot of anger fired up in David. 'Why? This is lovely. Can't we stay just five more minutes? Why do we have to leave so soon?'

Angela turned her head and gave him a look. It was confusion, condemnation, disappointment and other things. 'You sound like a schoolboy. A badly behaved schoolboy,' she said.

'I'm not a child!' he retorted. 'Don't speak to me like I'm a child!'

She guided him by the arm a little away from the other two. 'David, what is this? Go back and apologise to them. I don't care what excuse you give, just apologise. What's come over you?'

'Nothing.' He relented inside. 'OK.' He let the anger subside as he walked the few steps. He said, 'Sorry about that, I got a bit caught up in it all! Let's move on.'

Mrs George gave him a steely look, but Henry just said, 'You big kid!' in a friendly way, so that was all right. Angela watched him warily.

'What was that?' she asked as they walked on down the High Street, past shop windows full of light, colour, expectation and the mighty thrust of commercialism with something to celebrate.

'I don't know. I'm really sorry. It just came over me. I was really angry.'

'You know Myfanwy told you you need to find your anger? Well, surely she meant to confront it as well, not just accept it?'

'I don't know. Is that what's happening? I'm just letting out anger like steam out of a boiling kettle? I don't know. I don't think this is that.'

'But what else is it going to be? I'm not marrying an angry man.'

She meant that.

'Maybe you should go back to Myfanwy,' she added.

'I'm not going back to Myfanwy.' That had a touch of venom in it.

Angela just let it go. Externally, at least. She walked ahead a little.

David caught up with Mrs George, and said, 'And how are you, Mrs George?'

'A lot better than you, it would seem.'

'Have you forgiven us all for the ice cream incident?'

'As long as you never mention it again.'

'All right, then. Are you ready for Christmas?'

'Who's ever ready for Christmas?' she replied, wearily.

'Do you have any plans?'

'Dig a grave and fall in it, I should think. No, my grandchildren are having me, one lot from the 23rd to Christmas Day and the other lot from then to January the first.'

'Don't you enjoy seeing them? Isn't that something to look forward to?'

'I suppose so.'

He sighed, then looked across to see if she'd heard. She hadn't. 'Well, look at all this light and colour. Listen to the band and the carols. Don't you feel festive at all, Mrs George?'

'Oh, why do I bother?' she said, and forged ahead of him.

Annoyed at her, he muttered unpleasantnesses under his breath. Then he caught himself and said sorry to God. But he was miffed. It dented the festive charm of the moment, and what should be the festive joy of helping someone at Christmas. He sulked.

It was Wednesday, 21st December.

A foul stench with a shocking sharpness assaulted his nostrils. A huge retch bent him double, but he was empty. He wiped his hand across his lips, and they were slimy.

'Not again,' he said.

He stumbled from the wet sheets and dropped his pyjamas on the floor. The thought of all that cleaning up again was nearly too much to bear.

In the bathroom he stared blankly at some old, grey, dishevelled man who'd wandered in there looking for something. He spat down the sink and decided to go straight for the shower.

After that he attended to his teeth and bristles. He ignored the bedroom after dressing and went down for some tea. At least this time he didn't feel like he was losing his mind.

He sat outside with the big WOL mug of tea and stared at the view. It was a bright, Christmassy day, with birds to-ing and fro-ing in the trees across the field, and wispy white clouds holding up the light blue sky. It was mild.

So, what was the dream that was so terrifying him now? He thought he'd done with terrifying dreams. How many more levels of hell were there inside his being and mind?

Was he, really, getting anywhere?

See Myfanwy? Not on your life would he see Myfanwy. Weird woman. He didn't need her help and he didn't need Angela telling him to go and see her.

He sat and stared, relaxed his mind, and waited. He even prayed. Patiently – for he had learned to be still – he let it come.

The tunnel. Just a flash. Micky and him in the tunnel. Her looking up at him, holding his hand. Just a flash. That dream. Just like before.

Why? Why now? And was that making him bad-tempered?

What sense was in that?

He'd acknowledged the depth of that loss. The utter, sorrowing, deathly, stripping loss of her.

He thought about that for a moment, and a tear burned his cheek. Her little face looked up at him. Her little hand was warm in his. Such trust and companionship. So good to be able to be something to her. Be something. Was that what had made it hard for him to be 'real'? The loss of the person who needed him and for whom he 'was something'? For whom he was real? But he'd acknowledged all that, in seeing the loss of her. He'd accepted the loss of her.

So what was this?

He finished his WOL of tea and went upstairs, opened the windows, stripped everything with vomit on and put it in the washing machine, and used disinfectant and the carpet cleaner on the floor.

Doing it made him angry.

CHAPTER TWENTY-FIVE

It was Sunday, 25th December.

The big day!

David drove up to Angela's house because that was where they were all gathering for Christmas dinner, at 2pm so they could stuff themselves and then watch Her Majesty.

Angela opened the door with a big smile and they fell into each other's arms and kissed. Then she grabbed his hand and led him in, saying, 'Merry, Merry, Happy, Happy Christmas, my love. Come and have breakfast.'

He responded, 'And a Merry Christmas to you, dearest Angela.'

In the front room he saw his present to her of last year, in pride of place on the coffee table. The torsioned-glass rose vase, exquisite in form and tension, swirling up to its tender lip, out of which 'grew' the red rose on its green glass stem. She'd put water in the vase because it was more stable that way.

The tree in the corner was some five feet tall, with coloured lights in profusion twinkling and cascading, bedecked with a cornucopia of festive bits – baubles, tiny toys, reflective silver strips. Underneath it were many parcels, wrapped mostly in the same red and gold paper.

The room was lit further with more coloured lights hung from the central shade to the edges at six points. Cards hung down the walls in torrents of merry greeting.

They sat on the settee and she handed him a wrapped parcel. It was long, and square-ish in cross-section. He handed her his gift.

She said, 'Unwrap yours first.'

It was heavy. He pulled the sticky tape apart, hoping to get the paper to come off without doing any damage to whatever was inside. He succeeded, dropped the paper on the floor at his feet, and held up the box. On its side was a picture of a telescope for stargazing.

'I can gaze at my star any time,' she said, and kissed him on the cheek.

'You've been storing up that line!'

'That I have.'

'It's fantastic. I shall really enjoy using this. Thank you. Now open yours.'

She wrestled with the paper rather less daintily than he had, and it fell apart on her lap. The cardboard box gave no hint of what was inside. She looked at him, questioning, then opened up the end. Out slid the jewellery box.

She pushed the paper and card onto the floor and laid it on her lap. 'Oh, my goodness!' she said. 'It's beautiful!'

It was. Wooden construction with golden strips over the edges, and a marquetry picture on the top of a bird rising from a river with a tree in the foreground and a man watching from the other bank. The other panels at the side and back were of inlaid, parallel strips of cherry, walnut and maple.

She looked down into the lower right corner and spotted where he'd had 'A. A.' inlaid in ebony. It was a classy piece.

'Oh, I love it!' she said, hugging it to herself. 'Thank you so much. Now that I've actually got some decent jewellery, I shall have somewhere proper to keep it.'

They kissed, and laid back on the settee.

'Tea and croissants?' she said.

'Mmm!'

They went into the kitchen, where pots and trays seemed to be everywhere and it was already steamy and smelled of nice things in the oven.

'Turkey went in at half-five,' she said.

'You're a saint,' he answered.

She turned the microwave on to warm the croissants and started to make the tea. Then they sat at the big table where she'd made space and they enjoyed their breakfast together.

'Sleep all right?' she asked.

'Fine. You?'

'I'm always a bit suspicious when your answer is one word and goes straight on to asking me. Did you sleep well last night?'

'OK, I woke up in the middle of the night feeling sick, but I wasn't sick, and I have no memory of any dreams other than a little one about today and the family gathering.'

'Are you sure your Aunt Mary will get here OK?'

'She was insulted by the suggestion that she couldn't drive here perfectly well on her own, so what am I to do?'

'OK.'

'OK. What can I do?'

'Wash and peel some potatoes, in the time-honoured, old-fashioned way, in the sink.'

The church was full. The tree was lit by 1,000 white lights, all glowing steadily because people with epilepsy or migraines can find a twinkling tree of that size makes them feel ill. It also had loads of thin, brass hangings depicting the Gospel story of the nativity as they swung in the tiny breezes that people make, and which enter through ancient windows.

The usual greeting of one another went on for the full fifteen minutes before the service was to start. Bill and Mary Granger came over to them straight away.

'Glad to see you looking smart, Bill,' David said.

'For you, old boy. Mustn't let the side down.' He clapped David on the shoulder.

Mary kissed him on the cheek. 'Are you looking after my friend? You'd better or I won't let you marry her. I'll object when the banns are read.'

Barny the Reader came up to David in his white surplice and blue scarf and said, 'You all right with that reading this morning, then?'

David went blank. Had he forgotten a reading he was supposed to be doing?

'What?' he said.

'The Gospel reading? You haven't forgotten?'

David felt even more blank. Then Barny pushed him and said, 'Merry Christmas!' and laughed.

David laughed as well, a little. But actually he was irritated by the stupid joke. He looked at the red face puffed up with fat and jollity and felt a bubble of anger rise inside him. Stupid man.

It was clear the service was about to begin. David and Angela sat forward on the right, where they'd gravitated to over the year, but deliberately not in the same seats always. She took his hand and laid it on her thick, brown skirt. She cuddled herself against him, and he wriggled back to her.

The choir sang, the rector preached a short word, Holy Communion taken (not yet for David, as his confirmation was still to come in January) and a last hymn announced. Everyone streamed out and off to a day of gatherings and celebrations.

Angela parked in the driveway, leaving room for another car behind hers, and they went in. The house smelled fantastic. She went straight to the oven and had a look in. She checked the timer, closed the door and said, 'Phew! All good. Coffee time.'

David could see the white on Andrew's hand and on Thelia's hand as they stood outside the door. She was trying to get Andrew to loosen his grip. Andrew wouldn't even look up from the ground in front of him as greetings were exchanged.

'Here's your best friend, David,' Martin said to Andrew, while holding a large carrier bag in one hand and a bulky red box in the other, bending down close to him. But the whole torture of being so far out of his routine of time and place was too much and Andrew was resolutely silent.

They all trooped into the hallway and then into the front room. Before anyone sat down, Angela offered coffees and went off to make some, followed by Thelia. Andrew sat on the mat on the floor, and Martin put down his box of Lego beside him and his tablet on the coffee table. He kept the big bag of presents by him.

'Never ceases to amaze me that you bought that for Angela,' he said with a smile, indicating the vase. 'A man with that kind of taste is hard to find.' He sat on the settee.

'You wait till you see this year's offering. Andrew, what did you get for Christmas?'

The boy was silent, and looked sad. He had put on some weight, but he still had the mop of red hair and the angelic, freckled, pale face.

'Are you well?' Martin said, and David immediately wondered what Angela had been saying about him. 'Fine, thanks. You?'

'Pulled my back trying to rebuild the shed in the garden, but otherwise I'm OK. Busy as heck, of course.'

'Last Christmas you were in Dubai or somewhere.'

'It's always Dubai or somewhere. Sometimes I'm not even sure which!'

The coffees arrived. David lowered himself onto the floor next to Andrew. Angela sat on one of the armchairs and Thelia sat next to Martin on the settee. That left the other armchair for Aunt Mary if she arrived soon. Or ever.

'I was just saying what an incredibly tasteful gift that was last year,' Martin said to Angela.

'I know! He was trying to impress me. He did it again this year. Look at this!'

She fetched the jewellery box from the sideboard and handed it to Thelia, and everyone purred over how beautiful it was. David then fetched his telescope, still in its box, and stood there holding it as everyone enthused over how much he was going to enjoy that.

'Look, it's a telescope!' Thelia said to Andrew. He looked up at the box and studied the picture.

'Stars,' he said.

'Yes, stars,' David answered him. 'Tell you what, after we've had this coffee, how about you coming upstairs with me to set it up?'

'And look?' he said, almost catching David's eyes.

'Yes, and look, silly!' Thelia said. 'Speak properly sweetie or you sound dim, and you're really not dim.'

'Has to be dim to see,' he said, and everyone laughed.

'Good answer,' David said, squeezing his little shoulder in his festive red jumper. 'You're bright, and I can see that!'

Andrew stood up and jumped up at him, knocking the box to the floor, and squeezing David tight round his chest.

'Andrew!' he squeaked.

'Andrew!' Thelia repeated.

It felt like he was going to faint. A sudden rise of some desperation or something else caused David to push Andrew's shoulders, hard, as he said, 'Andrew! Get off me!'

Andrew fell to the floor with a painful-sounding thump, and everyone just stared, mouths open. For a moment David was standing over him like some horrific ogre. Andrew looked at the box lying there, then shut his eyes and a tear rolled down his cheek. The silence of the moment was awful.

'Andrew, I'm sorry,' David said, kneeling down to him, but he knew the damage was done. Andrew might never trust him again. A fragile and precious thing had just been crushed.

'Home,' Andrew said.

Thelia looked at Martin, who shook his head. She said, 'Andrew, you squeezed David too hard. He didn't mean to push you, did you David?'

'Andrew, no, I'm sorry. I really couldn't breathe. Please don't be upset.'

Angela stood up, looked at David with an unreadable but not pleasant expression, and said, 'I think we should leave you to it for a few minutes. Come on, David, let's have a look at lunch.'

In the kitchen she closed the door behind her and then turned on him. 'What the hell did you do that for? You *know* we mustn't ever push him away, and never, ever tell him to get off like that.'

'I couldn't breathe,' he said, lamely.

'It was a few seconds. You were hardly going to die. You won't be able to breathe after I'm finished with you. David, what have you done? You've never reacted like that before. What's come over you?'

'I know, I'm sorry.'

'I think you should stay out here and start on those sprouts.'

'Think about how I've behaved.'

'Something like that. I'll see what damage control can be done in there. I take it you're OK if we have to let him get your telescope out?'

'OK.'

Christmas dinner was still a little stiff. Crackers had been pulled with that sort of tense jollity that tried to hide animosities and enmities. In this case, what he regarded as a simple mistake but they judged to be a horrible injury to poor Andrew.

The telescope wouldn't even go back in its box since Andrew had stood on one of the lower tripod legs and bent it, and nobody dared to try to bend it straight again in case it cracked right off. Great.

He felt like everyone was silently accusing him, and the words formed in his mind. 'Look, I didn't *mean* to push him. It was a reaction, and I didn't *mean* to tell him to get off, and I'm really sorry and I'll try my best to make it up to him. But you lot can stop judging me for it or I'll just get up and walk home.'

He could imagine their stunned and embarrassed faces. Or maybe their blank expressions as they just let him go. Good riddance. Now we can have a happy Christmas Day together. Even Aunt Mary, who'd arrived in the last half hour, had been aware that something had happened just by the tension in the air and coaxed Angela into telling her.

He swore in his head, and bit into a roast potato. 'Lovely dinner,' he said.

Various noises of appreciation went round the table for the third time, except for Andrew, who just continued to stare at his plate. 'He'll eat when he's hungry,' Thelia said again, but they were all thinking, 'Poor little mite, now he can't even eat his dinner.'

They watched the Queen in stony silence and then the planned snooze was transformed into a brisk walk to blow the cobwebs off. Except for Aunt Mary, who said she should be getting off and got ready to go home. She seemed much softer off her own ground.

'Thank you so much,' she said. 'It was lovely to meet you all. And for my lovely presents.' She held up the bag containing some smellables and edibles, as one buys for an elderly lady you don't really know.

'Goodbye, dear,' she said to David. 'See you at the wedding. Do tell me if there's anything I can do.'

Was there a hint of, 'if it ever comes off' in there?

After the goodbyes they all put on coats and hats for a walk, though it was still mild. 'It might turn cold later,' Angela warned them.

So off they set. Andrew was on Martin's shoulders and showed no desire to ride on David.

They walked down past St Mark's to the fields. Others were making the same festive pilgrimage in search of forgiveness for the same festive gluttony.

'So, how are the wedding plans going?' Martin asked.

'Not bad at all, actually,' Angela said. 'Well, the church is booked anyway, and the rector says he might be around that day. Is there anything else we need to be doing?'

Laughter was followed by more from her. 'The choir are going to do an anthem. Even though they have plenty of special Easter things to sing. The choirmaster, Mr Dawkins, said they insisted. The reception is booked at Taylor's Estate, which is jolly posh but we are both pushing on ancient so you should push the boat out, I say. You're giving me away, Thelia.'

'I said I'd think about it.'

'And have you?'

'No.'

'What, not even thought about it or decided not to?'

'Not even thought about it. The answer's yes. Of course it is.'

Bright, low sun made them all squint as they walked. Andrew was playing with his dad's hair.

'Want a ride, Andrew?' David said.

There was no reply, or evidence of having heard. Martin, who was probably the most sympathetic of them, just looked at David and gave a little shrug.

Angela continued. 'The photographer is booked – from Starlight Galleries in town. The cars are booked. David wanted a horse and coach because of his age, but he settled for a nice limo from Minsters, the funeral people.'

'Just as appropriate, I'd say,' Thelia joked.

'Hoi! I never asked for a horse and carriage,' David corrected. 'I'm saving that for my funeral.'

'So, let's see,' Angela continued. 'The service sheet is all planned, same design as the invitations you got, designed by Leaf the Printers. Flowers by Ella Pickett, a friend, but at her commercial rate because I insisted and overcame. Though I have no doubt she'll throw in some extra bits for nothing. Dress is sorted after only twelve fittings by a woman I was recommended who lives in Reading. That travelling to and fro got a bit old a bit quick, I can tell you. But good value for the work she's done. She works from her own home but she has a real gift. Oh, yes, page boy. Any ideas?'

Andrew huffed.

'Yes, it's you!' Thelia said.

'Page one,' he replied.

'Let's see. Bill Granger, a good friend from church who's been part of our story this last year, is David's best man. Honeymoon is booked on a desert island with no name. What else? Did I say photos? Yes. Oh, yes, table decorations by the youth group leaders' team. It's going to be a surprise. I told them it'd better be a nice one. I think that's about it. We're staying at David's house, which will be our house, the first night, so we can come to church on Easter Day before we fly off to the island.'

'Isn't that a bit risky?' Martin said.

'What?'

'Coming to church to see all your friends the day after the wedding.'

'I don't see why.'

'Oh. OK.'

A light tea of cold meats, cheeses, crackers and small cakes was more relaxed than the dinner. Maybe it was his Aunt Mary whose silent condemnation had sullied the air? Or maybe a walk and a talk had done them good.

But by the time they left, Andrew still wouldn't engage with him, and that left David deeply saddened.

'I'm sorry, little guy,' he said, holding Andrew's arm as his dad carried him out to the car.

It was as if he wasn't even there.

'Never mind,' Thelia said, 'we've all made mistakes with him. He'll come round.'

She kissed him on the cheek, and once Andrew was sorted in the car Martin shook his hand. 'Nice to see you again,' he said.

They drove off and he and Angela went back into the house. It was just gone seven.

She linked his arm and said, 'Are you very upset about your telescope?'

'No. I'll take it to a shop in town and get them to look at it. I'm more concerned about Andrew. I hope I haven't really upset him.'

'Well, David, I think you did. We'll just have to hope he gets over it. Come on, don't let it spoil your Christmas Day. It's time to hit the mulled wine and put on the new *Scrooge* DVD.'

That lifted him. But underneath he was angry, because they had spoiled his Christmas Day. Even she had. They'd been mean when he'd intended no wrong. It was their fault Andrew had remained so silent with him. If they'd told him to get over it rather than sympathise with him it would have been OK.

Scrooge scowled and ranted.

David knew just how he felt.

Christmas to Christmas, it was like he'd come full circle.

Never escaped at all. Circling the plughole.
Merry Christmas and all.

CHAPTER TWENTY-SIX

It was Monday, 20th February. The Monday of half-term.

They were shopping together in town, this time without any of the elderly people they often took with them. In particular, they were looking for presents for Bill, Thelia and Andrew for the help they would be giving at the wedding. And something for Rector Colin for doing such a lovely job (which they were sure he would) and being so helpful in preparing them for the wedding and for married life.

Grey, damp, cold February had settled over everything, it seemed, since the New Year. People looked fed up. Parents seemed bad-tempered with their children. Children seemed bad-tempered with their parents.

David and Angela had traipsed around for an hour with no success, and he felt a bit tired so they sat on a bench in the High Street.

'Like a couple of old folk,' he said.

'I'm waiting for you. Old chap,' she retorted.

Through the window of a coffee shop David noticed a young mum with two small children. The children were climbing on and off their chairs, chasing each other around and clearly ignoring her occasional attempts to restrain them. She was a picture of misery. She sat with her forehead resting on her left hand, right over her big cup of coffee, and tears were actually dropping from the end of her nose into the cup. The children hadn't even noticed, or didn't really care.

David saw a picture of her husband, a nice man, being pushed away by her, desperate to get back. And he saw the woman's suspicions about him played out as it were in her head, right there.

'Lord, I see that. If she comes and sits right on this bench, I'll talk to her.'

Sure enough, she managed to gather them together and to get one of the girl's shoes back on, and dragged them out of the coffee shop. One or two folk watched them go, clearly relieved.

She dragged the little girl by the hand over to the bench, plonked her down on it and said, 'Now, Lucy, sit still! You are *going* to have your shoes on!'

David watched for a minute then said, quite softly, 'Hello, there, my name is David and this is my fiancée, Angela. May I speak with you for a moment?'

She looked up, still holding the shoe half on, and scanned his face. 'All right. What?'

'I see things. God shows them to me. I'm just an ordinary Christian from St Mark's, here in the town. I saw something as I noticed you in the coffee shop. Can I tell you what it is?'

She looked justifiably wary, but said, 'OK.'

'I saw that the thing you need most right now is your husband, who I believe is John, and I saw that he is desperate to be close to you, and he isn't having an affair, he's just suffering some depression from the state of things at home.'

'What?'

Angela knelt down and helped with the shoe. 'Lucy is a lovely name. My name's Angela.'

'Well,' David said, 'that's what I believe God showed me. You're projecting on to John what happened with your parents, and John is not the same as your dad. You are pushing John away and getting deeper and deeper into misery because you suspect him of having an affair, but he isn't, and you and he probably need to sit down and talk, or even get some counselling, and maybe a holiday if you can afford one. These two look like they're not at school yet.'

'They're not, more's the pity. You saw that? You don't know John?'

288

'I saw the situation, and I don't know John, and I'm suggesting a possible course of action. Look, here's my card. So you know who I am and you can contact me if you want to.'

'Huh. And you're his fiancée?'

'That I am. There, shoe is on again!'

Lucy swung her leg like she was quite pleased.

She took the card cautiously and looked at it. 'David, what's that? Sourbook. Nice name. So you say John isn't having an affair with that woman from work.'

'I don't know any details beyond what I was shown and told you. I'm only trying to help.'

'Strange way of going about it. OK. Thank you. You haven't got a message on what to do with these two, have you?'

'No. But my advice, for what it's worth as a man with no children, is have a rule with yourself. Once you've said "no", never change it to "Oh, all right, then!" That just rewards them for whining and teaches them that whining works. Think before you say "no" – whether you really mean it, and then stick to it.'

'Nice idea,' she said. 'Anyway, it was nice to meet you. I think. We need to be off.'

'Goodbye, then. I will pray for you all. Goodbye, Lucy, be good for Mummy, she needs you to do that, or she will be sad.'

Lucy hopped off the bench and skipped after her mum and brother down the pathway.

'Brilliant!' Angela said, taking his nearer hand. 'And very well handled, if I may say so.'

An hour later he felt the anger rising. He'd managed to control it fairly well in the last few weeks, though it had threatened to surface a few times. And he'd only woken in a tangled sweat twice in the last week, with no vomit. Maybe the anger and the dreams were connected – both worse or both better.

A woman pushing a double buggy round the big supermarket in town had met a friend and together they were now completely blocking the aisle he and Angela needed to go down to get to the bread. He could have turned back and detoured round the cakes, but he resented the way mothers with double buggies thought they could just have 'right of way'. So he said, 'Excuse me,' quite firmly as he approached them and then, because they didn't move quickly enough, he pushed the mother with his shoulder as he passed her.

'Sorry,' Angela said, behind him. Then she put a restraining hand on his arm and stopped him.

'David. You pushed that lady, deliberately.'

'They shouldn't be pushing those big buggies round the town expecting everyone to work their way round them.'

'Can you imagine the amount of work and stress that's involved in looking after two young babies?'

'Doesn't justify the way they push everyone else out of the way.'

'David! They don't push everyone else out of the way, and what you did to that woman was rude. What am I to make of you at the moment? You're hearing from God and getting unreasonably angry. I'm confused, I'll tell you.'

'Huh,' he said, and carried on.

Fifteen minutes later, at the checkout, they were behind a man with a basket of some five or so items, and an old woman who'd taken for ever to load all her items on the conveyor belt and then offload them into her push-trolley, and now as she searched in her purse for money she was chatting to the checkout girl like an old friend.

David was growing angry. Growing and growling angry. He commented internally that if the store assistant had half a brain she wouldn't be working here. Finally he snapped, and said out loud to the old woman, 'Excuse me! Some of us have a life we're still trying to live! Could we move it along here?'

The old woman froze, and Angela turned round and looked at him with shock and then righteous indignation. The worst sort of indignation. She pushed him hard in the chest so that he exited the queue, saying to the old lady, 'I am *so* sorry. I cannot imagine what's come over him. You take your time.'

Others were staring. She pushed him again, so they were free of the waiting queue, and said right into his face in quiet fury, 'What was *that*? You don't speak to people like that. What on earth is going on with you?' She grabbed the engagement ring. 'I feel like taking this off and throwing it at you.'

The sheer rage of her wrath took him aback. It moulded her whole image into something he hadn't seen before. He felt like hitting her. Punching her right in that furious face. His right fist actually balled slightly and his arm stiffened.

Angela jabbed him in the chest with her finger. 'I am not going to be a battered wife. You need to sort yourself out. I'm not marrying you just to end up abused by your anger. You're dangerous. Don't even think of contacting me till you've seen Myfanwy.'

She dropped their basket and stalked off. He kicked the basket across the floor and shouted, '*You* see Myfanwy!'

He hung his head as he went and picked the basket up, hoping people would stop looking at him. How could he go back to Myfanwy after what she'd said to him? After how she was with him the last time he saw her?

The perfect trap, he was in. Angela wouldn't speak to him unless he saw Myfanwy, yet he suspected if he saw Myfanwy she would be out to undermine his relationship with Angela. No way out. Circling the plughole.

It was Friday, 24th February.

Myfanwy was as brown as a bean. Bare knees and legs stretched from the bottom of her white chiffon dress, and bare, brown arms from its straps at her shoulders. Even her hair had attracted some highlights.

'Nice holiday?' he tried, but she didn't answer. She just waited.

'I'm here because of two issues,' he said, trying to look her in the face, at least. 'The return of some dreams, and anger.'

291

'In that case I'm surprised you're here. Am I not to blame for the anger – opening that can of worms and now there are worms everywhere?'

'Well, since you're asking, yes. But that's not to blame you. I can now see how much anger is in there, and it needed to find a way out.'

'Find a way out?'

'Be shown the exit.'

She laughed. 'I like that.'

'I do have a problem with you, though. When I left last time, you seemed genuinely upset, like some relationship we had was ending, like you had personal feelings for me.'

She studied him. 'What do you understand as the place of the relationship in counselling?'

He caught himself looking at her shapely brown knees and looked away. 'I should also say that Angela said I'm not to speak to her until I've seen you.'

'OK.'

'Because of the anger, not the dreams.'

'OK.'

'As to the relationship of the counsellor with the client, it has to be real but detached. There has to be genuine emotion involved, but not of any committed or romantic sort, which means affection is a grey area, I'd say. You have to be sure you are only reflecting me, not adding in your own baggage, of which there is always some. Because you're human. Allegedly.'

'All right, so what was happening when I last saw you?'

'It felt like you were expressing a personal sadness, like you'd miss me and you were jealous of my relationship with Angela.'

'And what was it really?'

'I don't know. You were feeling it. I only observed it,' he said, feeling quite proud of himself.

'Beware of fencing with me, you clever fellow,' she said. 'I will give you one answer and one answer only. I felt sad for you because I saw the potential that is in you and at the same time the depth of destruction and despair that could still befall you.

And that is all. And I will tell you immediately why you are getting only that one answer today.'

'As well as this one.'

'Don't fence! The reason is that you are at a very sensitive place in your journey of counselling, and if things are to be resolved in time for your wedding, you have to take full responsibility for all the answers. Responsibility in bringing them to light, and responsibility for owning them. Is that clear, David?'

He hated that she was speaking to him like a child. 'Yes, ma'am.'

'Good. A touch of anger there, I think. Tell me first about the dreams.'

He told her how they had changed from his dear little sister Micky *falling* on the live rail in the tunnel to being *pushed* by him. And him waking up screaming, vomiting, confused, terrified.

'What's the question we have to ask?'

'What is it showing me?'

'So?'

'That I wanted her dead. I resented her in some way and wanted to kill her.'

'Does that make any sense to you at all?' she asked, scribbling, pencil on pad.

'No.'

'What else could it mean?'

He tried to think. Nothing made sense. She waited. And waited.

'I don't know. Nothing comes to me.'

'Why would the content of the dream change?'

'Because I've discovered something new about what happened, which I haven't, or something in me has altered. Which could be.'

'What has altered?'

'Being with Angela. Overcoming the false allegation. Having a sense that God is using me.'

'Tell me about that.'

He explained about the insights and gave her one of his cards.

'OK. I see. You've left something out.'

Have I?' he said. 'Oh, yes, the anger.'

'Let's go there for a while. Describe it to me.'

He recounted some instances. She watched him closely as he spoke, and only scribbled after he finished.

Time was nearly up. She said, 'I am going to leave you with one question. You must discuss it with no one. Not even Angela. Not anyone you talk to about how you're feeling. We can meet again in a week. I'm having to squeeze you in now because you lost your regular slot. Are you ready for the question?'

'Yes, I suppose so.'

'Here it is. Who are you really angry with?'

'But…'

'No, David, session over. Who is the person you are really angry with? And, seeing as you consider yourself a clever fellow, here's another question that goes with it. What is the anger that destroys the world?'

David texted Angela after her work time.

'Hi, it's me. I saw Myfanwy today. Can we meet?'

A text came back twenty minutes later. 'OK, come round, I'll cook you a meal.'

'What time?'

'7pm.'

He walked up to her house through the dark and dreary evening. It seemed to sympathise with his mood. How had things gone so awry when they'd been so good? He looked back on their holiday, and all that sunshine, and all those good times together. Something was still at him. Something had it in for him and wouldn't let him go.

Levels of hell, inside him. Circling the plughole.

She opened the door and looked at him. He was unsure how to greet her and she seemed the same.

'Come in, then,' she said.

He left his coat on a hook behind the door and followed her into the front room. Like he was a visitor. They sat on the settee.

'What are we having?' he asked.

'Home-cooked fish, chips and mushy peas. Should please you. Listen, David, I'm sorry I was so angry with you the other day, but the truth is this anger frightens, and like I said, I'm not going to end up a battered wife. I've seen this anger in you too often now. And it felt like you were ready to hit me, having already pushed that lady. I don't like to be hard with you – it upsets me as much as it upsets you – but this is serious time now. We're due to get married in seven weeks.'

'I know.'

'And I'm prepared to continue planning for that, as long as you're seeing Myfanwy and you get something sorted out.'

'Hmm. I never told you what she said about you when our sessions ended before.'

'This is not some sort of competition between me and Myfanwy.'

'Interesting that you say that. Because it very much seemed that way to listen to her. I told her that for your sake I needed to stop seeing her, because she insisted on undermining my relationship with you, saying you were bad for me. She actually said, "I've never made you choose between me and Angela," which was exactly how it felt, especially when she hugged me with a tear in her eye and said, "We're not finished, you and I," and, "You will be back."'

'OK,' Angela responded, 'well done for standing up for me, but this really isn't a competition between me and her. She still needs to help you deal with the anger she's brought to the surface for you. You were never angry before. You were lacking in any basic human kindness when I first met you, but you weren't deliberately *unkind* to anyone. And you didn't flare up in white-hot anger. And you didn't frighten me with the expectation of violence. This is new and very bad. Come on, the food will be ready.'

They went into the back room and she served up the meal, sitting across the table from him.

'Listen, David, I'm not feeling very affectionate towards you right now. This meal is a way of saying I do still love you and care about you and hope we can get this sorted out. But you've really frightened me and made me doubt the whole basis of our relationship. To quote a cliché, I don't know who you are any more.'

'*I* don't know who I am any more,' he said.

She gave thanks and they started to eat. 'So what did Myfanwy say?'

David had a weapon and this was the time to use it. 'She said I can't discuss this with anyone and not even you. I think she meant especially not you.'

Angela ate and thought. 'OK, I'm going to trust her. I think you should trust her as well, even though I know you feel you have reason not to. It was she who put her finger on this anger. She can help you with the dreams. You need help fast. Nobody else can do it.'

He said nothing, but enjoyed a lovely bit of unbattered cod with tartare sauce on it.

'When are you seeing her next?'

'She's going to try to fit me in weekly.'

'That's only six sessions until the wedding. You'd better hope she works miracles. And pray for God to help her. Because I meant what I said. No resolution, no marriage.'

'What if she really doesn't want you and me to get married?'

'I trust her.'

'You've never met her.'

'I trust her.'

She had some lovely apple crumble and custard for them. Then coffee, still facing each other at the table. Then she ushered him homewards.

At the door he wasn't sure whether he wanted to kiss her or not. But she was resolute in any case.

'You are my love and I want to marry you,' she said, a dark sadness on her face in the dim light of the porch. 'But you need some fast sorting out, no question, and I can't help you there.

I'll pick you up for church on Sunday. Maybe we should have lunch out.'

'OK.'

'When is the new bedroom carpet being laid?'

'Wednesday.'

'And the double bed coming?'

'Friday.'

He went home.

It was Saturday, 25th February.

He woke in a dizzy swirl of fear and damnation, stuck to his sheets in a hell of slimy vomit, his insides aching and his mouth sour.

So this was how connected the anger was to the dreams. Spend a day talking about the anger, and wake up the next morning having dreamt the gut-wrenching dream of killing Micky.

Who was he really angry with? Was it himself? Possibly. That sounded the right sort of answer for a counsellor. Was it supposed to be Angela? To split them up? Could Myfanwy be trusted? And what was the anger that destroyed the world? The only answer he could think of was the wrath of God.

He couldn't face the day but he couldn't lie here in this.

He'd be better off dead.

Plenty of people would be better off dead, not least Mrs George, and he just had the misfortune to be one of them.

He literally slid off the bed and onto the floor, like some fat snake, lubricated by his own vomit. He disgusted himself. He stood and walked into the bathroom, shedding his pyjama skin into the laundry bin. He dared not even look in the face of the man in the mirror, but showered first.

The water was warm and good, cleansing, refreshing, like the love of God. He dried off, brushed his teeth and changed, and went into the spare room to dress as he'd moved all his clothes in there for now to keep them from picking up the acrid and so identifiable stink of sick.

This wasn't life. This was some kind of purgatory. How many levels of hell?

How many? And how did you know when you'd got to the bottom of them?

Was anger really better than depression? Would he, at this moment, rather go back?

And why didn't he wake up when he was throwing up? What torpor was this that held him so tight in his dreams in the night? He could choke to death in his sleep. Easily.

Everything was on the line. Literally. His marriage. His mind and sanity. His life. What was this deadly secret that refused to be unearthed but had had spades stuck into it that made it heave under the ground?

Heave. That was a good word for it.

CHAPTER TWENTY-SEVEN

It was Sunday, 26th February.

After the service in the morning he went up for prayer in the little side chapel. On duty with a man David hardly knew was Anna Lovren, whose insights had had a huge impact on him last Christmas when he'd first met her. He hadn't been back to her for help because he felt that being counselled by two people at once was unwise.

'Hello, David,' she said.

'Hello,' the man said, 'I'm Philip Gall. What can we pray about today?'

He sat between them. 'Well, I've been having issues with anger, and bad dreams, and they're affecting my relationship with Angela.'

'Nice and succinct,' Anna said. 'Let's pray. Is it OK if we lay a hand lightly on you?'

'Yes, go ahead.'

He bowed his head, and listened, and waited.

He heard them praying quietly in that language of heaven, that angelic tongue. Then Philip said, 'Lord, here is David. Lay Your hand upon him now for peace and healing.'

Then they continued praying quietly, and a peace flowed over David like a blanket from a father's hand. He felt like a small child on Daddy's lap, and it was so distinct he even felt like he was wearing pyjamas. And David recalled how God had said to him, so gently, 'You'll always have Me.'

Philip spoke. 'David, I see a picture, which you must weigh up as being helpful or not, but I'll tell you what it is. It's a bit nasty, I'm afraid to say. There is a big boil, on your neck, and it's causing you both pain and worry. It's red and angry-looking. But all the poison is in the boil now. It's full of pus that looks like vomit. And the last thing that has to happen – the *last* thing – is that it must be lanced. And that will be painful and unpleasant, but then it's gone. All gone. It may be tested, but it is then done away with. Like, the root has been reached, and finally dealt with. Does that make any sense to you?'

Tears started down David's face, and Anna pressed a paper tissue into his hand.

'I'll take that as a yes,' Philip said, his hand heavier on David's shoulder.

She drove them out to a little pub restaurant they knew near Illey. Not a sign of spring was in the February air. A dank dampness seemed to cling to everything from the sky to the trees to the ground. A light drizzle made the windscreen into obscured glass every so often. It was that irritating sort that didn't require the wipers on, but did need the occasional clearing.

They drove in silence. Heavy, it was, between them.

He looked at her ring, and wondered how it had come to this. At least she was still wearing it. Then again, did he really want to marry her? Was he angry at her? He was, a bit. She was treating him like a child again.

He recalled the sunny, Majorcan days when he'd given it to her, and compared them with the dreary scenes around them now, and the loss of that bright affection they'd had back then.

She put a CD on and played some nice worship music.

As they waited for their lunches to appear, she took his hand over the small table and, with a deep sorrow in her eyes, said, 'I do love you. I'm really sad about all this. But I can't marry a man that I fear.'

'I can't *be* a man that I fear.'

'What does that mean?'

'It means I can't control it. It just comes over me. It's like lust. You're doing it before you realise it.'

'I'm not sure the comparison is apt. Or that I want to hear about your problems with lust.'

'There you go again, criticising everything I say.'

She was quiet. The plates arrived and the two steak and ale pies with mash, veg and gravy were put in place. David picked up his fork, held it up to the teenage girl who was asking if there was anything else, and said, 'How hard is it to get a clean fork in this place? I would have thought that was pretty basic.'

She went red, and said, 'I'm sorry, sir. I'll get another one for you.'

She took the offending fork and came back with another. He accepted it, she walked off, he looked at it and bellowed, 'I don't believe it! Don't you even know what a clean fork looks like?'

Angela put a hand on his arm, everyone stared, and he said, 'Don't stare, I only want cutlery I can eat with, for goodness' sake!'

The waitress came back again, looking like she might cry, and Angela stood up and went to her. 'I'm really sorry,' she said. 'Don't let him worry you. Just get him a clean fork, please, and don't let it spoil your day.'

The girl smiled a weak smile, took the fork and went off. Angela sat down. When the girl approached with another fork, everyone was waiting to see what would happen next, but Angela whispered, 'I don't care if it's been dipped in dog poo and deep fried, you're accepting it.'

She offered it to him, he accepted it, looked at it and said, 'Thank you, that's fine. I'm sorry about my outburst earlier.'

She tiptoed away.

'How can I live with a man who does that when we go to a restaurant?' Angela said, looking almost as miserable as the girl. 'Am I going to spend the next twenty years apologising for you?'

'I hope not. Let's just eat,' he replied.

The idea had been to go for a walk together after lunch, but the drizzle had become heavier and the day more dank, so they sat in the car in the car park and talked. David found himself constantly distracted by the scenes of dripping branches and grey fields outside. They tempted depression, but he seemed immune to that now. Fear and anger had become his coin.

'I'm afraid,' he said.

'So am I,' she answered.

'What are you afraid of?'

'I'm afraid I've lost the man I loved and I don't even know what happened to him. And I'm afraid of getting married to the man who's replaced him, who makes me fearful of violence and anger and hatefulness for the rest of my life. I'm afraid that all the hopes I'd built up are coming undone and I'll be left with nothing. I'm afraid for you, because you're coming undone and you could be left with nothing. I'm very afraid.'

'I know. Every night I'm in a twisting turmoil of fear, and every day I'm acting in ways that are not me, and I hate it, but I can't stop it. Neither the fear nor the anger. I'm trapped in my own private purgatory and it's like I've already lost you because the relationship we had just isn't here any more.'

She started to cry, softly and quietly. He took her hand. 'Do you still trust Myfanwy? What if she wants me to identify that the person I'm really angry with is you, so she can split us up? What if she has some weird agenda? Why won't she let me go?'

'I still trust her,' she sniffed. 'I always pray for God to use her to get you sorted out. You have to stick with her. She opened up this anger, so she has to have the key to dealing with it.'

'That's not how it works. She can help me, but I have to find the key to dealing with it. I have to identify it, grasp it and use it to unlock the door into the root of this anger. And what will I find in there? Remember the dream about me standing outside the door, and it starts to bang and swell from inside the house, which is some "other place"? It's terrifying! It isn't easy, seeing her.'

'Good. Then it must be doing something. No Myfanwy, no marriage. You keep trying and I'll know I haven't lost you. But we can't cancel the marriage at the last minute. We'd have to give people two weeks, minimum. Saturday 1st April. And it won't be an April Fools' Day prank.'

'Not the best day.'

'We'll have more things to worry about than that.'

It was Friday, 24th March.

It was a Myfanwy day.

Four times that week David had woken in the slippery slew of his own deepest upwellings, feeling like he'd been emptied out.

But last night he didn't sleep at all. He went to bed at 11pm. He tossed and turned. He began to realise that he was actually fearing falling asleep, because of the dream. It had become so powerful that every time he thought of it his heart rate leapt and he ended up having to get out of bed and walk round and drink water to calm himself down.

He had stood, a number of times, looking out of his bedroom curtains at the moon, hanging high and holy in a clear sky. He'd got up at 3am and made tea and wrapped himself up and taken Bart out to sit with him on his bench and join him staring at that scene. It was magnificent. A silver and weightless lace laid over field and tree, shining in the semi-dark like it was some quite other place. Ethereal in its beauty. Yet it didn't call to him. And Bart said nothing. He was a wise bear.

It was a week, basically, to decision day. His visits to Myfanwy had disturbed him, challenged him, angered him, but not revealed who it was that he was really angry with. And she would not tell him. He had to discover it for himself. He'd thought of begging her, but that would just make him look weak, and needy. And assuming she really did know, she wouldn't tell him. She was resolute. *He* had to uncover it. Dig into that heaving earth and reveal it to his own sight. The horror. The *true* horror so buried that even the mention of it emptied him, and whose power of anger terrified him.

Still, at least he knew what was the anger that destroyed the world. He saw it in a buggy. A toddler whose whole body was contorted with a rage so powerful it made the little child jerk and kick and lash out and scream with a sound so grating it hurt. He let out a bellow of anger till his lungs were empty and then his face was red, his eyes swollen and blotchy, and tears and snot streaked his skin. He lashed out at his mum if she came within reach with such force that it probably would have actually hurt, and then he stuck three fingers in his mouth and bit on them as hard as he could, causing him to yelp and screech and then become rigid in a good imitation of a proper fit.

The anger that destroys the world. It wasn't the wrath of God. Well, not in this context. It was the anger of the small child. That wordless, screeching fury that you see in a totally frustrated young child, red-faced and thrashing about at being denied his wishes. An anger that seems to him so strong, so powerful, so destructive that it will destroy himself, Mummy, Daddy and everything around them, which is the whole world.

But why that was so significant he couldn't quite see.

He'd gone back to bed eventually, and kept Bart with him, hoping not to sully his lovely fur in the last of the night. But he still couldn't sleep. He looked at the ceiling. He looked at the wall. He stared at the clock. He put his earpieces in and listened to music.

He did the countdown thing. 'If I sleep now I'll still get four hours, and I can survive on that.' 'If I get to sleep now I'll still get three hours and a bit. I could maybe manage on that.' 'If I get to sleep now I'll only get two hours and that's nowhere near enough,' and so on.

At half past six he decided there was no point lying there any more so he got up, showered, toileted and dressed. He took toast and tea out to the bench in two jumpers and a heavy coat, because despite the arrival of spring it was still darned cold in the early morning.

A rabbit hopped along the bottom of the fence the other side of the road. The row of daffodils trumpeted glory, but he couldn't hear them. He heard the birds, in early chorus, but was unmoved by their calls to rejoice. Buds and baby leaves on the trees swayed and bowed in the intermittent breeze, like they were doing a dance. But it wasn't a dance he wanted to be part of.

A question popped into his head as if from somewhere and nowhere. It was, 'Do you know what "always" means?'

Did he know what 'always' means? It means for ever. Without end. Ah, but, it also means 'all the time'. 'Dependably'. 'Without fail'. Hmm. You are with me always, so that means both 'for ever' and 'in every moment'. OK, I get that. That's good to know. Thank You.

Breakfast finished, he decided to go for a walk. The air was brisk and cold, the day was waking as the world came to life around him in springtime hopefulness. Spring is hopeful. It speaks of Easter hope and hope of summer. So how come he felt bereft of hope and without a future that he could see?

And what was he doing to Angela? With whom he was angry, but also for whom he felt very sorry.

'David. I don't believe we can wait any longer.'

She had boots on up to her knees, and a blue skirt in a thick material, and a white blouse under a soft, fluffy, sand-coloured jumper.

She had no notepad on her lap, no pencil in her hand.

'David, have you had any notable insights yet?'

'No. I'm pretty sure it's not me I'm angry at, though I am and that makes a good psychotherapeutic answer. I'm pretty sure it's not Angela, though I am a bit angry with her. I'm sure it's not you, though you can be very irritating. It isn't my dad; it isn't my mum. It isn't any of our friends at church; in any case, I haven't really known them long enough. Unless of course I was projecting someone else on to one of them, but I'm not. It isn't God, though He and I have fallen out once or twice. It isn't the world in general or destiny or my bad luck. So, I'm full of "isn'ts". No "is-s".'

'What you've just said is enormously helpful. What did Sherlock Holmes say about once you've worked your way through everything that might not be feasible, whatever is still there must be correct? I believe we are right there. How does that make you feel?'

'Hopeful. Afraid. Uncertain.'

'I want you to relax because I'm going to put you into a light state of relaxation. Not hypnosis entirely, but a certain dissociation. Is that OK?'

'No. I don't want to be hypnotised, at any level.'

'Why not?'

'Because I don't trust anyone to be meddling in my mind without my conscious defences in place.'

'OK, that's fair. Though it means I have to play a dangerous game, sail close to the wind. We're out of time, aren't we? I need to get you to see and acknowledge what's been going on in you but I can only point, not show. If I show you, then it comes from me, and you probably won't accept it or deal with it. That will only happen if the revelation comes from inside of you. So I can point, but not too obviously.'

'What if you're wrong?'

'Then we've got nothing. Same as if I can't get you to see.'

'All right. What?'

She looked at him long and hard, and said, slowly, 'The person we're talking about must be someone in whom you are, or have been, emotionally invested. It's someone you're so committed to that the idea that you're angry with them is unthinkable. Even felt hatred for them. It's someone your own subconscious has tried to point you to. All the pointers are there, all the evidence is in place. You're just not "Sherlock" enough to see it. You resist it because it's unthinkably awful. But it's the truth.' She leaned forward and, with a look like anger and judgement on her face, she said, 'What is the truth, David?'

'You can't handle the truth.'

'Don't fence with me and don't mock me at the expense of your own sanity. I take my fee home at the end of the day. What are you going to take? What is the truth, David?'

He felt hot. His collar felt tight. Who? Who? Who?

She spoke again. 'Cast your mind far back. The most significant attachments are at the beginning, usually.'

306

His mum? Never a significant attachment. His dad? Only a friend, really.

'Oh, David! What is the truth? Which person in your past abandoned you and fled, leaving you in the biggest sorry mess of your whole life? What is the truth?'

Silence. 'What is the truth, David?'

Heat and confusion overcame him. Her words became distant. He wasn't still sitting on the chair.

And someone was crying out horribly, about something that could not be. Could not be.

It was too terrible.

He opened his eyes and saw carpet. And his fingers at his mouth were covered with watery snot.

And he took in a deep breath and cried out. Again. His body was bent like a foetus, and his eyes stung from tears. She was just watching him, from her chair, though a box of tissues was on the floor beside him.

'David. David. You have your answer.'

'I have nothing,' he croaked. 'I am nothing.'

'You've seen it and you just need to accept it. You told me yourself. But I still cannot tell it back to you. Stop resisting it. Stop fencing with it. Look. Remember.'

He wiped a tissue across his face. A sudden bolt of fear shook him. A deep shudder went through his entire body. A terror so sharp it took his breath away.

'No,' he said, softly. Then, 'No!' more loudly. Then, 'No! No!' he bellowed.

'Tell me again,' she said.

He cried. He cried so hard he couldn't speak. A heavy and desperate loss came over him and welled up from inside him, like he'd just lost Micky again. Lost and gone for ever. Her sweet face. Her little hands. Her trusting stare. Her comforting warmth on his lap.

'No, no, no! Not again!'

'For the first time, maybe,' Myfanwy said.

'No.' His throat hurt from some unheard pleading.

'Tell me, David.'

'Nothing to tell.'

'Now is the moment. Tell me and be free. Say it. See it. Remember it.'

He cried even more, wailing into the carpet.

She let him be for a while, then said, 'I've cancelled my next appointment, David, much to the annoyance of the person who was on her way. We are going to have this out. What did you see? Tell me.'

'Nothing.'

'Don't tell me nothing.'

'Nothing so awful... ever was.'

'All right. But it was, and all you're doing is acknowledging it. So tell me.'

'Why?'

'Why what?'

'Why did I feel that way,' he said.

'You tell me. You saw it all.'

'I never, I never...'

'David, this moment goes one of two ways. You refuse to tell me and it stays hidden, and we've got nowhere, or you tell me and we finish what we've been doing for more than a year. Which is it to be? Do you want to marry Angela or not?'

'Pull my guts out I will not say it. It cannot be... it cannot be...'

'And yet you saw it and felt it and it is. Tell me. You already said it, while you were clawing at my carpet. I heard you.'

'That was a mistake. That cannot be.'

He was empty of tears and cries for mercy. He gave his face another wipe and got up.

'There's a bathroom across the hall. I suggest you go and use it,' she said.

He left the counselling room, crossed the nicely carpeted waiting area and went into the toilet, where he relieved himself and washed his face. He looked at the haggard, shattered, red-eyed, red-faced old man in the mirror. Who was that sad fellow? Why did they keep wheeling him in here?

Back in his chair he cleared his throat and said, without having actually made the decision, 'I'm going to tell you. Somehow, I'm going to tell you.'

She looked surprisingly calm. 'Thank you, David, go ahead.'

He went to say it but tears welled up in his eyes and everything went misty again. It pulled his heart right out of him. 'Dear Micky. Dear, precious, lovely little Micky, who was my very life and I was hers. She… she did something I couldn't handle. She did something to me so terrible I've never recovered from it. Seems silly to say it now, but then, it set off the anger. The whole anger. The person I've been so angry at that I've pretty much… hated, is… it's… dear Micky. She abandoned me, and left me, and wasn't there any more when I most needed her. That was how it felt. That was how it was. It makes no sense maybe, but that's it.'

He looked down at the floor and wept a quiet stream of hot tears. He wiped them from the end of his nose.

'How many tears?' he said to himself.

'Enough to get to the bottom,' she answered. 'The lowest layer of hell. I believe you're there.'

They sat in silence for a moment or two, and something inside him settled.

'What's happening?' she asked.

'I don't know. Pressure is easing.'

'You've been in a state and I'm not going to let you go until you're a lot happier. Tell me again, what's happening?'

'Well, it's like I can see that anger for what it was. Not real. The anger that destroys the world. I was never really angry at Micky, in real life. I certainly never hated her, but then, it just felt like she'd abandoned me, and the only person close enough to me that I could attach that anger to was her, illogical though that seems from a nice safe distance, but at the time, in the mind of an eight-year-old, it was powerful.'

'Then what happened to it?'

'It was too painful to exist. That I should love Micky so much, and feel so sorry for her, and be so devastated by losing her, and yet feel such anger at her, that was too great a conflict. A dissonance, as you would say. The anger had to be subjugated by the love and the sadness but, like Freud said, it comes back. It's never really gone until it's faced. But facing it, seeing it for what it was, destroys its power. But only *I* could do that. *I* had to exhume it and lay my eyes upon it in order to see it for the thing it was. A paper tiger. An illogical thing. No insult to her or to her memory. Beneath this shattered exterior, I think I feel an incredible freedom. It's like its power is dispersed on sight.'

'You're babbling. But it's a good babbling. I think you're nearly ready to go home.'

Still, he left there half an hour later a broken man. Emptied. Cried out. Had the truth set him free? Or crushed him under a weight of knowing that would forever drag him down?

He sat in his car, staring. He drove home without even knowing. He sat on his bench without going into the house.

Why didn't it bother him now that he'd been so angry at Micky? Because now he saw it unclothed. It had been a child's anger. The anger that destroys the world. Now he could see that he only felt that way because he loved and needed her so much. It was his desolate lack of any other loving human being that left him without another avenue for his loss and grief. Everything for him was about Micky. His reaction to the sense of abandonment could only be directed at her as well. Everything was, had always been, about her.

It was no longer. He was free. Free of the stifling prison of the pain and anger of a desperate and abandoned child.

Budding trees waved at him a friendly greeting.

Daffodils all in a row marched past, trumpeting a glorious tune of order and freedom like a marching band.

Birds swooped and curved through a spring air bursting with the very scents of life that kept them aloft. They called to each other, but also to him, of places they'd seen that he should come with them one day to see. One happy day.

A burst of pink exploded a cherry tree into a ball of colour like you would pay £1,000 to create. All soft petals and dark bark, pink against black, magnificent in its huge declaration of hope.

He breathed in a lungful of the air and it nearly lifted him off the bench. It filled him with some exalted scent of very life, and as he let it go again, he relaxed inside into a joyous peace.

'Thank You, You who are with me "always",' he said.

He was hungry. Deeply hungry. Hungry for tea and something. Hungry for life. Hungry for Angela.

CHAPTER TWENTY-EIGHT

'You certainly look different.'

'We should go out to celebrate.'

'All right,' Angela said, slightly cautiously, 'but you know I'll be watching you.'

'You'll be watching me with proud affection,' David replied with a smile.

'I'm not sure I really get it.'

'I will explain all.'

They were sitting in her kitchen having a cup of tea. They got up to leave and she said, 'I know where we should go. The Plough at Lovington.'

'Why?'

'They are reputed to have the dirtiest cutlery in the kingdom!'

As they drove, he started to explain. 'Imagine you're frightened of balloons. You see a big, fat balloon. It's big, it's powerful, it's dangerous. But then it bursts. That was unpleasant. But look at it now. Small, powerless, curled up and dead. No longer a thing to fear. Actually, it's the same thing, but it looks and feels very different. When Micky died, I reacted with overwhelming loss and grief. It was a truly desperate sadness. A lonely pain. It felt like the only person I could take it to was dead. But to a child's mind, she had left me bereft. She had abandoned me. So there was a terrible anger. A child's extreme anger that feels like it will destroy the whole world. I was utterly conflicted. To the side of me that loved and wanted her, that anger seemed the most terrible thing in the world. The biggest, tightest, most dangerous and most powerful balloon there could be. So I buried it in a secret place in my subconscious mind. And I became wary of all anger. Getting in touch with my anger in order to stop being so liable to depression was like prodding the balloon. The balloon's hiding place was being uncovered. The anger started to seep out of it. But also, the fear of that revelation sent dreams. Dreams that pointed to the place – dreams of being the one who killed Micky. Warnings, perhaps, to leave it alone. Warnings that couldn't avoid conveying part of the truth – I was angry at Micky for abandoning me. Angry with a furious anger that was strong enough to be hatred. Of the very one I had ever most loved and needed. Whom to hate or hurt was the most awful thing I could ever imagine.

'Myfanwy had me reviewing my angers and hurts, and the people they concerned, making me narrow down who it was I was really angry with. The one I couldn't even include on the list. Once I'd narrowed it down to Micky, she prodded me some more, and let me unearth the truth. The balloon went bang. The shock nearly killed me. Her carpet will never be the same. But then I could look at it as an adult, see the illogic of it, the paper tiger that it was, the anger as that of a deeply hurt eight-year-old, not my anger here and now. It's a burst balloon. I loved Micky and I could never have hurt her, and the loss of her was the hardest thing I've ever had to face. Maybe ever will have to face. But now I see the anger of her leaving me for what it was. Its power over me is gone. Bang. Quick as that. I guess all those hard weeks of preparation also made it possible for the thing to disperse once it was seen by me.'

'And you feel like a huge weight has lifted off you?' Angela asked.

'More like I'm lighter myself. Full of helium. Ready to engage with spring and hope and life and to be at peace and not angry. Ready to marry you.'

'It sounds almost too good to be true.'

'You'll see.'

313

They ate on the patio, warmed by heaters, watching the dusk over the fields. Spring's bedtime hushed the nesting birds, blew the daffodils, shook the crocuses and fanned specks of pink and white in swirls from the cherry trees. Breathed in, it became a living waft of creation: lifting, filling, rejuvenating.

This was why she had chosen The Plough – not the cutlery, which was nice and clean. They dined on stroganoff and rice for him, and chicken korma for her, followed by Eton mess shared between them. He had a celebratory Merlot, or two.

Not the slightest inclination to annoyance rose within him. He was at peace. A happy peace. A deeply relieved peace.

As they drove home, she said, 'I believe you. All that tension has gone. I realise your shoulders have lowered. Your hackles, I suppose. I see in you the man I was with in Majorca, to whom I was happy to pledge my future and entrust my years. But are you up for a test?'

He looked at her cheeky face. 'Are you serious?'

'Yes, I'm serious. This is something I've been meaning to say but not dared to, and began to wonder if it even mattered any more. Are you ready?'

'Go on.'

'There is this one thing,' she said.

'Yes?' He began to get nervous.

'Bart – he has to go.'

'What? But he's just a bear!' David choked out, defensive of his friend.

'I'd be less insistent if you said, "It's just a stuffed toy." But he's more than that and you know it. I'm not saying he has to be thrown out. He can go to a good home, or a charity shop, but I'm not having him in our spare bedroom so when I chuck you out of bed you can go and lie with him and remember the "good times" and reflect on how much better things were before I came, and you can depend on his furry wisdom.'

'But he never did anything wrong!'

'There you go again. He has to go. I don't mind if it's somewhere you can see him from time to time.'

He was silent for a while. He searched his feelings. Bart had been a faithful friend and it just seemed wrong to have to cast him off. But there was not a hint of annoyance over it.

'Are you sure about this?' he said.

'Don't throw him out. Don't treat him badly. But you cannot keep him. For me.'

'Is that a fair request?'

'Yes,' she said, 'I think in the circumstances, it is.'

He was silent again.

'Andrew. I can lend him to Andrew.'

'You can *give* him to Andrew.'

He relented. Happily. Happy to do it happily. 'For you, my love, I will give him to Andrew in all perpetuity and to his progeny and successors, for being our page boy.'

'I knew you had it in you,' she said, and they both laughed as the last of springtime dusk slipped from the sky.

It was Saturday, 15th April.

The big day.

Like Christmas.

David was up at 5.30am because he couldn't see the point of lying in bed any longer. He was just too excited.

He wasn't surprised to see that there was a text from his best man, Bill Granger, on his phone. But it read, 'David. So sorry. On way back from Chester like I told you but left later than expected and car broke down near Birmingham. RAC chap says it'll take a couple of hours to fix. Should be with you in time. Sorry.'

David stared at it. Then he went into the spare bedroom and stared at the two suits, so carefully laid out side by side on the bed. Well, Bill had better get here in time. That suit wasn't going to fit many other people he knew.

All right, don't panic, that will be the glitch for this mission. Breakfast.

He went downstairs in his dressing gown, made tea and sat outside with it. How long before he could go and get some fresh croissants for a worthy breakfast? An hour or so.

The forecast was for a lovely day but at the moment it looked a bit drizzly over there, past the trees, towards that long stretch of the universe out that way. Hmm. Not to worry.

He had his usual electric shave, showered, brushed his teeth with infinite care, dressed in clothes that weren't involved in the ceremony, and checked his list again.

All good. Had the caterers resolved that problem with staffing? That was their problem, not his. He couldn't find them extra staff at the last minute.

Angela texted. 'You up?'

'Yes. Bill G stuck in Birmingham with car broken down! You OK?'

'Woken up with a bit of a cold. Sniffy. Red nose. Puffy eyes. Sneezy. Not too bad though. Make-up should fix!!'

'Love you however you look. Take some Co-codamol. Also give some to Thelia to keep on her. See ya later. I'm only waiting five minutes by the way then we're off to the pub.'

'I'll be there when I can. Love you. If I'm very late mine's a Merlot.'

He laughed as he looked at it.

Croissants. If he took his time getting ready, and pottered about a bit, and had a proper wet shave just to be sure, and walked very slowly, he should arrive not too long before the bakery opened at seven. He would pray as he went. Give thanks. A lot of thanks to give.

Goodness! It was his wedding day! How did that come about? It was that woman. That wonderful woman. His Angela, his angel. Who was about to be his wife, for always. He thrilled and tingled as he walked. What a day! 'O Lord, let it all go well, please, and keep us in Your care today, and everyone who's involved at all. And please help Bill with his car. I'm sure he's all upset and frustrated, so calm him, Lord, and help him not to worry or feel bad. Thank You.'

He arrived at the bakery only to find that on a Saturday they opened at 7.30am. His shoulders drooped. Ah well. Wander round town. He set off and remained calm and cool.

Then his phone rang. It was an unknown number. 'Hello, Mr Sourbeak?'

'Hello. It's Sour*book*. Who is this, please?'

'Yes, hello, sir, this is Jerry from Minsters, about your car.'

'Good morning, Jerry. I trust you have good news for me.'

'Well, not exactly, sir, no, I'm sorry. The thing is, the white limo was left out of the secure lock-up last night and it got scratched by someone, probably with their keys, I'd say. It's right along the side and on the bonnet and very obvious.' David's heart sank into his guts.

'The thing is, sir, our Angus says there's no way we can get a professional job done on it in time for the service today and he could only do a regular touch-up job with, well, touch-up paint. Would it be all right for your fiancée to travel to the wedding in one of our black cars?'

'But your black cars are for funerals.'

'Yes, I know, sir, but people do travel to weddings in black cars.'

'Yes, Jerry, but not in *your* black cars, and everybody knows that.'

'Well, the only alternative is to let Angus have a go at touching up the white paint.'

David took a deep breath. 'Fine. Tell Angus that I'm absolutely confident he can make such a good job of it that it will be a fitting car for my fiancée to be taken in on the biggest day of her life.'

'OK. Thank you, Mr Sourbrook.'

'It's Sour*book*. Thank you, Jerry, perhaps you can ring me in an hour and let me know how it's going. Of course, alternatively, one of you might know someone who's done a lot of touching-up paint and is a real wiz at it.'

'That's not a bad idea. OK, then. Thank you for being so understanding, sir. I'm sure we can knock ten quid off your bill. Bye for now.'

'Bye,' David said, and muttered, 'Ten quid!' He sighed. 'Lord, how many more things? Or perhaps I shouldn't ask.'

Eventually, at nearly twenty to eight, the bakery opened. David had watched them inside wandering around and chatting to each other for at least fifteen minutes, and kept looking at his watch, and his back was beginning to ache, and he reflected that if they said they opened at 7.30 they should open at 7.30, which was already later than on weekdays. But when the middle-aged woman in her uniform opened the door, he greeted her with, 'Good morning. I'm getting married today!'

She looked at him like he was a fool, as if anyone his age was going to get married, then said, 'Well, congratulations to you. You've been in here a few times with your intended, I'm thinking.'

'Indeed I have. We have. And we will be again. We're not moving away.'

'What can I get you, then?'

'A large latte and two butter croissants, please, to have here.'

He was nearly home when his phone rang. It was Angela. He could hear the tears in her voice. 'Oh, David! I've just tried on the dress and the seam's ripped! I knew all those dinners people invited us to would do this to me. I'm a great, horrible, fat hippopotamus!'

'You're not a hippopotamus,' he said, and she gave a tiny chuckle, amid the tears. 'But you are great. OK. First thing to do is take the dress off.'

'I've done that.'

'So you're standing there in your underwear?'

'Yes.'

'Ooh!'

'Focus, David.'

'Right, how long is the tear?'

'About four inches.'

'And where is it?'

'On my hip beside my big, fat bum.'

'You don't have a big, fat bum. You have a lovely bum. And how big are the cloth daffodils on your bouquet? Not the real daffs, the cloth ones.'

'About five inches across.'

'All right. Here's what you do. You and Thelia stitch up either side of the tear so it can't split any further, but leave it where it's separated. Then sew one of the cloth daffodils over the split. You might even do the same the other side after splitting it deliberately to give you an extra bit of wiggle room.'

'I knew I was right to ask a scientist!' she said. 'Got to go. Love you.'

He got home and put the kettle on. He was going to be having more caffeine than usual this morning. Good grief! Split dress, scratched cars, best man stranded, caterers short-staffed, coffee shop not open. It would try the patience of a saint. Which he was.

'Mr Sourbook. This is Jerry again from Minster cars. I'm afraid I've got some bad news for you, sir. Angus did the touch-up job but then found he'd used the wrong paint. He's used "ivory white" instead of "polar white". And it's a bit… obvious, you'd say. Are you sure you wouldn't rather use a black car?'

'Well, Jerry, in fact, no. I suggest you take the car to whichever garage you trust and explain your problem and ask them to do you a favour. Or you ring the stretch limo people and ask to borrow or hire their white one.'

'Well, there's an idea. All right Mr… Sourbook, I'll get on it and I'll get back to you. Bye for now.'

'Bye for now,' David said, and kept his sigh for after the call ended.

As he sat outside on his bench, with Bart beside him enjoying the spring air, his mobile chirruped again.

'Hello, Mr Sourbook? This is Starlight Galleries. Damien, I'm your photographer. You did say we could put up extra lighting in the church, didn't you?'

'No. I said they won't allow extra lighting. They never allow extra lighting. Not unless you're the BBC doing *Songs of Praise*. Don't you remember that little joke?'

'Ah. Right. That'll be why they're not letting us set up. Right. OK, I'm going to need some different equipment. But that's all right, don't you worry!'

'Good, thank you, Damien. I won't worry.'

The call ended.

'Don't worry,' David said to himself. 'We're a bunch of idiots and not one of us can get a simple job right, but that's OK because you're paying us. Are all weddings like this? Or do I attract a certain brand of incompetence? Still, chill. It's all OK. In God's hands, eh, you faithful old bear?'

Bart nodded.

He was helped.

'You know, don't you, that this is goodbye, faithful buddy. It's like I'm going off from my first family to my new family. Leaving home to get married and start a whole new family.

'Only, it's you that'll actually be moving, 'cos we're setting up home here.'

Bart looked sad.

By mid-morning, ten-thirty, David was getting anxious for word from Bill. His best man was supposed to be the one standing by him, helping him deal with all these frustrations. Well, it was an hour to the service.

His phone rang. It was Angela. 'Hello, my love. It's all done. It looks fabulous, and gives me enough leeway to actually sit down.'

'How useful!'

'Yes, and it looks like it was always intended with the bouquet, so all's well. How are you doing?'

'Do you really want to know? It isn't a pretty picture.'

320

'Oh? What? Has Bill arrived yet?'

'No. And no word. That's the worst thing. Then there's Minsters wanting to send you in a funeral car because their white one got scratched, the caterers short of staff, the photographer confused about lighting in the church, and… what else? Maybe that's it. I'm so glad all the flowers were done yesterday evening.'

'Are you coping?' she said, sympathetically.

'Yes, actually, rather well. I'm quite calm. Have the tablets helped your cold?'

'Yes, I'm a lot more comfortable and less snotty.'

'So lovely. I'll see you in an hour, as long as the church doesn't sink into a hole or the world doesn't come to an end. I'm beginning to wonder whether the Lord doesn't want us to get married after all.'

'Don't be silly. Of course He does. You're doing a great job.'

'Good thing someone is. All right, then, here we go. Bye.'

Next on the phone was Bill, ten minutes later. 'David! Dear chap! I'll be there in five minutes so get a coffee on, I'm parched!'

'Will do. Great news.'

'What?'

'Great news.'

'What great news?'

'That you're nearly here. I'll explain in five minutes.'

Bill accepted the coffee with uncommon gratitude and fell onto the settee. 'What a journey!' he said. 'I'm pooped, I can tell you.'

'Well, you're just in time to clean up, get dressed, and then we're off to the church, where hopefully the photographer hasn't stormed off in a rage, a white car that isn't falling to pieces will bring Angela, whose dress won't fly apart when she sneezes. Then we'll only have the caterers to worry about.'

'Dear chap, what *have* you been up to?'

They drove to the church with Bart in the back (wearing a seatbelt) at ten past eleven, and were greeted by the ushers, all of them church friends, including Anna Lovren. They had simply turned up with the service sheets and started handing them out, which seemed to David to be quite miraculous.

Men in suits and ladies in dresses and smart hats were everywhere. They said quick hellos as they made their way to the vestry and Rector Colin.

'In good time!' he said. 'Come in, and David, sit down and check over those two registers and that wedding certificate. Every name, every number must be correct. Take a moment over that. Bill, come with me and we'll confirm where you'll be sitting and I'll check the rings are ready.'

They disappeared into the church. David finished checking the three entries and then joined them. The flowers – mostly daffodils – were adorning every ledge, surface and pillar in a shower of yellow, orange and white. The smell of them was amazing. Not heavy, but fresh and breezy.

'All good?' Colin asked. 'I was just showing Bill where you two will need to be in about five minutes' time, at the front here, and then you'll just be waiting for Angela. Don't get fretful – most brides are late. Good. Registers perfect?'

'In every detail.'

'Good. Go and see some people before you need to come and wait here.'

David and Bill sat in their seats as the organ played and people filled up the pews noisily, chattering away.

David kept looking back to see if Angela had arrived. And looking out of a side window towards the sun and clouds.

Suddenly the music stopped and the rector walked up the aisle. He indicated to David and Bill to come to their places in front of him, slightly to the right, with Bill on David's right side, and the organ started to play Albinoni's 'Adagio'. The sweet music filled the church and everyone stood. David craned his neck round to see. There at the back of the aisle stood an angelic Angela, with Thelia beside her and Andrew behind in the most fabulous suit and shirt.

This was the moment. David had been watching a cloud parting the way for a shaft of sunshine which he reckoned would light her gloriously at the back of the aisle. She started to move forward, and the shaft of light didn't appear. He was no meteorologist – don't give up your day job. She approached one leisurely step at a time, as directed at their rehearsal, and he saw her beaming at him. No veil.

Closer. Closer. Andrew was smiling a broad smile at him as well, which he returned twice as wide.

She arrived, and the clouds parted so the shaft of sunlight circled them *both* at the sanctuary step. Now, that seemed right to him. She passed her bouquet to Thelia, who passed it to Andrew, and he stayed there beside her, holding it.

'You look stunning,' Rector Colin whispered to Angela. 'Are you OK? David, are you ready?'

For David, the words of welcome, and the promises, and the songs, were a blur of nervous ecstasy. All he really knew was that Angela was there and they were getting married. Even the rector's short sermon didn't really register. And then they were sat in the vestry signing books, and being lined up to process back out again to Mendelssohn's 'Wedding March' played magnificently with full gusto by the organist. Everyone was standing and applauding them, and then they were out in spring sunshine being surrounded and congratulated and photographed and manhandled.

The ride to the reception was a welcome hiatus, so they cuddled up and kissed each other and were quiet.

Then there was the line, in traditional style, because they wanted to make sure everyone was received properly, and the meal, and the speeches, and a rather saucy comment from Bill in his speech, that Angela was a truly wonderful gift that David couldn't wait to unwrap.

As soon as he could, David caught up with Andrew, and there was the most ferocious hug that flattened David's buttonhole daffodil, but he didn't even care. He fetched Bart and handed him over, much to Andrew's delight. He wanted to say not to hug him too hard, but the desire for it to be a true gift without strings attached overcame.

Wine and bubbles flowed, dancing began, the cake was cut and, as if in a blur of alcohol and friends, they were leaving and being driven back to their new home, David's cottage, soon after 11pm. Twelve hours after they'd set off.

They flopped onto the settee and he said, 'Welcome to your new home, Mrs Sourbook.'

CHAPTER TWENTY-NINE

It was Sunday, 16th April.

The big day.

The biggest big day of them all.

David woke up naked under the covers with a naked woman beside him. She was watching him with such fixed and tender affection that it almost made him want to cry.

'I saw your body,' he said.

'I felt your body,' she agreed.

'Just like the Bible says, no shame at all. Just like Adam and Eve.'

'We're just like Adam and Eve,' she said with a smile. 'No shame, no regret, no hurt feelings, no secret guilt. Just a pure and thankful joy. I love you.'

'I'm so glad we managed to wait. It wasn't always easy.'

'My goodness it wasn't!' Angela said. 'Men tend to let on when they're feeling that way, because it's expected for them to get hot under the belt. Women tend to keep it covered up because it's seen as slutty and shameful. But I agree it hasn't been easy. But I'm so glad.'

She stroked his cheek. He caught her hand and kissed it.

They both yawned, and laughed. 'What time is it?' she said.

He reached over and picked up his phone. 'Ten to nine. OK. Time to be up. I'll shower first then go and put the kettle on and start breakfast, and you can take your time.'

'Will you always be this gracious and thoughtful?'

'Of course!'

He showered, and found he could actually thank God in the stream of water for the tender exposure of last night, sensing absolutely no shame or guilt. He admitted to himself he was slightly relieved he'd actually managed it. At his advancing age.

Downstairs, he boiled the kettle and put on toast and two boiled eggs. He resisted Radio 4 because now he was a married man and his new wife wanted to talk to him at breakfast. Quite right too.

When she came down, they kissed and cuddled in the middle of the kitchen floor, then sat opposite each other at the little table.

They gave thanks for the food, then she said, 'All that trauma yesterday must have been quite a test of your calmness.'

'Oh! Phone call after phone call. And you and the dress! Which looked fabulous, I say again. But I can honestly say I didn't even feel a twinge of anger. Yes, I think you're right, it was a test, and as I sat there with Bill waiting for you to arrive, I recognised that fact. Tested and found fit for service.'

'Fit for service!' she laughed. 'Wedding service.'

'Fit for marriage.'

'You certainly are. I'm sorry I rang you up all panicky and tearful, almost like it was your fault.'

'Oh, you shouldn't be sorry. If I'm not here for you, who is?'

'Thelia. She did a great job, you know. And Andrew, he was so happy to see you when we came in the back of the church. And he loves Bart.'

'Who wouldn't?'

They ate quietly, then he said, 'You are going to have to wipe that smirk off your face.'

'Smirk?' she said, a little hurt. 'That's not a smirk, that's a *smile*, of wedded bliss.'

'It looks like a smirk of bedded bliss. Not that I have any problem with that at all. But we're going to church in an hour, and do you really want all our friends to see that expression? It's a bit of a giveaway.'

'Well, so? Why not?'

'You will be so embarrassed.'

'This must be why people go on honeymoon straight away. So their friends and family can't see the look on their faces the next morning.'

'Are you kidding?' he said. 'How many married couples do you think haven't made love until their wedding night?'

'Oh, yes, a tiny proportion, I suppose. OK, I will try. But if I glow, I glow. You should be glad.'

'I am glad. Perhaps my face doesn't have those glowy muscles.'

The church was still magnificent in daffodil splendour, and morning sunlight streamed through the stained-glass windows, creating patterns of glory all over the place.

They were mobbed and feted and congratulated. It was nice. Then they sat at the front where Rector Colin had asked them to.

Colin stood up, and everyone quietened. He looked around and smiled. 'Welcome,' he said. 'Today we have a special guest in our midst. Now, I know what you're thinking. No, I don't. I seldom know what you're thinking, and when I find out I'm often shocked. Anyway, enough of that rambling. We have a special guest in our midst – Jesus Christ the Risen Lord!'

He raised his hands and the organ gave a cascading crescendo of glorious chords, and everyone stood and began to wave their hands in the air and call out, 'Jesus!' 'Lord!' 'You're alive!' 'Praise Your Name!' and so on. This went on for at least two minutes, until the organ helped them to settle again. Everyone sat down and Colin said, 'Now *that's* how you do an Easter acclamation! But we have two other special guests – David and Angela Sourbook, who were married here yesterday but wanted to come here for Easter Day. They're sitting right at the front here where I asked them to, which is a lesson to all of us. All of you. Anyway, we're going to sing our first hymn together. It's a traditional one, "Thine Be the Glory", but we're going to sing it like it was written just before dawn this morning!'

Everyone rose, and such a rejoicing sound filled the church that the roof did indeed come off, spin round three times and lower itself gently back onto the walls.

Everyone sat down again. The service continued with some bits of 'essential liturgy', as Colin liked to call them, and then three readings, the first of which was the passage from Genesis chapter 2 about a proper partner for the man not being found among the animals but only in the creation of Eve, his wife.

And then Colin set up the lectern in the middle of the top chancel step for the sermon. 'I hope you'll forgive me on this holiest of all holy days,' a little cheer, 'this greatest of all great days,' a bigger cheer, 'this most excellent of all most excellent days,' a great cheer, 'if I start with David and Angela, because it is relevant, as you will see. David and Angela, come up and join me, please.'

They stood up and walked forward, hand in hand, and stood beside him on the step.

'Now, you didn't know I was going to do this, did you? In fact, we've never met before, have we?'

They nodded and people tittered.

'But I knew you were going to be here today because you told me every aspect of your wedding plans in relentless detail five or six times over a period of many months! Now I have a question I want to ask you, and it's a question based on the fact that you now have two new lives. Today is the beginning and celebration of all new life in the raising of Jesus Christ at the dawn of that first day of the eternal spring which is our everlasting home with Him. Yesterday you got married, and that means this morning you're tasting a whole other new life, especially given the number of years you both left it before coming to this point.'

There was laughter here and there.

'So there you are, glowing with the very first bloom of springtime love, especially you, Angela,' she bowed her head and giggled, while everyone else laughed, and David squeezed her hand. 'But before this new life, you both had another new life, the new life that Easter Day speaks of, and I want us just to acknowledge that first. Angela, you've been a Christian and a member here for how long?'

'More than ten years.'

'David, you came to faith more recently. Can you say when, exactly?' He held out a hand-held mike towards David.

'Not exactly. Over the last year, in bits and changes, but really fully confirmed by the Alpha course last autumn.'

'OK, you say "confirmed". You were actually confirmed by the bishop in January. So yesterday is a bit puzzling because I thought you were already a "confirmed bachelor".'

Everyone groaned, some tittered.

He turned now fully to David and said, 'So, David, you came to Christ more recently. It is still fresh in your heart and mind. While to you, Angela, it was some decade ago. To both of you I at last pose my question. On this Easter morning, the very day of new life, with another very profound new life beginning for you only yesterday – and I didn't say it's a fair question – which new life is the more valuable to you?'

He turned back to face the congregation. 'Bear in mind they were married just yesterday, and are glowing with the springtime of new love. It is a joy to see, amid all these daffodils. But now they have to answer honestly a testing question. Angela, I believe you should go first.'

He had been speaking through his clip-on mike, and he handed her the hand-held one. She looked at the congregation. She looked at David.

She looked at Rector Colin. 'It's like choosing between you and David!'

Everyone laughed. She turned to face the people. 'But it isn't. It's like choosing between my Saviour and David. It's like choosing between my heavenly Father, and David. It's like choosing between the One who died for me, and David. Ask me to choose between any other person and David, and my answer is David. Ask me to choose between belonging to my God Who loves me, saved me, holds me and without Whom I cannot live, and David, then it's the One who made me and has a part of my heart that no human being could ever inhabit. I choose the risen Lord Jesus Christ, right here among us, on His glorious day!'

The congregation rose in a great cheer.

When it subsided, she passed the microphone to David, who said, rather uncertainly, 'Thank you, dear.' Lots of people laughed again.

Rector Colin broke in and said, 'By the way, David, part of the reason for that first reading was that only Eve could truly partner Adam, and I agree with Angela's insistence that Bart your great teddy bear had to go to another home.' More laughter. 'Yes, I knew about that. You made the right choice to let him go. I'm sure he'll be happy with Andrew, who is now *your* nephew as well.'

'Thank you so much for that, Rector Colin. Hmm. Anyway, so, here I stand. Faced with you lot. Put on the spot. That's not a bad start for a poem. "Faced with you lot, put on the spot, the truth to share, with all laid bare." Needs work. Anyway, such a choice.

'Oh, you know, it would be easy just to say, "Well, of course it's Jesus." But I don't want to do that. Because maybe that isn't really honest. Not that I'm suggesting for a moment my good *wife*,' clapping broke out, 'has been anything less than honest. No, that would be a very foolish mistake on such a day. No, I tell you honestly, this day is the happiest I've been in I don't know since when. Such troubles I've been through to arrive safely at it! Such challenges! Such horrors indeed of mind and soul. You don't know. The amount of buried baggage I've been heaving around with me doesn't bear telling, and won't be told. So to stand here today, healed, delivered, married to the most fabulous woman, full of joy after all this, well, there are no words.'

He caught a glance at the rector, who was beginning to look a little uncomfortable. He hugged the microphone. 'So I have to tell you, as one who has been a Christian not long, who has depths yet to encounter of the endless love of God, who feels like one with merely his toes in the ocean of God's horizon-less kindness, I say, on this great day of all days, if I must choose one, I choose the One who has found me and brought me home – truly found me, and truly made me a home – the risen Lord Jesus Christ and Father God!'

The church erupted and the organ trumpeted and even the daffodils joined in. For nothing trumpets glory quite like a daffodil in spring.

You have to smile at daffodils. Yes, you do. You really do.

They were sitting in the airport lounge that afternoon in casual clothes. Because of their short-sleeved shirts, their arms touched from the elbows to their clasped hands. He loved even that touch of her skin.

Around them, people were coming and going, children wide-eyed or moaning, books being read, music listened to on earpieces, food being eaten, but they just sat, content at a depth no one could possibly see.

David noticed a man of about thirty approaching them, looking intent. He stopped and said, 'You're newlyweds.'

Angela tipped her head forward and put her hand along her forehead like the peak of a cap and said, 'Is it still that obvious?'

'No,' he said, 'it's not obvious at all. Hi, my name's Thomas. I'm from a church in Luton. You might have heard of it. Anyway, God sometimes shows me things, and I believe He just showed me some things for you. Can I tell you?'

'OK, go ahead,' David said, intrigued but slightly wary. Why hadn't he mentioned which church? Was he just a little odd? Or was he being cleverly enigmatic because if you knew the churches there you'd know which one, and if you didn't know them, what was the point of a name?

Still standing there and looking awkward in a gangly fashion, Thomas said, 'First I saw you, sir, playing a video game. It was one of those that has levels. And you reached the end of the very last level and sat back all happy and let go of the controls with a smile on your face. Does that mean anything?'

David smiled, a great and relieved smile. 'More than you could possibly know.'

'Then I had a word for you both, *together*. It was, "God's blessing is on you, and you will *see* and *heal*, together." That's it. Just that. I'm Thomas from Luton. Yes, good things do come out of Luton,' and he was off.

David and Angela stared at each other in amazement, and David said, 'Well, there's a revelation!'

No, this is what was spoken by the prophet Joel:
'In the last days, God says,
I will pour out my Spirit on all people.
Your sons and daughters will prophesy,
your young men will see visions,
your old men will dream dreams.
Even on my servants, both men and women,
I will pour out my Spirit in those days,
and they will prophesy.'
Acts 2:16-18